"I'm Not Letting Magellan Get His Hands On You Again. Not Ever."

His eyes flickered from blue-gray to green, and, briefly, to glittering black. Nikodemus was playing with the top button of her sweater, not even thinking about what he was doing, she thought. All he'd done was trace some lines with his fingertip, but her skin felt hot wherever he'd touched her. Her gaze met his. Could he be any more gorgeous? Apparently, yes.

His smile was pure seduction. He unfastened the top button. "What do you think, Carson? The two of us. Should we?"

She blinked. A proposition. He'd just propositioned her.

"Come on, sweetheart."

My God, she was actually thinking about it. He slid a finger between the halves of her sweater until the second button stopped him.

"You're making me hot," he whispered. "Hot and bothered." His hand was inside her sweater now, and more buttons were open. "Let's do this."

Why not, she thought. One way or another, she was probably going to die pretty soon. If not directly from Magellan's poison then from the withdrawal and if that didn't get her, then Kynan would find her. Why not see what sex would be like with Nikodemus?

She lifted her hands and drew her fingers through his hair . . .

MY WICKED ENEMY

CAROLYN JEWEL

FOREVER

NEW YORK   BOSTON

Copyright © 2008 by Carolyn Jewel
All rights reserved. Except as permitted under the U.S. Copyright Act of 1976, no part of this publication may be reproduced, distributed, or transmitted in any form or by any means, or stored in a database or retrieval system, without the prior written permission of the publisher.

Cover design by Claire Brown
Cover illustration by Craig White
Book design by Giorgetta Bell McRee

Forever
Hachette Book Group USA
237 Park Avenue
New York, NY 10017
Visit our Web site at www.HachetteBookGroupUSA.com

Forever is an imprint of Grand Central Publishing. The Forever name and logo is a trademark of Hachette Book Group USA, Inc.

Printed in the United States of America

First Printing: August 2008

10 9 8 7 6 5 4 3 2 1

*H*uge shout-out to Megan Frampton, who read this book in the raw. (Hah!) Ahem. I fixed that stuff, okay? Also to Kathy Alvarez for doing much the same. As ever, my family comes in for a big thank-you, too, especially Nathaniel, who puts up with a lot from his mom when deadlines are nearing. (Those cooking skills will serve you well in future, I promise!) To my big sister Marguerite, you'll always be older, but you'll also always be the best. Thanks as well to Sherril Jaffee and Noelle Oxenhandler, English professors extraordinaire, and to the students in English 530 who read early chapters. I can't go without mentioning Jake, Jasper, and the Fudgester for all that shared chair time: I've perfected the art of sitting on the edge of my seat so as not to disturb your cat and doggie naps. My editor, Michele Bidelspach, is a saint; a big thank-you to her for all the insights and suggestions. Last but by no means least, to my wonderful agent, Kristin Nelson. And she's nice, too!

GLOSSARY

Blood-twins: A bonded pair of fiends who share a permanent magical connection. They may be biologically related and/or same-sex. Antisocial and prone to psychosis.

Copa: A plant derivative of a yellow-ochre color when processed. Has a mild psychotropic effect on the Kin, who use it for relaxation. For mages, the drug increases magical abilities and is highly addictive.

Cracking (a talisman): A mage or witch may crack open a talisman in order to absorb the life force therein and magically prolong his or her life. Requires a sacrificial murder.

Demon: Any one of a number of shape-shifting magical beings whose chief characteristic is, as far as the mage-kind are concerned, the ability to possess and control a human.

Fiend: A subspecies of demon. Before relations with the

magekind exploded into war, they frequently bonded with the magekind.

Kin: What fiends collectively call each other. Socially divided into various factions seeking power over other warlord-led factions. The Kin connect with other Kin via psychic links, often collectively. They typically possess multiple physical forms, at least one of which is recognizably human.

Mage: A male who possesses magic. A sorcerer. See also *magekind*.

Magekind: Humans who possess magic. The magekind arose to protect vanilla humans from the depredations of demons, a very real threat.

Mageheld: A fiend or other demon who is under the complete control of one of the magekind.

Severing: The act of removing a mageheld from the control of a mage or witch, through the use of magic.

Talisman: A usually small object into which a mage has enclosed the life force of fiend, typically against the fiend's will. A talisman confers additional magical power on the mage who has it. Sometimes requires an additional sacrifice. See also *cracking* (a talisman).

Vanilla: A human with no magic or, pejoratively, one of the magekind with little power.

Warlord: A fiend who leads some number of other fiends, who have sworn fealty. Usually a natural leader possessing far more magic than others of the Kin.

Witch: A human female who possesses magic. A sorceress. See also *magekind*.

My Wicked Enemy

CHAPTER 1

Someone was following her. Carson recognized him from her stop at the sidewalk coffee vendor twenty minutes ago. She was at a Chinatown intersection, waiting for the walk signal to change color. And so was he. The same man. For one thing, his height was unmistakable. People crowded the corner, waiting like she was. When she glanced over her shoulder, she recognized him because she'd seen him twice already. His gaze swept across her, and she looked away quickly. Her heart beat so hard and so fast she had to breathe through her mouth. Streaks of color flashed at the edges of her vision, a sure precursor to total debilitation. If Magellan had sent him, she was as good as dead.

Please, she thought. *Don't let me have an episode. Not now.*

Her coffee was long gone, even though she clutched her empty cardboard cup, and she still had a splitting headache. In an hour, maybe less, she'd be prostrate, unable to do anything but lie in a darkened room and wait for her *episode* to fade. The outside clamor wasn't helping. She wasn't used to the noise or the sheer number of people around her. Carson rarely spent time in public. Almost never. By herself? Absolutely never. Even if she weren't being followed, she'd be keeping her arms in close, her empty coffee cup almost touching her chest. On edge and at sea no matter what. Now she wasn't sure she'd be able to stay on her feet long enough to make it back to the doorway where she'd spent the night.

More than anything, she wanted to go home, take a shower, and curl up in her bed, in her room, in her house and feel safe. Her longing for the familiar brought a lump to her throat. She couldn't go home. Ever. Instead, she knew things she wished she didn't and had seen things she wished she hadn't. Yesterday she'd been living in a Tiburon mansion with the staff of fifteen it took to look after Álvaro Magellan. Today she was in San Francisco with a hundred dollars and clothes that used to belong to someone else.

The light changed. For half a breath, no one moved. Two cars and a bike messenger zoomed through the intersection on the red. Normal, everyday people surged forward, and Carson went with them. The man following her crossed to the opposite side of the street. Halfway down the block, the crowd thinned. Carson stopped outside a jewelry store and stared at the window. But she watched his reflection in the glass, not the display, trying to think what to do.

The tall, muscled, long-limbed man in faded jeans, an old T-shirt, and cowboy boots looked too scruffy to work for Magellan. She wasn't one of the paid staff, but she worked for Magellan, too, just like everyone else in the house. Álvaro Magellan took on the *yes, sir* type. But the words *yes, sir* would never pass this guy's lips. His jeans were pale along his thighs and white at his knees. A two-day growth of beard shadowed his cheeks. He had the kind of dark hair that probably lightened several shades someplace with a real summer. A haircut would not be amiss.

The shop window didn't reflect the color of his eyes. He was too far away for that, but she could see him slouching against a wall like a Calvin Klein model. Her pulse slowed enough for her to breathe through her nose again. Her headache got worse. She took a few steps along the display window but moved her head to keep his reflection in view. For all she knew, he was some lowlife looking to snatch her purse. If she was lucky, that's what he wanted.

She moved to the next store, pretending interest in a series of porcelain cats. She didn't see Mr. Cowboy Boots's reflection in the window anymore. Maybe he'd settled on someone else's purse.

The proprietor of a sidewalk display of Long-Life Happy Balls held out a hand and circled the chiming metal balls around his palm. She looked up to acknowledge him, but his face vanished behind streaks of orange. Her skin prickled in a wave from the top of her head to the backs of her legs and along her neck. Cantonese pitched and rolled in her ears, and for an instant she understood the words. Then the meaning flashed out of her head, and all she heard was the impenetrable rhythm of a language born on the Asian subcontinent. Cantonese was dying out in China, displaced by Mandarin. But here, in cities like San Francisco, with Asian populations that immigrated during the gold rush and after, Chinese meant Cantonese.

Traffic sounds whirred in the background, horns blared, wheels rolled over asphalt, engines accelerated. Carbon particulates gave the air a sharp scent. Pigeons cooed from eaves, and she heard the Doppler shift of conversation and tinny vocals from iPod earbuds as people flowed around her. Music from one of the open shop doors floated over the noise. She concentrated on breathing, but her headache didn't recede.

"Well, well, well," said a voice behind her. The words were soft and mellow. "If it isn't Magellan's witch."

Her symptoms vanished in a single instant of clarity. The streaking colors, the distorted sounds, the chill in the pit of her stomach blinked out of existence. Her thoughts cleared. She was miles from home. In San Francisco. In Chinatown. Half a block past the intersection of California and Grant streets and about a mile from the doorway where she'd spent last night. If she were to keep walking, she'd end up in the bay. Magellan knew she was gone, but he didn't know where. He couldn't. He'd never imagine she could make it all the way into San Francisco on her own. He thought she was helpless. Yesterday, she left everything behind, her purse, her clothes, her books, and her medication. All she took was the cash she'd snatched from the drawer on her way out. Today, a stranger was following her. He wasn't one of Magellan's suits. And he wasn't a purse snatcher because he knew Álvaro Magellan's name.

Carson turned, and Mr. Cowboy Boots smiled at her with a friendly, open grin. "Every girl just loves to be called a witch," she said. "Thanks so much for the compliment. Really." Close up, he was even better-looking than she'd thought. "Who are you?" she asked. "And why are you following me?"

"Hm," he said with another friendly smile, but drawing out the sound so it was plain he was going to lie. "Nikodemus."

"No last name?"

"No."

The pain came back, throbbing again, along with the sensation that her hair was electrified. When he said his name, his eyelids lowered halfway, but his gaze moved from her head to her feet and then back, at last, to her face. She'd been around men enough to know that, among other things, his perusal was a sexual assessment.

Nikodemus.

Nikodemus. What a crock. She tightened her grip on the scuffed black purse she'd pulled out of a bin at Goodwill. Her knees shook. Her body felt like it might just float away. He *was* good-looking, she hadn't mistaken that. He also wasn't what she expected of someone with a name straight from one of Magellan's papers. His eyes were gray with a hint of blue. His jeans fit tight around lean hips and thighs. Probably Nikodemus wasn't his real name. The name was probably his way of convincing her he knew Magellan. Another shiver streaked through her. He was dangerous. That much she knew. She pushed past him, heart pounding.

"Where are you going?" he said to her back. "That's pretty rude, you know."

She took maybe three steps, and there he was, walking backward on the sidewalk in front of her so she had to look at him and everyone else had to get out of his way. Her breath caught in her lungs, and the deficit made her light-headed.

"Sweetheart," he said, extending his arms wide. His voice invited her attention, begged for it in a beguiling tenor. "Why are you walking away?"

She kept walking but dug in her purse for a dollar. Her fingers shook. If anyone was watching and she gave him a dollar, maybe they'd think he was panhandling her instead of deliberately meeting up with her. She looked for money in the bottom of her bag, her fingers brushing the object nestled at the bottom, and she flinched. The little figurine felt hot. "Whoever you are, go away." Her voice trembled, too. She found a dollar and stopped to extend it to him. The paper quivered in the air. "If you're a friend of Álvaro Magellan, I don't want anything to do with you."

He clutched his chest with both hands and pretended to stumble. "A friend?"

"Quit bothering me." She glanced around like she was looking for a police officer. "Take this. Go away. Please."

He smiled. Despite the scruffy appearance and too-long hair, his teeth were white and even. "Thanks." He took the dollar. "Carson."

When he moved his head, she noticed he wore a star ruby in one ear. The cabochon winked like an eye in the shifting light. She froze, arrested by the thought of the gemstone watching her.

"Don't you think we ought to talk about what you're doing here? All by yourself?" he said.

"No. I don't."

"I do." He must have been six-three at least, which made him a foot taller than her. The odds were against her. Considering her headache was shifting toward the debilitating, she wasn't going to outrun him, let alone win a physical struggle. He leaned toward her. "Magellan is number one on my hate list, Carson. If he's on yours, too, we really need to talk."

Her knuckles hurt from squeezing the strap of her purse. She stared up and into his face, a lot farther up than she expected. "Not here."

He smiled. "I'm starving," he said. "How about that restaurant across the street?"

Five minutes later, Carson was staring at a menu, with no idea what any of the words meant. She had no connection to the culture that understood spring rolls or General Tso's chicken or ma po tofu. Magellan never ate out, and, therefore, neither had she. Sometimes the staff ordered out, but she never got invited. She lived in a no-woman's land. Not exactly on staff, but definitely not one of the family, either. She sat on the chair facing the wall, but perched sideways because she wasn't stupid enough to put her unprotected back to a door she couldn't see. The dim light in the restaurant eased her headache a depressingly small amount.

Nikodemus slouched on the chair against the wall. Heads had turned when they walked in, male and female heads, because this was San Francisco, and he had the kind of presence that made people stare. She found that disconcerting. He grinned at her, not even bothering to look at the menu. "Carson Philips, as I live and breathe."

She gazed at him, at a loss for words. If her head wasn't pounding so hard, she might already have figured out why he was calling himself Nikodemus. With no last name. That wasn't a name you just picked at random. Not when that name featured prominently in the myths Magellan studied. He'd written an entire paper on the subject of

Nikodemus and the rituals attributed to his worship. The thing is, this Nikodemus, or whoever he was, didn't look all that dangerous now. He was young. Much closer to her age than Magellan's. He looked like someone who'd be fun to be around. He looked like someone who'd be interesting to know.

"Talk," he said.

"You must be from Harvard or Yale," she said.

He snorted. "Hardly."

She concentrated, but she was seeing flashes of color again. She willed them to go away. "A collector? Someone who lost out to Magellan at an auction?" She peered at his face through streaking colors. "Someone who *acquires* artifacts?"

He grinned. "No, no, and no."

Their waitress came. He ordered in Chinese without looking at the menu. This time she didn't get even a glimmer of understanding. The words and their meaning remained impenetrable. Carson pointed to an item that was cheap and didn't sound too exotic. Afterward, there wasn't anything to do except look in the teapot to check the color of the water, even though it was too soon for it to be drinkable tea. She leaned back. Nikodemus was watching her, his head tipped to one side. Her headache made her feel stupid and slow.

"Why were you following me?" she asked.

He cocked his head and looked at her like she was stupid, and maybe right now she was. She could hardly think straight. He shrugged. "You're Magellan's witch."

"At least you're not calling me something worse." Carson threw herself against her chair and then wished she hadn't. The sudden movement made her head hurt. "I'd appreciate it if you didn't call me that."

"I think you know what I mean."

She rubbed her temples. "Actually, I don't."

"Let's see if I can clarify for you." He pretended to think. "Carson Philips, you're a witch."

He sounded like he meant something more than name-calling by that, but his exact meaning refused to come clear in her overstimulated brain. She wondered if he'd read Magellan's paper on Nikodemus. He must have. "Right," she said. "I'm a witch about like you're a fiend thought to have first manifested in the Gobi Desert five thousand years ago."

He didn't even crack a smile. "I like the weather here better."

"Hardy har har." She guessed he was about thirty, maybe younger. "How did you find me?" she asked.

"Why are you running from Magellan?"

"Who said I was?" Her fingers trembled, so she pressed her palms to the white tablecloth and stared at the backs of her hands. "Can't a girl go shopping if she wants?" She sounded light-hearted, but her hands looked tense. She tried to relax her fingers and couldn't. He knew she was running from Magellan. How? How did he know anything about her, a stranger, when she barely knew the people who lived with her? After what she'd seen, she didn't know if she could trust their waitress, let alone Nikodemus with no last name.

"Maybe I can help," he said. And when she looked up, she couldn't stop the absurd thought that maybe he could. He leaned toward her. "Why don't you start by telling me about Magellan."

She couldn't feel the right side of her head anymore. Staring at the star ruby in his ear helped her focus. The throbbing pain dampened. "My parents died," she said.

"I've lived with him since I was eight." *Lived with him* was about all it had been, too. Álvaro Magellan had been about as distant as any person could be from a child. "He made sure I knew he had a legal obligation to take care of me. If it hadn't been for my parents naming him my guardian or whatever, he wouldn't have had anything to do with me. So he fed me. Put a roof over my head. Paid for my clothes. Gave me an allowance. There was a string of nannies until I was twelve, a new one every year just about, and I was constantly warned never to bother him. Ever. There were huge areas of the house I was forbidden to enter. God forbid he should ever accidentally see me." She snorted. "I was closer to the cook than Magellan."

He pulled the paper wrapper off a pair of wooden chopsticks and broke them apart. "Bet he had you homeschooled."

Why was he so certain? "I couldn't go to a regular school."

"No letting the likes of you run free in the world."

She wasn't sure what he meant. *The likes of you.* Just like she wasn't sure what he meant by calling her a witch. She didn't want to know. "A normal school would have been too stressful for me."

"Right," he said. Only he didn't sound like he agreed with her.

"It's true." She'd spent her childhood and most of her young adulthood going to specialists who did tests, who poked and prodded her and handed out pills in a rainbow of colors that did nothing to stop the headaches. They got worse, and their sequelae longer lasting and more severe. "Idiopathic migraine with accompanying fatigue."

"Uh-huh."

She licked her lips. He made her feel like her life was

a lie. Which, actually, it seemed to have been. "He spent a lot of money on specialists."

"Yeah, Magellan's a great guy." He examined his chopsticks. Gray eyes with a hint of blue. Like the sky before morning had completely arrived. Really pretty eyes, she thought. "Upstanding citizen. The fucker."

"I don't think he liked children very much."

"Like I said."

Carson breathed in slowly. Did his dislike of Magellan give her sufficient reason to tell him more? And if so, how much? She didn't know. All she knew was she spent last night in a doorway, and hating Álvaro Magellan wasn't such a bad thing to have in common with someone. "His work comes first."

"His work." Nikodemus didn't sound mellow anymore. He threw the chopsticks on the table. His T-shirt, imprinted with the text "Alcatraz Federal Penitentiary," fit snug against his torso. Whenever he moved, muscles flexed somewhere. "You help him with his work, don't you?"

She winced because his voice hurt her ears. "Sometimes. He's famous, as you must know. Preeminent," she amended. She thought about leaving and almost stood up. Except, if she left, what then? "He's the world's foremost authority on the desert-fiend myth." She tried to decide from his expression how much he knew about Magellan and his arcane expertise. She couldn't tell. "People write to him constantly, asking for his opinion on some artifact or source of the myth. Wanting reprints of his papers. They write in with all kinds of crazy ideas. Someone has to answer the mail and keep things organized."

Nikodemus stared at her too long with eyes that held more than just the chill of anger. She held his gaze. Looking away first meant you were weak. It was like admitting you were less, and she never let anyone make her feel less. Not even Magellan. Nikodemus's eyes were a fortress. He could look out, but she'd never get in. She checked the tea again. It was still too pale to drink. "You think he studies myths about desert-fiends?" she heard him say.

Carson looked up and locked gazes with him again. He didn't seem so affable now. "Of course that's what he does." It wasn't. She knew that now, and Nikodemus, or whatever his real name was, seemed to know that, too. Her body started to shake. She didn't know what was safe to say or do.

He shook his head. "That's rich. That's really rich, Carson. Next thing you'll be telling me you don't deserve to die."

CHAPTER 2

*T*he waitress, a pretty Chinese woman no older than Carson herself, brought their soup and spring rolls, which didn't look much like rolls to her. Nikodemus looked the woman up and down. In leisurely fashion. Their waitress couldn't take her eyes off him. Carson knew about men and flirting. Sometimes, not often, one of the men who worked for Magellan flirted with her. And once he'd had a visiting scholar stay with him for a while. That went a little beyond flirting, so she wasn't entirely ignorant about men. The waitress—she was really very pretty— said something to him in Chinese. He replied in Chinese, and the two of them laughed. He watched the waitress walk away.

There was silence while they ate their soup. She didn't touch the rolls, but Nikodemus did. He wasn't exactly handsome, it was just his physical presence. Well, yes, actually, he was handsome. Just not like Magellan's assistants, with their Italian suits and short hair. Carson couldn't help but stare at a man so different from the ones she'd grown up around. Long hair, for one thing. The earring. An easy smile. A confident air.

When he was done with his soup and the spring rolls—he ate them all, including hers after she declined to try them—he looked at his wrist. He didn't have a watch, but the motion conveyed his meaning. His gaze was intense on her face. The star in his earring flashed in the light. "Tell me why you need my help, and while you're at it, you can add in why I shouldn't kill you right now for helping him in his work."

For an instant her world contracted. "I don't understand," she said when she realized she hadn't misheard the threat. Her chest fluttered, and she had trouble breathing again. All she could think was he wouldn't try anything in a restaurant. Not in public. Her head hurt, a stabbing pain behind her eyes. He wasn't going to help her. All this time running from Magellan and she ended up with someone else who wanted to kill her. Underneath the table, she scrubbed her sweaty palms on her jeans. "I haven't done anything to you."

"What's to understand?" He moved his head to get his hair off his forehead. His hair was a dozen shades of brown. If he kept it properly short, it wouldn't bother him. "All you have to say is Nikodemus, I want—whatever it is you want—and you shouldn't kill me because—whatever you think that is. Easy."

The waitress brought their entrees. She gave Nikodemus a slip of paper and spoke in a stream of Chinese that included the English words *cell phone*. She placed a fork by Carson's plate while Nikodemus slipped her number in his wallet. His gaze sidled to the waitress as he picked up his chopsticks. He'd ordered something with tentacles, she saw. It smelled foreign and savory. He helped himself to rice and spooned some of his food onto the rice. She picked up her fork. Bits of fried chicken with vegetables sat on her plate in a shiny, sticky red sauce. Her stomach turned. She wasn't hungry anyway.

"How bad can it be?" he asked. He sounded sympathetic, and despite everything, because of everything, she wanted that to be true. She wanted someone on her side. She didn't want to be alone. "Just say it. I can't possibly think any less of you afterward than I do already." He waited while Carson tried to figure out how to start. The thing was, she couldn't reconcile her urge to like and trust him with the fact that he'd threatened to kill her, all in his easygoing voice. Like it was no big deal. Like he had every right to feel that way. She should leave him to the waitress. Except he'd follow her and kill her, right? She swallowed the lump in her throat and almost couldn't.

"Okay, then," he said after she'd opened and closed her mouth twice. "Maybe this will help. This morning, the top items on my to-do list were these." He held his palm in front of his face. "Eat breakfast." He made a little check motion on his palm. "Get laid." Another check mark on his palm. "Kill Álvaro Magellan. Did not do that." He went back to his meal. All Carson could do was watch, hypnotized by his beautiful eyes. "You're on that list, too. In fourth place. Kill Carson Philips."

"Me?"

"Yeah, you."

"Why?" She used her fork to rearrange the food on her plate. He had to be either an academic or an artifact dealer. She couldn't make herself accept any other possibility. Since he didn't seem the scholarly type, she figured he had to be a dealer. Of the shady variety. "Did I write you a rude letter? Tell you we didn't want to buy your fake Babylonian figurine straight from the grave of Hammurabi himself?"

"If I had an artifact, it wouldn't be fake." His gaze locked with hers. "Maybe today I can get three out of the four. I'd rather kill Magellan, but offing Magellan's witch would make this a top-ten day for me. Does that help? Because despite any impression you might have of me, Carson, I am not patient."

"Why do you keep calling me a witch?" she said softly.

One eyebrow lifted. His chopsticks stopped halfway to his mouth. "Sweetheart, you are in some serious denial."

Carson was shaking again, so she put down her fork and clasped her hands on her lap. "All right," she said evenly. "Whatever you say. I'm a witch." She wondered if his behavior was normal. She might not get out much, but she read books and magazines. She read the paper. She even watched TV sometimes. God knows Magellan wasn't a role model for normal behavior. Nikodemus knew that, she kept thinking. He knew an awful lot about Magellan. "I need help," she whispered.

He cocked his head. "Why?"

She looked Nikodemus in the eye and said, "He's insane." There wasn't any other explanation. At least not one she was prepared to broach just yet.

He ate a bite of tentacle. "Insane like he thinks he's a potted plant, or insane like a crazed killer?" He glanced at the ceiling, pretending to think. "Oh, wait. He is a killer." His gray-blue eyes returned to her, colder than before. For a moment, she thought she saw something else in his eyes. Movement of some sort. But that was crazy. Nobody had eyes like that. "Seriously, Carson, talk, or else all you're doing is wasting my time, and that pisses me off."

Orange flashes filled her vision. Nikodemus touched her shoulder, and the throbbing pain eased. She knew, intellectually, the two things—his touching her and her pain easing—were unrelated, but that didn't stop her from making the connection.

"Carson," he said in a softer voice. "Talk to me. I can't help you if you don't talk to me."

The gentleness of his voice struck hard. He didn't mean it, but she was desperate to believe he did. She forced herself to look at him and discovered she was a wretched liar. Lying meant keeping track of what she said and remembering when reality had to be altered to fit any lie she tried on him. What she told or didn't tell. Her head hurt too much to lie. Half-truths would have to do. "I think he believes in fiends and magic."

He scratched his chin, nodding. "Explains the hobby."

"Is your name really Nikodemus?"

He made a face. "What difference does that make?"

"Well, it's just . . . a coincidence, I suppose." On her lap, her fingers curled into fists. She thought about Magellan's paper on Nikodemus and the ritual he'd described in it. She started feeling shaky again, as if the world was going to dissolve around her. "I think he believes there really is an ancient fiend called Nikodemus—"

"Potted plant, is he?" Nikodemus had a European face with a hint of something else. His cheekbones were high, his mouth sensitive. Not Spanish, she thought, but something exotic. Some unusual blend of heritage. But no way was he Chinese.

"You don't study the myths, do you? You just collect the artifacts, am I right?" she asked.

"What myths would that be?"

"About fiends. Desert-fiends, I mean, not the kind from the Bible. His fiends came first. He's obsessed with them, you know."

His mouth quirked, then stilled. "That's a pretty funny obsession, if you ask me. No wonder you ran away from him."

"They can control a person's will and even take over their bodies."

"Ooh, scary," he said, not looking at all scared. He glanced around the restaurant. "How many pod people do you think are here?"

"They're evil incarnate." She leaned toward him, her attention on his face, alert to any change that would tell her he didn't think Magellan was crazy at all. "But a mage, a sorcerer, can control them and keep them from harming people." *Or a witch,* she thought. A witch could control them, too.

He looked at her, totally calm. "Is that right?"

"I think he's convinced fiends exist and that they can be controlled with the proper magical . . . baloney." She wriggled her fingers in the air.

One eyebrow arched. "Baloney?"

"Hocus-pocus." She mustn't let him think she believed any of this. She stood firmly on the side of rationality and logic. Any other position was pure insanity. "Artifacts, incantations, all the things Magellan collects and writes about. Mystical stuff our ancestors believed in up to a few hundred or thousand years ago."

"Supernatural creatures who take over a person's will, like in *The Exorcist,* you mean?" She nodded, and he laughed. "That's a bunch of bullshit, Carson. Do a three-sixty with a human's head, she doesn't keep calling you names. She dies." He put his hands around his throat and made a choking sound.

She wanted to laugh, but she couldn't. Her stomach was acting up again, churning away. He reached for her, touched her shoulder again, and she felt better just from the distraction of the contact. "What if Magellan has started believing in fiends? I know it's ridiculous, but what if he's gone insane?"

"Well, now," he said, letting his fingers slide off her. Almost immediately, her headache pulsed again. "All that stuff about fiends living among us, that's pretty interesting." He poured himself tea. Was he smiling? She wasn't sure. "To be honest, so far I haven't heard anything to make me think he's insane. There are plenty of normal, sane, but misguided people who believe in that kind of shit."

Carson surrendered to the tremble of her breath through the words. She couldn't stop her emotion, but she kept her body and expression still. "I saw Magellan kill a man."

"A man?" Nikodemus tipped up her cup and filled it, too.

She lifted her hands, remembering the sheen of red on his fingers. "Yes. It was a man."

He pushed her tea toward her. His fingers were slender, with nails almost too long. She remembered reading somewhere that guitar players kept their nails long. She wondered if he was a musician. Teacup in hand, he leaned against his chair and stared at her with one arm folded over his chest. "Are you saying he thought the guy was one of those desert-fiends?"

"Maybe." She stared at the table. "Maybe, yes."

"What's a fiend look like? Are you sure it was a man?" His gaze held hers. She'd never seen eyes of such a pure, piercing color. That, along with her headache, made her dizzy. Someone with eyes like his could take your heart with one lingering glance.

"Yes, of course."

Something flickered behind his eyes. "How do you know?"

"Because it wasn't a woman. Because it was someone I knew." She took a deep breath, and even though she wanted to, she didn't tell him the rest. He already wasn't convinced about anything she'd said. "He used to work for Magellan. Magellan told me to go to my room, and I did. But I didn't stay there." She couldn't tell him anything else. What if she was wrong? What if she was the insane one? "I ran."

"Why didn't you call the police?"

She knew her hesitation made her seem deceptive. A liar. But she had to be cautious. With her head hurting the way it was, she needed more time than usual to get her thoughts together about what to say and what to leave out. She shook her head. "I called on my cell, but when his car came down the hill, looking for me, it rang, and I threw the phone away. I was afraid they'd find me if I kept it with me." She took a steadying breath. "So, I got on a bus and ended up here." All of which represented a gross understatement of the most terrifying night of her life.

He drank some tea. The space around them got very quiet. Whatever he was thinking wasn't pleasant, she thought. After another sip, he put down his cup and said, "Are you fucking with me, or could you be for real?"

"What do you mean?" A breeze cooled her cheek when the restaurant door opened. She pushed away her plate with its sticky blood-red sauce. The smell was making her ill, and she could not afford to be sick. Not now. "Magellan killed a man. I saw it. I saw him do it." The clench of the body, the sound, the awful sound that still grated in her ears. "According to you," she said in a low voice, "maybe it's not the first time."

"No shit, Sherlock." He took another bite of his lunch.

She stared at the ruby in his ear. Star rubies were critical to the ancient rituals Magellan was working so hard to reproduce. Was that a coincidence, too? The way Nikodemus's name was a coincidence? His eyes flickered, and nobody's eyes flickered between colors, from gray-blue to silver-black. She said, "Maybe I'm the one who's going insane."

Nikodemus leaned back like he didn't want to be too close to a woman who was losing her hold on sanity. "What else, Carson?"

She closed her eyes, seeing the room with Magellan in the center, blood glistening on his hands, dripping down. Horror rushed up as fresh and new as ever. "Please help me," she whispered. He was calling himself Nikodemus. His eyes weren't normal. That had to mean something. She choked back a sob. This was no time to break down. She had to hold herself together a while longer. "I ran away from Magellan, and nobody ever leaves him."

He reached into a front pocket of his jeans, pulled out a hundred dollars, and threw it on the table. "Incoming," he said. He grabbed her hand and yanked her to her feet.

"If you want to live until you convince me you're serious, move."

Carson turned her head, and her heart dropped to her stomach. Two men had just come into the restaurant. They looked like investment bankers. They wore dark Italian-made suits and polished oxfords, and their hair was short. Very short. One of them wore sunglasses. The other had a hand shoved inside his suit jacket, reaching for something. She recognized them both. Kynan and Tibold. Magellan had recently hired Tibold, but Kynan had been with Magellan forever, and he'd always frightened her. He was big and heavily muscled, with pale brown eyes so beautiful your breath caught until you saw the hate behind them. He had a way of looking at her that made her feel like she was naked.

Neither of them stopped for the pretty waitress who'd given Nikodemus her phone number, and they ignored her gesture to an open table. Their heads swiveled, looking around the restaurant, searching.

For half a second she refused to believe she was in danger, but then the part of her brain responsible for self-preservation took over. They were looking for her, and that couldn't be good. Kynan saw her first, and the moment his attention locked on her, her spine turned to ice.

"Magellan doesn't mess around, does he?" Nikodemus said. "He sicced the big dogs on you." He pointed to a glass door with a heavy push bar across the middle and the words "Fire Exit" in big black letters on the upper pane. "That way."

Tibold shouted when she and Nikodemus headed for the exit. Tibold slammed into the waitress, and they both reeled back. A bowl of rice went airborne. Kynan jumped onto a table and launched himself. He seemed to stay in the air an inhumanly long time.

Customers shouted and dove for cover from flying food and broken glass and plates. Nikodemus upended their table and kicked it toward the leaping man. Then, hand clamped around hers, he hauled ass out the fire exit with her stumbling behind him, trying to keep her balance. They exited onto a narrow street closed to traffic, the alarm blaring.

"Magellan sent them," she said. She was shaking again, worse than before. Thinking about what Kynan would do to her if he caught her made her sick. "They're going to kill me."

"You're a fucking genius," Nikodemus said. He shot a glance at either end of the street, then back to the exit door. He didn't say anything. He didn't move. The hair on the back of Carson's neck stood up. Goose bumps prickled along her forearms.

The alarm cut off.

Light seared her eyes, just once, like a camera flash going off. Kynan, by far the larger of the two, reached the fire exit on the run. He put out his hand to press the crash bar and nothing happened. He punched the handle again, but the door didn't budge. Tibold joined him. His sunglasses were gone. Kynan stared through the glass and connected with Carson. She took a step back. Kynan's mouth contorted in rage. He redoubled his assault on the door.

Nikodemus laughed like he'd known the door was going to jam and was enjoying the hell out of watching the two men bang away on it. He grabbed her hand and pulled her toward the cross street. Carson ran to keep up.

Behind them, something exploded. She stumbled as

the air around them concussed. He grabbed her, spun her around to put her back to the brick wall, and flattened himself against her, his torso trapping her with her head toward the restaurant side where the fire-exit door had exploded. She breathed in his scent, a desert-dry heat that rose from him and enveloped her. At least her head stopped pounding. She could feel the hum of his breath in and out of his lungs. Glass, bits of masonry, and metal rained down.

"Kynan's coming for me," she whispered. Magellan had taken Kynan off his leash and sent him after her. She shook because she'd always known there was something fundamentally wrong with Kynan.

"Breathe," Nikodemus said, stroking a hand along the outside of her arm. "Don't panic on me. You're just picking up their emotion, that's all. A couple of mageheld fiends, Carson. Nothing I can't handle." She realized she'd been chanting her fears out loud. *He's coming to kill me. He's coming to kill me. He's coming to kill me.* His body pressed against hers. "Do you need me to take control, Carson?"

That got her attention. Her head cleared, and so did some of her terror. This whole situation was just insane. Completely insane. She wanted to be far away from here. Her muscles twitched with the urge to run. She needed to be away from the nightmare her life had become.

He pushed off the wall as Kynan and Tibold charged into the alley. The light hit their eyes just right and turned their pupils shiny orange. She was seeing things now, because people's eyes didn't change color. No way. Tibold jerked back like he'd been hit. With a grunt of surprise, he fell hard on the pavement. Kynan never missed stride. Tibold sat on the ground, hands pressed to his chest, gasping like he couldn't breathe while Kynan charged on, staring at her the whole time.

What was left of the metal push bar from the door had landed near Carson's feet. She grabbed it, because something was better than no weapon at all. The metal chilled her palm.

Nikodemus ran toward Kynan, then spun and, using the force from his spin, coldcocked him with a furious backhand. She heard the crunch of bone giving way. Nikodemus kept moving until he was behind Kynan. He wrapped his arms around Kynan's neck and chin and wrenched hard. Kynan threw him over his shoulder and staggered, blood pouring from his broken nose. Meanwhile, Tibold was back on his feet. He propelled himself at Nikodemus.

Carson screamed a warning, and that made Kynan's head whip toward her. His broken face was healing right before her eyes. He pointed at her and grinned.

Nikodemus had Tibold in a headlock. His arms strained. Bone cracked, and when Nikodemus let go, Tibold's body hit the ground and didn't move. Nikodemus knelt and did something with his hand. The body jerked once.

Someone roared. Kynan, Carson realized. He shot toward her so fast she didn't have time to think. She swung her metal bar as hard as she could. She was going to die, she thought. But not without a fight.

The jagged end of the bar caught Kynan's cheek and tore through his skin. He grabbed his face, eyes burning like a furnace, and Carson felt the world turn upside-down. She couldn't move. Her brain was locked tight against her. Kynan's eyes boiled as red as the blood oozing over his fingers.

"Don't worry," Kynan said. "I'm going to take my time with you. It might be hours before I kill you."

Behind him, Nikodemus was on his feet. He didn't look any friendlier than Kynan. He flung out a hand, and Kynan's body bowed toward her. Her paralysis shattered. Kynan whirled to Nikodemus, who was circling around them.

Carson's headache returned with a vengeance. She was practically blind from the pain. Her stomach burned. Her mouth tasted bitter, metallic, and sour. Her vision wavered. No matter how hard she blinked, Kynan looked more like a deformed lion than a man. His eyes glowed; his upper face protruded, or maybe his jaw receded. He started running toward Nikodemus. Steam rose from his feet. Beneath her the pavement rippled.

Kynan snarled, a rumbling sound that buzzed in her ears and vibrated in her chest. He leapt toward Nikodemus, arms outstretched, fingers curled into talons. Carson grabbed her metal bar with both hands and darted toward Kynan, shouting with inchoate rage. She swung the bar with all her might and hit the back of his head with a crack like a gun shot. Her joints hurt from the impact. Kynan staggered.

Heat bubbled around her, burning her. Her skin sizzled, and she was sure her head was going to explode like the fire-exit door. Pain enveloped her, and she screamed. The heat came from Nikodemus. It gathered around him, coalesced, and flashed outward. She didn't see anything, but she felt the push on her body like a punch. Kynan flipped head over heels and hit the ground, sliding backward, smoke curling out of his mouth and wide-open eyes. He lurched to his feet, normal now. No animalistic face or body. Only his normal, beautiful, hate-filled face. Carson held her bar like a baseball bat.

"Come on!" Nikodemus sprinted, grabbing her wrist as he passed her. She clenched the length of metal as they exited onto the main street and slowed to a normal pace. He pushed through the crowd, jostling people as they went. "You can drop that now," he said.

She looked at the bar. "No."

Nikodemus shrugged. "Suit yourself."

Down the hill, a No. 1 California bus moved through traffic, less than a block away. Bodies pressed in on her, carrying her toward the bus stop, whether she wanted to go or not. Nikodemus was ahead of her, moving through the crowd easily because he was tall and acted like he owned the sidewalk. The pain in her head was a dull ache, but she still had the visual disturbances and the sensation that the air around her was crackling with electricity. Her fingers and palm hurt from gripping the bar, but she didn't want to be without a weapon ever again. Having a weapon was all that kept her from breaking down.

Nikodemus was past the bus stop. He looked over his shoulder, saw how far back she was, and stopped. Carson headed for the unaware crowd at the bus stop. She wanted out of here. Away. Far away from Kynan and visual hallucinations and exploding doors. Sweat trickled down her back, and her shoulders were one huge knot of tension. Someone bumped into her, pushing to get ahead of her in the line of waiting riders.

The bus stopped and the door whooshed open. Nikodemus scanned the crowd, looking away from her for just a moment. One advantage of being short was she fit into a gap in the line of passengers. She got on, dug out quarters, and paid the fare. Standing room only. Her jaw clenched. So many people, bodies pressed together without regard to age or gender or propriety.

On the sidewalk, Nikodemus headed back the way they'd come. She walked to the rear of the bus, into the thick of people who lived every day of their lives without wondering if they were going insane. Nikodemus scanned the street, and then he shoved a man with a briefcase and shouted. He whirled. His mouth was tense, eyes darting everywhere. He called out again. Her name.

As the last passengers paid their fares, panic grabbed her by the throat. He'd fought in that alley and kept Kynan and Tibold away from her. From her. She was insane if she thought Kynan wasn't going to find her again. He wasn't going to give up. She knew it. As for Nikodemus's intentions, if someone was going to kill her, better him than Kynan.

At the last minute, she leaned over the seated passengers and banged her fist on the window. Nikodemus turned around. Their gazes met, and swear to God, she felt like he was right there in her head. He dashed for the bus and got on just as the doors were closing. He flashed a Metro card at the driver and joined her at the back of the bus. He stood close. Too close. No more than six inches between their bodies, and there wasn't room to back up.

Nikodemus smiled. "You whacked Kynan a good one," he said.

She tilted her chin so she could see his face. "He deserved it."

His smile flashed into a grin. "You can play on my team anytime."

The bus lurched and headed up the hill. And Carson's

head was full of Nikodemus, who might or might not be five thousand years old.

She gripped her metal bar and prayed he wasn't planning how to kill her.

CHAPTER 3

Nikodemus grabbed the witch's hand and got off the bus at Polk Street, an area transforming from down-and-out to up-and-coming. This was a commercial/residential area: restaurants, used bookstores, a corner grocery, a bakery, a chain store with a pharmacy. Most of the upper stories of the buildings were apartments. She kept a step behind him, but he could tell she was having trouble walking a straight line.

He turned around and drew her toward him. She came without resistance. He pressed a finger to her forehead. The noise of traffic receded. No more distant sirens or people talking. Just a moment of perfect silence he wished would last forever. Her eyes were heartbreakingly clear. An intense gaze, even filled with pain. Considering Kynan Aijan had been trying to kill her, she was holding up damned well. "You gonna be okay?" he asked.

She swayed toward him, not as unsteady as before,

but not entirely steady, either. "Sure," she said. And then she laughed, but not like something was funny. "Unless you decide to kill me, after all."

"I don't kill people when they're helpless. You have my word on that." He smiled, because he wasn't sure how much she knew, which he guessed was jack shit, and how much she was figuring out on her own, which was possibly more than he thought. "It's okay," he said. Damn, but she was pretty. Exactly his type. He put his arms around her and drew her close. Her metal bar banged against his leg. "Honest."

"Why should I believe you?" She clung to him like they were soon-to-be-lovers only she didn't realize that's what he was thinking. Okay, maybe she did. She pushed away, fighting back tears.

"Sweetheart." He brushed the back of his fingers along her cheek. She didn't turn her face to the contact. Too bad, because her skin was soft, and the contact gave him a rush. At the moment, her magic was practically nonexistent, and that made her feel enticingly human. "Who else do you have to trust? More to the point, come to think of it, who else has your back where Kynan is concerned?"

She looked into his face, staring hard because it was getting dark and she didn't see as well in the dark as he did. "Nobody."

"Then why not me?"

"I don't know you," she said softly. She touched his earring. Wasn't that just like a witch to go straight for the object of power? "You could have let Kynan take me. But you didn't. Why not?"

"A grave misjudgment on my part," he said, smiling so she'd know he was joking. Kind of. "But then, I'm known for my open mind. Look, you can trust me, but if you decide for whatever reason that you can't, then whack me with that bar, okay? Deal?" She nodded, and he took her hand in his, and they started walking again. Slowly, until she was steadier on her feet.

They walked uphill past Lafayette Park, turned a corner, and continued along a treelined street to his narrow Edwardian with no front yard and twenty steps to the door. At the top of the stairs, he pulled a set of keys from his pocket and fit his key to the lock. He stood aside to let her in. While he bent for the mail, she looked around. His house had good proportions and he watched her take in the high ceilings, the chandelier overhead, the hardwood floors, and the wooden florets around the windows and doors. She appeared fascinated by the medallions painted with woodland faces that interrupted the straight line of the crown molding. Had she guessed what they were? To the left, stairs led to a second floor. A hall extended rearward to the right of the stairs, and through an arched passage on a hard right, he could just see the bowed windows of the room that fronted his street.

Mail in hand, he flipped on the light. Carson closed her eyes and kept them that way. When she opened them again, she stared hard at the nearest painted-face medallion. She rubbed her eyes. "Where is this?"

"Home, sweet home." He tossed the mail on a table by the door and reached around her to turn the locks. The deadbolt clicked into place. His spine turned to ice, and he whirled, expecting to get hit with something deadly, but the witch had her head down, shoulder against the wall, and was holding on to her bar like it was her only friend in the whole world. "You okay?"

She nodded. She wasn't okay, though, any idiot could

see that, and Nikodemus liked to think he wasn't an idiot. She was a witch, after all, and sensitive to a lot of things here. He lifted a hand toward the ceiling and the faces in the medallions went quiescent. "You want to put that thing down yet?"

She shook her head and straightened. Her eyes didn't quite focus.

After a bit, he said, "What's the matter with you?"

"I have a headache." She cradled her purse to her chest, the metal bar across her body. She was a little thing, really little. Didn't look dangerous at all. "A migraine, and I don't have my medication with me."

He pushed her shoulder, herding her deeper into the house. "I'll give you something to help."

"Regular medicine doesn't work."

In the arched hallway leading away from the door, darkness coalesced and solidified. He was used to it, but Carson came to a dead halt. He turned around. She took a step, stumbled, and caught herself with a hand to the wall. The bar clanked onto the floor.

"That bad, huh?" Nikodemus touched her upper arm and steadied her. She'd hardly eaten at the restaurant, just some soup. She was probably light-headed from lack of food. "Come on."

She let him lead her to his kitchen. He didn't turn on the light for her, and she seemed grateful. He took a bottle and a plastic jug of dark liquid from his refrigerator and filled his favorite mug from the container. He handed it to her. The word *STUD* was stamped in gold letters on a green background. She didn't take it, so he drank half before refilling it and handing it back. "You're not the only one who gets headaches." He pressed the mug on her. "Perfectly safe. An old family remedy," he said. "It'll help your head, I promise."

She took the mug. "What is it?"

"A traditional cure for what ails you." Nikodemus watched while she sniffed the contents. "Smells awful," he said. "But it works. Sit down." He pointed to a chrome table and chairs tucked into a nook. While she did, he opened an ice-cold bottle of Asahi Black. He sat cater corner to her with his legs out straight and crossed at the ankles. "I use brown sugar to sweeten it," he said after she took her first swallow. "Doesn't help much."

She swallowed and tried hard not to make a face. He did his best not to let her see he knew. For a witch, her manners were impeccable. She set her feet on the bottom rung of her chair. "Is this where I say it tastes like chicken?"

"Is that a joke?"

She ducked her head and stared into her mug for a bit. Then she said, "Yes. Actually, yes it was. Sorry if I offended you."

He waited a beat, then said, "I was beginning to think you didn't have a sense of humor. Tastes like chicken. This shit tastes like swamp water." He laughed, and so did she, a little. She had a nice smile. Not that a nice smile meant anything. "I was getting hives thinking about sitting around here with you never laughing at my jokes." He took a sip from his beer. Condensation made tracks on the bottle and dammed up around his fingers. He looked at her from over the top of his beer. "I'd offer you one, but you need to get rid of your headache first." He waggled his eyebrows. "Then I can get you drunk and take advantage."

The witch laughed and drank the rest in one long,

horrible swig. "Good girl," he said when she showed him the empty mug. He took it and put it on the table. He tipped his head toward the hallway. "Come on, I'll show you my mad scientist laboratory while we wait for the juice to kick in."

She stood up. "If you're going to kill me, I have to say you're the nicest, most polite killer I've ever met."

"Thanks," he said, touching his chest for effect. "That means the world to me. It really does." He was having a hard time believing he was amused by her or that he actually wanted to make her laugh. She followed him out of the kitchen, watching him walk, a fact of which he was very much aware. "That was the kitchen," he said. "Living room." He pointed ahead of them with the hand holding his Asahi Black. A drop of water rolled down the bottle and fell, twinkling, to the floor. At the edge of the room, he switched on the lights. This time, she didn't need to close her eyes. "Chainsaw in here."

She looked around. "The bloody ax is where?"

"Spare bedroom."

She laughed, genuinely. Jesus, she was really something when she smiled, wasn't she? He kept watching her from over the top of his beer. "I've always had a thing for girls with green eyes," he said.

Carson opened her mouth to say something but didn't. She was very good at hiding her thoughts. He wondered what was going through her mind. *Thank you, I'm glad I have green eyes.* Or was it, *Don't touch me or I'll scream.*

He leaned against the wall opposite, arms crossed over his chest, watching her without saying anything. He had the impression she was listening intently, but the house was as quiet as an abandoned temple. "How's the headache? Any better?"

"Yes. It is." She touched the side of her head. "What's in that stuff?"

"I told you. Secret family recipe." He used his upper back to push off the wall. "You ready to talk?"

CHAPTER 4

*T*alk. She took a step back. *No,* Carson thought. No talking. Talking would take them in unfortunate directions. "Yes."

Still holding his beer, he grabbed her hand and led her to the room off the entrance. Even with the cowboy boots, he didn't make noise. He had a fluid walk, graceful, like a dancer. At the restaurant his graceful motion had turned to deadly power. No. It hadn't. None of that happened.

The decor here was homier and more inviting. The green velvet sofa looked comfy. There were two matching chairs and a black leather recliner, battered in a comfortable way. He put his beer on the glass table and sat on the sofa, knee up, booted foot on the green-velvet cushion. He took a cell phone from his back pocket and set it next to his beer. There was a flat-screen TV on one wall. She recognized the Wii on the table next to the TV because Magellan's employees played constantly. Wiimotes and Nunchucks were on the table. He rested an elbow atop his knee and let his hand, with its long and slender fingers, dangle down. He was all long legs, lean thighs, and ripped abs. The muscle was impossible to miss from this close. No wonder he wasn't afraid of Kynan. "The chair is for you," he said. "It's better if you're not too comfortable."

"Okay." Her mouth went dry. She dropped her purse to the floor and sat on the chair. It wasn't comfortable. She stared at the ceiling. Faint in the plaster she could see bronze stars that ran in a pattern along the ceiling and down the wall into a copper pot placed so that it looked like the stars were spilling into, or maybe coming from, the pot.

"I'm going to give you the benefit of the doubt." He was serious now. His good-humored smile was gone. It had never occurred to her he wouldn't trust her. The idea startled her, that she wasn't the only one with reason for distrust. What else had she overlooked?

"What do I seem like to you?" she asked.

"A green-eyed witch who almost got her head taken off by Kynan Aijan."

She gripped the sides of her chair. "You know him."

"Magellan doesn't sic Kynan on someone unless he's serious about doing some damage."

"Kynan hates me. He always has."

"Well, yeah. You're a witch."

Carson blinked.

"I'm not going to off you, if that's what you're thinking. All I'm looking for is the truth."

"I told you the truth."

"No, you didn't. Not all of it, anyway." He cocked

his head. "How about you tell me everything you remember from the last normal thing you did up to right now."

Carson huddled on her chair, but it didn't help the cold in her bones. "Nothing is normal about my life."

"Normal for you."

"The last thing I recall is being in my room."

"When?"

"Yesterday. I had a headache. A bad one, and I was trying to open my medication, only my hands shook so hard I couldn't. I was sick to my stomach." She touched her head. "I couldn't see very well, either. Magellan doesn't like for me to bother his assistants, and it was the cook's day off. I went looking for him." Downstairs, barely under her own power. Crying from the pain and from the fear something deadly was wrong with her. And then, the moment she opened the downstairs door, normal stopped. "I'm not crazy," she whispered. "I know what I saw." And she did know. She did. That was incontrovertible. "I know what I saw."

"You saw Magellan. And?"

She watched his face when she answered. How much more she said depended on what she saw there. "He was standing over a body."

"What happened next?"

Carson sat on her hands so he wouldn't see them shaking. "He had a stone knife." Thinking about the knife kept her mind off worse things. "Catalogued as having come from the Thar Desert. I'm fairly certain the knife was stolen. From a dig." She sucked in a breath. "Magellan stabbed him with the knife."

"And?" Not disbelieving. Not horrified. Not sympathetic, either.

Horror lapped at her, as if she'd just now walked into that room and stood there, staring at someone she knew, whose body didn't look right anymore. A body that didn't look human. Carson brought herself under control. But then, that was the whole point, right? The body hadn't *looked* human. The emotional cataclysm of that night had affected her ability to correctly process what she'd seen. She was experiencing some sort of cognitive dissonance and now remembered the scene in monstrous terms because the event itself was monstrous. In measured words she related almost everything that happened.

"Nobody disobeys Magellan." She wasn't a naturally fast talker. She'd always spoken with deliberation. Words needed careful choosing. Especially now. "He never raises his voice, but you know when he's angry. It's awful." She leaned forward, knees pressed together, balanced on the edge of her chair. "And he was angry with me. I'm not supposed to bother his assistants. And I'm not supposed to disturb him when he's working downstairs. Until then I never had. But I had to do something." She ran her hands through her hair. "He was angrier than I've ever seen him before. Tibold was there. He walked me out." She shivered at that recollection, too. Odd, though, how she felt better telling him about it. "He opened my medicine for me. After he left, I was afraid to take the pills." She glanced at him to see how he was reacting. His face was calm. Unreadable. "Because I knew, I just absolutely believed I wasn't safe anymore. I couldn't stay. So I ran. Away. Out of the house." She took a trembling breath. "I ended up here."

"With only the clothes on your back."

"Yes. That's right." She looked at her legs. Until now, she'd never owned a pair of jeans. "But these aren't my clothes." She unwrapped her fingers from the sides of her chair and clasped her hands on her lap. "I knew he'd keep looking for me, and I wanted to look unfamiliar. Magellan doesn't like to . . . lose things. And then you followed me." Nikodemus, a man with the name of a five-thousand-year-old fiend, nodded. Their eyes met, and she felt a pull between them, as if he were tugging on an invisible string. But she just couldn't say it. She didn't want to say out loud what was in her head. "So, if I had to pick one of us to be crazy, I guess it's me."

"You're not crazy."

In her head she could see Magellan with his blood-red arms, and she could feel the chill of the room. All over again, the light in Magellan's eyes glittered with madness, and the thing in the room that was a man and then something else, something inhuman, and then dead. She'd felt the life go out of him. It. The monster. Nothing could erase those memories. Not even if she lived to be five thousand herself.

"Is that all?"

"Yes."

"You sure?"

She looked away, then back. "Yes." Her heart pounded so she could hardly speak, and when she did, the words came in a whisper. "I keep wondering, Nikodemus, if the myths about desert-fiends are real, what that makes you."

He seemed to think about it. "Warlord without port-folio?" Carson studied him, unable to tell if he was joking. Was she about to take a leap into a madness of her own? He shrugged. "The kind of creature Magellan likes to kill, I suppose."

"If you were from China, you'd have brown eyes." She stared into his blue-gray irises.

"Why?" he asked. "Seriously? If there was such a thing as a fiend, Carson Philips, why assume it has human geographical or racial patterns of appearance?"

"Then why assume they'd look human?"

He cocked his head at her. "Good question."

"You look normal to me," she said. "A normal, everyday person." Her voice abandoned her, and she took a sip of his beer without asking. Cold, biting chill.

"I like to think I'm above average, actually, but that falls within range of normal, don't you think?" Nikodemus put his elbow on his upraised knee. "Let's say I'm one of those desert-fiends."

His smile sent a chill down her spine. He wasn't normal. She knew that, but she couldn't make herself admit it out loud. "Okay."

"Know what I'd do?"

Carson whispered, "What?"

"I'd get in your head. Bend your will. Just a little. Enough for me to see what I need to. Then I'd find out for sure what you are."

Neither of them said anything for a long time. She felt a point of pressure on her forehead, and she jerked her head back, neck muscles tight. "Can a fiend do that?"

"Oh, yeah," he whispered, all soft and tender.

"What would it be like?"

"Fast," he said. "You wouldn't like it much, but the fast way I'd be done sooner. Slow isn't quite as unpleasant overall, but the part that isn't fun for you lasts a lot longer. I'm good either way. Your choice. Fast or slow?"

"Fast," she whispered. Her mouth was bone-dry, but she still had to wipe her palms on her jeans.

"You sure?" he asked.

She nodded. This was crazy, she thought. Crazy to talk as if any of this could actually happen.

She felt a tap on her forehead, a burst of pressure. Behind her eyes, she saw stars, and then there was someone else in her head. Instinct told her to fight, and she did. With all her might. His attempted invasion intensified, burned behind her eyes and in the back of her skull. Her throat felt like it was on fire; her blood heated beyond endurance.

"Sweetheart," she heard him say. He sounded as if he were a long way away. "You gotta let me in or this is just going to get worse. I don't want to hurt you." His voice softened. "Please?"

She opened her eyes. Nikodemus looked sad, as if he were on the verge of tears. She saw his mouth form the word *please*. Worse than this agony? Despite the screaming protest of her better sense, she stopped fighting him.

She got a sense of relief—it wasn't her own relief—and then Nikodemus came on, taking over, ripping through her mind, looking for anything that indicated deception. She was choking, she couldn't breathe. Her head was on fire. He pushed deeper, lightning fast. Faster than she could react if she'd been able. Memories raced through her head, images without control, emotions without context, brought up, discarded, examined dizzyingly, sickeningly fast. Her ears throbbed with sound, a roaring protest at this violation of everything that made her Carson Philips.

Through it all, Nikodemus sat on the couch, still with an elbow resting on his upraised knee. Silver fire flickered behind his eyes. Sensations blasted through her, searing.

"You are so totally fucked," she heard Nikodemus say.

CHAPTER 5

Nikodemus grabbed his cell phone and punched in a number. While it rang, he studied Magellan's witch. She was out cold and would be for a while, considering how thoroughly he'd been rooting around in her head. That sort of indwelling tended to cause a hangover effect. Man, he felt sorry for her, and impressed that she'd been so adept at keeping him out. A survival skill, he speculated, from years of living with a house full of fiends? The ringing stopped.

"Talk to me," said the voice on the other end.

"Durian. I need you here."

"Check."

He closed his phone and went back to studying Carson Philips. No denying she was totally hot. Small but stacked, you might say. Proportionally long legs, teeny-tiny waist. Exactly what he liked in a woman, human or otherwise. Too bad her life was so royally screwed up, or he'd be wanting to get something going with her. Humans, even if they were witches, were a funny lot, bound as they were to their corporeal bodies and short lives. Of course, most of the magekind had the nasty habit of extending their lives by any means necessary, which invariably meant murdering his kind. Which was exactly why Magellan and his witch had landed on his to-be-killed list. They were enemies, mages and his kind, but Magellan was really, really good at killing. If the mage got any better at it, even he might not be able to stop him.

Psychically, the witch made for an amazing high. Once she'd relaxed and let him in, looking around was easy. Coming out was not. She felt really, really good. They were a good match that way, even if she was magekind. Possibly because of what she was. His enemy. Evil. Evil, however, didn't whack a mageheld fiend on the back of his head in an attempt to protect a fiend who wasn't mageheld. Misguided scrappy little thing, she was. Musta never gotten around to reading the Guidebook for Evil Mages, even though she'd lived with the guy who could have written it. He went to the kitchen and grabbed another beer. Back in the front room, he sat on the couch with his feet on the coffee table and his open beer in his hand.

He shook his head, but it didn't make the queer tightness in his chest go away. He never had emotional reactions to humans, but he was having one with Carson Philips. Hormonal ones, sure. He had them all the time. He got as sexually worked up as the next guy, but this connection to Carson Philips? Feeling sorry for a witch? No way. He couldn't let that happen. He'd lose everything. Besides, he hadn't felt sorry for a witch in more centuries than there were letters in the words *drop dead*. He drank his beer in silence, thinking about a pair of gorgeous green eyes and a witch who just didn't have a clue.

He felt Durian approach the house. The proximity of another fiend was presaged by a sort of electrical charge, a ripple through his consciousness that put him on alert. By now, Durian was feeling that same ripple, a little stronger for Durian, since Nikodemus outranked him in power.

When the knock came, he ignored it long enough to piss off Durian. His cell phone did a little dance on the coffee table. He had it on vibrate, so the damn thing sounded like a bumblebee. He ignored the phone and walked to the door. "About time you got here."

Durian snapped closed his cell. Always a natty dresser, he had on black trousers, a black cashmere shirt, and shiny, very shiny, black loafers. He had brown eyes and long brown hair that looked black until the light hit it. "About time you opened the door, Warlord."

With a nod, he acknowledged Durian's respect of his position, empty though it might be right now. There weren't many warlords left, not after centuries of predation by the mages. Hell, even fiends were getting scarce. "Beer?"

"Thanks," he said. They went to the kitchen, and Nikodemus got another Asahi Black from the fridge. Durian popped the cap, fit his mouth to the top, and drank. "Ah. That hits the spot." Nikodemus walked back to the front room with Durian behind him. "So, what's got you all worked up? Is there a problem with the meeting? Somebody say they weren't coming?"

In seven days, three warlords were coming to San Francisco, willing, at last, to talk about stopping their infighting for a common effort against the magekind. Some stress there for sure about convincing the kin to work together. So it was saying something that he wasn't worked up about the meeting right now. He actually had other things to worry about. "No," he said over his shoulder. He went in and pointed to Carson. "Her."

Durian stopped next to Nikodemus, gave him a sideways look, and took another pull from his beer. Like most fiends, he was tall and athletic in his human form. His hair was loose tonight, not tied back, and it reached past his shoulders. These days fiends were especially proud of their long hair, given short hair meant you were screwed. Durian rarely had to use his considerable abilities to convince a human woman to volunteer for bed duty or a little of the emotional connection fiends found so compelling in humans. He just flashed a smile and fluttered his big brown eyes, and that fueled most any woman's desire. "She's not dead. You've got that going for you."

Nikodemus picked up his beer. "Yeah, there's that."

"Passed out, huh?" He lifted his bottle in a toast. "That's some serious loving there."

"You don't recognize her?" Understandable if he didn't. Her hair partially covered her face, and her closed lids hid her gorgeous green eyes. Every fiend in a hundred-mile radius of San Francisco knew Magellan's witch had green eyes. She was legendary for them. He would have thought Durian would feel the thread of magic in her, stunted though it was. God knows he did.

Durian shrugged. "Should I?"

"That's Carson Philips."

Without his smile, Durian didn't look so affable anymore. In fact, he looked downright dangerous. Easy to believe now that he was a born killer. "Is that so?"

"Says she ran away from Magellan." Nikodemus sat

on the couch again, stretching his arms along the top of the cushions, a palm curled around his beer. "I found her about half an hour before Kynan did. He had orders to kill."

Durian's eyes opened wide. "Kynan Aijan?" Nikodemus nodded. The other fiend leaned back, impressed. "Why isn't she dead?"

He waved off the subject. "Dumb luck? There she was walking downtown, not bothering to hide what she was, and I'm thinking, who the fuck does she think she's going to bag with that lame come-and-get-me act? Some low-level kin gofer?" He drew his eyebrows together. "The closer I got, the more chaotic she felt."

Durian snorted.

"True tale." He held up a hand. Carson wasn't moving, but her magic fluctuated from high intensity to practically nothing at all. Distracting. And enough to make Durian's head snap toward her. "Relax," Nikodemus said. "She's at least twenty minutes from coming to."

"What is that?"

He nodded. "Exactly my point. No way is she helping him. How can she when her magic is like that?" That was the strange thing about Magellan's witch. Everybody assumed she was Magellan's partner in crime, but she just didn't have the ability. "She's like that when she's conscious, too. Burn-you-to-a-crisp magic. No magic at all."

Durian rubbed his arms through his sweater. "What's wrong with her?"

"She doesn't know shit about anything. Or about us, either," Nikodemus said. "Just a bunch of bullshit book facts. From what I can tell, Magellan never let her get near the real stuff." He crossed one ankle over the other.

"Except maybe once." The problem of Carson Philips was getting more complicated by the minute. "It got a little obvious while Kynan was trying to kill her that something major was up." He remembered his beer and drank some. It didn't taste as good as he needed it to. "Kynan Aijan is after her, and she's like a goddamned puppy."

"Right," Durian said. "A wolf puppy who's going to grow up with sharp teeth and a predator's instinct."

He shook his head. "Well, that's just it, Durian. She's not. It's too late for her."

"How so?"

"She thinks she has migraines. I've heard of mages doing this kind of thing to their own. He obviously did it to her." He stretched and looked over at Carson, still out cold. "Mage finds some young witch or sorcerer with plenty of power. They have to get them young, before they've come into their magic." Durian's look of revulsion was priceless. "Feed the magelet enough of the right drugs, and then cut the magelet off. The power is still there, but the kid can't get to it. Ever."

"But the mage can?"

He nodded. "For Magellan she's like having his own personal reserves to call on when he needs it. Until the poison kills her, that is. Or else all that pent-up magic. I'm guessing she doesn't have much longer." The thought made him a little sad. She didn't deserve this. Nobody did.

"She really can't pull?"

Nikodemus sorted through the information he'd gleaned from scouring Carson's mind. A born witch, and he'd found no indication she'd ever pulled magic in her life, not even a suggestion that she knew what she was. Durian waited for him to come out of his reverie. He didn't want to. There were some good moments in there. He shook his head. "Her power ebbs and flows like crazy. When it's ebbing, she feels vanilla. Totally human." He stretched again and tried not to react to the witch's sputtering power. "She could almost pass for normal. But come high tide, she's got headaches and shit from the magic she can't touch. Starts stumbling. White as a goddamned sheet. I thought she was gonna pass out on me at least once."

Durian studied Magellan's witch for a while. "That must have been distracting."

His shoulders slid lower on the couch. "Yeah." A mage's magic had a widely known attraction for fiends. The magic felt good. Gave you a tingle down low. These days you learned to control the reaction, or sooner or later you got too close and ended up with a shaved head, enslaved to some mage until he decided your life was over. The days when fiends could trust the magekind were millennia past. While a fiend was enslaved, the short hair was permanent, a side effect of the magic. The permanent buzz cut made it easy for mages to tell which fiends were enslaved and which were free for the taking. Durian was right. He ought to kill the witch on principle. What was the old saying? The only good witch is a dead witch. Or something like that.

"And she doesn't know what she is? Nobody ever told her? She never figured it out?"

"Why would Magellan tell her anything? The whole point is it's easier for him if she doesn't know shit. He's the one who fed her poison until there was no hope of her ever touching her magic. She's gonna die because of him, the bastard." He drank more beer. "You think he'd tell her all about it? What Magellan's done to her is just all kinds of evil." He shook his head. Hell, he did feel sorry for her. "In a sick sort of way, she has a lot in common with us."

Durian stared at him. Hard.

"That's called irony, Durian," Nikodemus said. "Magellan's screwed her but good, and just like his magehelds, she's not going to survive it."

"You have my respect and fealty, Warlord. I will fight with you when the time comes."

"Well, that's good." Because he had to.

"I don't care what the mage was giving her or what it did to her. She's a witch. She ought to be dead. One less of them in the world is one less enemy for us to kill when the time comes."

He made a face. Like he didn't know Carson was a witch or what her kind did to his. He knew he shouldn't be making excuses for her. But she'd whacked Kynan Aijan across the back of his head when she didn't have to do anything. And she did it even though she was clueless and defenseless against the fiend. "I hate the magekind same as any of us. I'd be happy if they all shriveled up and died in the next five minutes, but I still think what Magellan's done to her is sick and perverted."

At last, Durian sat down. How long had he known Durian? Not as long as some. Just since he came to San Francisco, but Durian was solid. And smart enough not to get caught. Smart enough to understand, as Nikodemus did, that their kind needed to get their collective acts together if they were going to survive. No more of this clannish refusal to work together. The remaining warlords needed to join forces against the mages. There was no other way out of the annihilation the kin were facing. Durian was the first to join him when he decided the time had come for him to pull together a fighting force. A clan. No more freelancing, lone warlord for him. Warriors fight. Warlords lead. It was time for him to lead. He needed Durian, his intelligence and his skills. Durian wasn't afraid to think out on the fringes. The guy had a way with the other warlords. The whole meeting would never have come off without his skills.

Durian smoothed his pants leg. "Kill her now, Nikodemus, before she runs back to her lover and begs his forgiveness. And then tells him all about us."

He shook his head again. "No way. She's scared to death of him. And besides, Magellan never made a move on her. He gets his rocks off with Kynan." He stared at the label of his beer, feeling sick at some of what he'd seen in her head. "That's a memory of hers I could have done without. She saw them once. Kynan was giving him a blow job. Her boyfriends, all two of them, she met through Magellan. Probably mages, but there's no way to be sure about that. Neither of them lasted long." He swallowed more beer, but it didn't drown the taste in his mouth. He knew for a fact Kynan didn't swing that way. Some did—in that regard fiends were no different than humans—but not Kynan. He was strictly hetero, and if Magellan was fucking him, then it wasn't Kynan's choice. Nothing ever was with a mageheld fiend.

"Just how deep were you in her head?"

Nikodemus plucked at his shirt. Really deep. So deep he wasn't sure he was completely out yet. "She's a scrappy little thing." And a liar. Not that he blamed her, but still, she hadn't told him everything.

"Scrappy." Durian drank more of his beer. "You're losing your objectivity." His voice rapped out his displeasure. "She's a witch, Nikodemus."

"A witch who can't pull. How can she be dangerous if she can't pull? Magellan wants her dead, and she believes Kynan's going to find her and make it happen. Based on what I saw, she's not wrong." Durian's expression was unreadable. "The kill order had to come from Magellan."

"Why, if she's going to die anyway?"

He shrugged. "What Magellan did to Carson is borderline unlawful among the mages. There are certain mages who, if they find out about it—*snick*." He slashed a finger across his throat. "If she's dead, there's no evidence."

Durian sat forward to put his beer on the table. "Why did you call me, Warlord?" He stared at Nikodemus. "If you want me to babysit your scrappy little witch, I decline." His eyes flashed. "With all due respect. I don't want anything to do with her."

"Not her." Durian owed him. In a karmic way, Durian owed him. Durian had sworn him fealty, so it wasn't just a matter of him calling in favors and Durian being honor bound to pay them back. Durian was magically bound to give Nikodemus the aid he requested. Just as Nikodemus was bound not to make capricious or self-serving requests of those who were sworn to him. Warlords who did soon found the bonds weakening. Nikodemus turned his head and looked at his friend. "I need you for something else, Durian."

He sat up straight, gaze fixed on him. Durian blinked, once, and his pupils were huge. Yeah. That was Durian's thing. He said he'd given up the killing that made him feared among the kin, and maybe he had. He'd have been hunted down and taken in Copenhagen otherwise and, if not dead, then serving some Danish mage. "Kynan's out there. Without Magellan stuck to his rear." A warlord himself, and not to be lightly dismissed. Kynan Aijan was scary as hell, and right now he was playing on the wrong side. "I want you to find him and take him down. Permanently."

Durian grabbed his beer by the neck and spun it. "For being Magellan's fuck buddy?"

"Killing him is the only way to call him off. I want the witch alive and Magellan dead." Nikodemus heard Durian's heart beating. He was getting permission to assassinate one of their own kind, and the fiend was glad, the way a drug addict was glad for another fix. "If Kynan's dead, Magellan is vulnerable." And that was true. "Carson Philips will get me close enough to take him." Because, yeah. Once a fiend gets a taste for killing, he never really loses the desire. "He's out there. Without Magellan. Find him and take him down."

He let go of the bottle. "My pleasure, Nikodemus."

Nikodemus told Durian where Kynan had been the last time he saw him and where he and Carson had been when he managed to get her stunted magic shut down enough for Kynan to have to work at tracking her. Kynan was going to find her eventually, and Nikodemus didn't want him carrying out Magellan's orders. The witch was going to be useful to him. "There's nobody better than you, Durian."

He rose, all six-foot-plus muscled length of him. His eyes sparkled. "Doesn't mean it's going to be easy."

"No fooling." The problem with mageheld fiends was you couldn't feel them. Other than fiends who belonged to the same sorcerer, a mageheld fiend was cut off from his own kind. No back and forth the way he and Durian had with each other right now, feeling each other slip in and out of each other's minds. Magehelds were practically human in their inability to connect, the poor bastards. He felt another flare-up from Carson. High tide right now. Her witch magic was seriously cranking him. Had to be the magic, right? What else could it be? At this rate, he was going to have to do a little self-pleasure to get through the night.

Durian felt it, too. At freaking last. "She's waking up."

"Yeah. Any minute now."

Durian took a long breath. "I don't like it."

"You don't have to. Just be careful and call me when it's done."

Durian gazed at him for a while, then bowed his head and pressed his first three fingers to his forehead. "Warlord."

After Durian left, Nikodemus relaxed against the couch and let Carson's magic flow over him. He felt the draw all the way to his balls, and he imagined what it would be like with a woman as beautiful and forbidden as Carson Philips. He'd get her naked slowly, kissing and caressing all the parts he revealed, touching her until she was melting in his arms. Making love to her would be sweet, because that's what she was deep down. Slow and easy for their first time, because Magellan had damaged her so badly—he happened to know her sexual experience was limited enough that she thought she wasn't all that wild about men and their needs. Later, when she knew how good sex could be for her, they could try a few things. But first, they'd do sweet. She needed somebody to show her what that was like, to have a lover who thought of her first.

Carson's eyes fluttered open.

CHAPTER 6

*C*arson fought the urge to throw up. The effort took all her concentration. All of it. Colors streaked behind her closed eyes, intense purple, violent green, and orange against dead black. When her stomach eased up, she cracked an eye and saw the strap of her purse. That made no sense. God, she felt wrung out. The moment she tried to focus, her head spun, full and empty at the same time. If the vertigo didn't stop, she'd be sick to her stomach. She closed her eyes. At least the sensation of the room spinning out of control stopped. The inside of her skull burned.

Isn't that what Nikodemus said he would do?

Nikodemus. He was real. A fiend out of the Gobi Desert. And he had made her feel like he was in her head. He had been. He'd taken control of her and had done whatever he wanted to.

He was in the room with her right now.

Adrenaline flashed through her. That got her eyes

open again. This time the streaking colors didn't take over her vision. Her purse strap did. She wasn't on her chair anymore. Her cheek pressed against an unforgiving floor. One arm was trapped under her stomach, and her fingers were numb. Her other hand lay palm-down on the floor. She managed to roll onto her back. The room started to spin again. A line of pale bronze stars floated on the ceiling, a dizzying perspective until the sensation that the stars were moving passed. She sat, flexing her fingers to get the feeling back. Pins and needles shot up her arm.

Nikodemus gazed at her from his couch, his eyes intense but his face calm. Remnants of the energy he'd sent into her flashed and sputtered like a dying electric current. He crossed his arms over his chest and continued to watch her. For the space of a breath, he blurred at the edges. The whites of his eyes were lost to shadow, and even when they'd returned to normal, his pupils burned silver-black. Impossible, she thought. Then again, not impossible at all.

She blinked. His clothes were the same, faded jeans, T-shirt, and cowboy boots, but his bronze-blond hair was dark brown now, almost black, and instead of reaching to his shoulders, it hung past his shoulders to his waist. Like hers. His stubble was gone in favor of a baby-smooth shave, and the shape of his face was sharper and prettier than before, with the fair skin of someone with Black Irish in his gene pool. Like her. He had a long nose and a stubborn mouth. It was a face of character, this masculine version of herself. His eyes were green, a dark, mossy green. Like hers. She blinked again and he was back to the scruffy good-looking man she'd first encountered.

He stood but didn't help her up. She didn't blame him.

She ranked second only to Álvaro Magellan on the list of people he wanted to see dead. If she hadn't come back from the abyss he'd left her facing, he'd have one less to-do item. He didn't want her here any more than she wanted to be lying on the floor of his living room feeling like she'd been seared from the inside out.

You are so totally fucked.

Something in her head buzzed, or maybe it was in her chest. She couldn't pin down the feeling, only the newness of it. The strangeness of it. The inside of her head pulsed, but this pain was different from her headaches. The entire inside surface of her skull felt tender and inflamed. She decided to stay where she was. If he was going to kill her, there wasn't any point to getting up. She stared at the ceiling, breathing through her open mouth. Underneath the sleeves of her sweater, her skin prickled. "Well?" she whispered. "What am I?"

It'd be nice, she thought, if he knew.

Nikodemus moved toward her. This time she heard his boots on the floor. Heel tap, soft sole. Heel tap, soft sole. Then his head blocked her view of the stars glowing on the ceiling. He held out a hand. "Alive."

"Am I?"

He grabbed her upper arm and hauled her to her feet. "Yeah, you are. For now."

Her legs wobbled, but Nikodemus steadied her with a hand under her other arm. Her head started buzzing again, and when she closed her eyes, giant purple streaks crossed the field of black behind her lids. The room came almost right after a deep breath. Nikodemus led her to the couch, and she sank onto the cushions, head lolling back. The room spun. Pretty spinning stars on the ceiling.

He grabbed her purse and dug in it until he pulled out

a carving about three inches high, black basalt with the body of a man and the head of a wolf. "Care to explain this?" he asked.

"It's Sumerian," she said. The figure had ivory sclera and obsidian rounds for pupils. The irises were gold. The subject stood one foot in front of the other, robes so delicately carved she could practically see them moving. She licked her lips. "Magellan stole that, too."

"What's it doing in your purse? Taking a vacation?"

"I suppose," she said slowly, "that I stole it from him." She reached out and took it. A spark streaked through her hand, strong enough to be painful and make the tips of her fingers tingle. The sensation worked its way up her arm, all the way to her shoulder. Her fingers went numb again. "Ouch."

"What?"

"Static electricity, I guess."

"You felt that?" He leaned forward, staring at the carving. "That's very interesting, Carson."

She transferred the figurine to her other hand so she could shake out her arm. Her other hand tingled, too. The stone was warm on her palm. In addition to the warmth, it was unusually heavy for its size. Up close the carving was even more detailed than she thought at first glance, down to the locking pattern carved into the hem of its robe. "This is why Magellan is after me," she said. "I stole it from him because he thinks he needs it for the rituals he's been writing about. The one he was trying that night. I thought if I took it, maybe he wouldn't try killing anyone else."

"That's damn noble of you." Nikodemus ran his fingers through his hair and left his hands clutching his head. "Do you know what that is?"

"A talisman. A good luck object for the bearer. In the world of the desert-fiends and their worshippers, used as a way to communicate with a personal god or perhaps a revered ancestor."

"Close enough." He let go of his head. "There's a myth about this one that makes it special."

She kept turning the figurine in her hands. The material looked like basalt, but it wasn't as cool to the touch as it should be. If she were prone to flights of fancy, she'd have said it felt warm from the inside. "Really?"

"There's a fiend inside, locked there by a mage. Only a mage can release him. So the story goes."

She didn't look at him, even though he was far too close. She rubbed a forefinger up and down the black rock. "It's not uncommon for a culture to develop myths about objects they endow with human or godlike characteristics. But I'm sure there's more to your story than that." Carson waited for him to continue.

"Yeah. There is. A lot of mages today would give their firstborn child in order to release the fiend inside that thing. A mage like Álvaro Magellan would want to crack this wide open and take the power into himself." Carson's pulse thundered. "Anybody who studies the past knows there's a price to pay for everything, especially power. You have to take a life in order to crack this thing open and get at the spirit inside. And if the mage succeeds and lives through the aftermath—trust me, that's not a given—he'll become invincible. Possibly even immortal."

"That's what Magellan wants," she whispered.

Nikodemus tipped his head, exposing his star-ruby cabochon again. "Of course, the mage can't kill just anybody."

"No?"

"He'd have to kill someone like me."

Her heart clenched. "Are you really from China?" she asked, looking at him from under her lashes. "The Gobi Desert?"

"What do you think?"

She ran her gaze up and down him and couldn't tell he wasn't just like her. He stood close, too close. If she moved her knee even an inch, she'd hit his leg. "I don't know anymore."

"The world has changed, Carson. We pass for human most of the time." He rubbed his upper arm. "Adapt or die."

"What do you really look like?" When she closed her eyes, she saw the creature on the table. She saw the room where Magellan had stood with red dripping down his arms, the tangy smell of blood in the air. The thing dying on the table had looked into her eyes, and his rage and despair pierced straight to her marrow. No one should die like that. No one.

He spread his hands. "This is the only form you need to worry about." He didn't back away. He was too close. Way too close. Making a point.

"What now?"

"That, sweetheart, is the question of the day." Her body twitched from wanting to back up, but she didn't want to concede the territory. "Hell, that might even be the question of the century. What am I going to do with Magellan's witch now that I've got her?"

"Take me back to the store you got me from?"

He didn't laugh. Didn't even crack a smile.

She shifted her butt backward, but to maintain the moral victory, she didn't move her legs. Was he going to just put her out on the street for Kynan to find? The thought induced more than a little terror. She'd be alone. With a dwindling supply of money and Kynan out there looking for her. Hunting. Her throat closed up. Nikodemus was right. She was fucked.

He sat on the couch, and she scooted away, as far as possible while still maintaining her dignity. He stretched an arm along the top of the couch and rested an ankle atop his knee. "Even if I thought it was in my interest to let you go, which it isn't, there aren't many places where Magellan can't find you." He leaned over her, invading her space again. He had such a wonderful smile, and he could poison it faster than she could blink. "Could be there's none."

She moved. Like him, she sat sideways on her end of the couch, one knee drawn to her chest. He looked completely the way she remembered, and she wondered if she'd imagined seeing him with black hair and green eyes. "People disappear all the time."

"To find you, all Magellan's fiends have to do is use their natural affinity for a human with magic. The way you were telegraphing, a baby could have found you. You're lucky Kynan didn't find you first."

"Telegraphing what?" She ran a hand through her hair and wished she had a tie for it.

He put his near arm along the top of the sofa, fingers stretching toward her. "Magic, Carson. It's our sixth sense. It's how we survive. We can't live without connecting to magic one way or another."

"This is absurd." Carson rested her forehead on her knees and shivered like there was a blizzard in the room. "There's no such thing."

Nikodemus shot off the couch and started pacing.

Carson turned her head to the side and watched him. He stopped midpace and stared at her. "Magellan's been fucking with you. Mages like him don't leave anything to chance. Everything you are or are not is calculated." He frowned at her. "You are totally—hell, what's the word?" He snapped his fingers. "Innocent? Naïve?"

She lifted her head.

"Clueless. I'll be honest. I didn't expect that. You don't know the first thing about Magellan or what he is or what you are."

"I hate him." It felt good to say the words. She hated Álvaro Magellan with white-hot passion.

He threw himself onto the leather chair, hands clasped behind his head. "If I were you, I'd be wondering what the fuck Magellan did to me." Nikodemus looked at the ceiling, and Carson could have sworn the stars started to glow. He was maybe two feet from her, but she refused to look away even though he was glaring at her now. "Everyone knows you're his witch. Helping him. His right-hand man." His attention flicked to her chest, and boy, oh, boy, was that glance unsettling. "So to speak. You resonate, Carson, and most fiends just can't resist."

Carson didn't say anything for a while, because she didn't trust her voice not to break. She wasn't crazy. Why didn't that make her feel better? "I didn't know. I didn't know what he was doing until the day I ran away." She rubbed her temples. "No wonder you want me dead."

"If it's any consolation, now that I know you weren't helping him on purpose, you're off the kill list."

"Lucky me," she said. So she could go out there with Kynan looking for her. "Does that mean I can leave now?"

"You go out there unprotected like you were today and

you better believe that big fiend of his is going to find you. If he does, you'll wish I'd offed you instead."

"I have a little money." She hugged her knees to her chest. "I was thinking of going to Los Angeles."

He didn't say anything for a while. Neither did she. "Okay," he said. "Look. I know you're not a normal witch. I know what Magellan's done to you." He cocked his head, and she had the feeling he was being careful with his words. "So here's the deal."

"A deal."

"I'm offering you my protection. My oath," he said, emphasizing the word, "that I'll do everything in my power to keep you safe."

"In return for?"

"You don't have to do anything. You've proved yourself to me." He leaned toward her. "We both know if you go out there by yourself, you'll just get killed. Hey, you took on fucking Kynan Aijan for me. I'm not letting him or Magellan have you. It's as simple as that." He looked thoughtful as he shook his hair behind his shoulders. "Although . . ."

"Although?"

"I could use some help with Magellan." He grabbed his beer and finished it off. "You don't have to. No pressure, Carson."

"I'll help," she said after another long silence. "If I can."

"Thanks." Nikodemus set the carving on the table. "I do mean that." He looked at the ceiling. "Shit. I cannot believe I'm saying thank you to a witch."

"I'd be dead if it weren't for you," she said.

He walked to her, but he didn't say anything. He stared into her face like he was memorizing her. His eyes looked normal. Gray irises with a hint of blue. But they weren't normal. He wasn't normal. Her skin crawled with the cold inner knowledge that he wasn't human and that he was letting her feel the difference. "You and I are just totally wrong."

The air between them seethed, and the buzzing in her head started up again. Underneath the sleeves of her sweater, her skin prickled. She rubbed her forearms. "Well, to be honest, there isn't much right about my life at the moment."

Slowly, he lowered himself to the couch, straddling her with one hand on back of the couch. He touched her cheek with the side of his thumb. "I'm sorry about all this, Carson."

"Me, too."

He traced a circle on her forehead. "What happens to you if you don't take your meds?"

"I don't know." She swallowed hard. "I've never gone this long without. Lately, I have to take them more and more often in order to stop the pain." His finger started a line from the center of her forehead to the end of her nose. A burst of warmth followed his fingertip as he continued along the space above her mouth and then over her lips. Whatever he was, desert-fiend, liar, psychotic, he'd saved her life today.

"Can you get more?"

"I take several different meds. Mostly prescription. Ergotamines. Triptans. Isometheptene. Feverfew. We rotate them. When one stops working, we use another one. And then go back." His finger continued down her chin, over and then to the underside and along her throat. She felt like he was drawing a permanent line on her. Marking her. She wasn't sure what she thought of that, but she had the vague sense that maybe she should mind more than she did.

"You sure that's what you've been taking?"

She pushed him, but he didn't budge. He started tracing another line, above her eye and down, like a prison bar. For a while she was sure she was going to throw up, but she concentrated on the air around her and the nausea went away. Nikodemus kept drawing his line, and after a bit, she didn't feel sick at all. Being this close to him made her too aware of his masculinity, of the rock-solid chest underneath his shirt and the hard thighs on either side of her legs.

"I think I'm addicted," she said. Her fear took over, and the confession tumbled out of her. "Whatever he's been giving me, I think I'm addicted. I've thought so for a while. You know? Like some kind of paranoid looney. I'm not normal, I know. Normal people have friends and go to school, and I've never done any of that. I'm practically the only woman in a house full of men, and I almost never have sex." She laughed, but to her ears the sound was morose.

He started a line down the right side of her face.

"I keep trying not to take the pills, but I can't." A sob came up, viciously choked back. "I can't not take them. But I don't have my meds with me. I was stupid when I ran away." She kept talking too fast. She knew it was stupid, but there'd never been anyone to listen before, and Nikodemus seemed to really be listening to her. He honestly wanted to help her. "I'm crazy, because I thought he was poisoning me, and so I left it behind on purpose."

"He was, Carson. I'm really sorry."

Her breath stopped when he finishing telling her how Magellan had been using her. And then something in her head just went *click*. How much help would he have to give her if she'd been poisoned? "I'm going to die, aren't I?"

He didn't answer, and Carson had to fight off a wave of panic. She didn't do a very good job. "Hey," he said. "Hey. It's okay." He drew another line that went just outside the corner of her eye. "Remember my oath? We'll find out whether there's something we can do to keep you alive, okay? I promise."

"How?" she whispered. Arcane knowledge about fiends stuffed her head from the incidental reading she'd done, all the time thinking how quaint ancient beliefs could be. Magellan had written about fiends' names, ranks, titles, and powers and the objects that drew them. He'd described the manner in which they could be restrained, the worship they had once enjoyed, the precise nature of the sacrifices made to them. Words, inflections, and phrases that gave to or took power from them. All of it was stuck in her head, only it wasn't some ancient religion practiced by a class of elites. It was real. Fiends were real. Even the ritual Magellan had been performing the day she ran away was real. Her stomach curdled. "Why would you want to help me?"

His eyes flickered to something besides blue-gray. He didn't say anything—he just got really quiet. The air between them chilled. "You don't get it, do you?"

She shook her head.

"I'm not letting Magellan get his hands on you again. Not ever. And you're not going out on the street without any protection from Kynan or even some other mage. You're with me now. I'll protect you. Because you'll get me close to Magellan." He held up two fingers. "Scout's honor, Carson."

"Are you ever serious?"

"All the time, sweetheart." His eyes flickered from blue-gray to green and, briefly, to glittering black. He played with the top button to her sweater, not even thinking about what he was doing, she thought, unaware that she was having some inappropriate thoughts about him. All he'd done was trace some lines with his fingertip, but her skin felt hot wherever he'd touched her. Her gaze met his. Could he be any more gorgeous? Apparently, yes. His smile was pure seduction. He unfastened the top button. "What do you think, Carson? The two of us. Should we?"

She blinked. A proposition. He'd just propositioned her.

"Come on, sweetheart. Can't you feel it? It'll be good between us. Really good."

My God, she was actually thinking about it. She really must be crazy. He slid a finger between the halves of her sweater until the second button stopped him. "How do I know you're not bending my will again? Making me want you when I really don't?"

"You may be fucked up here"—he tapped the middle of her sternum—"but there's nothing weak about your mind." He went back to her sweater, holding the second button between his thumb and forefinger. "You put up a hell of a fight. It wasn't all that easy getting in. Not until you let me." He slid the button free. "You'd know if I was bending you now. You'd feel me pushing you."

She took a breath, and Nikodemus's finger brushed the swell of her breast. Her breath stopped again, but this time for a different reason.

"So, the thing is, Carson," he said with a smile that turned her bones liquid, "if you feel like you want me, it's because you do." He'd leaned closer to her, and now her head was resting against the back of the sofa, and he was looking into her eyes. And his hand was sliding over her, cupping her breast from the outside. She could hardly breathe, it felt so good. "You're making me hot," he whispered. "Hot and bothered." His hand was inside her sweater now, and more buttons were open. "Let's do this."

Why not, she thought. One way or another, she was going to die pretty soon. If not directly from Magellan's poison, then from the withdrawal, and if that didn't get her, then Kynan would find her and take care of her. Why not see what sex would be like with Nikodemus?

"I swear I'll do it right."

She lifted her hands and drew her fingers through his hair. She sizzled from the contact.

"Carson. Christ. You're beautiful. You really are."

For some reason, that made her want to cry. "You're beautiful yourself," she said. Why not have a real life before she died?

He smiled again, slow and sweet. "Oh, yeah."

But then his cell phone went off, and he swore and reached back to snatch it off the coffee table and flip it open.

Even before Nikodemus said, "Talk to me," she heard what sounded like incoherent screaming over the phone speaker.

CHAPTER 7

Xia let his Harley coast down the street. Fortunately, the place where he'd been told the talisman had been taken was on a street with an incline, which meant he could get pretty close. He stayed back of the actual house he was supposed to hit. Lights were on in the front, but that wasn't a problem. He had all night. He parked, pulled off his helmet, and stuck it on the rear pannier. He ran his hand over his head. Even years later, he still felt the shock of his shorn head. The part of his being that no longer belonged to him burned hotter in his chest. Anger pulsed in the void, hot and bitterly sharp.

He waited in the increasing dark. As he'd been told to expect, there was a mage in the house. Too bad he hadn't been released from the stricture against harming mages. He followed instructions, not because he was a good, obedient boy, but because he had to, with no improvisation unless it involved him living another day closer to the moment when he'd kill the mage who had him. Magic came out of the house in erratic spins of energy. Maybe the fiend who lived there had already lost his soul. Ooh. Poor bastard. Maybe the mage was shaving the poor fuck's head right now. He settled back on his motorcycle to wait and see if he had company in hell.

Xia was good at waiting. Waiting gave him time to think about how he'd kill his own mage one day, if not the one inside Nikodemus's house. He put up his feet and took out his knife. Rasmus, the Danish mage who controlled him, didn't care about the knife, because he knew Xia couldn't use it against him. Lucky him, Rasmus didn't see anything wrong with occasionally releasing him from the prohibition against harm to mages long enough to take out some other mage in his way. One of the only perks of his life since the day he was betrayed was getting sent after a mage. Mage killing—his favorite job. Get in some practice with the knife, test its limits, look for flaws in the magic. He spent hours honing the edges to fatal sharpness. There weren't many flaws left. Maybe tonight would be one of those rare nights when he'd be allowed to off one of the magekind. He let the fantasy run for quite a while.

About an hour after dark, the garage opened and a cherry Mercedes convertible drove out, a male at the wheel. Long hair. All right, so that was a surprise. But then again, he recognized Nikodemus, and no warlord was going down easy. Especially him. The mage he'd been told about was still inside, though. And alive.

Not long after the warlord left, a pizza delivery car pulled into the driveway. Some skinny-ass human loser got out. Xia put away his knife and sat up. He took care of the loser. Nice and quiet. He'd never remember what happened to him. He waited for the car to drive away before he picked up the pizza box and balanced it on one hand. "Showtime," he whispered.

The mage actually answered the door. A witch, just like Rasmus said, and damned if Rasmus wasn't right that she was limited. She didn't have any of the attitude the magekind usually had. She was soft where every other mage he'd met was hardass. She had green eyes. Big green eyes, and she was hot, bodywise. Pretty face, too. Her eyes went wide when she saw him. Well, yeah. Xia knew what she was seeing, and he liked that she was afraid of him. Big guy in motorcycle leathers stands at your door and you're some tiny chick with an ugly sweater that didn't hide a primo rack, yeah, you ought to worry. Even a witch was physically vulnerable. "Pizza," he said.

The witch opened the door to let him in. Was she an idiot? He stepped in. No surprise, the warlord's house was proofed. The minute he stepped inside, the imps reacted, chittering and objecting to the mage-bond in him. Either she didn't know what that meant or she wasn't smart enough to pull her power. Xia got a little sexual spark down low. Was this his lucky day or what? She was just as young and inexperienced as he'd been told. Really young to have so much power leaking out of her. His entire spine sizzled. Oh, yeah. This really *was* his lucky day. The witch didn't know what to do with her magic.

"It's paid for, right?" she asked.

Xia improvised when he realized she didn't know what he was. First, though, he needed to get past the goddamned imps before they ruined everything. "All paid for. Nikodemus called me. He didn't want you here alone and asked if I'd bring it over instead of having it delivered to you cold." He lifted the box to his face. "Smells great."

She stood aside, and Xia gave her another long perusal when she wasn't looking. Small women weren't his style, but he could make an exception for a witch with a nice ass to go with her rack. He walked in, past the imps, and found the front room, where the light was on. "Don't forget to tell Nikodemus I said hi."

"He won't be long. You can tell him yourself."

"Sure." He put the pizza on the coffee table and flipped open the box. Good pizza smell. Nikodemus went for quality pie. "Have some." He took a dripping-with-cheese slice and handed it to her.

"Thanks."

Xia stood there, watching her devour the pizza, and he was totally turned on. Well, he was a fiend, wasn't he? He just naturally responded to the magekind. Her magic spoke to him, got him worked up whether he wanted to be or not. A woman with an appetite. Well, goddamn. He got it at last, why the witch was hanging around Nikodemus without taking him down. Nikodemus had a link with her. Now that he was close, he could feel the sliver of a connection recently severed. Nikodemus was one fucked-up fiend, making it with a witch and letting her live afterward. If it had been him doing her, she wouldn't be around to talk about it later.

"Please. You have some, too," she said, gesturing. "Sit down."

"Thanks." He got a slice for himself and sat on the couch. Not too close to her, no sense bugging her out. A fiend and a witch doing the nasty. Well, just goddamn. Nobody ever accused Nikodemus of not having balls or never crossing a line or two or a hundred. He put his feet on the table, unzipped his leather jacket, and slouched down on the sofa. She was done with her pizza already and reaching for more. He wiped his palm on his shirt and stuck out his hand, "Xia, by the way."

"Carson." She put her hand in his, and hell if he didn't get a flash of heat all the way up his arm at the contact. He was improvising already, why not improvise his way under her clothes?

"I'm going to get a beer. You want one?" This particular improvisation required him to act like he knew the house and belonged here. He knew about Nikodemus. There weren't many fiends who didn't at least know about him: the only warlord without a clan of fiends surrounding him. Rumor was he was building up and the other warlords were freaking at the idea. But before he did anything with the witch, he needed what he'd come here to get. Get his theft out of the way, and he could improvise a little more. The only problem was, where the hell was it?

"Help yourself." She shrugged and eyed the pizza.

The television was on, Mortal Kombat frozen on the screen. "You game?" he asked.

"I was trying, but . . ." She sighed. "Mostly nothing happens."

"Wanna learn? Here, have another slice." He leaned forward and grabbed a big slice for her. Then he took off his jacket and tossed it onto a chair. He was wearing a blue tank top he knew matched his eyes. She took a big bite. "Hell, did Nikodemus forget to feed you?"

"I wasn't hungry before." Yup. There went the green eyes, up and down his arms and the abs you could bounce a quarter off of.

Xia stared at her. "You're pretty." A true statement.

She was, and he was getting worked up around her. Physically and otherwise. Except her magic was fucked up something serious. Nikodemus's doing? If she was into kink, he wanted some. Bad.

Carson's cheeks turned pink. Kind of cute if you cared about that sort of thing in a witch. He didn't. "Thank you," she said.

"After I get us a beer, I'll whoop your ass at Mortal Kombat. How about it?"

She looked at him, all innocent like she'd never *pwn3d* a fiend in her life, and said, "Okay."

On the way to the kitchen he detoured around the house. But he didn't get any sense of the talisman he was supposed to steal. The witch was supposed to have stolen it from Magellan, a wily bastard mage if ever there was one. Rasmus was hungry and smart, and he wanted what Magellan had. Strike that. He wanted what Magellan used to have. Rasmus intended to get tight with Magellan, because whoever found and cracked the talisman was going to be one beefed-up mage and Magellan was the only one who knew the ritual. Rasmus's exact instructions were to steal the talisman from the witch. Instructions that, come to think of it, gave him a lot of leeway. If he got close enough to the talisman, Rasmus said, he'd feel it like an itch under his skin.

The witch had followed him on account of who the hell knew why. Whatever the reason, he didn't like or trust it. Now she was standing in the archway looking all small and helpless and a total wet dream for him. No question he wanted some of what she had. "The kitchen's that way," she said.

"I was just checking something out. I forgot something the last time I was here." He felt a flicker of power, but it wasn't coming from the witch. The skin on his arms crawled. Had to be the talisman. Had to be. The witch was looking at him funny now. Fuck. Did she know?

"Are you cold?" she asked.

"A draft, I guess."

Her pretty green eyes weren't suspicious at all. He went past her, close so that his torso slid across hers, which got him thinking about something else, all right. He got the beers and came back. She was on the couch again. He sat next to her, closer this time. She gave him a look, a little sideways shift of her gaze. He used his thumb to pry off the cap and handed her one of the Asahi Blacks. Then he did his. The cap flew off and hit the floor five feet away. Ice cold. She picked up the Wiimote, and while she was distracted, Xia let himself soak up the magic he felt coming from her. She didn't even notice what he was doing. His belly did a little flip-flop. Nice. And this time Rasmus wasn't around to stop him.

Yeah, a little tension because he hadn't done what he was supposed to yet, which was find the talisman, but nothing he couldn't deal with. He was feeling a lot more tension over the witch. No wonder Nikodemus had her here. He let her magic work on him. If it weren't for the void in his core, he'd have been in some serious bliss.

He took away her Wiimote and put his hands on her shoulders, up close by her neck. Her gaze lost some focus, the way humans' did when a fiend got in close. His leathers creaked when he bent toward her, and swear to God, he couldn't decide what to go for first. The mind fuck or the body one. He could hear her heart pounding, feel the anxiety in her. Getting in ought to be easy.

"No," she said. Her eyes were more alert than he expected.

"Oh, yes," he whispered back in a voice intended to soothe and seduce. "You're so pretty, Carson." *Too fucking bad,* he thought. "I can't figure out why Nikodemus would leave you here all by yourself."

"A friend of his is in trouble." He shifted on the couch. She frowned and scooted away. He looked for another way into her head and didn't find it. "Cut it out," she said. She brushed away his hands. "Either you stop, or you leave."

"My bad," he said. "It won't happen again." Damn, but she had some serious defenses. Rasmus had told him she was limited, but she felt like she had enough magic in her to blow away the Danish mage without trying very hard.

She smiled. "So, how do you know Nikodemus?"

"Are you serious?" He grabbed his beer and took a nice long pull. "Everybody knows Nikodemus."

"All right, then, what do you do for a living, Xia?"

The witch was being so polite he could gag. "What the fuck is that supposed to mean? What do I do for a living. What do you think I do?"

Her eyes stopped being soft, and he sat up straight, hands in the air. She sure looked like a mage now. "I don't know," she said. Her magic cranked up until he thought his head would explode. "Pizza delivery boy? Model for House of Leather?"

Crap! Did she ever give up? "Don't you know anything? I work for a friend of Nikodemus's. They go way back."

"What do you do for him?" She squinted and rubbed the back of her neck.

"A little of this. Little of that. Whatever the hell he tells me do to."

"You're a gofer."

"Among other things, yes."

"By any chance, do you deal in artifacts?"

He went still. "Sometimes."

"I suspected as much." The witch leaned forward, attention fixed on the knife fastened to the side of his jeans. "Like your knife. The hilt is exquisite. You really shouldn't be wearing something that valuable. I don't think I've seen anything quite like it. Where on earth did you get it?"

"It's mine." His body had a predictable response, and he shifted on the sofa.

"May I see it?" She held out a hand. Just like a mage, always ordering people around. "Please?"

With one hand, he pulled his blade free of its sheath. Her palm closed around the lapis hilt. Her eyes got big again. "Ouch!"

"Watch yourself," he said. He took back his knife. "It's dangerous." She shook out her hand. He had an erection the size of the Empire State Building. In his head he saw himself inside her, inside human heat and wet. He held the blade to the light. "Watch this. I'm not going to hurt you. I promise." He took one of her hands and extended her arm. He was shaking with anticipation. How long since he'd done this? Knife clenched in his hand, he pushed up her sleeve and stared at the tracery of blue veins in the tender inside skin. The slender blades of his knife intertwined, wound around each other, each edge a thousand times sharper than any human-made steel. How many years of slavery did each of those carved-out edges equal by now?

Her eyes got big again when he put the tip of the blade over her arm. He tightened his fingers around her wrist. He wanted this so badly he was afraid his trembling would make him miss the vein he wanted. Jesus, he was useless. He got himself under control and stretched her arm to the side, against the couch. The anticipation opened him wide. He touched the blade to her skin at the very spot he'd picked out.

"You barely touched me," she said, staring at the growing dot of red on her arm.

Hunger came to life in him, blossoming like a new rose. Blood quivered on her pale skin. He brought his head close to her arm and breathed in. The dot of blood welled and ran into the crook of her elbow. Now he ached. Ached. His tongue touched that scarlet edge. The taste burst over him. Wild and bitter. He'd be seeing true just from this little taste of her blood. He pressed his mouth to her skin and tasted deeper. Deeper and deeper. Sweet, bittersweet taste.

"What are you doing?" She pushed at his head and nearly succeeded in pulling her arm free. "Stop it, I said."

The throb of the garage door opening broke his trance.

Fuck.

He was totally out of time. He grabbed her head, knife clutched in one hand. "Where's the talisman?" he said.

"I don't know what you're talking about."

He was pretty sure she was lying, but there wasn't time to scare her into telling the truth. "The thing you stole from Magellan. Where is it?"

The car shut off. Xia jumped back, chest heaving, breath burning in his lungs. He didn't have long, and now duty tore at him. He had to betray his kin yet again. Every goddamned day of his life he was an enemy to his kin, but this was the lowest he'd ever been, forced to steal a talisman he knew would be used as a weapon against his people. Once Rasmus cracked this thing open, he was going to make his current power look anemic. He yanked on Carson's arm and pulled her off the couch. No more delaying.

"Hey!"

Dragging Carson behind him, he burst into the hallway where he'd felt the shiver along his skin. He followed the sensation down the corridor. Goose bumps broke out along his arm and all down his back. Wherever it was, it was damn close.

He didn't have time for more than a cursory inspection of how Nikodemus had warded the talisman. He slashed. The edge of the blade severed the wards without finesse. A piss-poor job. He was going to leave signs. Too bad. His orders hadn't included leaving no trace of his presence. He snatched the talisman from the niche it was hidden in and got burned by a flash of white heat. "Fuck!"

But he had it. The carved stone heated his palm, burned him, actually. Teeth gritted against the pain, he headed for a back window, holding Carson. Magic came off her in waves, and Xia was convinced she was going to blast him.

"What are you doing?" she asked. She stared at his hand and the talisman. A door opened somewhere in the house. The warlord was home. Xia shoved the talisman in his pocket. The magic inside was unstable, because it remained hot. "Give it back. It's not yours."

"It's not yours, either, witch." If he were free, he'd kill her and be done with it. He saw her intention of warning Nikodemus before she knew herself what she was going to do. He grabbed her arm and twisted it up hard until she squeaked with pain. "Any noise from you, and you're dead."

With his free hand, he ducked her head down, and they both went out the window.

CHAPTER 8

Carson fell hard on her hands and knees when Xia pushed her out the window. The landing knocked the air out of her, and she was trying to get a breath when Xia grabbed her around the waist. She was still gasping when he put the point of his knife to her throat. She was terrified and convinced Magellan had sent him. How else would he know about the talisman?

"Not a word," her captor said.

Any minute she expected him to plunge his knife into her chest. But he didn't. Xia dragged her with him along the narrow path between the side of the house and the house next door. She saw a light go on in Nikodemus's house. On the street, Xia marched her up the hill to a chromed motorcycle parked under a tree. His arm squeezed, compressing her ribs. One-handed, he fished a roll of duct tape from one of the panniers. He put a length over her mouth, then plunked his helmet over her head. She bent at the waist, trying to knock herself free of his grip.

But, in a rapid series of moves, he turned them around so her front was pressed hard against his back, yanking her by the wrists to force her arms around him. He wrapped her wrists with duct tape and then maneuvered them onto his motorcycle. Terror ground at her heart so hard she thought it would burst. With her behind him, he released the brake and let the bike roll downhill. He used his feet to keep them upright. They were blocks away before he started the motor.

He headed the bike up hills so steep she tightened her arms around him just to keep from sliding off the back. His ribs moved with laughter. She was losing all sense of where they were or how long they'd been driving around the city. Cold whipped through her when he stopped the bike on a dark, empty street: commercial buildings, warehouses, buildings made of stucco and tin. Not much traffic.

This was where he was going to kill her. She took slow, deep breaths. Panic would only get her killed faster. With his feet planted on the ground, he cut the tape between her wrists but maintained his hold on one arm. She flexed the other, willing the circulation to start up in her fingers. Her feet didn't reach the ground, but at the first opportunity, the very minute her feet hit pavement, she intended to run for her life. Still gripping her wrist, Xia turned just enough to snatch the helmet off her head. The edge scraped the back of her skull.

"Get off," he said.

With trembling legs, she slid off his bike and had to concentrate in order not to fall. His fingers remained clamped around her wrist. She ripped the tape off her mouth and drew in fresh air. If he was smart, he'd drag her away from the street. Between the warehouses, or maybe through a fence to a back yard. Fear made her body feel too light, but her head was clear. She kept her weight on the balls of her feet, prepared to dash if he let go or loosened his grip. Into the street was best, she decided. Across the street and into the dark of the largest of the structures.

He pulled her toward him, eyes raking her up and down. "I'll find you again," he said. "Wherever you go, I'll find you."

"I haven't done anything to you." Belatedly, his meaning penetrated. He was letting her go. She stared into his shadowed face. Clarity came to her, a flash of certainty, fueled by what Nikodemus had told her and what she knew from Magellan's texts. Xia was a mageheld fiend. His will did not belong to him. Some mage, someone like Magellan, controlled his actions. She stepped close and put a hand to his cheek. "I'm sorry for what's been done to you. It's wrong. If I knew how to fix it, I would."

"Back the fuck off, witch," he said. He slapped away her hand. The corner of his mouth curled. "When I'm free, I'll hunt you down and kill you. I'll kill every mage you ever knew. Everyone you love."

"Give me back the talisman." She held out her hand as if he owed it to her. As if he was nothing and she was queen of the world.

"Just like every other mage," he snarled. Anger twisted his mouth and turned his eyes an eerie, interiorly lit blue. "You don't control me, witch, so the answer's no."

"Give it back before Nikodemus finds you and takes it back."

"Fuck off." One-handed, he shoved the helmet on his

head, cutting off her view of his insanely blue eyes. And then he reached over and pushed her hard enough to send her flying. Her feet left the ground, and she landed hard, scraping the backs of both arms through her sweater.

Stunned, her ears rang with the sound of him revving the motor. She turned her head away from the exhaust. As she watched him go, all she could think about was that he had the talisman and that right now, Nikodemus must believe she'd stolen it and was halfway to Magellan with it, betraying him the way mages always betrayed fiends.

The sound of the motorcycle receded. She was alone. Far away, traffic whooshed along a freeway structure. But this street was silent.

She sat up, slowly, to work her way past the bruises, and stayed on the curb until her head stopped spinning. When her eyes focused, she pulled off the bits of tape still stuck to her wrists. She stood and assessed her condition. Nothing broken, but a great deal was scraped or sore. Her headache, which at Nikodemus's house had nearly vanished, was coming back full force. Great. She shivered. She had no idea where she was. The combination of wind and fog numbed her joints, and now that she wasn't distracted by the thought of being murdered, the cold penetrated straight through her. She had no money. Her purse was at Nikodemus's house. She checked her pockets anyway. Nothing.

Carson started walking. Downhill, since Xia had ridden so far uphill to get here. The streets were wide and dark, not many lights, just locked-up chain-link fences and the smell of cooling asphalt and roof tar. Her everyday world had turned into a dangerous place. She was smack in the middle of a war. If Nikodemus was right and she really was a witch, she had the awful feeling her side wasn't the good guys.

She tripped over a metal pipe, a short length, a little longer than her forearm, rusted out at one end. She picked it up because there was no other weapon at hand. Whether Nikodemus would come after her she didn't know, but somewhere out there Kynan was looking for her. She wasn't going to be unarmed when he found her.

Every so often a car drove past her, blasting music so loud the bass pounded at her ears. One of them slowed down. She ignored the stares and shouts and gestures and kept walking, gripping her pipe. Head down, she counted her steps and headed for the distant lights and sounds of traffic.

The downhill was getting to her knees. Her thighs hurt and her shoes pinched, but she kept walking. The street leveled out for a bit and became residential. Some bars, none too clean from what she saw, a restaurant with dingy walls and paper instead of tablecloths. But mostly homes in various stages of disintegration. Sheets over windows, peeling paint. Barred doors. Her stomach rumbled. Another car pulled even with her and kept pace. A shiny black BMW. She tightened her fingers around her pipe, prepared to—she didn't know what. Bash someone over the head with it if she had to.

She heard the electric hum of the Beemer's passenger window sliding down. She walked faster. Colors flashed behind her eyes. The car door opened while the vehicle kept moving, and someone jumped out, running a few steps to keep his balance. She turned, pipe raised, and her blood froze.

Kynan grinned at her. He made a motion to whoever

was driving the car, and the door swung shut. He grabbed the back of her upper arm. "Gotcha," he said.

He was much, much taller than her. Carson brought up the pipe, but he caught it midswing and crushed it into so much powdered rust. He stopped walking, forcing her to stop, too. She drew a breath to scream, and he grabbed her, hand over her mouth, while he stood with his head cocked, studying the buildings. She worked her mouth open and tried to bite him, but his palm was over her mouth, not his fingers. He dragged her up the stairs of a stucco building with a battered mailbox at the top of the cracked stairs. Someone had taped a For Rent sign in the street-facing window.

Once she realized he was taking her inside, she fought. But he was much bigger and stronger, and when she started kicking, he just picked her up and threw her inside, hard enough that she hit the floor and rolled several feet.

"Leave me alone, Kynan." She scrambled to her feet, eyes darting every which way, looking for a way out. Somewhere to run. "Magellan will never know if you let me go." Her plea might have been spoken in ancient Egyptian for all the effect she had on him. They were inside an empty house. Vacant. He walked to her and grabbed her by the shoulder in a merciless hold. He marched her through the house, away from the windows and toward the back, where darkness seethed with malice. She twisted and brought up a knee, but he slammed his body against her. Her head hit the wall hard and opened a cut along the side of her head. Warm blood trickled down her temple. Carson prayed Nikodemus was angry enough to come after her.

"You seem to have figured out a few things since you ran off," he said.

"Yes," she said. She focused on keeping her breathing even. "Yes, Kynan, I have. I know what Magellan did to you. I know you're not free." Words bubbled up, low and desperate. "I'm a mage—maybe I can fix that."

He laughed. "Carson, you couldn't touch your magic if your life depended on it." He slapped a hand on the wall above her shoulder. "You forget, I've been watching Magellan poison you since I brought you to the house. You're expendable, Carson. You always have been, and when you're gone, he'll just send me out to get him another witch or mage to use up."

Her stomach felt like a rock. Nikodemus had been telling her the truth.

"Seems like you know a lot now. So maybe you know what this means: I've been released from the prohibition against harming one of the magekind." He put his head by her ear. "You do know what that means, right?" He grabbed one of her hands and pinned it against the wall. "Did you manage to find out about that?"

She stared into his gorgeous eyes. Thick black lashes. Golden-brown irises. "It means Magellan sent you to kill me. It means you have no choice." She dropped her voice. "You never have."

"You learned fast while you've been free." His mouth came closer to her ear, close enough that his breath heated her cheek. He licked blood from her temple. "What's it like, Carson? To go where you want, when you want? To look around and know you can do whatever the hell you want?"

Her head was pounding again. She might just float away from her body. "I hate him, too," she whispered.

"He told me to bring him your eyes and your heart when I'm done."

Carson stared back at him. She wanted to be sick, but she wasn't going to give him the satisfaction.

He pressed her against the wall, trapping her there with his arms and body. He was erect. He rolled his hips against hers to make sure she knew his physical state. While he leaned against her, he traced a finger along her lips. "Every time I looked at your mouth, I imagined you on your knees. Did you know that? In my head, you're always naked, and you're touching me, your mouth on my body, and I can do anything I want. What I want. The way I like it. I'm going to have your mind, Carson, and when my cock is hard inside you, I'm going to make you come. You'll hate it, you'll hate every second of every minute while I bring you."

She felt him slipping into her head and threw up a wall, the way she had when she was trying to stop Nikodemus.

"It won't last, Carson." He growled. "You can't hold out on me forever."

"I hate him as much as you do."

He snarled, a sound more animal than human. "Nobody hates Álvaro Magellan as much as I do. Not even you." She felt his presence around her, heavy and monstrous and trying to get into her head. *Walls,* she thought. Her mind was protected by a wall. The sense of him receded. "I killed your parents for him, Carson. I'm the one who took you from your loving family and gave you to Magellan. Poor little orphan. Raised by the man responsible for your parents' murder."

She shook her head.

"On your knees, Carson. The way you saw me with

Magellan." He pushed her down. "Do it. Just like that. That's how we're starting. You do to me what I have to do to him."

Carson fought to keep her mind walled off. She might not be able to use her magic, but Kynan was right about one thing. She was free, and she could do whatever she wanted. "I'd rather die."

CHAPTER 9

Nikodemus smelled pizza when he came in with Durian. The whole business with the phone and the yelling was an annoying fuckup. Durian had called to report no progress and then dropped his phone in the john, hence the screams of anguish before everything cut off.

"The witch still here?" Durian said.

"Yeah." *Good,* he thought, smelling the extra garlic and basil. At least Carson had had something to eat. The imps were jumpy, but considering Magellan's not-really-a-witch was in the house, no wonder. She amped him up, too.

"You sure?" Durian had been all over the city, and he still looked like he'd just stepped out of the pages of *GQ*.

He was sure, except, actually, he couldn't feel her. Not a thing. An exhausted human could do that, sleep so hard he couldn't be felt. "She's probably asleep on the couch, dead to the world. She's had a hard couple of days.

Makes sense she'd fall asleep after getting some food in her stomach."

"Sure."

She wasn't in the front room.

But a quarter of a large pizza and two bottles of beer sat on the coffee table. The television was on with the sound off, frozen on a scene from Mortal Kombat. One of the beers was empty. The other one hadn't been touched. Not more than a sip or two at best. Cold. Not icy anymore, but still cold.

Durian picked up her purse. Black leather, battered and shapeless, the stitching coming loose. "This hers?"

"Yes." From the corner of his eye, he saw a red dot on the floor. His pulse shot up to two hundred. A drop of blood. Just one, a perfect circle on the floor. He knelt by the droplet. Not fresh enough to be warm, not old enough to be dry. He touched the drop and brought his finger to his tongue. Carson's blood, no question. Even stale, the taste worked on him. He let his body react, and his magic roared to life. He didn't do anything to bring it down. The imps chittered loudly.

"What is it?" Durian asked.

"Carson's gone." The house was empty. No mage. No Carson Philips. No talisman, either. An uneasy feeling settled on him. That drop of blood suggested too much that wasn't pleasant. "I don't feel another fiend, do you?"

"No." He felt Durian go on alert, gathering his magic, letting the constraints of a human body dissolve enough to pull additional power. Nikodemus had already done the same. A sweep of the house didn't take long.

"Looks like your little witch robbed you blind," Durian said when the two of them stood in front of the empty niche. Nikodemus tried pretending the talisman was still there, but his indulgence lasted about three seconds before the disaster sank in. The thought of a mage with the kind of power the talisman would confer turned his blood to ice.

"No, she didn't." His defense of her came out without him even thinking about it. Now, that was a shock, to realize how strongly he felt about the witch. Well, fuck Durian's attitude.

"She's on her way to Magellan right now," Durian said. "Or else off by herself, killing one of the kin on her own."

"I want to know what happened here," Nikodemus said. "Then I want to find her." There was no way she could crack the talisman on her own. She couldn't. And he just didn't believe she'd go running back to Magellan. No way.

Durian bent on one knee, examining the floor. "You got fooled, Warlord. That's what happened."

"Only another fiend could have gotten through my wards." Durian didn't argue, because it was true. "And since we didn't feel so much as an echo of a fiend here, whoever took it must be mageheld."

"Of course. She's a witch. She probably has dozens of magehelds at her command," Durian said. He looked over his shoulder at Nikodemus. "She summoned one and let him in to do it for her." He got up and scrutinized the hallway. "There were two people." He knelt again to run his fingers over a spot of the floor. "Heavy boots here."

"Fiend?"

"Impossible to say. Mageheld if it was, which we have already surmised." He touched another spot. Nikodemus didn't see anything, but this was Durian's speciality. If you were going to be a good assassin, then you'd better be a damn good tracker. Durian had honed skills most fiends didn't. "Smaller feet here. Fresh. Human. Female." Durian lifted his chin and swiveled his head, breathing in during the entire motion. "Large male. In human form, but not human. I agree, mageheld. Much smaller female. Easy to pin down. Your human witch."

Two sets of feet. Big mageheld fiend. Tiny little witch who reacted to the talisman like it was hers to crack. Add two and two and you could end up with him being an idiot fooled by a pair of green eyes. Only that wasn't what had happened. Carson Philips wasn't like other mages. He'd been in her head, and he knew different. No way had Carson stolen the talisman. "What about the blood?"

"Could be a hundred explanations." He stood in front of the niche, eyes closed. "Accident. A struggle. Or maybe she likes to give her fiends a taste. I've heard some witches like a worked-up fiend between their legs." Durian faced him, eyes open. "This was a snatch and grab. Done quickly. Hastily, even." He frowned. "The weapon that cut through was more than capable of delicacy. He was in a hurry." He started walking again, toward the window at the end of the hall. At the window, he stood motionless except for breathing and the movement of his eyes. "From that spot to the window, he was carrying her. They went out here. Her first. Then him."

"Kynan?"

He shook his head. "Maybe. No way to tell."

"You want my version?"

Durian settled his weight on one hip and nodded. "Certainly, Warlord."

"Kynan lusts after Carson so hard his dick is in a permanent hard-on. He gets sent after her with orders to kill.

He finds her, because he's Kynan Aijan and he can find a barnacle on your ass if it has mage-magic in it. But he's not going to do it right away. Hell, I heard him tell her he was going to take his time."

"How'd he get in?" Durian asked. "This house is proofed."

"There was a breach when she opened the door for pizza." His oath was working on him. She was out there somewhere, and he had to find her. "Kynan was close enough to sense her. He went after her. Got in. Attacked her. Takes the talisman on the way out with her because he knows Magellan wants it back and it'll give him major points."

Durian shrugged. "Maybe."

"Carson can't pull. Even if she wanted an army of magehelds, she couldn't manage it any more than she could crack the talisman on her own. Find Kynan, and we'll find the witch and the talisman," Nikodemus said.

Durian lost the trail about two blocks downhill from the house. "He'll be taking it back to Magellan after he kills her." Kynan or some other mageheld had stopped touching the ground then. He stood in the middle of the street, scowling. "You touched the witch, right? Her mind."

"I had permission." Helping yourself to someone else's mind was taboo among fiends, but they always recognized extenuating circumstances. This was one of them. He'd been so deep in the witch's head, with a little luck, he'd be able to get a lock on her general location. The closer she was, the more accurate his ability to find her. The problem was she'd know it, and if she couldn't be trusted, or someone else already had control of her, they were fucked. So much for the element of surprise.

"If we're going to find her before she takes the talisman to Magellan, we don't have a choice," Durian said. "Sweep for her."

Nikodemus let his magic burn in him until his skin ached to be free of this form. With the reversion to a more elemental state, he felt Durian like a flame. He also felt Carson. Very far away. Still in the city, though. The lure of her mind was sweet, like a drug. Someone had taken her from his house and that pissed him off. "Got her."

He and Durian went back for the car. He let Durian share his connection with the witch. Took them forty minutes to get to her. And forty nanoseconds to spot the fiends in the shiny Beemer parked in front of the building she was in. Mageheld fiends, because he couldn't feel them. Their appearance gave them away. Clue one: ninety-thousand-dollar car in a crappy neighborhood. Clues two and three: two freaks inside the car with short hair and suits. Magellan should have pasted labels on their foreheads.

The lack of mental awareness cut both ways. Inconvenient as hell not to have a connection to them. He couldn't get in to shut them down without being close enough to touch. But they couldn't feel him, either. That gave him and Durian an advantage to work.

Nikodemus kept driving, turned the corner, and pulled his car into a spot near the house behind the one Carson was in. "What a dump," he said when they were out of the car and looking into the back yard. Everything sagged. Cement for a back yard, with dandelions pushing up between the cracks. Water pooled around the back stairs. "I want them both back, Durian. The witch and the talisman."

Durian's expression said he thought it was too late. "I'll take care of Kynan, Warlord. The witch is your problem."

Nikodemus grabbed Durian's chin in one hand and let his power scorch him. "You call this fealty?" he said softly. "I told you what I want. You damn well better help make it happen."

Durian's eyes flashed. "My apologies, Warlord."

"Accepted."

"We go up." Durian pointed. "You take the back. No sudden moves. Recon only until we know what we're facing."

Nikodemus nodded.

Getting in was sliding on ice. Smooth, cold, and fast. He let his form change just enough to use his greater agility and climbed the side of the house. The window sash came up easy once he broke the lock. Thank God for skinflint landlords. Inside was a dump, too. Mold dotted the new paint, and the carpet was just butt-ugly. He moved toward the stairs, keeping his magic on tap and his senses wide open. Durian was waiting at the bottom of the stairs. When Nikodemus came down, he got hit with a blast of Carson's fucked-up magic so hot he practically fried on the spot. And just when he concluded Durian was right and she'd screwed him royally, pretending she couldn't use her magic, the heat turned to ice and sputtered out. Hot magic, cold magic, and no fucking control. He didn't get how she'd lived this long. That kind of hot/cold swing ought to have killed her a long time ago.

He followed Durian past a laundry room with bad plumbing and curling linoleum. An indistinct male voice broke the silence. He started to get anxious, because he was remembering the look on Kynan's face when he saw

Carson. You didn't have to have a connection to know what he wanted from her. Kynan Aijan had a serious jones for the witch. They went around the corner, two cold and silent shadows.

He was creeped out at being so close to Kynan without feeling him as kin. It was unnatural. Freakishly wrong. The feeling went straight through him. He got the chills just thinking about what it must be like to lose his ability to connect. Rage built up in him. Absolute fury. Fucking magekind were animals, what they did to fiends. Kynan couldn't feel them, but he still had his other senses, and he was going to figure out he wasn't home alone with his lady. When the fighting started, his buddies out there in the Beemer were going to come in. Not the greatest odds, but he'd faced worse in his life. He had faith Durian could take down the other two when they came in. He stopped in the doorway. He felt Durian go on point, too. There was blood, and the smell hyped them up.

No way Carson had gone willingly. Blood trickled down the side of her face. Scalp wounds could bleed like crazy, and the smell was distracting Kynan from what, more than obviously, was an attempt at a mind-fucking rape. She had her clothes still, so, thank God, Kynan hadn't gotten to the physical stuff yet. But mentally, he had her just about nailed down. He'd be scouring her mind right now except Carson, even cut off from her magic, was holding him off by sheer force of will.

He signaled to Durian to go around the side, taking the primary attack, because this was exactly what Durian was trained for. But Durian hesitated. Nikodemus knew he was pushing it, doing all this to save a witch and expecting Durian to do his part. But no way was he going to let Kynan break Carson. No fucking way. He took the point himself. Durian he'd deal with later.

Carson turned her head, and Nikodemus's gaze locked with hers. Jesus H. Christ. He was in her head so fast he got dizzy. Accessing her was the equivalent of turning on a garden hose and getting a fire hose. Holy shit. She didn't say anything, but she didn't have to. Her eyes spoke for her. Fear. Relief. And a defiance that about burned him. And what do you know? He could feel Kynan through Carson's magic, even though Kynan was mageheld. And that gave him an advantage over the fiend he'd never expected to have.

In the instant before Kynan got that he had company, Nikodemus struck. He pushed his magic through Carson, feeling the burn on the way.

Kynan flew across the room like a bottle rocket. The house shook when he hit the floor. For good measure, Nikodemus locked the two bozos in the Beemer. A little mojo to the door, and the two in the car were trapped. He shut down Kynan, amping up the control, because using Carson let him get at Kynan in a way he couldn't have otherwise. Fucking-unexpected-A. Took about thirty seconds to lock down the entire situation.

Durian knelt and went through Kynan's pockets looking for the talisman. That left the witch for him, except he had all he could handle trying to hold on to Carson and keep his magic going. Durian came up empty and whirled on Carson. She was pushing herself onto her hands and knees, shaking off the effect of Kynan's attempted indwell. "Where is it?" Durian shouted.

Carson lurched to her feet, one hand on the wall for support. She looked at Durian with a deceptively calm expression. "He's not the one who took it," she said. Her magic sputtered and died, and Nikodemus lost his lock on Kynan and his fellow magehelds. Fuck. Kynan was twitching.

"Liar," Durian said.

"Watch it!" Nikodemus shouted.

Kynan shifted. Full power. The building rumbled with it. His hand shot out and seized Durian by the back of the neck. Kynan went flying again, this time because of Durian. The two in the Beemer broke free. Through Carson, Nikodemus could still feel the magehelds, just barely, a faint echo. Not much, but enough to get prepared. The two outside pounded up the front stairs, busting open the door. Nikodemus got one of them before he made it inside. The second one made it halfway across the room before Durian cut him down. A nice, clean, efficient kill, worthy of an assassin. Poor mageheld fuck never had chance.

Nikodemus figured that staying in Carson's head wasn't going to break taboo any worse than he already had, not having asked her permission and all. If he didn't, there were going to be more bodies in here in half a second. He pushed his magic through Carson again, hard enough to make her gasp, and then he jumped Kynan's mind, working practically blind, since she was now at squirt-gun levels, magically speaking. His recent touch of the fiend helped him direct the attack blind. Kynan went down again, but he was still twitching. This wasn't going to last long.

"Go, go, go!" He grabbed Carson and booked it for the car. Durian sped after them. Not even he was crazy enough to tackle Kynan right now. He caught up when Nikodemus had to slow to get Carson over the back fence. They sprinted for the street. On silent communication,

Nikodemus split off for the driver's side while Durian got Carson into the back. *Wham, wham.* The doors slammed shut. Inside, the scent of Carson's blood filled the air and started a thrumming in Nikodemus's body. A fresh, rich scent. Durian was probably no better off.

"Floor it," Durian yelled.

In the rearview mirror, Nikodemus saw Kynan vault over the fence. Carson's magic ricocheted like those fireworks that blossom outward and fade and just when you think the show's over, more color rushes at you. "Durian! Get the bleeding stopped. Now." At this rate, Kynan could call himself a cab and find them. He was afraid to use Carson to pull again—she was fading fast.

"I'll take care of it, Warlord." His voice sounded strained, and yeah, that made total sense what with Carson at high tide and bleeding, to boot. Carson yelped, and she and Durian disappeared from the rearview mirror.

CHAPTER 10

The back of Carson's head hit the rear passenger seat with a thud that crossed her eyes. She lay lengthwise on the seat, no seat belt, one foot on the floorboard, the other jammed up against the opposite door.

The man Nikodemus called Durian grabbed her shoulders and pinned her down as the car took off. His eyes flashed red, and then he was hard against her body, suffocating her. Her heart crashed against her ribs. She couldn't breathe even though she could get air into her lungs. The point of her elbow collided with the door, and she saw stars. He was heavy, pressing down hard to hold her in place. His eyes glowed like gold on fire. A fiend. Like Nikodemus, Durian was a fiend.

The car leveled out, but Durian didn't let her go. She got her arms up to push him away. As soon as she touched him, a growl rumbled from deep in his chest, but she could breathe now.

"Where is it?" Durian said between gritted teeth. His

fingers tightened on her shoulder. His growled words answered the question of whether she'd been rescued: not really.

"I don't know." He wasn't going to let her up, even though the car was moving steadily through traffic. She tried to hook him in the ribs with her elbow, but he leaned away at just the right moment. "He took it."

"Who? Magellan?"

"No!"

"Durian," Nikodemus barked from the front seat. "I can still smell blood. I don't care what you have to do, get it under control!" The car took a corner too fast, and her body pressed against Durian's outside thigh. The fiend pulled his shirt over his head and wadded it up against the side of her head.

"Ow."

"Don't move, witch," he said. His pecs bulged. Like Nikodemus, he was ripped.

The pressure hurt her bruised head, and while she was distracted by the pain, he tried to get in her mind. Carson pushed back, and Durian grimaced.

"That's better," Nikodemus said from the front.

No. Way. Just no way. She wasn't letting him in her head. Behind her forehead, a bubble of pressure released, and the effect, whatever it was, cut Durian off. She put herself behind the walls that had kept out Nikodemus and Kynan before and locked gazes with Durian. She whispered, "Stay out."

The car slowed. Durian stared at her and relaxed his grip on the back seat. "Christ," he muttered.

"Hell of a rush, isn't it?" Nikodemus said from the front. "Just don't overdo it back there. Keep her under wraps. That's all you have to do."

"Warlord." Durian never took his eyes off her. His hand covered her mouth as he leaned over her, and Carson just wasn't strong enough to stop him. She shoved at him, hands on his bare chest, but it didn't help. His hair fell over her as his mouth hovered over her cheek, breath hot on her skin.

She yanked her head hard to the side, and his hand slipped off her mouth. "If you want to know something," she said in a low, hard voice, "all you have to do is ask."

Durian backed off. "Who did you let into the warlord's house?"

"He said his name was Xia."

"Rasmus's fiend," Durian said, glancing toward the front of the car.

"Shit," Nikodemus said. He slammed on the brakes, and Carson and Durian ended up on the floor amid a blaring of horns. He fell hard on top of her, knocking the wind out of her. Adrenaline rushed through her. She brought up a knee, and she ought to have collided with his crotch instead of his kidneys, but his head jerked back, followed by his upper body.

Nikodemus had flung his arm back, fingers tangling in Durian's hair. He pulled up hard. "Get the fuck off her, Durian." Horns blared. "Carson. Up front."

Durian howled in protest. Carson wriggled out from under him as Nikodemus pulled over on a tree-lined street of Victorian-era homes. Nikodemus had one foot jammed hard on the brake to keep the car from rolling down the steep incline. She slithered over the seat, heading for the front passenger side. "Watch your head, there. Not you, you dumbass." He put a hand on her backside and pushed her the rest of the way over. She landed with her head over his lap. "You okay, sweetheart?"

She sat on the front seat, holding tight to her emotions, shaking as she struggled to fasten her seat belt. He released the emergency brake and looked over his shoulder to check for oncoming traffic.

"I guess."

Durian growled, and if Carson hadn't known the fiend was there, she'd have thought there was a grizzly bear in the car. "Let me out here," he said.

"Kynan can wait," Nikodemus said. "We need to get on Xia's ass."

Durian fell silent. "As you wish, Warlord." The note of respect in his voice was absolutely genuine. "But I still need a few things before we go after Xia."

Nikodemus nodded and punched the button that released the lock. "See you back at my place, Durian." The fiend got out and bowed to Nikodemus before he closed the door. Nikodemus reengaged the locks. "He is fucking pissed at me."

"I'm sorry."

"Not your fault. He just doesn't care for mages. Can't say as I blame him. Much." He touched her shoulder. "It won't happen again."

They drove back to his house with his arm on the back of her seat. Every now and then, he touched her nape or fiddled with her hair. Whenever he did, she felt like she had right before her first kiss, shivery and nervous and worried about what he meant by it. She had no idea what to do or even if she ought to do anything at all. He didn't say anything even after he garaged the car or when they went into the house by a side entrance. Her head hurt, but this time it was because she'd hit it hard when Kynan threw her against the wall.

He closed the door behind them. He didn't look angry

or like he was planning how best to kill her. But then, how was she supposed to know what was going on behind his eyes? She wasn't the one who could insert herself in someone else's head and look around for something interesting. They were in the rear of the house. Near the kitchen. There were painted medallions here, too. She was convinced there were real bodies behind the faces and that if she turned her back on them, they'd come to life and leap on her. Her head ached where she'd been cut.

She followed him into the kitchen. Nikodemus wrapped his arms around her, and held her, and she let him because he made her feel safe. Relief hit once they were inside. She was safe now. Her legs wobbled a little. "Tell me, Carson. In your own words, if you don't mind."

"Xia told me you called to have him pick up the pizza instead of having it delivered. He said he knew you." His body was warm, and she had to work hard at not pressing herself against his solid strength. He didn't seem to mind having her close, though.

"I didn't call anybody but the pizza place, Carson." His voice was moderate, a trace of tension, but no anger. "I told them to deliver."

"He said he was your friend." She tipped back her head to see his expression. He didn't look angry. But how many times had Magellan exploded with no warning? The thought made her heart leap. She took a step back, then another when all he did was tip his head.

"Didn't you recognize him as mageheld?"

"Mage what?" She put her hands to her temples and rubbed. "No. No, I didn't."

"Mageheld. It's what we call a fiend who's controlled

by a mage. Mageheld. Like Xia. He's mageheld to Rasmus. The way Kynan is mageheld to Magellan."

"He didn't look any different to me."

"It's not how we look. It's how we feel to each other. Chances are you did feel him, but you didn't know what it was." Nikodemus put a hand behind her arm and walked with her toward the fridge, where he poured her a glass of his headache remedy. "Those of us left free can't feel the mageheld. But a mage can. The short hair's a dead giveaway. Mages shave the fiends they enslave."

"Oh." She thought about all the short-haired men in Magellan's house. Fiends. All of them enslaved. She took the cup and steeled herself for the taste. "Thank you." She took a sip and shuddered.

"Shit does taste like swamp water."

"Yeah." She finished her swamp water, thinking about mages and fiends and what Xia's short, short hair meant, and wondering what she would have been like if Magellan hadn't taken her. Would she have her own private army of mageheld fiends? It was an unsettling thought. Nikodemus touched her cheek. Just a brush of his fingertip, but it sent shivers down to her toes. She ducked her head so he wouldn't see her reaction and found herself staring at the empty mug on the counter. Magellan lashed out unexpectedly all the time. She prepared for the same from Nikodemus.

"Xia's been around a long time. And mageheld for years," Nikodemus said. "For longer than you've been alive."

"What about Kynan?" she asked. She pressed her fist to the countertop. Maybe if Magellan hadn't raised her, she'd be after Nikodemus, too.

"Him, too." Nikodemus stayed close to her, and it

was distracting that her body was so aware of him. She missed the comfort of his arms and wanted him to hold her again, even though she felt like she was betraying him just for having the longing. "I don't understand why mages hate fiends. Why do they—why do we do that to you?"

Nikodemus sighed. "A long time ago, fiends got out of control with humans. The world was different then. I'm not saying it never happens now, but we got our act together and put a stop to it when the mages started fighting back. Even after, though, when we were . . . more circumspect with our interactions, the mages just never stopped coming after us."

Carson chewed on the inside of her mouth. He stared at her, and her stomach momentarily took flight at the thought that he wanted to kiss her. He was close enough to.

"There was blood on the floor when I came home." He proceeded to give her a thorough once-over. He wiped her head with a damp cloth.

"Ouch."

"Hurts?"

Carson saw stars. "Yes."

"Sorry." He inspected her neck and shoulders as far as he could without rearranging her clothes, touching intimately, but without intimate intent. He pushed up one sleeve of her sweater, then the other. She found herself staring at a bruised puncture in the crook of her elbow.

She looked at her arm. "He was showing me his knife. It hardly hurt. But then he went all strange."

"Blood is exciting for us." He waited, and Carson made sure she didn't react. "The smell. The color. But especially the taste. That's why I was yelling at Durian to keep you from bleeding. We were both getting cranked."

"Oh."

"In passion, Carson, whether it's love or hate or just plain lust, the taste, smell, and color of human blood bring us closer to our elemental natures. Closer to whoever we're with. In a good way or a bad way, depending on how you feel about fiends. Some of you like it." His hand came away from her. The pads of his first and second fingers glistened with a smear of red. "And some of you don't." He walked to the sink and turned on the faucet to rinse his fingers. He wiped his hand on his jeans. "It was natural for him to want that. If it were me, I would have wanted to do the same."

She allowed the words to sink in, tried to understand them separately and without emotion. Her stomach felt like a clenched fist as she looked at his fingers, now clean of her blood.

"It's what fiends are, Carson. We're a warrior species. Blood and the glory of battle make us alive. For us, living without that connection to blood and kin is worse than being dead." He came back to her and stroked the bruise on her arm. With you, for a while, Xia probably felt like he was free." His eyes were so beautiful, she thought. She could gaze into them forever. "A few thousand years ago, human sacrifice was common enough. It's not now because the world changes. The magekind treat us as if nothing ever changed for them. To them, we're evil. Monsters they either control or kill, lest they be killed themselves."

"The magekind," she said, stretching out the syllables. The air vibrated between them. "You mean my kind. People like me."

"Yeah, Carson," he said softly. "I do. Sorry. But that's how it is. You and I are enemies."

"Why? I've never done anything. Why do we have to hate each other?"

"You're different, Carson." He put a finger to the inside of her eyebrow, following the arch with the tip of his finger. Carson closed her eyes. A thread of otherness was in her head, vibrating just enough for her to know he was there. She opened her eyes and flashed back to her earlier sense of Nikodemus as not human. She felt that from him now. Stronger than ever. "You're not like Magellan," he said.

He was staying out of her head now. She studied him. If she'd had the ability to see inside his head, she would have looked. Gladly. "What's Rasmus going to do once Xia gives him the talisman?"

"You know the ritual," he said quietly. "You saw Magellan do it. At the very least, you read about it."

"A sacrifice to release the spirit trapped inside. A murder."

Carson was getting all too familiar with mages and their relationship with fiends. She forced herself to think this through, to compare what she knew of the ritual with what Nikodemus had told her about fiends and mages and what she had observed and reasoned out on her own. She looked Nikodemus in the eye. "I assume Rasmus's strong enough to survive the aftereffects?"

He leaned against the counter, long legs crossed at the ankles. "Rasmus is strong enough, trust me on that one."

"How bad will that be?" She had an idea about that, unfortunately.

"If Rasmus, or Magellan, for that matter, cracks the

talisman it's possible . . . likely, he'd have enough power to take a warlord without help. You'll have to take my word about how bad that makes it for us." He raked his fingers through his hair, and the light glinted off his earring. "Go clean up while we wait for Durian to get here. Upstairs. First door on the right."

While she was heading up the stairs, Nikodemus's cell phone went off. She heard the device vibrating all the way from the front room. She slowed when she heard Nikodemus say, "Talk to me." The next thing he said was, "Fuck," in a low, emphatic tone.

She returned to the arched doorway. Nikodemus had his back to her, and he was pacing, listening to whoever had called him.

"Tell him I said to stay put. No. I said no." He listened a while longer. "If he already left, why'd you let me think he hadn't?" More listening. "Never mind. I'll take care of it. Thanks. No. You needed to call. You did. We're square that way." He closed the phone and stood motionless, squeezing his hand so hard Carson expected the phone to burst apart.

"What happened?" she asked.

He turned around. "Durian went after Xia by himself."

"Did he find him?"

He stopped squeezing his cell and the room got ten degrees hotter. She felt the pressure of his mental energy. "He followed Xia all the way to Rasmus."

Carson kept the eye contact. "We're going after him, right?"

He laughed. "A witch who can't pull? Get real."

She stayed exactly where she was, aware for the first

time in her life that she had a purpose. "I felt you when you were fighting Kynan. You used me. My magic."

His cheeks flushed. "If I hadn't, you'd be dead."

"I said I'd help you." She touched his arm. "So why not let me?"

He searched her face. "Even if it kills you faster?"

"I'm offering, Nikodemus. Don't be an idiot," she said. "Just don't."

He stuck his cell in his back pocket. "Back there with Kynan? I pulled some fucking amazing magic through you. Amazing."

"So?"

"The problem, Carson, is your magic is all over the fucking place. I can't risk you shutting off just when I need you, if you get my drift."

She stared at his still-clenched fists. His fingers clenched and released, clenched and released. "You can control a human, can't you?"

His eyes narrowed, but she was certain, almost certain, that she saw a leap of anticipation in them. "It's called an indwell."

"And you could do that with me."

"Yeah," he whispered.

"Would that work?"

He took a breath. "I wouldn't need to be in total control. But I'd need it to be permanent. So you can't shut me out."

"I'm still offering," she said.

His eyes flickered through shades of blue, gray, and black. "Come here." She walked to him and he took her wrist, bringing her forearm parallel to the floor. "I'll keep my promise. You know that, right?"

"I know.

"This should do." He drew the side of his fingernail out from the puncture Xia had made, leaving frost in his wake. They watched her blood pool in the crook of her elbow. "Look at me now." His voice felt like smoke. "This is the important part. It works better if you're looking at me. Don't block me, okay, Carson?"

She nodded. He pressed a fingertip to her forehead, and a spark leapt from his finger to her skin and into her head. His eyes changed from gray-blue to silver-black, and Carson didn't dare look away. Panic rose up, but she kept her mind open. Vulnerable. Nikodemus slid into her head, and when he was there, he brought up her arm and fit his mouth over the reopened cut. Her body clenched at the same time he swallowed. His other hand cupped the back of her head.

When he lifted his head, he was alive in her mind. She breathed when he did; her heart beat when his did. Without question, he could do anything to her, ask anything of her and she would do it. He didn't, though. He just gazed at her, growing more vivid in her head.

"Holy fuck," he breathed. His hand still cupped her head. Their bodies were just inches apart. Carson licked her lips, and his gaze followed the movement of her tongue. "You like that?" he whispered.

She nodded.

His presence in her mind flared, and in another breath, they were physically synchronized again. He wasn't controlling her—he was just there. Incredibly *there*. She raised up on her toes to press her lips to his. He hesitated, but then he responded, and his physical state echoed her own. His mouth opened over hers, and God, he felt so good. So right. His thumb moved over her cut, pressing down as his tongue slid across hers. Slowly, he drew away. Reluctantly. He bowed his head and pressed his forehead to hers, hand still cupping the back of her neck. His breath rattled in his chest. "Next time tell me no, Carson, or you're going to find out exactly why fiends make better lovers."

The wry remark got her past the longing to kiss him again. Nikodemus receded from her head but didn't disappear. "I think we better get going," she said. She was wobbly inside, but she didn't feel like he was controlling her. Mostly, she felt normal, if you counted her wild desire to kiss him again and see where they ended up as normal. Which for her, wasn't. But, then, she'd never met Nikodemus before, had she?

"Trust me," he said. "You'll know if I take over."

"Let's not waste any more time, Nikodemus."

Rasmus lived in the Berkeley Hills, across the bay from the city, on Wildcat Canyon Road, a winding road on the ridge above the University of California. Nikodemus's Mercedes took the turns smooth as silk. It was full-on night now, but foggy, so there wasn't any moonlight. Streetlights were few and far between. They went around a corner, and then Nikodemus jammed on the brakes hard enough to snap Carson's shoulder belt tight. He backed up to a car parked off a soft shoulder, a Volvo that had seen better days.

"Durian's." Nikodemus closed his eyes and shook his head. "I can't feel him."

"Maybe we're not close enough."

"Maybe," he said in a low voice. He gripped the steering wheel and didn't say anything for a while.

Carson put a hand on his shoulder. "We'll find him."

"Let's go," he said.

Her mouth was dry as dust as they parked on a verge

choked with weeds and blackberries and walked uphill along a one-way-at-a-time driveway. Carson's pulse beat hard when they cleared the last of the trees that shadowed the pavement. They were here. Her feet slowed without her thinking about it, so that Nikodemus ended up several steps ahead of her. In the dark, he seemed taller and more imposing. Confident, too. He moved silently, unlike her, the perfect sneak thief.

A few feet from the gate, he waited for her to catch up. They waited in the shadow of a pine for Durian to appear, but he didn't. After perhaps fifteen minutes, Nikodemus threw an arm around her shoulder and drew her in close to whisper. "Change of plan, all right?" She nodded. "Without Durian, we have to approach this differently, so listen up." His breath warmed her ear. "Unless something goes wrong, and it won't, no killing tonight. I'm not after Rasmus. We're going in cloaked. His fiends can't feel me, regardless, and given that I have you on tap, I can hide both of us from the mage. All I want is the talisman. We get that, find Durian, and we're gone like we were never here. Okay?"

"And if we don't?"

"Plan B is if I let go of you, you make nice with Rasmus while I take care of business. Let him think whatever he wants. You're both mages. Talk shop or something. Say anything. Lie. Cheat. Steal. Just keep him distracted. Can you do that for me?"

She nodded.

Nikodemus slipped his hand from her shoulder to the back of her neck and looked her in the eye. When their gazes met, that spot in her head tingled with awareness of him. "Plan A first, Carson. You lay low and I keep you under wraps. I'll pull when and if I need to. If we can't get the talisman that way, we go to plan B. I'll still have you, by the way, so don't try anything stupid. You're a witch, and magehelds have to defer to you. Demand to see Rasmus. Acting like a bitch should be plenty convincing. Okay?"

She nodded again.

"Either way, I'll get the talisman, find Durian, and get us out."

"Is there a plan C?"

Nikodemus smiled. "You bet. Run like hell. You ready?"

She wasn't, but she nodded anyway.

"That's my girl. Balls of steel." He turned to the gate and muttered something Carson couldn't make out. An echo of air brushed back at her. The gate swung open. Her incipient headache vanished like someone had wrapped a blanket around it. She knew the pain was there, but she couldn't feel it. He looked at her sideways and blew on the tips of his fingers. Nobody came out to investigate. Carson stared at the house, straining to see and hear. Was the mage in there murdering a fiend right now? Could she really have grown up to do something like that?

The top of the driveway opened onto a flagstone-paved area large enough to hold several cars. There was one car, a dark Jaguar, and a motorcycle.

The mage's house was three stories of gray stone with olive trees and a tulip tree in the front as the centerpiece of the landscaped garden—all the signs of wealth Magellan so loved himself. A portico light was on, but only two windows were lit, both of them on the third floor, where, if the house was anything like Magellan's, the assistants had their quarters. One window flickered with television glow. Carson shivered. At the front door her heart pounded so hard she couldn't get a breath. She burned with the desire to thwart Rasmus, not because of Nikodemus but because it was a vicarious strike at Magellan.

Nikodemus put his head by her ear again. "Durian's here. I can feel him now. This is going to be a piece of cake. Let's roll."

He moved first, soft and substantial as shadow, so silent he might have been a true shadow. She crossed the threshold after him, every nerve in her body taut. Her head throbbed. She was dizzy, and every so often some snatch of information came to her that originated from Nikodemus. His impressions tangled up with hers, and she ended up disoriented, trying to separate his from her own. Somewhere in the house, she heard a noise, a scratching sound. Like a dog walking over a wooden floor. The smell was horribly familiar. Blood. Blood mixed with the musty gunpowder odor she'd encountered the night she walked in on Magellan.

"We're too late," she whispered. Rasmus had already started the ritual. She couldn't tell if the wrongness was in her or if it came to her from the house or even from Nikodemus. Her legs shook, and every time she closed her eyes, her stomach turned somersaults.

"Don't make me do all the work here. Focus," Nikodemus said.

She nodded and tried to filter out her fear. Whoever was watching television changed the channel. The sound cut off mid-sales-pitch and then blasted on rock music. One of the Dane's fiends, so Carson assumed, came down the stairs, shoes muffled on the carpeted surface, then thumping on the landing. At the bottom of the stairs, he flipped a light switch. The click was louder than it ought to have been. To Carson, he looked human. As human as Nikodemus, come to think of it. He looked past them, even though seeing her and Nikodemus standing there should have stopped him cold.

She watched him for some sign of what he really was. He wasn't as tall as Nikodemus or as broad through the shoulders, but he had muscles. He wore sweatpants and running shoes and nothing else. From the look of him, he was fresh from a fight. Blood trickled down the side of his face from a cut over one eyebrow. He kept walking. Carson gave a silent sigh of relief.

The conversation downstairs got louder and angrier. The acrid smell in the air thickened. "Fuck," Nikodemus whispered.

As they turned the corner into a living room, the sound of running thundered. Nikodemus hissed and caught Carson's arm. She concentrated on breathing, on keeping calm. Even he flinched at the noise, and that made her feel better. He pulled her close. Her arms slid around him, actively thinking of him in her head, helping her stay low. "No," he muttered. "No, no, no."

CHAPTER 11

Nikodemus didn't feel Durian anymore. Not even a glimmer. Fuck. He was Rasmus's mageheld now, or as good as. He tensed as Rasmus's big fuck of a mageheld, Xia, came down the stairs. Like the other fiend, he was wearing sweats and running shoes. A black tee stretched tight across his chest.

On the bottom stair, Xia hesitated. His eyes burned neon blue as he scanned the room. Beside him, Carson held her breath so hard Nikodemus felt it when her brain started telling her to take a breath. Xia glanced downstairs and then back, eyes blazing with suspicion.

Xia walked a slow perimeter, and at the front door, he stopped and ran his fingertips over the wood from top to bottom, paying more attention to the door knob. Even Nikodemus held his breath and prayed his camo would hold against the mageheld. But at last, with a final sweep of the room, Xia headed downstairs.

At the same time, he and Carson let out a breath. "Jesus,

he's one nasty fuck," Nikodemus said. Carson started to say something, but a shrieking howl from lower in the house froze them both. The sound continued longer than he could imagine anyone making a noise so soul-piercing. Magic, a mage's magic, turned the air to lead.

"Durian," she whispered.

But it was too late. Way too late.

Carson clutched his arm as the waning howl slivered the air. The sound cut off, leaving them in horrible silence. Without thinking, he slid his hand down her arm until he was holding her hand. He curled his fingers around hers and gently squeezed. He steadied her until she was used to the sensation of him affirmatively touching her inside her head. He went deeper. "We aren't going to be unseen this time," he said, keeping his head near her ear and speaking softly. "If—things don't go so great, I'll be pushing my magic through you, and you're going to feel it. Like this."

The amount of magic in her wound him up. The stuff was like some kind of dark and twisted lake, and if he had time, he would have explored. He wanted to kill Magellan. Jesus, she was just a kid when he started with her. As with sexual maturation, you had to castrate early if you were serious about stopping a mage's magical development.

He worked to keep the anger from his voice. "You're not going to freak out if that happens?"

"No."

He pulled as much magic as he dared. He wasn't worried about magehelds picking up on him. The fiends here couldn't feel his magic if he handed them a glass of it to chug. It was Carson who worried him. He was confident he had her shielded from the mage, but the more magic he pulled, the higher the risk of his accidentally exposing her. One of the magehelds was bound to figure out some of the mage-magic didn't belong to Rasmus. Or worse, he'd slip up and Rasmus would figure out he had uninvited company.

No living without risk, right? Besides, she was his secret weapon. On the way down the stairs, the air kept getting heavier and thicker. His skin crawled. Somewhere down there a mage was pulling some serious magic.

Another scream lifted the air. Despair and pain and outrage and terror all wrapped up in an awful sound tearing at his heart. He wasn't the only one to feel the despair of that sound. Carson clapped her hands over her ears, bowing her head to her chest, shoulders hunched over. Even a human mage who couldn't touch her magic reacted. Durian was being murdered, his soul torn apart, his body separated from his magic. They didn't have much time left.

At the bottom of the stairs his head pulsed with an additional awareness. To the left, a corridor led to a chrome-metal door closed tight. Nikodemus slipped past her and stood with his palms pressed to the metal surface. The reflection was warped and almost as useful as his access to Carson's sense of fiends, mageheld or not.

"Double platinum," he said softly. "Layer of crushed rubies in between. Typical paranoid mage behavior. Nothing magical passes in or out of a door like this." Crap. He'd really been hoping to get a sense of what was going on in there. "There's no way I'm getting us through that." He turned his head and saw her shaking. She had balls, though. He felt her getting ready. Fatalistic, thinking, for Christ's sake, that whatever happened to her next was payback for letting Xia into his house. She was wrong. But that's what she felt.

Her eyes went wide, pupils huge. Smart lady. He didn't even have to tell her it was time for plan B. He couldn't help admiring her nerve. She had to be terrified, but she swallowed once, walked up to the door, and knocked.

He released his camo of her just as she tried the door. It opened, and then it was too late. He didn't have time to tell her there were two mages inside. Not just one.

CHAPTER 12

The door swung back and, reluctant to touch anything, Carson darted inside before it closed, Nikodemus's words echoing in her head. *Keep your cool, and they'll only see you.*

Her nightmares confronted her. The smell of blood and acrid smoke of pulverized rubies was so fresh and sharp she was astonished she hadn't smelled it before. Durian lay on a long, chrome table, his head shorn nearly bald. One naked arm hung off the side, his feet off the other end. Blood congealed around his body and dripped to the floor to form a pool already drying at the edges. Her stomach clenched.

Several inches of the metal table extended past Durian's head. The talisman sat on the edge of the table above his head. The carved figure pulled at her attention so hard she had to concentrate to look anywhere else.

Two men stood on the other side of the table. Rasmus was tall with pale skin and a narrow nose set in a gorgeous face. Blue eyes as gorgeous as the rest of him. Long white-blonde hair fell past his shoulders, thick and straight, to the middle of his back. He wore black pants and a black turtleneck.

Magellan stood beside him in a custom-made suit, English-tailored double-breasted gray wool. His chocolate eyes were set deep over a nose that bespoke an Aztec ancestor in his Brazilian-Portuguese heritage. Blood spatters made a diffuse arc across his coat, white shirt, and sky-blue tie.

Two fiends she recognized from home stepped forward, mouths tight, bodies tensed for action. Magellan raised a brilliant red hand to stop them, and they did. She'd never seen anyone disobey Álvaro Magellan. Xia stood just behind Rasmus, arms crossed over his chest, legs apart.

"*Boa noite,* Carson," Magellan said. "What a pleasant surprise to see you again."

"I wish I could say the same."

"You left so suddenly." His eyebrows drew together as he tried to pretend he was puzzled. "Without telling me what upset you." His voice fell. "Oh, yes, we have missed you. Very much. But tonight, you will come back to us? *Sim?*"

She licked her lips. "I don't think so," she said.

Magellan's gaze darkened. "We shall see. Regardless, you have arrived just in time." He held a knife in his other hand—it wasn't Xia's knife—and lifted it slightly and at an angle to Durian's throat, ready to plunge down the glinting blade. Durian twitched even though Carson couldn't fathom how he could still be alive. Not when Magellan had sliced open his chest.

From the corner of her eye, she caught a flicker against

the wall, sometimes there, other times not. Nikodemus. Her head told her it was him. Neither Magellan nor Rasmus gave any sign of noticing, and Xia might as well be a statue. But Xia's gaze constantly tracked the room. Carson walked toward Rasmus and Magellan, away from Nikodemus.

Rasmus made a motion in the air. "Good evening, Ms. Philips." His English was perfect. "Welcome to my home." His voice was a honeyed bass, familiar and terrible in its beauty. Magellan had a voice like that. He smiled. "Álvaro has told me so much about you."

Her chest went cold inside. Rasmus's attention was on her, looking her up and down with such concentration she was convinced he didn't know about Nikodemus. Magellan, too, watched her with a cold and scornful smile. The chill around her heart and the spark of heat in her head told her Nikodemus was drawing on her. Xia's eyes narrowed. Rasmus frowned. "She is—I disapprove of this, Álvaro."

"Her condition is not your concern." Magellan gestured with his blood-covered hand. "Come here," he said as if there were no doubt of her obeying him. Maybe there wasn't, because she took a step closer, provoked by an inner compulsion to stare at the carved black figure on the table.

"Ah," Rasmus said, seeing the direction of her stare. "You are drawn to this. Despite your—alteration." He picked it up with a graceful movement, ignoring Magellan's scowl. He balanced the figurine on his palm. "As am I. Lovely, isn't it?"

"Yes."

"I told Magellan that's why you took it."

"She can feel nothing, Rasmus."

"Perhaps she cannot touch her magic, but that doesn't mean it isn't there, acting on her. Or even on her environment." He looked like he'd swallowed something rotten. "On the subject of what you have done to her, Álvaro, you and I must agree to disagree."

If she were to stretch out her hand, she could touch Durian's chest. And if she dared, she could lean a little farther and snatch the black figurine off Rasmus's palm before he could prevent her. Her fingers itched to touch the carved surface again. Instead, she touched Durian's neck. The frost around her bones deepened. His pulse beat against the pads of her fingers, weak and thready, but there. His eyes fluttered open, pain-filled, and yet there was also a flame of hatred. "This is wrong," she said. "It's evil and wrong."

"You are ignorant," Magellan said. "He will destroy some human if he's not controlled. It is his nature."

What if she wasn't fast enough to snatch the figurine? Magellan turned his head to her, and she brought her hand to rest on the metal edge of the table. He took the carving from Rasmus. Behind him, Xia drew his knife and started flipping the blade, hilt to tip, catching it each time between thumb and forefinger. She was close enough to see the carved details. "It's exquisite work," she said to Rasmus. Was she fast enough to snatch it from Magellan? Close enough? "Nineveh, I think. First millennium."

Rasmus's upper lip twitched. "May I call you Carson?" He didn't wait for an answer. "We are very close to unlocking the power this lovely object keeps hidden inside."

"It's only stone." It wasn't, though. A pulse of awareness came from the object, pulling at her in an oddly familiar manner. To her right the light rippled, and she couldn't stop herself from looking. Her lack of restraint betrayed them. Xia came to attention. "Stone," she said in a clipped tone. "That's all it is. A bit of stone carved by someone thousands of years dead."

"If you wish to believe so, you may." Rasmus looked at Magellan. "Now that your witch is here, Magellan, I presume you no longer need my assistance."

The figurine was still between Magellan's thumb and index finger. She could reach it. Years and years of obedient fear of crossing Magellan blocked her off from the resolve she needed. By the time her hand shot out, it was too late. The talisman was locked behind Magellan's closed fist.

"I can use her, *sim*." Magellan's eyes blazed. "But I may need you to restrain her for me. She has not been taking her prescriptions." He scowled. "This will be the last time ever she is useful to me. You needn't be careful."

"Of course." Rasmus began to mutter under his breath. "Come, Carson," he said. Pain flashed over her, and she saw through streaks of color.

She stumbled back, clutching her head between her hands, and then the pain stopped. It broke apart. Her vision returned to normal.

"Forgive me, Álvaro," Rasmus said. His mouth twisted. "I don't know what happened." Rasmus's magic worked around her again but didn't touch her. Her gaze involuntarily went to the shimmering air that marked Nikodemus's position.

Magellan's head whipped around. "What are you looking at?"

She clapped her hands to her head again, but the pretense came too late. Magellan glared at Rasmus. "Treachery of yours, Rasmus?"

"I assure you not," Rasmus said in a voice that was no longer pleasant. "Xia? Is the witch looking at something we should know about?"

The fiend's eyes bored a hole in her. Right through her. Like he'd already settled on how best to kill her and all that remained was to do the deed. His mouth pulled down at one corner. "She did not come here alone. There's no way."

"Is that true? Have you brought a guest, Carson?" Rasmus asked.

Magellan set the figure on the table by Durian's hip, far from her reach. His attention shifted to his left, squinting hard. He pushed the knife into Durian's chin. "Draw even an atom more of power, fiend," he said out loud, but not to the precise place Nikodemus was standing, "and this one will be irredeemably lost."

Something eased up in her head. A pop sounded in her middle ear. Nikodemus releasing his power. He came into her view. Xia caught his knife by the hilt this time and let it settle into his hand. A muscle in Magellan's cheek twitched. He hadn't realized Nikodemus had gotten so close. He covered the reaction well. Carson watched Magellan's eyes go wide. "Nikodemus?"

"Fuck off, mage." Nikodemus sank to a half crouch, his irises solid silver flecked with black.

"Do nothing as of yet, Rasmus." He lifted a hand toward the other mage, but his attention was riveted on Nikodemus. "There is no limit to what I could accomplish with Nikodemus himself at my command."

"You don't own me yet, mage."

With the tip of his knife, Magellan drew a line in

the air, downward along Durian's chest, stopping above where his heart would be. The frost in her turned to ice. "What did I tell you, fiend?" Magellan held the point of the knife to the gaping wound in Durian's chest.

"That was hardly magic," Nikodemus said. His voice was bereft of silk or warmth. He was himself turned to stone inside to speak with a voice like that. Carson knew what he was going to say before he spoke. "Do what you will, mage. There's nothing left to save of this one."

Magellan's hand shot out and grabbed Carson by the hair, yanking hard enough to lift her off her feet. She bit back a cry as she landed on the bare metal end of the table. "And her?" His grip on her hair brought tears to her eyes. "Is she in your control? Answer me, or your servant dies right now."

Clink.

She turned her head in the direction of the noise and saw the figurine had fallen over. Durian's fingertip stretched toward it. Pressure built behind her eyes. Xia's face and upper torso were at the periphery of her vision. He was waiting. Lying in wait, and Nikodemus was drawing hard on her. She was ice inside. Solid ice. She pushed everything out of her head. Everything except the carved black stone and Durian's reaching fingers.

Something happened. She didn't know what, but Magellan said, "I make no idle threats, fiend." The knife was at her throat now.

"Go to hell," Carson said. She reached for his arm, trying to block him.

His arm plunged toward Carson's chest. She was stone, too. Just like Nikodemus. Time focused for her, each second a life of time in which to choose. She angled the heel of her palm at Magellan's wrist.

Her ears exploded in sound. Streaks of vivid crimson and midnight blue saturated her vision. The only reason she knew she'd connected with Magellan was the clang when the knife point slammed onto the table. He yanked on her again, pulling her across Durian's lower torso. The smell of blood sickened her. Her hands flailed, slipping in blood. Through a veil of shifting colors, she watched Durian's fingers reach for the figurine. She shut out everything. Xia. Magellan. Rasmus. Durian. Even Nikodemus. Durian shoved the figurine at her. She closed her hand around it. Her palm sizzled with heat, and an electric charge shot up her arm.

Time returned to breakneck speed.

Magellan captured her wrist in a grip that made her clench her jaws to keep back a scream. No way was she going to give Magellan the satisfaction. No way. Nikodemus was in her head, his emotions huge, overwhelming her.

"Xia," said Rasmus, "subdue the fiend Nikodemus."

Magellan's gaze slid back to Carson. "It is of no use to you," Magellan said, twisting her wrist to a point beyond pain. Both her arms went numb from the elbows down. He pressed the knife to the side of her throat. "Release it." His voice was metallic to her ears. "You can do nothing with it. You don't have the ability."

She glared at him with eyes of cold hatred. She didn't care if he killed her. All she wanted was to destroy Magellan. His grip on her wrist bent her in an awkward position with no leverage. One swipe of his knife would spill her lifeblood, dark and red, to join Durian's on the floor. She felt the air move as his knife descended, as if the blade were heavier than it ought to be, with a weight that pushed air before it. She jerked back in the nick of time.

The knife sliced the air centimeters from her throat. Magellan pulled hard on her wrist. The shock boomeranged to her shoulder and back down. She expected to feel the knife next but felt nothing. Maybe dying didn't hurt. Maybe the shock of a mortal injury kept you from feeling anything.

Wham. Something heavy hit the wall hard and shook the room. Nikodemus had managed to throw Xia, and the big fiend was picking himself up off the floor.

"One move," Magellan said, "pull any magic at all, fiend, and I'll kill her right now." Carson, on her back, saw Nikodemus poised to leap for Xia. The stream of awareness flowing between them stopped.

"Don't listen to him," she said, ignoring Magellan's knife and his grip on her. A wave of anger overtook her. Her entire life up to now had been a lie. A lie. Nikodemus was the one to show her the truth. She didn't care if Nikodemus used her up, as long as Magellan didn't get what he wanted. "I'll never forgive you if you do. Never."

The mage twisted her arm until her shoulder joint pressed unbearably against the socket. The tip of his blade sliced across her wrist. But she kept her hand clenched tight around the little figurine. "Let go," he snarled. "Or I'll cut off your hand. You—" He indicated one of his fiends. "Kill Nikodemus."

A fiend let out a keening cry and rushed across the room.

"No!" With a massive rush of adrenaline rocketing through her, Carson hurled herself toward Magellan, catching him unprepared and somersaulting over Durian's body. The mage didn't let go of her wrist, but he stumbled back, and Carson's momentum brought her the rest of the way over the table. She crashed onto her back and only just kept her head from cracking on the floor. The numbness in her arms spread. Magellan must have cut her badly. The corner of her mind that wasn't terrified knew she was going into shock.

Nikodemus leapt onto the table and unleashed a stream of blinding heat at the same time she inhaled burning air. The fiend attacking him went down with a crack and didn't move again. She saw Rasmus's body fly across the room. He landed ten feet away on his hands and knees. The energy came from Nikodemus—she felt the cold leaving her for him. Magellan shouted, but his grip on her wrist didn't lessen. Above her, Nikodemus's eyes flashed silver. Xia caught the bulk of that flash. He bled from a cut on his cheek.

Magellan yanked on her wrist, the one clutching the stone carving. The talisman in which a mage had imprisoned a fiend. Above her, she heard him say something and saw Nikodemus somersault backward, thrown by an invisible hand. His knife descended again. Her wrist burned icy-hot, and she convulsed, a scream shredding her throat. Magellan lost his grip on her hand and she hit the floor. Why? She rolled, awkward, heart racing, clumsy with fear. Pain cut her off from everything except the jangle of injury.

Magic boiled through the room, raging with such force it pushed through her like Niagara Falls. Not cold any longer but burning hot. A counterpoint warred with his magic, battering her, combusting the air she breathed. Memories came on, one image after another, a kaleidoscope of colors and shapes, people and scenes that belonged to someone else's life. Unimaginable pain lanced through her. A surge of energy burned her inside, leaving just enough space for the pain.

All she could do was lie on the floor and struggle to make her lungs work. Nikodemus shouted, screamed at her to focus, and she didn't know how or why. Without warning, the heat in her flashed out again. Air condensed around her and vanished at the point where her fingers curled around the figurine. Like a slap at the back of her head, it was over. Feeling roared back; all the saved-up pain hit her brain at once.

She would have puked if she hadn't been paralyzed by the agony. When the sensation eased up, she rolled onto her back, cradling her arm against her chest, afraid to look, afraid Magellan had cut off her hand. She couldn't feel anything below her elbow.

Magellan lay on the floor, eyes open. Very much alive but unable to move or, it seemed, speak. Xia wasn't much better. He was on his hands and knees, head down, arms trembling. Rasmus had collapsed, and two fiends lay dead.

Nikodemus helped her up, but she couldn't stand without swaying. Her head was a whirlpool inside, thoughts and feelings churning cold, then hot. He caught her around her waist, stopping her from falling to her knees. His biceps flexed against her back, and his strength comforted her. "Whoopsy-daisy," he said. He glanced at the mage and Xia. "This is going to last ten minutes, tops. Fifteen if we're lucky."

"Durian," she said. "What about Durian?"

"There's nothing we can do."

She went up the stairs on legs of rubber. She tried to move her fingers and couldn't. And then came a horrifying recollection of hearing about ghost pain and stories of amputees feeling long-missing limbs. "Nikodemus," she said in a voice thin with terror. Her eyes were stuck on his. "Tell me I still have my hand. Tell me he didn't cut it off."

He looked but kept them moving. "You have two hands, Carson."

"Thank God." What if he was lying? She laughed, a crazy sound. The truth would wait for later.

They headed for the door. Outside, Nikodemus muttered something, and Carson thought she might have seen a glow around the edges of the door. He was sealing it, she thought. Sealing it so they couldn't easily be followed. Every minute's delay worked for them and against Magellan.

The pain in her arm was so intense she couldn't tell where she hurt most. Her wrist? Her fingers? Her palm, where the sharp edges of the talisman cut into her skin? The pain remained icy-hot. He loosened his hold on her arm, but she had Jell-O for legs, and he grabbed her quickly.

"You okay?" Nikodemus waited for her to nod. "Good," he said. "Because we've moved on to plan C. Run like hell."

CHAPTER 13

To Nikodemus's magic-heated body, the outside temperature felt twenty degrees colder than when he'd walked up Rasmus's driveway with Carson Philips at his side. He moved quickly, supporting Carson and keeping to the shadows. Her pulse fluttered in the back of his consciousness, faint and thready. She'd been hit by magic strong enough to take apart the room, and at the moment, her mind was blank. So was her magic.

She kept her feet under her but walked with her shoulders hunched over, clutching her injured wrist to her chest. Magellan had been serious about cutting off her hand. Fuck only knew what shit the mage had put on his blade. He was just the sort of bastard who'd poison his knife to make things hurt more. The thought sent a shiver through him. What if that was part of her problem?

By the time they reached the bottom of the drive, he was freaking about the possibility she'd been poisoned. He didn't bother asking why he cared what happened to

a witch. He'd long ago stopped thinking of her as his
enemy. She was, fucked up as it seemed, his ally. His.
Hadn't he just watched her face Rasmus and Magellan,
with him completely confident that she would put everything on the line for him? And she had. She was one
tough little witch.

Right now, she wasn't doing so hot. Though she walked
doggedly beside him, keeping pace who knew how, his
link with her was to a mind in a state of chaos and on the
edge of physical breakdown. He gripped her upper arm
when she tripped. That earned him a glare.

"I'm not helpless," she said. But her coordination was
failing. Any fool could see that. Well, you had to admire
her spirit if not her sentiment.

"No," he said easily. Blood covered her sweater.
"You're not helpless. But sweetheart, you're slowing us
down when we ought to be hauling ass. Let me help you
so we can get out of here before Magellan regroups and
sends his good buddy Kynan after us."

"I'm fine."

"You're not." He propelled her forward. "Quit telling
me you are. You'll get us both killed with that shit." So
what if she was pissed at him? He went deep into her
head and did what he needed to get her moving faster.
And when he did, his stomach hollowed out. Whoa. He
was looking down a lava crater and her magic was seething magma about to blow. Had to be magic from Magellan taking a whack at her. She kept up with his longer
strides, but her body moved herky-jerky even with his
assistance. She lost her balance.

"Right, sweetheart," he said, catching her in time to
prevent another fall. "Fine. You're absolutely fine." At

the car, he released her to fish out his keys. She fell to her knees on the edge of the roadway and threw up.

Doubled over, she put a hand on the ground to steady herself, keeping the other tucked against her torso. Her supporting elbow wobbled and gave way until she was on her haunches, chest to her thighs. His link with her flashed on, strong enough to make him dizzy with the effort of keeping her in check. Whatever the hell Magellan had thrown at her was taking her down, and badly. Her magic came full-on, cut off, sputtered back, ramped up, then cut off again. Carson collapsed.

"Oh, fuck." He knelt on the ground next to her. Blackberry thorns caught his jeans, and he withered them to dust without hesitation. He didn't know much about human physiology, except that humans were frail compared to his kind and slow to heal when they were injured. He got nothing from her mentally. Nothing. Anxiety constricted his chest. He touched a hand to the side of her throat to reassure himself she wasn't dead, just shut off.

He got her into his arms and finagled open the passenger-side door. Inside, he got her seat belt fastened. Her head lolled back, but she was conscious again. Barely. Twisted magic swirled in her, out of control, a hurricane without an eye. He recognized his magic in there. Stood to reason some of his magic would be there. Magellan's, too, and that's what was wreaking havoc inside her at the moment.

Out here in the damn boonies of Wildcat Canyon Road, there wasn't anyone to see him vault over the car. The interior light came on when he got in the driver's seat. Push in the key, start the engine. Carson's breathing changed. Shallow, rapid pants, gusts from the storm raging inside her. Fresh blood darkened her sweater. He smelled the copper tang. Hell. He didn't know enough to understand which was the bigger threat, her physical injuries or the magic trying to find a way out of a human body unable to absorb it. Getting the fuck out of here was at the top of his to-do list, but she might bleed out on the way.

He twisted on the seat and lifted her arm away from her chest. Blood scent rose from her sweater, some of it Durian's, but more of it hers. She let him stretch out her arm, but her hand stayed fisted tight. The slice across her inner wrist was deep. The edges gaped, and blood pooled in the valley. With each beat of her heart, blood welled from the wound. The smell hit him hard. Sweet, sweet scent of blood.

"Am I going to die?" she asked.

"Die on me, and I'll put you in a world of sorry." He looked around the car for something to bind up her wrist. Nothing. He jumped out and found an old shirt of his in the trunk, left over from something or other. He got back in and grabbed her wrist. A shirt bandage wasn't sanitary; humans were susceptible to infection, but if he didn't get the bleeding stopped she wasn't going to live to get infected.

She opened her eyes. "I don't want to ruin your car."

"I'll send you the bill, Carson," he said. It was all he could do not to bend his head to taste her. She was a goddamned walking high to a freak like him. So, yeah, maybe he did taste a little. Maybe he did shudder with the warm taste of his kind's ancient prey. But he stopped, didn't he? It's not like humans didn't have their own predatory instincts to satisfy now and again. From up the hill, a motorcycle engine started up, a loud Harley motor. He wrapped his shirt around her wrist even though there was more to be had. He got himself under control. She didn't deserve to die. Not because of him. Not after the way she'd put herself out there for him.

He slid back to the driver's seat. Foot ready to hit the gas, he did what recon he could. Nothing ahead but deer, raccoons, and some bats. He heard the motorcycle before the headlight appeared in the rearview mirror. Nikodemus killed his lights and clamped down hard on Carson's magic.

"I need my medicine," she murmured. He knew she was feeling high, because that's what happened to a human who was still alive enough to know what was going on during a near total indwell. He didn't know how else to keep her alive, and right now he was so close to being in full possession of her that he might as well be indwelling. Wouldn't that be something? Indwelling in Carson Philips. He doubted she'd ever let him. But wouldn't that be nice?

He buckled up, grabbed the steering wheel, and shifted into neutral. His Mercedes rolled downhill. He didn't start the motor until he'd steered around the corner. The ER was out of the question. All kinds of freaks staked out Berkeley's Alta Bates hospital. If he took her there, they'd have every mage in the county down on them. He headed for downtown and one of those twenty-four-hour places likely to have a first-aid kit and needle and thread. Halfway down the hill, she started bleeding again, and when he touched her forehead, she was burning hot. "Shit."

She was fading in and out, psychically speaking. Magellan's magic was killing her. He had a good idea now what she'd been poisoned with and that she was having a reaction to that, too. Which meant he was going to have to take a risk. Great. If he was going to keep her alive, he had no choice.

Twenty minutes later, they were on Solano Avenue and he was looking at what must be the last independently operated twenty-four-hour pharmacy in the state of California. He cut off the engine. This wasn't safe. Rasmus was the ranking mage in the East Bay, but with Carson seizing up the way she was, he couldn't wait. She needed human first aid, and besides which, he didn't know how much longer he'd be all right with the smell of her blood so strong and her magic switching between AC and DC. He faced her and thought she was one of the most beautiful women he'd ever seen. "You stay put. I'll be right back."

She was slumped on the seat, but her eyes opened partway. She nodded, and then her eyes slowly closed. He took on Durian's form, shaved head included, and got out of the car. He hoped this would work.

Inside the pharmacy, a balding man of about sixty looked up from a computer screen when Nikodemus set the little bell above the door to tinkling. A plastic name tag above his breast pocket read "Harsh" in squared-off red letters. Nikodemus got nothing but human from him, which was creepy, seeing as this was a mageheld pharmacy. Was the old guy human or not?

Nikodemus smiled at Harsh. The front of the store was shelves of human products, divided between snacks and sundries, toothpaste, deodorant, and over-the-counter medicinals. A selection of condoms lined one wall. Right by the home pregnancy kits. Yeah, give me an extra box of Trojan Ribbed, please. So he could save Carson's life and then spend the next few days of his life making love to her. He had a fucking serious thing going for her. Way beyond anything safe.

Harsh the pharmacist sat behind a counter in the rear of the store with shelves of prescriptions waiting to be picked up by humans who didn't know the pharmacy wasn't legit. Blue light flickered on the old guy's face. A stack of manga sat to the side. One of them was open facedown on the counter. "You're here late," said Harsh. Funny, he didn't sound like an old fart.

Nikodemus shrugged.

"What can I do you for?" He picked up a can of Red Bull and drank from it.

"Copa. Pure if you have it." He grabbed the biggest first-aid kit he could find, then went to look for a sewing kit.

"Huh," said Harsh. He sent a longing glance in the direction of his manga. "You mageheld gofers always want pure."

"How about some gum, then? Does that help the monotony?" Nikodemus reached into his pocket and pulled out a crumpled paper. He pretended to squint at it. "And uh, penicillin."

"You got a scrip for that?"

He lifted his hands. "Boss treating you like shit, too?"

"Still an asshole," Harsh said, toasting him with his Red Bull. "To asshole bosses. No allergies to penicillin?"

"Do I care?"

"Penicillin it is. How much does the patient weigh?"

He thought about Carson and her tiny but stacked frame. "One ten soaking wet."

Harsh looked at him, giving him a long stare. "I hope she's good in the sack."

Nikodemus looked out the window at the car. He could barely see the top of Carson's head. The pharmacist hopped off his chair like he had a brand-new set of titanium hips and knees and headed for the back. "Yeah," he said. "Asshole bosses are the worst." He stayed back there a long time. Long enough that Nikodemus found the sewing kit and had his purchases on the counter, ready to ring up. He glanced out the window and saw, oh, shit, Carson getting out of the car.

"Hey," Nikodemus called. "My asshole boss is going to be plenty pissed if I don't get back with the pure. She seriously needs her shit tonight."

"A minute," came Harsh's voice from the back.

Nikodemus looked out the window again. The back of his neck itched. No, he didn't like this one bit. Harsh came out with a translucent brown bottle in one hand. "This stuff's hard to handle, you know." He had brown eyes, gold-flecked, youthful in his sixty-year-old pharmacist body. He set the bottle on the counter but kept his hand on it. "Copa's dangerous. You want to watch what you do with this."

"Hopefully she'll overdose and all my troubles are over." He reached for his wallet.

The little bell over the door tinkled. *Fuck.* Carson came in, arm crossed over her chest, fist still clenched. The blood on her sweater had darkened to red-black. She looked at Harsh and then at Nikodemus. "I can't move my fingers," she said in a low voice. "I've been trying since you came in here." Her voice never wavered, and her expression remained as calm as her voice, but her panic-edged eyes were fever-bright. "I can't move my fingers."

The pharmacy was on a corner with glass windows

fronting the main street and the cross street. A dark Jag with tinted windows pulled up and parked on the cross-street side of the store. The engine roar of a motorcycle sounded from outside. The Jag's rear driver's-side door opened. The man who got out wore a suit. The other three were muscle.

Nikodemus faced Harsh. "You fucking ratted me out."

Harsh lifted one shoulder. "I'm just another mageheld bastard like you, right? Gotta do what the boss says."

The mage and his fiends walked toward the store. Magellan's figure was unmistakable. He recognized Kynan, too. "No," she said. She shook her head. "No."

He reached for her good arm but missed because Carson took a step toward the pharmacist. Nikodemus locked the front door against the approaching fiends, but there were four this time, and one of them was Kynan Aijan, a freaking warlord. Playing games with the door wasn't going to buy them enough time, considering his pal Harsh could be counted on to interfere with any attempt to slip out the back. Magellan wasn't stupid. There'd be fiends at the back, too. Probably with Rasmus and his monster, Xia. Harsh, in fact, was already moving toward the half-door between his domain and the store proper, fast enough that his stack of unread manga toppled. He jumped over the dutch door. Goddamned spry for a senior.

"You." Carson pointed at Harsh. Magic built up in her so fast even Nikodemus was taken by surprise. She walked forward, and before Nikodemus could stop her, she touched Harsh's chest. The air went cold and then hot. Harsh jerked backward like he'd been punched. With a grunt, he grabbed his chest, staggering against a shelf of cold remedies. Whatever she'd unleashed against him knocked him out of his human guise.

As a fiend, Harsh the pharmacist was an impressive physical specimen. He stood just over six feet tall, long-limbed, densely muscled, and ready to fight. Shaved head all the way. Just fucking great. He was big enough to kick some ass. Nikodemus crouched, prepared to take him on. Except he could feel Harsh, and that shouldn't be.

"Fuck," Harsh said. He pulled his hands away from his chest and stared at them like he expected them to be covered in blood. "She cut me."

Nikodemus didn't have time to react, because Magellan's fiends reached the door. They couldn't open it. Kynan grabbed the front mageheld by the collar and threw him out of the way. He whipped his elbow against the plate glass and *bam*. Glass flew everywhere.

CHAPTER 14

Kynan reached through the broken window, swept away the remaining shards of glass, and destroyed the door frame. His compatriots followed. One faced Carson and pulled a gun from inside his coat, locked and loaded. Guns killed. Nikodemus didn't want to get this far only to lose Carson to a gun. He grabbed her hand and swung her out of the way at the same time he sent a blast of killing shadow toward the fiends at the door. The gun never went off, but Carson rocked back and fell to her knees.

Nikodemus let go of her and brought his forward momentum into the first of Magellan's fiends, snapping his neck. He struck the second even harder, with a backhand to the nose after a kick that shattered the fiend's kneecap. That one went down shrieking. Nikodemus went in blind and closed down everything. Ruthlessly. Without remorse. Sometimes the best he could do was send a mageheld fiend home to freedom.

With a roar, Harsh charged, and Nikodemus whirled

to face this new threat. The fiend shot past him, taking down Rasmus's last creature with a vicious slice of a talon across the throat. Blood arced into the air. Nikodemus punched into Kynan's mind as hard and fast as he could, never easy with one of the mageheld. He had to go off memory. His best almost wasn't enough.

Carson, meanwhile, had scuttled across the floor and had the gun in her uninjured hand. She trained it on the space once occupied by Kynan, but the big fiend was down for the count right now and not coming home to papa anytime soon. Her eyes were wide and startlingly green in her face, but she wasn't shaking. She looked calm and controlled. He had the feeling nothing would have kept her from missing. She lowered the gun.

"Come on, sweetheart." Nikodemus grabbed her good arm and headed for the door. Harsh reversed direction and snatched the prescription bottles and Nikodemus's other purchases off the counter. Then he sprinted after them, shifting back to human form, though not as an aging pharmacist. This guise was nearly as tall as his other one and significantly younger.

On the deserted street, Magellan leaned against the side of his Jag, a hand-rolled cigarette in one hand. To get to the car, they'd have to get past Magellan and the rest of his goons. Carson raised the gun one-handed. Steady as a rock.

"Carson," Magellan said in a low voice. "I admit I am impressed you are still alive. But don't be a fool. You can't start a battle where humans will stop talking about gang wars and start talking about shape-shifting monsters."

She frowned hard and flicked the safety on with one finger.

"Good girl," Magellan said with a sneer.

Right then and there, Nikodemus decided he hated Magellan more than anything on the goddamned planet.

"Now, give me back the talisman. *Por favor.*"

Harsh shouldered himself in front of Carson like he intended to take a shot for her. Guy thought he was some kind of cowboy. The wind changed direction and blew sweet-smelling smoke toward them. Definitely not tobacco, but Copa laced with weed from a few miles north where the National Forest system doubled as illegal farms. Magellan was self-medicating his magic. Probably had to now that he didn't have Carson. Fucking addict. He'd bottom out soon, but in the meantime, Magellan was twice as dangerous. Nikodemus kept a grip on Carson's arm because she was unsteady on her feet again. He slipped the car remote from his pocket and pressed the button. The headlights flashed.

Rasmus came around from the back of the store, six fiends following. Xia was one of them. Harsh growled.

"Keep a lid on it, pharmacy boy," Nikodemus whispered.

Rasmus's gaze lingered on the newly freed fiend. "Well," he said. His raised eyebrows betrayed his surprise. "Isn't this interesting? I thought I felt something."

"No," Nikodemus said. "It's not interesting at all."

Rasmus looked at Magellan like he could burn a hole through him at thirty paces. "Was this your doing? He was a useful creature to me."

"No," Magellan said. He drew on his cigarette. "I don't know what happened to your fiend. Perhaps he wasn't solidly yours in the first place."

"And Ms. Philips? Perhaps she was never solidly yours, as well?" Rasmus asked. His gaze stayed on Carson. Nikodemus let himself slide to stone.

Magellan grinned and exhaled Copa-laced smoke. It wasn't a nice grin at all. "She appears to be in need of medical attention."

"Everything's under control," Nikodemus said.

Magellan lifted a hand and pointed to Nikodemus's car. One of the fiends edged forward, and Nikodemus, working blind again because he couldn't get much pull through Carson in her condition, cut off his power. Much easier with this one than with Kynan. The fiend was still mageheld, but he shuddered to a stop. Yeah. The problem with enslaving your help was they didn't want to help you. Nikodemus smiled at the mage. At least this guy wasn't a threat for the foreseeable future. "Touch my car," Nikodemus said, "and you won't live thirty seconds past your second mistake."

Another fiend moved out of the shadows behind Rasmus and Magellan, and planted himself between Nikodemus and the Mercedes. This one's magic flared hot. He wanted a fight, which was only his nature running true. Like most of the mageheld, he was conflicted even when compelled to do as commanded, because he also wanted to end the mage's miserable life in bloody fashion. Nikodemus held eye contact with Magellan and said, "Get your boys out of my way or I'll freeze this one the way I got your big boy in there." He inclined his head toward the pharmacy.

"No." Carson's whisper echoed in Nikodemus's head. Her magic swirled, heating enough that it fired him with exquisite pain. She was close to being out of control. Nikodemus wanted, just for a moment, to let the heat come. He wanted the magic in her at the same time he wanted to bathe in all that energy, drink it, eat it, consume any and all of Carson's life force that he could take, whether it killed her or not. Not many humans survived that kind of intense contact with a fiend, at least not with their faculties intact.

"But she is very ill," Rasmus said, hands spread wide. His remaining fiends held back. "Leave her with us, and we'll see she is treated appropriately. In her limited condition, she cannot be much use to you."

"Sorry, mage. She doesn't want to go with you," Harsh said.

Magellan took a deep draw on his cigarette and exhaled the too-sweet smoke. Carson coughed and waved away the smoke. Harsh backed up behind her, looming over her like a very large, very protective Rottweiler.

"She is in no condition to know what's best," Magellan said. He tugged on his French cuff.

"I'd hate to off another one of your boys." Nikodemus cut off a third mageheld. Then another, in order to make his point. In his head, he felt Kynan stirring back to consciousness. Shit. That guy was not going to be as easily dealt with. He held his power at the edge of his control. They needed to get this going. One option was to let loose and see who was standing at the end. He hoped it didn't come to that.

Magellan's grin slipped. His remaining fiends stared at Nikodemus. The ones he'd cut off staggered, disoriented and about as useful as an unarmed human. Which is to say, not useful at all. "You haven't got what it takes, either one of you. This is what you might call a standoff." Nikodemus smiled. "You stand off, or I'll kill all your boys."

Magellan's power flashed. Instinctively, Nikodemus drew on Carson. Deep in his chest her changed magic burned him, poisoned, twisted, and now with an edge of something else along with the chaotic remnants of whatever had happened to her at Rasmus's house. He cut off the remaining fiends. And it was easy. He didn't even break a sweat.

Carson stood by him, holding the gun and swaying, eyes wide, pupils so big they obliterated her irises. If he took much more, she'd die right here and now. A low, thrumming growl came from his throat, a match for the energy ripping through him. Behind them, Kynan came out of the pharmacy.

"Keys!" Harsh's voice boomed in the still night air. He shoved the first-aid kit down his pants and held out his hands like he was a wideout and Nikodemus was Joe Montana down six points with a minute left.

Nikodemus threw the keys at Harsh, who snatched them out of the air but kept his legs and arms pumping for the driver's-side door. He sailed over the top of the car and landed with a thud on the street. Nikodemus grabbed Carson, and they ran past two senseless fiends to the car. At the curb, he yanked open the back door, shoved Carson inside, and jumped in after her, pulling his feet back in time for the door to slam shut. Harsh landed in the driver's side. Kynan threw himself at the car. The vehicle rocked.

"Whooo-hoo!" Harsh yelled.

Nikodemus rolled Carson to the floor and threw himself on top of her. The engine thundered to life. His head hit the edge of the seat as Harsh swerved into the street, dislodging Kynan from the hood. Harsh hit the gas and kept going.

Nikodemus kept Carson's head down and looked out the back in time to see Magellan gesture ferociously. Kynan ran down the middle of the street, arms and legs pumping. The mage's other fiends were pretty much useless. "Lose him," he said to Harsh. "Then head for the city."

A motorcycle engine screamed just as they turned the corner. From the front seat, Harsh saluted.

The car shuddered around a tight corner. Nikodemus braced himself over Carson. For the next twenty minutes, he stayed on the floor with Carson, keeping her under tight control until the engine smoothed out and Harsh said, "Bay Bridge here we come, boss."

Only then did Nikodemus get them off the floor. He had to help Carson buckle up, because she still didn't have the use of her arm, then himself, too, in case any cops were on the prowl for an easy ticket. "You're bleeding," he said. Carson shook her head, a tight movement of her chin. "Liar." He took her injured hand and examined the wound. His makeshift bandage was long gone. Her fist was clenched so tight her tendons stood out like wires. "Relax your fingers."

She shook her head. And damned if her fingers weren't locked tight. He didn't dare push her. The slash across her wrist was deepest toward the inside edge, and he could see where Magellan's knife had hit bone. They approached the toll plaza, but they had FasTrak and didn't have to stop.

"When we get home, we'll get you some real-deal first aid, okay? But I don't want you bleeding all over my car."

"Get her arm above her heart," Harsh said.

Carson lifted her arm. "I'm not bleeding."

"Liar."

"Only a little."

He squirmed on the seat but couldn't get his knees unbent because the driver's seat was all the way back. "So, sweetheart." He slid an arm around her, amazed that she was both conscious and lucid. "What the hell did you do to my man Harsh?" Nikodemus glanced in the rearview mirror and saw Harsh's eyes on them. He'd buckled up, too, and kept the car at an even seventy-five in the middle lane heading for Yerba Buena Island.

"Nice to meet you, Harsh." He leaned forward and stuck a hand into the front-seat area. His goddamned knees hurt. "Nikodemus."

Harsh had a good firm grip. "I know who you are, Warlord."

She looked at the back of Harsh's head for a long time. "I can feel you," she said. "But not in my head like Nikodemus." She kept her wrist pressed to her chest. "Why?" She looked at Nikodemus. "Why do I feel Harsh like that?"

"Because," Harsh said. "You severed me from Rasmus." He changed lanes and accelerated through the tunnel. "In a manner of speaking," he said matter-of-factly, "Carson, I belong to you now."

"No!"

They both jumped, Nikodemus and Harsh, at her vehemence.

"Interesting," Harsh said. "But it's not at all the way I was held by Rasmus."

"Did she really sever you?" Nikodemus asked. Because if she had, that was really fucking something. Maybe even a little scary, come to think of it.

"Yes. She did."

How did a witch with no access to her magic manage to sever a mageheld fiend? Why didn't he get even a whisper of what she was going to do? "You sure it was her?"

"Yes."

"I'd say it couldn't be done, except I feel you, and I didn't before. Damn good work for a witch who can't pull, wouldn't you say?" He slumped sideways against the seat, trying to get more room for his legs. "She didn't sever you, Harsh. She couldn't have."

"It was her. I felt her do it."

"What does that mean?" Carson asked. "Sever?"

Nikodemus put an arm around her and got a little tingle up his spine when she leaned into him. "It means Harsh isn't mageheld anymore. It means someone separated him from Rasmus and now he's free."

"How?"

"No fucking idea, Carson." The idea that she could have severed a mageheld fiend made him queasy. She couldn't pull, so how in the name of pick-your-favorite-deity could she have severed anybody from anything? They'd need an army of help if Carson Philips got her magic back. "Welcome home, Harsh."

Harsh nodded without smiling. His nonpharmacist human form had short, very short, auburn hair and cheekbones a male model would kill for.

Nikodemus said, "Clean sever or not?"

Harsh shifted to maintain his speed up the grade. "Clean. Rasmus felt the rebound." His eyes flicked back to the rearview mirror. "I can feel her, you understand?"

"How? Is she holding you now?"

"That's not it," Harsh said. "It's a clean cut."

"Huh."

"I think I'd know, Warlord, if all that had happened

was I exchanged one mage for another. And so would you."

When they were on the west side of the span, Nikodemus gave Harsh directions to his house. "It's not like with Rasmus." Harsh said that last word like it tasted bad. "It's just . . . I can feel her, that's all." Their gaze connected again in the mirror. "That all right with you?"

No. Actually, it wasn't. Harsh the goddamned pharmacist thought Carson was with him. "It's not like I can do anything about it."

Like hell he couldn't.

CHAPTER 15

*I*nside the house, Nikodemus caught Carson right before she collapsed. His pulse banged like he was caught in a nightmare. If it weren't for his arms around her, she'd have slid to the floor. "Shit, Carson, don't do this." The words rushed from him, born of panic. "Sweetheart," he whispered as he cradled her against him, "Please, sweetheart." His oath ripped him apart. "I don't know how to fix a broken witch." Considering the way her magic was coming on—all wild and topping out like he'd never felt from her before—he wasn't even sure her magic was still broken. A not-so-quiet part of him thought that even if she was fixable, the very last thing he ought to do was try to repair the damage. He'd just be turning her into the wolf Durian had feared. A more violent part of him couldn't let her die. Wouldn't. Couldn't bear it.

He was acutely aware of how fucked up it was for him to be holding a mage in his arms, trying to figure out how to keep her alive. But that's how things were, and he'd always preferred to deal with the reality he faced. She wasn't like the rest of the magekind. Without Carson, he'd never have gotten the talisman away from Magellan. Not in time. He owed her. Fucked, sure, but true nonetheless. He owed her, and that was true sideways and upside down. What's more, she was worthy of the oath he'd made.

Her injured arm was pressed between them, near her chest, hand fisted tight. Her body quivered relentlessly. "I don't feel good," she whispered against his torso.

Nikodemus stroked her hair with one hand and with the other fished in his front jeans pocket for the Copa. Damn. Harsh had the stuff. He was holding the first-aid kit, too. "Harsh."

"Warlord?" He was standing right there, and Nikodemus had been too lost in what was going on with Carson to notice. The other fiend bent in a respectful bow that didn't seem natural to him. He didn't know what the hell Harsh was, but he wasn't a low-ranking fiend, he was certain of that.

"Copa." Nikodemus held out a hand. Carson's condition was scaring him.

"I'm not sure that's wise."

He waggled his fingers and kept a pleasant expression, though he was on the edge of making a point about Doing It Right Now. Goddamn it. "Don't make me come and get it from you."

"It's poison."

"And she's a witch." He snapped his fingers. "The magekind take this crap all the time to get their magic ramped up. She needs to be ramped up. Trust me." He wriggled his fingers again. Her magic was sputtering out, and something else that just didn't feel right was cycling up, and it scared the hell out of him. "Feel that, Harsh?" Harsh nodded. "Magellan hit her with something nasty. Whatever it is, it's riding her hard. She needs her magic or that shit's going to kill her." He held out a hand for the Copa again, but Harsh didn't hand it over. "You have a better idea?"

"Yes." He tapped the first-aid kit. "Clean her wound, stitches if she needs them, then shoot her up with a full-spectrum antibiotic to kill whatever bug is spiking her temp. I'd give her morphine if I had it, but right now I'd settle for five hundred milligrams of ibuprofen and something to help her sleep."

"Thank you, Dr. Harsh," Nikodemus said. Fuck no was Harsh some low-ranking fiend. "Let's just do that while she dies from the magic that's killing her right now. Maybe the antibiotic fairies will bring me a syringe full of that full-spectrum crap you want her to have. Hell, maybe they'll bring the opium fairies with them." He sliced a hand through the air. "Do I look like a goddamned human doc to you?"

Harsh remained calm. His eyes were hooded. "In fact, Warlord, you do not."

"I got the first-aid kit, didn't I? In five minutes, if she's still alive, we can start using it on her. Now," he said in a low voice, "give me the fucking Copa, or I'll rip off your arms and stuff them where the sun don't shine." Harsh handed over the pills without another word. "Thank you."

He bowed. Damn low. But no fingers to his forehead to signify respect. Nikodemus's instinct to exact obedience from a fiend flared up. "Warlord."

Carson's head tilted back on her neck, exposing the length of her throat to him, like a supplicant female of his own species, a thought that made him feel like a pervert. She wasn't a fiend. It was just the strain of the moment that made him think she felt like one. "It's okay," he whispered. His oath to keep her safe worked him hard. "I've got you."

And he did. He wasn't in control of her or anything extreme, no indwell going on, not that he didn't want to, but he was there. Her breath warmed the lower portion of his sternum while he popped the lid and shook the Copa onto his hand.

"Here." He handed her the dark yellow wedge, but her mouth went stubborn and her eyes were definitely suspicious. Right. Shit, he was an idiot. Magellan had been feeding her poison for years. No wonder she didn't want to take anything. "It's Copa," he said. "Fiends take it to get high. Mages take it for the boost it gives their magic. It'll stabilize your magic so we can concentrate on your physical injuries, all right?" He waited until she processed that and decided whether to believe him. "Tastes like chicken, I swear."

She dry-swallowed the wedge like a pro.

The minute the Copa hit her stomach, he felt the drug surge out of her and wash back along his link with her. Black and perverted. Whatever had happened to her magic back there, he'd never felt anything like what he was getting from her now. The crazy-wild fluctuations slowed.

She lifted her head, and he got a full-on look into her wide-open eyes, along with a shot of her twisted magic. The Copa was already turning her eyes a dense, otherworldly green. Like the deep bottom of a cold, cold lake. He wanted to swim there a long time. A natural reaction that he shut down hard.

Elsewhere in the house, the imps reacted to Carson's magic and his jacked-up state. Her mental energy sizzled, unfocused and reeking of fear, exhaustion, and pure-D chaos. She was heading for a systems crash. Stood to reason, considering everything she'd been through tonight. He needed to get her someplace where he could uncouple their connection, fix her arm, and, like Harsh advised, let her sleep off the effects. He hoped there wasn't going to be any permanent deficit for her. That happened sometimes. Some humans just never recovered.

Her magic amped him hard. Inevitable, really, but he had himself under control. Purple shadows surrounded her eyes, and her skin was too pale, even for him, someone who liked pale-skinned humans a lot. Not that he didn't sample widely. He did and enjoyed the hell out of himself every time. Pale skin did it for him. An opposites-attract kind of thing, in a manner of speaking. Her magic evened out, twisting up with the other crap swirling around in her. His belly got taut.

Wouldn't he like to do her that way? Him all dark and not-human and her pale as ivory, and this time with poisoned magic seeping out of her and her wide Copa-tainted eyes crazy with passion. He reined himself back, but Jesus shit, he could smell blood, and her scent, and it about drove him out of his mind. The zing of her magic crackling back to life ramped him even higher. She felt more like a witch than ever, and he responded like a fiend. Blood lust and body lust. He wanted what she had.

"She's crashing, Warlord."

"I know that." Whoa. She looked really, really pale. Her knees buckled, and he caught her up. The imps chittered in his head. He ignored them to get a hand behind her knees and sweep her into his arms before she fell. "Upstairs. Bring the first-aid kit."

He took the steps two at a time because she was out cold before he'd turned around with her in his arms. Harsh was right behind him with the first-aid kit. What a good boy scout. Her eyes fluttered open when Nikodemus got her settled on his bed. Harsh cracked open the kit and started rummaging through it, muttering to himself.

Through her socks, her feet were ice-cold. He had blankets somewhere. In case he ever had human guests. But that hadn't been for a while, and he wasn't sure where he'd put his stash. He found a blanket stuffed in a drawer and yanked it out. Nikodemus lay the blanket over Carson's lower body, tucking the ends under her feet. Harsh had her wrist exposed now, and they both reacted to the pungent scent of fresh blood. Two fiends smelling blood. Never a good thing. But Harsh got himself under control, and Nikodemus had been under control for longer than Harsh had been alive.

Harsh dumped the contents of the first-aid kit on the mattress. "Primitive crap." He rummaged through the stuff with a deep frown. He was all business now. "There's nothing here. I'm supposed to fix this with a few bandages and some gauze?"

"Work with the first-aid kit you have, pharmacy boy. Not the first-aid kit you want." Nikodemus kept his connection going with her. He didn't dare cut off from her until she was psychically stable, and right now she wasn't.

Harsh sat on the bed and pulled Carson's hand onto his lap. He turned on the bedside lamp, angling it to get the beam directed where he wanted it. The wound gaped. Her eyes opened, and she just looked like she was too small and too delicate to make it through what was happening to her. She hadn't complained yet. Her shoulders were up around her neck, and her jaw was clenched tight. Not even a whimper.

"Can you do something for her pain, Warlord?"

Nikodemus went into Carson's head. She was one massive raw-ended nerve. He got her into a mental place where he could put himself between her and the pain. Her physical state flowed through him now, and he ground his teeth just to keep from screaming. How had she lasted this long?

Harsh looked up. "Thanks." His attention went back to Carson. Already her shoulders were relaxed. Nikodemus felt like his arm was going to come off. Shit. Her wrist looked bad. Much worse than he expected. Her sliced wrist oozed blood. Dried and drying blood coated her fist and wrist. Harsh turned her arm toward the light. "Can you move your fingers?"

She shook her head.

"We're lucky he was going at her from the side. Otherwise he'd have cut through tendon." Harsh glanced at him. "She needs a plastic surgeon."

"No docs. You know that."

"This is going to leave a scar no matter what I do." He used his teeth to rip open a packet from the first-aid kit.

"How far do you need her out?" Nikodemus asked.

"Under. I don't want her to flinch. Can you do that?"

"Yes."

Harsh threaded a needle from the package in the sewing kit. "I can't believe I'm doing this. It's medieval, for God's sake. Shit. Whatever happened to her burned her, too."

He prepared himself. This wasn't the way things were

supposed to work. In the old days before there were taboos, when a fiend messed with a human, he let the human take the pain. This time, the white-hot torment was his. Because whatever the hell she turned out to be, a permanently broken witch or a mage who could pull magic, he didn't want her to die. He was so amazingly fucked. Twice over. It wasn't like he didn't have his own defenses against the magekind. There was a reason he'd been around this long without getting taken. He wasn't all that worried about Carson taking him down, and besides, he just didn't believe she'd try it with him. By accident, maybe. But even if he could work out some kind of cold-war-like détente and keep Carson in his life, he'd have to give up his hopes for drawing the other warlords into an alliance.

A fiend with a witch for a lover wasn't going to be seen as very trustworthy, but so the fuck what? He'd find another way. He was getting ahead of himself, though. First, she had to live through this.

One day at a time, he told himself. Maybe even one minute at a time. He pressed his back hard to the wall while Harsh took tiny stitches that felt like hot metal in his body. He ground his teeth and just fucking held on.

After what felt like a hundred years, Harsh snipped the last knot and inspected his work before he applied several adhesive strips in a nice little Frankenstein pattern over skin that was now yellow with the substance from the wipe in another foil-wrapped packet. Harsh gooped her up with more antiseptic and wrapped her wrist with gauze, using the crappy first-aid-kit scissors to cut the gauze. He sifted through the packets on the mattress, tore open two more, and shook out pills. "What I wouldn't give for some Demerol."

Nikodemus kept his arms crossed tight over his chest. "Still waiting on the drug fairies."

Harsh ignored him and dropped the pills onto Carson's good hand. "Take these. They'll take the edge off." She swallowed them without water. Harsh dug in his pocket and pulled out the other prescription bottle. "Penicillin next." She dry swallowed them, too. Like a champ. Now that her wrist was fixed up, Harsh examined Carson's clenched fingers. "Can you move them yet?" he asked.

Carson nodded. Nikodemus came closer. He wanted the talisman safe. No matter how fucked things were for her right now, he didn't regret going to Rasmus's. Because of Carson, Magellan and Rasmus weren't able to crack the talisman. She deserved a medal for that. She really did. She looked at him. "I got it back for you," she said.

Slowly, she leaned toward Nikodemus and held out her hand, still fisted, fingers down, until he stuck out his hand, palm up. Totally worth it. As if her fingers were rusted at the joints, she pried open her fist. She grimaced.

Black sand and a fine crystalline grit rained onto his palm. Light refracted off the mound on his hand, scattering into tiny rainbows. His entire being clenched on him, a vise crushing the life out of him. He felt sick, actually, deep inside his body.

Harsh bent for a look. What is it?"

Nikodemus said, "A disaster. A fucking disaster."

Why the hell weren't they all dead or mageheld?

CHAPTER 16

Nikodemus unfurled Carson's fingers. More of the glittering debris clung to her skin, and he carefully brushed away the remains. Smack in the middle of her palm was a charcoal smudge. A black line ran from the edge of the mark toward her wrist, where it vanished under the gauze. He put a hand on the underside of her arm, careful not to touch her anywhere else, and pushed up her sleeve. "Oh, fuck," he whispered.

"What is that?" Harsh asked.

He grabbed one of the wipes off the bed and scrubbed until he'd removed every trace of dried blood on her skin. It didn't change anything. On the inside of her forearm, an undulating black line streaked up her arm from the mark on her palm along her pale skin all the way to where her sweater bunched up on her lower arm. Even though the line wasn't to her elbow yet, he understood now what he'd been feeling from her since they left Berkeley. A fucked-up attar of fiend and mage.

Eyes big and dilated with the Copa and painkillers and whatever was happening to her now, Carson's gaze locked with his. "It's moving," she said.

He didn't say anything. Couldn't even find the words to describe what he was feeling right now.

"Blood poisoning causes a red streak," Harsh said, his gaze moving between Carson and him. "Why is this black?"

"It's not blood poisoning," Nikodemus said. He drew in a deep breath and snatched up the crappy scissors to cut off the sleeve of her sweater. The line on her inner arm was about three inches from her elbow and climbing.

She closed her eyes and shuddered. She was stifling an enormous store of emotion. This wasn't just a line of black, and she knew it. Yeah. Now she knew it. When she opened her eyes, they were full of mute appeal. He had no assurances to give her. "You know the myths are real," he said. "You know what Magellan was trying to do. The talisman cracked, Carson. But not inside Magellan. Inside you."

"But Durian wasn't dead," she said.

"Two other fiends died there, Carson." Killed by him, as a matter of fact.

For a while her gaze stayed on his face, and he wondered if she felt the same heat he did as their connection flared. She propped her uninjured arm atop her raised knee, leaning against Harsh. His connection to her told him she was trying hard not to panic.

The line was heading straight for her heart and from there to her brain, where the energy that had been released from the cracked talisman would seep into her body and psyche, to the very center of the magic she was unable to touch. If he didn't figure out what to do soon, sometime in the next twenty-four hours he was going to be disposing of a body. Magellan or Rasmus might have survived this, but Carson wouldn't. He watched and felt her panic, and then she got control and shut herself down. She drew in another breath and stared at her arm and the streak of black. He tried to ignore the fist clenched around his heart.

"All right," she said. "All right." This time she whispered the words. She looked at him. "What's going to happen?"

Nikodemus pressed a fingertip to her forehead, hoping he could help her settle. The magic in her twisted him all around. "I don't know, Carson."

"You're lying. Don't lie, Nikodemus." He scrubbed a hand through his hair. Carson took a breath and let it out in a short burst. "I'm going to die anyway, Nikodemus. What difference does it make what you tell me?"

"A fiend wouldn't die from Magellan's poison. And right now you're at least partly fiend. I think that's why you're still alive."

Her eyes opened wide. "Am I going to die or not?"

"I don't know. Everything I've ever heard about this says you wait and see what happens." You died or you mastered the magic. There wasn't any choice there. And he didn't see how Carson could master any magic, human or fiend.

Harsh brushed something, maybe nothing, off his pants. "I know someone." He licked his lips and glanced away in time to avoid Nikodemus's look.

"What?" Nikodemus said.

"I know someone who might be able to help." Carson's head shot up, too. "I'm not saying it's certain, but *maybe* is better than waiting around to see what happens."

"Who?" Nikodemus said. Was he suspicious? Hell, yes. But Harsh was right. Maybe was a lot better than sitting around waiting.

"They live about an hour north."

"They?" His bad feeling ballooned. The possibilities had just gone from a couple to exactly one. And it wasn't a fun one. "Who, they?"

Harsh looked everywhere except at Nikodemus. "I've known them a long time. From before Rasmus."

"Just two random buddies of yours who can fix something like this? Oh, no . . ."

After a silence, Harsh sighed. He met Nikodemus's eyes at last. "They're stable, Warlord."

"I have my issues with blood-twins." Nikodemus put up a hand to forestall whatever Harsh was going to say. He couldn't be talking about anything but blood-twins. "I don't want to hear it. Fine. They're stable. But are they stable enough?"

"Last I saw them, yes."

"Brothers or sisters?" Nikodemus asked. He really, really wanted to hear Harsh's blood-twins were same-sex.

"Brother and sister," Harsh said.

"What the hell kind of fiend has blood-twins for friends?" Carson looked between the two of them. Nikodemus tried to recover some of his calm. "Are you nuts?"

Harsh's eyes got a faraway expression. "I don't know, Warlord."

"Do they have the magic for this? Because I'll tell you right now, unless they do, it isn't worth the risk."

"They do."

"What are you talking about?" Carson asked.

Nikodemus gave her the highlights. Just as there were

human twins who chose the same clothes or bought the same car even if they lived on different continents, so there were fiends who were psychic twins in addition to being physical twins. Blood-twins. If the effect was weak, they hid what they were. Their magic was symbiotic, doubled and redoubled by the other, typically far exceeding what a single fiend could pull. Blood-twins could do things most other fiends couldn't, and they shared their lives the way they shared magic. They were notoriously unstable and antisocial because they didn't need anyone else. They didn't swear fealty and almost never hooked up with warlords. Blood-twins didn't play nice. With anyone. They were borderline psychotics. End of story. Except Harsh was right. A pair of blood-twins might be able to stop whatever was killing her now.

They'd have to be crazy-desperate to ask a blood-twin for help with anything. He looked at Carson and just knew if she died, his heart was going to shrivel to nothing. Everyone would think he was the same Nikodemus, but he wouldn't be.

One minute at a time, he thought. One step at a time. He'd worry about the future after he knew if there was going to be one that included her. If he was throwing away his dream of leading an alliance against the mages, so be it. He could work it in the background. Through Harsh, if he wanted to, and maybe a few others who had reason to trust him.

He tossed Harsh his cell phone. "Call. Tell them we're on our way."

CHAPTER 17

Harsh had the car idling when Nikodemus followed Carson out of the house. She was wearing an old shirt of his, since her sweater was ruined. A ragged hole in the back of her jeans leg exposed a patch of bare thigh. Nikodemus pulled his gaze away from her leg and threw the duffel he'd packed with a few necessities into the trunk. He calculated the time he had left until he'd know if he needed to do something about his meeting with the warlords. An hour to get to the blood-twins. Say, half a day, maybe a whole day, to get Carson severed, and then back to the city for her to recuperate, leaving him with, at worst, a day to prepare for meeting with the warlords. Doable. Not optimum. But doable. Even without Durian.

He opened the rear passenger door for her.

"Thanks." Her mouth was tense and worried. Well, he was tense and worried, too. They all were. She got in and clicked her belt on one-handed. Nikodemus got in the back, too. So far, so good. Carson wasn't suffering badly. The painkillers helped enough to keep the pain Nikodemus was still intercepting to a tolerable level. She'd made it downstairs on her own, which was more than he'd expected. The Copa had stabilized her magic. Perfect. Right. Not.

Up front, Harsh revved the motor. The former pharmacist had taken liberties with Nikodemus's closet, but without looking as sexy as Carson did in his shirt. Harsh's pilfered jeans, the new ones Nikodemus hadn't even worn yet, didn't fit, given that Harsh was a couple of inches taller. He'd also cut the sleeves off Nikodemus's favorite threadless.com tee, "Stick Figures in Peril." The bastard. He should have looked like a total freak, but what he looked like was a rich guy slumming. Odd, that. He wondered what Harsh had been before he got caught up in Rasmus's axle. He wasn't a warlord. That, Nikodemus would have known. The guy used to hang with blood-twins. Did he eat nails for breakfast, too? He was fucking hard to read, that was a fact, and Nikodemus wasn't sure if that was due to Harsh's connection with Carson or if the oddness was something he'd always had. He was certainly comfortable driving an expensive car. He didn't have any hesitation about where things were on the dash or anywhere else in the car. Like he used to own one himself.

"Everybody buckled up?" Harsh asked.

"Yes, Mom," Nikodemus said. Carson laughed, and he saw Harsh's eyes flick to the rearview mirror. Of course she laughed. That wasn't her T-shirt ruined up there. His link with her was still open, and he left it that way. If she had some kind of reaction to the fiend-magic working its way into her, he wanted to know.

Harsh plugged an MP3 player into the car's sound

system and started up Mozart's Jupiter symphony as he brought the car into traffic. Just great. He'd been a busy boy when he wasn't ripping off his closet. He was ruining his tunes, too. "Death Cab for Cutie better still be on there, pharmacy boy."

"Relax," Harsh said. He turned up the volume. "101 North, here we come."

Nobody talked for a long time. Nikodemus wasn't much of a Mozart fan, and he thought about setting up the DVD player so he and Carson could watch Jet Li kick the shit out of ancient Chinese brigands. But Harsh had said they were only heading an hour north, and that wasn't enough time to give the wu-shu master his due. He slumped on the seat, arms crossed over his chest.

The longer this went on, the more thoroughly he saw how fucked he was. Carson reached over and touched his knee, and he slid his hand around hers. Her fingers were hot, and his sense of fiend-magic from her was cranking him up. Fiend and mage from the same person. Wild. He opened his connection to her, and she didn't object. Scrappy thing, she was.

He was having a hard time adjusting his worldview to include a mage he didn't want to kill. Life really sucked when your nearest and dearest hatreds got confronted and failed to stand up to the test. God fucking damn it. He owed her. No problem there. There were worse mages to be indebted to; like, every other one in the world besides Carson Philips. Nikodemus stroked her shoulder. Through the fabric of her shirt he felt a tingle in his hand, a zing of fiendish magic tainted with mage-magic.

It was beyond lousy for him to feel kinship with Magellan's witch. Not so long ago he'd been happily ranking his top three ways to kill the woman. Now he wanted to save her life. He didn't just *want* to save her life. He *needed* to. Every time he looked at her, so pale and subdued, with that freaking line snaking toward her head, he could hardly catch his breath. He stroked her temple, just a circling motion of his fingertip. In the Copa-subdued chaos of her head he caught flashes of her mageborn magic, but she felt like kin, too. He didn't want to hope, and he sure as hell knew he shouldn't be laying plans for them, but shit, he couldn't give up. He just couldn't.

She swallowed like her throat hurt. "It's hot in here," she said. "Aren't you too hot?"

"Harsh," he said over the Mozart. "Crank the AC, would you?"

A minute later, cool air wafted over them. He stretched out her hand and pushed up her sleeve—his T-shirt sleeve hit her elbow—to check where the black line ended now. Answer: midbiceps. It might be slowing down a little, but unless he was mistaken, the line was darker. He followed the line with his fingertip. Underneath his fingertip he felt a swirling magnetic pulse. Pure kinship. But the mage in her called to him, too.

He leaned against the seat and closed his eyes. *Reason,* he thought. He needed reason and logic to help him through this. She was human. He wasn't. She was a witch, or at least she'd started out that way. He was a fiend, and fiends and the magekind were natural enemies. Except he didn't give a fuck about her being a witch, and besides, she was something else now, too, wasn't she? Carson leaned her head against his shoulder and goddamn reason to hell. This was what it was. He put an arm around her shoulder and kissed the top of her head. "You okay?"

"I have a headache," she whispered.

"It'll be okay, sweetheart. I promise." He popped out more of the ibuprofen and gave it to her, because he was distracted by how much she was hurting.

Thirty miles later, Carson had dozed off and the shopping malls and cities had given way to open land. Another five miles and he saw the sun rising over oak-covered hills. They left Marin County for Sonoma County, and for several more miles, aside from the occasional dairy barn, there were no houses.

"How's she doing?" Harsh asked.

"Sleeping." He pushed up her sleeve. The line reached to her shoulder joint. "How much farther, Harsh? We don't have much time."

"Not far." Harsh kept the speed up even after he left 101 for a narrow road that wound through countryside. Nothing but open land, cows, sheep and horses, and wildflowers bursting into morning color against the green. Before long, they turned left onto an unpaved private driveway. They drove farther into the hills, bumping over ruts the whole way until, at last, they descended into a valley.

The road ended at a turn-of-the-nineteenth-century farmhouse with several outbuildings in the back. Harsh parked in a graveled area behind the house next to a rusting pickup. Nikodemus and Harsh got out. "How'd a pair of blood-twins score a place like this?" he asked.

"It's mine," Harsh said. "Land used to be cheap here." His eyes darkened. "I didn't expect to be gone so long."

The pit of Nikodemus's stomach clenched, because now he got what he should have gotten right away. He let blood-twins live in his house? Harsh wasn't just everyday friends with them. No one let blood-twins this close without being way more than friends. "Which one,

Harsh?" Nikodemus asked. He was pissed that Harsh hadn't mentioned he was doing the twins.

"Fen," he answered softly. "The sister." But of course Harsh would have ended up the lover of both of them. Had to, if the relationship was going to last. There was no way someone got between blood-twins. The bond between them was all-consuming. They were strictly a two-for-one deal, no outsiders allowed. All of which meant Harsh was in a hard place. He seemed to know it, too. They weren't going to accept him back. Not with his bond to Carson.

"Let's go inside," Nikodemus said. "And find out where we stand."

"Control, Warlord," Harsh murmured.

He ramped himself down. If he didn't get as vanilla as possible, the twins would be entitled to assume the warlord in their yard was here to attack, and their little meet-and-greet would be over before the door closed. He wished like hell Durian were here. He'd know how to deal with this situation. He'd persuade the blood-twins of whatever it was they needed to be persuaded of and have them convinced the agreement was their idea. With Nikodemus supporting Carson, they went inside through a door that put them in a kitchen. Just your basic everyday kitchen.

Uh, not exactly.

Viking range. Marble counters. Oak cabinets and a chrome fridge. Copper pots hung from the ceiling. There was a butcher-block table in the cooking area and a set of expensive knives on the counter. Somebody sure liked to cook. The twins were seated at the kitchen table. Nikodemus couldn't separate them magically. They felt identical in that respect, but that wasn't unusual with blood-twins.

Harsh slicked his hands over his head, then froze with his palms cradling his shorn skull. "You never get used to it," he said softly.

The male at the table was the poster boy for fiendkind; a tall, muscled man with straight brown hair caught back in a loose ponytail. Five eerily intense cobalt blue stripes ran down the left side of his face, tattooed in varying widths from the midline of his left pupil outward to his temple. The line that bisected his eye colored the white of his eye, too. He stared at the table and gave no sign that he gave a shit about their entrance. Good-looking guy, though. His body was fit and hale. He looked like he could go out and bale hay or brand cattle or snap some mage's neck without breaking a sweat.

Once Harsh was in their club, the male half of the pair would have taken on his sister's reactions to Harsh. All of them. Friendship. Longing. Lust. Love, if that's what it was.

The sister, Fen, was brain-numbingly beautiful. She wore her dark red hair slicked back from her face so that when he finally got over her perfect bone structure, he had the unpleasant shock of taking her hair for buzzed short. But it wasn't. A thick red braid hung down her back. Tiny silver hoop earrings went all around the outside of one ear, and dozens of narrow silver bracelets hung on her wrists. Her blouse was white gauze. Her bra was red. Very red against the porcelain skin of her cleavage.

Fen stood up. She had the body to go with the face. Lean. Athletic and long-limbed, she moved like a ballerina about to go *en pointe*. One of them, probably both, was pulling magic hard. The male didn't stir.

"It's me," Harsh said.

Fen looked from him to Nikodemus and then to Carson. "Harsh."

She had a sexy voice. Nikodemus felt the zing of magic from the twins, and besides the fact that Fen was gorgeous, he knew why Harsh had fallen for them. He'd have been tempted himself. Those two had some potent shit together. For the first time since they got Carson in the car, he thought there was hope.

Fen's gaze lingered on Carson, and her expression tightened. Her sky-blue eyes didn't focus, but Nikodemus didn't for a moment think she wasn't taking in every detail to be had from them. Five copper-colored stripes of varying widths circled her forearms. He caught a suggestion of nystagmus in her pupils, a rapid jitter of focus.

Carson's magic sputtered. Adrenaline surged through him when he got a blast of mage from her, followed immediately by a totally warped sense of her being kin. He slipped an arm around her. Her skin burned with a dry heat that had to be sapping her energy. They were lucky she was still on her feet.

Fen's mouth tightened. "Why come back after all this time?" she asked Harsh. Fen's stare at Carson wasn't a curious look. She looked at Carson like she hated her. Nope. She wasn't happy. Not happy at all. How many women, blood-twin or not, wanted a long-lost lover to come home bound to some other chick?

"I wasn't free before," Harsh said. He took a step forward but stopped short of moving past Carson. Big mistake. Harsh made it look like he didn't want to move past Carson. Fen's gaze shifted to Carson and stayed there. Harsh addressed the male. "Iskander?"

Carson gripped Nikodemus's arm with fever-hot fingers. Her attention fixed on Iskander. Nikodemus, with his connection to her still active, felt the avaricious longing so typical of the magekind for the kin. Man, could you spell trouble with that. Iskander lifted his head, and Nikodemus got a shot of heat when the male fiend and Carson locked gazes.

Something here stank like dead guppies on a hot day. Iskander looked at Carson as if he was getting a major hard-on, and Fen looked like she wanted to shove Carson down the Grand Canyon. If the fiends weren't blood-twins, the different reactions might have been normal. But they were, and the divergent reactions weren't.

"What is he?" Carson whispered. Her fingers gripped his arm tight enough to distract him. "Nikodemus, what is he?"

Good question, Nikodemus thought.

CHAPTER 18

$\mathcal{F}$en sent her magic sniffing after Carson. Nikodemus let her play a while, got her frustrated, then crushed her attempt to break in. Any other time, Carson could have handled Fen on her own. Her mind was damn near proof against fiends. But this wasn't just any time, and nobody, especially not some whacked-out psycho blood-twin, was taking on his connection to Carson. Fen's eyes went wide when the blowback hit. He made sure it was enough for Fen to get the message to stay the fuck out.

"Who are you?" Fen asked.

"Someone you shouldn't piss off," Nikodemus said. That made two things that didn't add up. Blood-twins who didn't share a response to someone they met, and now Fen asking him what he was. She freaking ought to know. She ought to have known what Nikodemus was the minute he got in the door, if not sooner.

"Warlord," Harsh said. Playing the diplomat so Fen

wouldn't blunder into some serious hurt. How warm and fuzzy for Harsh to be protecting the psycho he loved.

He felt sorry for Harsh. Seeing the two of them reminded him that being in love was nothing but physical and mental misery. Coming home after a long time away and finding out everything, including the love of your life, had changed for the worse, sucked. This bullshit was exactly why Nikodemus had told himself he'd never fall in love ever again. You just ended up making excuses for someone. Excusing the inexcusable. Love plain made you stupid. The problem was, he was worried he was looking at his own case of stupid coming on. He wasn't exactly making excuses for Carson, but it was damn close. She'd behaved courageously the entire time he'd known her—not what you expected from one of the magekind. This whole thing had him fucked up bad. Get her fixed and get him cured. Right. Then they could get on with their separate and incompatible lives.

The male, Iskander, went on staring at Carson like he'd never seen a woman in real life. Ridiculous. His sister was about as hot as any female got. They were blood-twins. Of course Iskander was doing his sister. So why, when his sister was telegraphing emotion, was Iskander not reacting in like fashion? He should be. The two of them should be reacting as one. He checked Harsh. "You said they were blood-twins," Nikodemus said.

"They are." Harsh reached up to smooth back the hair he didn't have anymore, stopped, then crossed his arms over his chest.

Carson's magic was spinning out of control again, one minute nerve-shredding, ball-shrinking mage, the next eerily like one of the kin. "I thought mageheld fiends had short hair," she said. She took a step toward Iskander but looked back at Nikodemus. "Don't they?"

"He isn't mageheld, Carson," he replied. But it sure as hell freaked him out that she had the same mistaken thought about Iskander that he'd had about Fen. He could feel them, though. They weren't mageheld. They were just freaks.

Fen's pale blue eyes jittered like tectonic plates were meeting back there and producing a nine point nine on the Richter. Then the tremor stopped, and Nikodemus felt her power spread toward him. She might be skanky as hell, but she had some serious mojo going on. This time, he let her magic touch him. The creepiest thing was the way Iskander didn't react. Not even a flinch when his sister pulled all that power. "Keep her away from my brother, Warlord."

Nikodemus drew Carson back, tucking her against his side while Harsh sat across from Iskander. He stretched out a hand and touched the other twin's hand. "Iskander?"

At last, Iskander looked away from Carson, but his expression was dead. His eyes were the same color as his sister's, sky-blue, but there was no spirit behind them, no anima. He was empty inside. If Nikodemus had passed him on the street, he would have taken him for a human with an interesting choice of tribal tat.

"How long has he been this way?" Harsh stroked Fen's arm.

"Since you left." Fen sat down hard, elbows on the table, hands clasping the back of her bowed head. The stripes around her forearms turned coppery red. After a silence, she lifted her head. "Some days are better than others. He'll say a few words. He dresses himself. Keeps things neat. Most days he's like this. Doesn't talk. Hardly even moves."

Harsh's hand slid down her arm. "I'm sorry."

Fuck. It was all Nikodemus could do to keep himself from swearing out loud. "Are you telling me they're broken?" Broken blood-twins weren't going to fix anything.

Iskander's head jerked up. His blank blue eyes flashed, and for a moment, he looked whole. A burst of magic came from him, effervescent and scalding hot. Psychotic. Totally out of control.

Beside him, Harsh stiffened. Iskander looked straight at Carson, his eyes alive. Knowing. Carson shook off Nikodemus's arm and walked toward Iskander, palm out. The male half of this fucked-up set of blood-twins waited calmly. His eyes started to glow, deepening in color from sky-blue to cobalt. The air crackled with magic.

"Don't touch him, witch!" Fen jumped from her chair and her hand shot out, fastening around Carson's gauze-wrapped wrist just as Carson was about to touch Iskander's chest.

Things happened so fast Nikodemus couldn't block the pain that crashed over them both. Carson fell to her knees, eyes wild with agony, but Fen kept squeezing. Nikodemus fronted Carson, got her pain down to a dull roar for her and a searing burn for him. He pulled magic and, through his link with Carson, got a dose of her magic, deep and vibrating. Fiend and mage. A fucking rush. Fen twisted Carson's wrist, and they all caught the scent of her blood when her stitches tore. The level of tension rocketed to the moon. Nikodemus roared. He had Fen cut off before she finished calling Carson names.

"Let go of her, right now," Nikodemus said through gritted teeth. His body thrummed with Carson's pain and the hunger for blood, fresh and hot, streaming down the back of his throat. Harsh froze on his chair, nostrils flaring. Like Nikodemus, he was hyped to the max. The only one who didn't move was Iskander. "Trust me, fiend," Nikodemus said in a low voice. "You don't want me pissed off."

"She tried to touch us." Fen kept her grip on Carson's wrist and pulled more magic. Nothing happened. Nikodemus smiled at her. Fen hissed. "The witch tried to touch my brother."

Nikodemus cut off her air. Fen's eyes bulged. "I said, let go."

The tats on Fen's forearms glowed hot red, but she released Carson's wrist. The pain backed down a notch, and Nikodemus replied by giving Fen enough air to keep living. She tried to pull free of Nikodemus's block, but no way was he letting her go that easy. As far as he was concerned, she could fry in her own backwash. He made sure Fen understood he could crush her like a bug and that he was considering doing it. Freaking blood-twins. They were crazy, all of them. Even the fucked-up ones were a goddamned menace. The room sizzled with magic. But it wasn't coming from Fen. He had the sister locked down tight, and that ought to mean Iskander was, too. It sure as hell wasn't Carson. She was on her feet again, cradling her wrist across her chest and panting, at total low tide.

Harsh jumped up. His chair clattered to the floor. "Iskander?"

Nikodemus shot a glance at Iskander and saw his eyes alive and fixed on Carson. She stared back at Iskander with fever-bright eyes. She took a step toward him, reaching again. Bright red stained the gauze around her wrist. Her foot caught in Harsh's overturned chair or she might actually have made it to him, and, well, Fen probably would have tried to kill her with her bare hands. As it was, Nikodemus grabbed Carson by the shoulder and hauled her back.

Whatever the hell was wrong with these two fiends, Nikodemus no longer doubted they were real-deal blood-twins. He could feel the twinned power in his bones, shivering along his spine and through his head. Then somebody turned off the tap and the magic cut off. The life in Iskander's eyes faded away.

"Let go of me, Warlord." Fen bowed her head and touched the tips of her first three fingers to her forehead. "I'm good now."

"The witch is under my protection, fiend." Hell, but he was turned on, full of desire for Carson. "You understand that now?"

"Yeah," she said. "Message received." The tats on her arms were fading, but Nikodemus didn't let go until the glow died out.

Carson's magic flipped on, and all four of them felt it. High tide on the mage side but fluctuating with a fiend's magic. Just totally fucked up. His balls got tight and full. Just as fast, the magic shut off. The skin on the back of his neck rippled. He caught her just in time to keep her from collapsing to the floor.

"Upstairs," Harsh said. "First door on the left."

While Harsh ran outside for the first-aid kit, Nikodemus got Carson into an upstairs bedroom with an attached bathroom. The blood-twins stayed downstairs. Someone had done some remodeling here. Houses this old weren't naturally convenient like that. On the bed, Carson curled into a ball and shivered. He sat beside her just as someone tapped on the door.

Harsh came in with Nikodemus's duffel and the first-aid kit. Carson's magic flooded the room. If she'd had any focus, she'd have killed somebody. She sat up, hands clawing at the black line circling her throat.

"I can't breathe," she rasped.

CHAPTER 19

*H*ours later, the black line was a jet necklace around Carson's throat. The end disappeared under her hair at the nape of her neck. Thank God the choking sensation had passed without actually killing her. For a time, if he'd wanted, Nikodemus could have tracked the line all the way from her palm up her arm, to her shoulder, around her neck, to the back of her head. From her palm to her shoulder, her skin was now pristine. The tail end of the streak was visible at the top of her shoulder joint, having drawn upward after the leading end stopped at the back of her neck. Wouldn't be too much longer before the line was gone from sight. He put an arm around her back, holding her up. She quivered continuously.

He was in the bathroom with her at the moment, with Carson on the floor by the toilet, having recently puked until all she could do was dry heave. Harsh stayed in the doorway, silent but there, while Nikodemus knelt beside her. He wished he could rip out his heart right now, because watching her fade away like this, with him not being able to do anything to stop it, was pure hell. He couldn't help the chilling conviction that this must be her final decline. After holding on for so long, her mind and body had simply reached the end. Once the line was gone, she'd die. The morbid thought refused to unstick itself from his head. His breath made a lump in his throat, and he felt himself splintering; part of him teetered on the edge of black panic, and the other cooly observed that he was losing it, and that if he fell into that looming abyss he might never be whole again.

He didn't know how the fuck this had happened to him, going as psycho as Iskander over Magellan's witch. But here he was, looking at his total devastation. Well, right now, Carson was alive, and he was going to cling to every second that passed until he couldn't anymore. Carson lurched and hugged the toilet. He felt her ribs contract, but she didn't throw up.

His link with her kept going in and out. One minute he could swear she was kin, and the next he got pure mage. Other times he was right there in her head like nothing was wrong, and then, wham, all he got from her was her physical state. Then emotion, a mental shriek, and the now-familiar mix of fiend and mage. And sometimes, like now, their connection just fizzled out until he got nothing, and he'd smother under a tidal wave of panic that she was gone for good.

"You care for her, don't you?" Harsh asked. He was wearing his own clothes now, and it seemed he was a clothes hound like Durian had been. Olive cashmere sweater. Silk-blend pants. Shiny shoes. Everything fancy and expensive.

"If it weren't for her, Magellan would have succeeded."

He turned his head and glared at Harsh. Harsh's attention was on him, but not judgmental, which made things easier. Nobody liked a judgmental stranger watching them crack up.

"She's the one for you, isn't she?"

"Yeah," he said, because he was too tired to deny it. Somewhere along the line, he'd totally clicked with Carson. Spend some quality time in a girl's head and watch her pull your ass out of a raging fire or two, and you could fall pretty damn hard. Nikodemus looked at Carson again. With her head down, her hair bared her nape. The spot where the black streak was gathering was darkening and condensing. "If it wasn't for her," Nikodemus said softly, "we'd be facing a mage who could take a warlord without breaking a sweat."

Harsh didn't say anything for a long time. The line was disappearing at a faster rate. Nikodemus slid onto the floor next to her. She was falling apart physically. Psychically she was a category-five hurricane. He pulled her into the crook of his arm, and she collapsed against him with a moan. She was so small, and most of her life she'd never had anyone to watch over her or care what happened to her. Just a goddamned mage, using her up. He couldn't even remember the last time he wanted to protect someone with his life. The moment was here, and he was powerless to save her.

"I don't know what to do for her," he said. "If she were one of us, sure, but she's not. She's not made the way we are." He let his head fall back against the bathroom wall. He didn't want to think about her dying.

Harsh chewed on his lower lip for a while. Just when Nikodemus was going to tell him to contemplate his navel someplace else, he hunkered down next to her. He grabbed her wrist, not the one Magellan had tried to slice through, and concentrated. "Look," Harsh said, "what if the problem isn't the magic?"

"Meaning?"

"Maybe the problem is her body. She's not a fiend. Her physiology is human."

"Thank you for that news flash," Nikodemus said. He touched the gathering circle of black on Carson's nape. Energy flowed back to him; nothing but fiend.

Harsh must have felt it, too, because he sucked in a breath and let it out. "If she were a fiend, this would be a mild flu for her instead of bubonic plague. Her body isn't made like ours, and that's what's killing her."

"Point?"

"There's a hospital in Olompali. It's small, but they might be able to do something for her symptoms. You've done all you can for her psychic condition. Now we need to treat her physical symptoms."

"She can't go to the hospital." He caught Harsh's wrist. "Don't you think I'd have taken her if that were possible? You know what we are and what happened to her. She can*not* go to the hospital. She'd die there for sure."

"I understand that." Harsh's brown eyes were so calm Nikodemus could hardly stand to look in them. "But what if the hospital comes to her?" he asked.

"What are you talking about?" He reached for Harsh's thoughts, prepared to tear through them without permission or remorse, except Harsh reared back, stopped only by Nikodemus's iron grip on his wrist. The other fiend threw up a clumsy but effective block. He could rip through without effort, but he waited, out of respect, an inch and a half from being goddamned impolite. This wasn't the first time he'd gotten the feeling Harsh wasn't what he seemed. Not a warlord. Not a blood-twin psycho himself. He'd know if Harsh were that. But not just any old fiend, either. Your average fiend didn't hang with blood-twins. Nikodemus held Carson tighter and wondered if Harsh could be trusted. "What gives with you, pharmacy boy?"

Harsh sighed. "I'm on staff at UCSF. At least I was before I got taken."

"On staff." He had to think a minute before he remembered how that worked among humans. "The University of California at San Francisco? The Medical Center?"

Harsh nodded.

"You're a doctor?"

"An oncologist. Specializing in cancer disorders of the blood."

"You treat humans with cancer?" Fiends weren't supposed to have human jobs. Mixing with humans got you exposed or taken. Fiends blended in with humans when they had to. But they lived on the edges of their society, like urban wildlife that went unnoticed, only with their own banking system—until someone saw a coyote eat the family cat. The kin passed for human, but they weren't and never would be. Humans were a source of psychic energy, an ancient and traditional prey.

"I'm not an ER doc, Warlord."

"But you went to a human school. Medical school." His heart about leapt out of his chest, punching enough emotion that Carson stirred. He waved a hand. "Never mind how you managed that, given what you are. You're a human doc." He squeezed Harsh's wrist until his eyes reacted to the pain. And he did it on purpose. "Go to the hospital and get what you need to save her."

Harsh swallowed hard. "I'm not that good."

"Not that good a doc?"

"No, not that good a thief." Harsh jerked his arm toward his solar plexus, but Nikodemus didn't release him until it was plain Harsh wasn't getting free without his consent.

"You're a fiend. Explain to me why not. Slowly, so I understand."

"Until I was twenty-five, I didn't know what I was. Nobody did. Including my parents."

"You grew up with humans?"

He nodded. "It wasn't until I met Fen that I knew what was going on with me. She was the first of the kin I ever met. Iskander was the second."

Nikodemus's head rang like he'd been whacked by a two-by-four. A fiend raised by humans. As a human. "No wonder you're messed up."

"There's a lot of things you take for granted, Warlord, that I never learned. A lot of things I'm not good at."

"No wonder you got taken."

Harsh didn't answer right away. Uh-huh. There was a universe in his silence. Starting with an excuse for a red-headed sociopath? "I'll give you a list of what I need."

"Right. You do that."

Nikodemus finished at the hospital about three o'clock, having had to close off his link with Carson in order to concentrate on ripping off the place without anyone seeing or remembering he'd been there. With a trunk full of stolen supplies, Nikodemus headed back to the blood-twins' home. He was lucky the Sonoma County Sheriff's Department wasn't patrolling this section of the county roads. After he left the city limits, he never let the needle fall below sixty. He reached for his connection with Carson the minute the farmhouse came into sight. Not even a glimmer of feedback. The back end of the Mercedes shuddered at sixty-five but leveled out at eighty.

Fen was on the front porch when he revved the car around the last corner and then jammed on the brakes. She jogged down the steps. *Yeah,* he thought, *she's gorgeous, but she ain't Carson.* "The mage is still alive," she said like it was killing her to give him the news. "I'm here to help you carry the stuff." She lifted her arms in a graceful ballerina pose. So far, Nikodemus hadn't seen her do anything that wasn't elegant. "That's all."

On the way up the stairs, he got a blast of fucked-up magic from Carson, and then their link settled into a stream of what felt normal for her. Thank God. He wasn't too late. He and Fen unloaded the gear in the bedroom.

"Hey!" Harsh said when Fen dropped the box she was carrying from waist height to the floor. "Watch it. Some of that's fragile."

Nikodemus couldn't get over the fact that Harsh had been raised by humans. Talk about a dysfunctional childhood. Fen bent her knees and dropped the next box pretty much the same way. Nikodemus reached over and grabbed the rest from her. "If any of this is broken," he said, "you go back for more."

She headed for the door without another word. Typical behavior for a blood-twin, but knowing that didn't make her easier to deal with. Nikodemus really didn't like her, and she was the one who introduced Harsh to his people? It was a miracle Harsh wasn't a full-blown sociopath. Fen stopped at the doorway and watched Harsh tearing through the jumble of supplies. Her bracelets jingled softly. "Human medicine isn't going to help her survive this. Let her go, Warlord. Why prolong the inevitable?"

"Get lost," Nikodemus said.

"There's a lake." Her bracelets jangled some more. "You can dump her body there."

Harsh grabbed a plastic bag of clear liquid with "Ringer's lactate" written across the front, along with a bunch of measurement marks and fine print. "Fen, you're not helping. Nikodemus, did you remember the blood pressure cuff?"

"Thanks for the tip," Nikodemus said at the same time, only he was looking directly at Fen. "Now get the fuck out. If you put it on the list, Harsh, it's in there." He pointed to one of the boxes. "Look in that one."

Harsh set up an IV, took Carson's blood pressure, looked into her eyes, and down her throat. And whatever other crap a human doc did to find out what was wrong with his patient. And then he drugged her up with something he said would keep her from barfing and help relax her out.

Nikodemus sat on the edge of the bed, opposite from where the IV hung off the curtain rod. The black line was gone but for a dime-sized circle of jet an inch or so above the nape of her neck. He held her hand and did his own examination. Her mental state was not good. Magically speaking, she was closer than ever to total chaos.

From the bed, Carson moaned and scratched the spot where the IV needle went into her hand, but Harsh had anticipated that and used enough tape to cement it in for a year. So he let her dig at it for a while. After a bit, her eyes closed. But she kept breathing, and Nikodemus didn't lose their connection. She wasn't asleep, she was just concentrating like holy hell. He helped when he could.

Harsh checked her eyes and her pulse again. "And now, all we can do is wait."

They settled in. Harsh checked the IV a couple of times, but mostly he sat on the floor organizing the gear Nikodemus had heisted for him. Syringes. Needles. Triplicate-form drugs. Ringer's solution. Pills of various shapes and colors. Gizmos for looking inside her head. He hoped some of this stuff would help her.

Carson slept. Or maybe just went under the drugs, and that gave Nikodemus a respite from her chaotic state. Harsh took the opportunity to unbandage her wrist and stitch it back up with a different needle and real sutures. She must have been under, because she didn't even flinch, and he got only the faintest sense that she knew what was going on. Harsh took her pulse. Then he got the pressure cuff on her again and started pumping.

"So?" Nikodemus said when Harsh took the stethoscope out of his ears.

"So, now she has low blood pressure instead of sky-high pressure."

"Is that good?"

He watched Harsh search for the right words. "Let's just say it's not a disaster."

Nikodemus lay his hand on her temple and concentrated the way Harsh had done with the BP cuff. "She's hunkered down inside herself."

Harsh was back on the floor organizing his pills, fingers moving quickly as he sorted bottles and boxes. "I'll leave the magic to you, Warlord."

"I've seen fiends who didn't last this long," Nikodemus said.

That got Harsh to look up. "You've seen this before?"

"With fiends. Not humans. It's the only way to save a fiend who's been imprisoned like that. Mages used to do it to us all the time. They'd separate a fiend from his magic and bottle it up. The container confers power on whoever possesses it."

"Like a genie in a bottle?" Harsh asked.

"There's no three wishes. Just permanent magic. The mages started playing around and found out they could absorb the fiend into their bodies. Fen and Iskander taught you about that kind of indwell, right?" Harsh nodded. "In Carson's case, the indwell was forced. For fiends, if we're strong enough, we survive. Same with the mages. Only a few can these days. Magellan. Rasmus. Dharma in Indonesia. A few others." He studied Harsh. "We live longer than humans. A mage who takes on a fiend like that gets the magic and the longevity." Nikodemus sighed. "Most of the knowledge was lost during the human Dark Ages. But then the troubles broke out, and a few mages got motivated to rediscover their glorious past of oppression and murder without any of the restraint of their ancestors. Talismans show up every now and then, but making them these days is considered old-fashioned. Today's mage prefers to mainline. We just try to keep the talismans away from the magekind."

Nikodemus turned back to Carson. She lay on the mattress, arms around her head, barely breathing. He drew her hair away from her face and neck and braided it so it would stop sticking to her skin. Strands slid across his fingers like silk. When he finished, he wiped her face with a towel. And then he settled himself next to her on the mattress. He massaged the knots in her shoulders and thighs, but there wasn't much relief he could give her. The assimilation was inexorable. He'd known fiends who'd taken on an imprisoned fiend and didn't survive as long as she had so far. He kept telling himself that. She wasn't dead.

Harsh had his gizmos and pills all organized and laid out on a dresser. He looked over his shoulder at Nikodemus. "I can feel her, Nikodemus. Better give her more Copa."

He got up and dug the bottle out of his pocket. He pried it open. Damn childproof caps. "Carson," he whispered. He put a knee on the bed and leaned over her, daring a stronger link with her, a tendril of a connection, wispy as mist, that slid right in. She reacted to his voice, and to the link, too. "Take this."

She did. Dry swallowed it just like a fiend. Or a mage. Whatever the hell she was. He was jumpy with the desire to do something. Anything. He needed to do something. But there wasn't anything he dared try with her in this state. He hated that. He looked at Harsh. "Want some?"

The fiend propped his hands high up on either side of the doorway. Raised by humans. And introduced to his heritage by a pair of blood-twins. The poor fuck. "No, thank you."

He looked at Carson, lying on the bed, pale and sweaty. Barely breathing. "Can't you give her something else? Isn't there something in all that crap that will keep her alive?

"I can't give her any more opiates," Harsh said. "Not yet."

"We're going to lose her, aren't we?"

"In my opinion, if she's going to die, it'll be soon." He lowered his voice. "If," he said. "I said if."

He squeezed the bottle of Copa. "If she was a normal human, how long?"

"An hour. Maybe less."

CHAPTER 20

Carson? Hey, sweetheart.

Carson lapsed deeper into her dream state. In her semilucid, not asleep, not awake, state, she wasn't sure if the voice was real or in her dream. Something about the words made her think she ought to respond.

Get the fuck out if you can't be helpful.

Someone leaned over her, breath warm against her cheek. Soft lips pressed against her forehead.

I need you, Carson. Please. Don't leave me.

She tried to open her eyes, but nothing happened.

"Carson?"

God, she had to work at lifting her lids, and when she did, her sense of perspective got lost in a jumble of lines and angles that refused to resolve into shapes she understood. She blinked. Someone was leaning over her. She fought to bring the face into focus.

Nikodemus brushed away the hair on her forehead. "I

need you to wake up, Carson. Can you do that for me?" His voice dropped low and plaintive. "Please?"

She lifted her hand and touched his chest with her good arm. How strange, she thought. Nothing happened. There wasn't any flow of energy from her to him, no roaring heat in her veins. Why not? Nikodemus put a hand over hers. "It doesn't do any good with you," she murmured. "You aren't mageheld."

"Carson?"

Her brain came slowly alert. Everything processed in slow motion, as if her mind didn't want to give up the place she'd been. And then she was here. Present. Now. With Nikodemus. Elsewhere in the house, Harsh was sitting on a bed, holding his head in his hands. She felt Iskander, and as she recalled his face to mind, she could swear she felt stripes down her face, too. Her body ached. Every breath hurt. Her thoughts scattered.

Nikodemus dug in his pocket and pulled out a brown prescription bottle. He popped the cap and shook a small triangular pill onto his hand. "Here." The earthy smell reminded her of his headache-remedy tea. He held the tiny pill to her lips. She tried to take it from him, but her hand shook too hard. The material started to crumble.

She opened her mouth, and he slid the pill onto her tongue. She shivered at the sharp, pungent taste. Nikodemus sat on the edge of the bed, one leg on the mattress, the other on the ground. She felt as if she were in a foreign country and had just recognized Nikodemus as someone from home. He was kin. Where on earth had that thought come from? Her skin was dry and hot.

"You're very sick, Carson. You know that, don't you?"

"Yes." Her heart tensed up. She was dying. Because of Magellan.

He smoothed her hair behind her ear, and his finger lingered there. "The talisman you took from Magellan cracked open, and everything inside it went into you. Do you remember that?"

She nodded. Her head was a boulder on the pillow.

"Harsh thinks you're dying." He stretched out her injured arm, unfolding her fingers so he could touch her palm. A faint grayish-black spot was all that remained of the mark the talisman had left on her hand. "He thinks you're not going to make it."

"But Magellan didn't get the talisman." She turned her trembling hand over, palm up, palm down. Pain incinerated her, and for a while all she could do was wait for the burn to subside. She lay her head against the pillow. Her body was empty. Whatever magic was consuming her had taken just about all there was of her. "It was worth it," she whispered.

"Carson," he said. "I think there's a way to keep you alive."

She had to be careful where she looked. Her depth perception kept wigging out on her. There was something wrong with her inner ear, too, because if she moved her head, she got dizzy. His gaze fixed on her, but she lost his eyes in a haze of gray and blue and charcoal shadows. A thread of fear worked its way through her.

"Listen to me," he said. "Just listen, okay?" He put his mouth by her ear. "I don't want you to die. You can't die on me, Carson. Do you get that? Nod or something if you get that."

Her head moved on the pillow, and it took about all her strength.

"I feel you as kin now, and if you're kin, you can swear fealty to me. We'll have a permanent connection that I think will stop the talisman's magic from killing you." He spoke in a low, quick voice. "If it works, you'll be my creature afterward, sharing a part of me. There's always a risk things won't work the way they would if you were really kin. But I don't think that's what will happen." He clenched his teeth. "You need to understand it's not a one-way thing like we had going when we were at Rasmus's. This thing puts an obligation on us both. There's no going back from this. It's permanent."

Her vision started going out again. She blinked hard and got his face back into focus. His eyes were hard. Chips of blue-gray slate. She nodded.

"One last thing. This is taboo. You may feel like kin, but you're magekind, Carson, and totally fucked up, excuse my French. I don't think anyone's going to approve of this." He gripped her hand. "Just nod if you're okay with that. If you can't nod, then squeeze my hand."

She swallowed. "When?" she whispered past a desert-dry throat.

"Now. There's no time to wait." He took in a long breath, and with a hand on her chin, he pushed her head to one side to expose the side of her throat to him. "Say this, Carson; or just think it really hard. Either works. *I promise on my blood that I will be faithful to you, the warlord Nikodemus. I will never cause you harm and will observe homage to you against all who oppose you, in good faith and without deceit.*"

With each syllable came a pulse in her head, a deeper awareness of Nikodemus. Her sense of him grew larger in her mind. Denser with each word.

When she finished, his fingers tightened on her chin.

"Well done, Carson Philips," he said. He helped her sit up in the bed, and she wasn't wracked with pain. His strength flowed into her. Nikodemus traced a line on her throat with the side of his fingernail.

At first she didn't feel anything but his contact with her and a tingle in her skin. Then a cold pain rose up. She flinched as the sensation got bigger in her head. He held her immobile, one arm around her waist, the other cupping the back of her head. He was strong. Much stronger than she expected. She fought to stay calm. He overwhelmed her. Nikodemus bowed his head and inhaled. Blood trickled down her collarbone, a slow streak of heat on her skin. His hand on the back of her head tightened, pulling back to stretch her neck taut. He whispered, "Let me in, Carson."

At first, she didn't know how, but she remembered the first time he was in her head and how she'd relaxed her mind. She tried that now. She was caught off guard by the abrupt sense of him coming to her. He pushed his magic into her, a trickle at first, then more. His head bent, breath warming her, and he touched his mouth to the cut he'd made. His tongue moved, tracing, moving away, back into his mouth. She knew the moment he tasted her blood because a spark of shimmering heat rolled through her. He moved downward, mouth following the trail of her blood, tasting, closer to her collarbone, and then he kissed her there, right where her blood was pooling, tongue touching, lapping. The zing of the contact rocketed through her. Pressure built in her head. His teeth scraped her, nicked her skin, even. The energy he sent into her worked its way into all the interstices of her body.

She moaned, a sound of sensual longing. She wanted

him to sate himself on the taste of her blood. His body along hers felt good. Warm and alive.

He let up the pressure on her chin, and Carson turned her face back to his. She felt light-headed, shaky. His chest expanded slowly, then contracted as he let out the breath he'd taken. With his hand still holding her chin, he turned his head to the side, too, and scored his neck until a line of red appeared, then brought her to his neck. The scent of his blood rose in her nose as she lowered her mouth. Her stomach roiled, and she had to fight to keep down the bile.

"Finish this," he whispered. "Finish this or it's no good." He held her close, intimately, as if they were lovers. The heat of his body spread into her; the scent of him shook her to her bones. Her palms pressed against the muscled wall of his torso. She trusted him. More than once he'd saved her life.

She held her breath and pressed her mouth to his throat, hands on his chest, trying to keep her balance. His hand on her head pressed down. She opened her mouth and touched his skin. His blood spread over her tongue, hot and tart, too everything. Too hot, too bitter. Too sweet for her to bear. He blossomed inside her, and then it was like they were mortise and tenon, a perfect fit.

Her world changed. She connected with Nikodemus, mentally and physically. Heat rocketed through her, and she felt a twist in her body that echoed back from him. His neck arched, giving her better access. Her body stopped hurting, and the taste of his blood wasn't abhorrent anymore. One of his hands stroked her back, pressing her against him until she relaxed and slid her arms around his shoulders to hold on.

"Yes," he said in a low, drawn-out whisper. His hand

on the back of her head pulled back, turning her head away. Carson thought he meant to take more blood from her and exposed her throat to him again. He slid his hand underneath her hair to the back of her head and, with spread fingers, turned her head back to his.

She gazed into his face, into his blue eyes backlit with a glow of silver. The moment stopped being about her fealty to him or the steps that had given them a permanent connection and started being about something else.

He brought her head closer with a light enough pressure that they could pretend there wasn't any at all. But his head moved toward her until his mouth hovered over hers. He was letting her choose what happened next. She closed the distance between them and pressed her mouth to his. Blood mingled on their tongues, his and hers. He shifted on the mattress, and their bodies were closer yet not close enough.

His mouth was tender over hers, and at the same time he kissed her, his magic flowed over the connection between them, taut as a wire on the verge of snapping. His fingers wrapped around her throat, gently holding, then sliding down, over the curves of her breasts, along her stomach, to her ratty blue jeans. He wasn't retreating. He was kissing her, gently, sweetly. Actually kissing her, parting her lips, moving his tongue into her mouth.

Nikodemus pulled back. The moment he let her go, she lost her hold on where she was. The extra dimension was there again. More of everything. More color, shape, sound, overwhelming her. She swayed, and Nikodemus caught her before—before what? His touch soothed her, helped her focus the additional sensations.

"I'm not saying no," she said. He got up anyway. "Don't go," she said.

"Never." He pulled the Copa out of his pocket, shook out three more pills, and put the bottle on the table beside the bed. He sat and touched a finger to her neck, and she caught his wrist and tugged him toward her. "You sure you want to do this?" he asked.

Carson nodded. "Yes."

"All right, then." He gave one of the pills to her and took the other two himself.

CHAPTER 21

Arousal flooded Carson, spine-tingling, blood-boiling arousal. She fell deeper into Nikodemus's embrace. His kiss was nothing like what she was used to. Nothing at all. The softness of his lips melted her, sent her into a kind of sensual overdrive. How could someone so big and hard and relentlessly masculine kiss with such heartbreaking tenderness? His mouth covered hers, her tongue moved into his mouth, and she inhaled the scent of him, tasted the Copa.

With every passing second, she felt better, stronger. She leaned forward until she was pressed against his chest, her fingers curling into his hair, soft, thick, and warm over the backs of her hands. Nikodemus pressed his palm to her lower back to shift her up, bringing her knees on either side of his hips and swinging her onto his lap. She wriggled closer.

His hands pushed upward, along her spine, taking her shirt with the motion, keeping her on his lap with the pressure. Cool air brushed over her shoulders. He leaned back a little, scanning her up and down, devouring her with his eyes.

"Nikodemus," she said. Her sense of him tickled in the back of her head. She ran her hands down his back, over and around the muscles of his spine.

"I like women who are small like you," he said in a soft, low voice. He had his hands well underneath her shirt, on the bare skin of her rib cage. "Want to know why?"

"Yes." The way Nikodemus looked at her and touched her right now was different from anything she'd ever felt before. His gaze was hungry, full of anticipation, and his hunger transferred to her, too, when she'd never been all that wild about sex before. Nikodemus slid his hands to her front, and she grabbed on to his shoulders to keep her balance. A jolt zinged through her fingertips and shot straight to her belly. Between her legs she was wet and heavy with desire. He had his hands on her breasts, right over her bra, holding her.

"I get worked up when the woman's small, and I'm not. Especially when she's a witch." His eyes flashed silver. "Guess what, Carson?"

"What?" She leaned forward, into his hands. She saw his eyes change from blue-gray to glowing charcoal-black.

He brought his mouth within inches of hers. "I'm feeling really worked up right now."

"Me, too," she said.

His breath whispered against her ear. "You ought to be totally off-limits, Carson, but I really, really want to do you."

She looked at him, and through the little thrill of seeing his planed cheekbones and parted lips, she said, "I think I should do you."

"Oh, yeah?" He pushed her back enough to slide his mouth down to her throat, pausing at the cut he'd made. He leaned forward, and she had to hold on to his shoulders to stay put, but with a little awkwardness, she got closer to him. His teeth closed on her throat, not hard, but not exactly gentle, either. A scratchy moan rolled out of him. "Oh, that's nice," he said. "Carson." His voice was tense. "Goddamn. We shouldn't be doing this, but just—goddamn."

A whole jumble of emotions came at her too fast for her to absorb. He ramped them down. Her heart felt too big for her chest, because she'd gotten a glimpse of how he'd felt, and what he'd done to keep her from dying. She held his head between her hands and waited for him to meet her gaze. Any future she had, she owed to him. "Thank you, Nikodemus. For everything. For saving my life. For finding me in the first place."

He held her with one hand and with the other drew a line from her throat to the top of her jeans. She still had on his borrowed T-shirt; it was loose and too long. His hair fell lovely dark bronze past his face to his shoulders. Any minute now, she was going to drop off the earth with the sheer intensity of her feelings. He raised his gaze to her. His fingers spread over her back, holding her weight.

"Jesus, Carson." His torso bowed toward her. "Jesus, I can feel this totally fucked-up magic in you, and I want it so bad I hurt. I fucking swear I hurt."

Maybe it was the Copa that made her feel like she was expanding outside of herself. Or maybe it was her connection with Nikodemus, because she felt that, too.

An awareness of him in her head. After he lifted his head, Carson leaned forward and kissed him, leading for the first time in her life, savoring his mouth, touching his tongue with hers. The mental contact rippled through them both. The sensation made her even more aware of the two of them. That he was male, and she wasn't. The room seemed to get smaller and her need for him even greater.

"Like it?" he asked softly. He slid his hand down her back until his fingers slipped underneath her shirt. On her bare skin.

"Yes."

"This is just a taste of what it's like between kin, Carson. We connect like this. Do you want more?"

"Yes."

This wasn't like before, when he'd reached inside her and scoured through her thoughts, when he'd held her frozen, unable to move, uncertain if she'd be able to catch another breath. This time his deliberate and purposeful presence in her head didn't feel like an invasion to be resisted at all costs.

Nikodemus said, "Just so you know, this isn't just about the magic and you swearing fealty to me. It wouldn't be like this if we didn't have some chemistry already." He tilted back so she didn't fall when he let go of her to slide his hand around to her belly. His stomach muscles went taut, the muscles of his upper legs, too, holding them like this. He caressed her, teased until she thought she would explode. His torso was warm and firm. Her palms landed on his muscled shoulders, sliding down the backs of his arms and around his biceps.

"Yeah." He closed his eyes and lowered them both to the mattress, her T-shirt pushed up around her stomach.

And then he shifted to lay his hips against hers. She responded with a want from deep inside her. Her fingers closed around his upper arms. She arched again. Deliberately. In her entire life she'd never, ever deliberately teased. She'd never dared to ask for what she wanted and hardly dared now.

The energy between them just about melted her. She put her hands on his shoulders and drew her palms along the unfamiliar curves and indentations of his body. Heat built in her, hotter yet when she caught a glimpse of his face, the intense concentration of his expression. When her spine was flat to the mattress again, his eyes popped open, locking with hers. Carson felt a flash of something alien. A consciousness that didn't process the world like she did.

"Does that bother you?" he asked. That he wasn't human couldn't have been more clear. "I was careful before, but now I don't give a fuck. I want to see where this goes, okay?"

"Okay," she whispered. Her surroundings had shifted somehow. Changed in some subtle way that had her struggling to identify what was different. She saw more clearly, color was more saturated, her sense of smell was better, her hearing more acute. There was a moment, just a moment, when she felt her emotions as if she were outside herself. She felt a hunger, an extra-sense that wanted to dive into his magic. Her body leapt at the sensation, and then the feeling attenuated. Her focus shifted to his mouth.

He sat up, straddling her hips, and fingered the top button of his jeans. "I need to be naked." His hair hid part of his cheek, but there was no hiding the impish smile. "Don't you think?"

"Yes," she said. She wanted to touch him, to taste him, to have her mouth on him, to wrap her arms around him while he slid into her body. She wanted to hurry in case he changed his mind. "I do think you need to be naked."

He grabbed the bottom of his shirt and pulled it up and over his head. The waist of his jeans hit low, and Carson feasted on the sight of his body, pecs, abs, the taper downward to his belly and hips. His skin was golden-brown everywhere. The buzz between them tweaked her higher and higher.

His smile did something wonderful to her inside. A melting something. He put a hand on the waist of his jeans and thumbed the fastening. He was aroused. Very much so. Her attention tracked his fingers unbuttoning his 501s. Underwear, she discovered, was not a choice he made. He laughed at her surprise. She knew his desire; she could distinguish his from hers and that freed her even more. He wanted her. He was aroused because of her. He wanted her body beneath his. He wanted her human warmth and emotion feeding him, slaking his thirst while they had intercourse. They could do anything, she thought as he worked the last button free. Anything at all, and no one would ever know Carson Philips had been wicked and depraved.

"Anything you want," he said. His voice was low and determined, as if it were important to him that she believe him. "Any way you want it."

With his fly open, his jeans rode low on his hips. She drew in a breath as he got to the last button and stopped. He caught her wrist. Carson looked into his eyes. His fingers squeezed her wrist. "Touch me. Please."

"My pleasure, Warlord." That made him laugh softly

until she put her palm over him, holding him gently. He pressed forward into her hand. Her reaction to him, to touching him and having him arch into her, seeking more from her, made her giddy. She hadn't ever been this bold before. Nikodemus didn't make her feel awkward at all. His penis had an unfamiliar breadth and length. With her heart beating hard and her chest tight with reverence for the experience, she explored him with her fingertips and her hand, gently gripping, harder when he squeezed her wrist.

"Fuck, yes," he said.

She raised up on her knees and put her other hand on his abdomen. Her injured palm ached, but she didn't care. "You're so warm," she murmured.

"Touch my balls, too," he said. The words came out on a low breath, almost a moan. Had she brought him to this? Her hand delved down to skin ever warmer. His chest expanded, and his eyes closed halfway. She felt the weight of him on her fingers and stroked him. "Oh, yeah."

He kissed her, roughly at first, a little out of control, his hand around her wrist showing her the movement he wanted. When he stopped it was to lift his hips and push at his jeans until they slid off. He shucked them off and grabbed her around the waist again. "Know what I like best about human women?"

She didn't care about the answer, because she was trying to decide what she liked best about warlord fiends. He was naked, and he was beautiful. Long-limbed, muscled in a way that made her think he was quick and strong. Sculpted. He let her look at him. What little body hair he had was golden-brown. So beautiful she was afraid to touch him.

He laughed. "I like the way human bodies can't change, the way their minds feel when I'm inside. And with you, it's doubled. I can feel your magic, Carson, and I feel you as kin, too." He looked her up and down. Keeping one hand on her side, up high and underneath her shirt with his fingers touching her side. "Carson," he murmured. "Tell me you want this, too."

She wasn't used to being looked at with such lust. His fingertips brushed across her, tightening her body in places she hadn't known could react like that. Nikodemus wrapped her in his arms, and somehow they ended up on the mattress again, only with her on top of him, supporting her weight on her arms, desire streaking through her like fire.

"Jesus God," Nikodemus said. His reaction flared in her head, and for a disconcerting series of seconds or minutes or hours, she saw herself through Nikodemus's gaze. She looked sexy. Wanton, even, with pale skin and dark green eyes.

"Sweetheart, yes," she heard Nikodemus say. "Like that. Just like that." The intensity of his expression scared her. Her heart beat slow and hard against her ribs, her breath uncontrolled. The sizzle of energy in her head caught her up. Nikodemus pulled himself up, pushing up her shirt, his mouth on her stomach while he worked on her pants.

Her breath hitched, caught in her chest. She didn't understand what had happened to her, how her body could have reacted like that. She surfaced from the mental tidal wave and realized Nikodemus's hand was on her face, slowly caressing her. She leaned down to kiss his shoulder, her hair falling forward, as she bit down a little, smelling the heat of his skin and the blood underneath.

"Oh, fuck, that's nice," he said.

"Yes," she whispered. "It is."

He let go of her and reached between them to unfasten her jeans. He was present in her consciousness, but not in a way she understood. Even without eye contact, they connected viscerally. But when he looked up, his gaze pierced her, and he came alive in her head. His emotions flared so intensely she wondered if he was even aware she felt him. If that's what this was. The sensation was too new for her to be sure of anything.

Head back, he let out a low, sighing moan. The mental connection between them ratcheted up. Sex had never been any big deal to her before, but now she thought she'd die if Nikodemus didn't make love to her.

A noise behind her broke the intimacy. She ignored it until the back of her neck prickled. She pushed away the disturbance and concentrated on Nikodemus and his mouth, and her hands on his body, sliding over muscle and sinew. Nikodemus replaced his mouth with his fingers and turned his head toward the door. "Look what the cat dragged in," he murmured.

"Carson?" said a male voice.

She jumped and then realized she was tangled up with Nikodemus. His eyelids lifted just enough for her to see a flash of blue-gray on its way to turning black. "Ignore him. He'll go away once he realizes he's interrupting."

"I can feel her," Harsh said, his voice nearer, a little shaky. "She feels like a mage, but like the kin, too. She's bound to you, and now I can feel her like she's kin. The closer I get, the more I know what she's feeling. Both of you. It's killing me." Harsh came to the edge of the bed and touched Carson's shoulder. His fingers were cool. For God's sake, Nikodemus still had a hand on her breast. "I feel the warlord in your mind, Carson Philips," he said in a low voice. "So much that there's no room for me." The air around them quivered.

"Go away," Nikodemus said. But he quickly pulled down her shirt.

"I missed this," he whispered. "Being with other fiends. When you're mageheld, all that's gone. It's like dying a little every single day. Only you can never die and stop the misery."

Nikodemus kept his gaze locked with Carson's. "Go downstairs, Harsh," he said. "She's not ready for this. She doesn't understand how it is with fiends. Not yet."

But Carson had reached out and touched Harsh's arm because he looked so sad. The tips of her fingers tingled at the contact, and she felt Harsh's mental presence in her head. He longed to be physically and mentally close with others of his kind. She lifted her hand, and the connection cut off. When she touched him again, the sensations flooded back.

"What is that?" she whispered.

Nikodemus's presence in her head got wound very, very tight. "It's what fiends are, Carson. We connect mentally. We need that connection to be whole and healthy. She stretched out her hand again, and this time when she touched Harsh, his eyes changed. From chocolate brown to scarlet and then back. His face changed. His skin changed, and Carson was sure she was hallucinating. She snatched back her hand.

"He's been free all this time," Harsh said. He hadn't changed. He hadn't. "This is how it always is for him.

He's never been cut off the way I was. Isolated from everyone he loves or could love."

Nikodemus threw an arm back and grabbed on to the headboard, bringing them both up, him and Carson and then Harsh, his hand locked on Harsh's chin. He kept an arm around Carson. "No more freelancing for you, Harsh."

Harsh went icy. A regular glacier.

"What's the problem, Harsh?" Nikodemus said. His voice had lost all trace of that silky warmth. "Can't I trust you? Because if I can't, you aren't getting near Carson. I'll personally see to that, Doctor Harsh. You want this so bad, then you join me. Formally. The way it ought to be done."

"Of course, Warlord." Harsh inclined his head, and when he lifted it, he recited the oath Carson had already made. At the end, she thought she felt something from Harsh, a sense of peace and acceptance. Of being where he belonged. Only this time, she wasn't touching him.

Nikodemus's biceps bulged when he opened a cut on the underside of Harsh's jaw. Bright blood filled the score, and she felt a leap of hunger at the scent and the color. She wanted to be closer to the smell, to breathe it in and let the taste spread over her tongue. Nikodemus pressed his mouth to Harsh's jaw, and Carson tasted copper in her mouth and gasped at the rush of Harsh into her head, brought there by Nikodemus. Harsh's arm came up and he wrapped a palm around the back of Nikodemus's head and held him there.

The sizzle went deep in Carson's body, and it didn't stop even when Nikodemus released Harsh physically and came fully back to her. She caught a glimpse of Harsh's face. His eyes were dazed and unfocused, his mouth damp, lips parted because he was breathing as hard as Carson. Nikodemus held out his arm and drew the side of his finger along the bend in his elbow. Blood welled there, and Harsh bent and tasted. She felt the psychic lockdown that cemented Harsh's oath and bound him to Nikodemus.

Harsh bent over them. "He's bound you, too," he said to Carson. He came closer to her, his breath warm against her temple, stirring strands of her hair. "And it is splendid, Carson Philips."

She put her hand over Harsh's, and he filled her head until she gasped at the onslaught of sensation from him and Nikodemus, different from anything she'd felt before, darker feelings, bigger, wider, and at the same time incredibly compressed. She felt joy at being with her own kind at long last. More than anything, she wanted to touch Harsh and Nikodemus, to taste their blood on her tongue, to have her skin against theirs. An image flashed into her head, an instant only, of the three of them making love, Harsh touching Nikodemus, kissing him, and then her and—

Nikodemus changed.

He grabbed the fiend's arm, breaking their contact. Her vision snapped back to her body. "It's too much for her, Harsh," he said. "Some other time, when she understands more about what she is now."

"Warlord . . ."

"Harsh." Nikodemus turned around, and Carson felt the edge of his anger. "That's enough. Enough."

"She's not safe when you're this distracted," Harsh said.

Nikodemus leaned forward and grabbed Harsh's face in his hand. He stared at Harsh, and Carson knew Harsh wanted to kiss Nikodemus, because she felt his desire. She also knew that Nikodemus no longer intended to make love to her. That when Harsh had said it wasn't safe, he was right, and Nikodemus had changed his mind.

A violent warning moved from Nikodemus to Harsh. "Get. Out. Of. Here."

CHAPTER 22

Xia crouched low, out of sight of any sharp-eyed fiends. His blood responded to the witch with a painful pull. He tasted her all over again. Tangy sweet blood. He'd been having dreams about her ever since he snatched her out of the warlord's house. At first, just the daydream kind. The recollection of her would come up at random points in his day, and he'd think, Hell yeah, she tasted good, and wouldn't it be nice to have more? Then thoughts of her, explicit ones, sexual ones, came while he was working on his blade, destroying his concentration. The witch was invading his life. He was starting to hate her almost as much as he hated Rasmus.

Right now, however, she was at the mall in podunk Olompali, California. Shopping. Accompanied by the warlord Nikodemus and Harsh. None of them had any idea he was watching them. Rasmus and Magellan had called out an army to take them all if they could orchestrate it. Rasmus had the point right now, and he was a powerful mage, no doubt about that. But Xia wasn't sure he was powerful enough to take down Nikodemus. Privately, he thought the best Rasmus was going to get was the witch and maybe Harsh.

As expected, the warlord and Harsh stuck to the witch like a mageheld fiend to his master, a fact that meant grabbing her again wasn't going to be easy this time. Every now and then Nikodemus would get an intense look about him. Xia couldn't feel what he was doing, but he could guess. It's what he would do if he were out here in public with Magellan's missing witch: send out pulses of magic to check for the presence of fiends and mages. Didn't do him any good. Even a warlord like Nikodemus couldn't feel a mageheld fiend, and Rasmus and Magellan were keeping themselves out of range.

He followed the three through the mall. A shopping trip for the little witch. How precious. They were tireless. Goddamn. How many stores were they going to hit? He had on his leathers again, and when he let himself get distracted by her, sometimes he made too much of an impression on the humans. A few of the female ones would have tempted him before, but he wasn't in the mood. Not since he'd gotten a taste of Carson Philips.

No doubt about it, her magic was a hell of a lot stronger than it had been before. Magellan's ritual had gone awry, a real fuckup, what with the witch interfering as she had. Now that he was close enough to her to feel her magic, Xia thought she felt disturbingly fiendlike. Even a hint of the kin slivered his soul. It was impossible of course, since she was a witch and he was cut off from his kind. The only fiends nearby were Rasmus's other magehelds, and Xia could sense them only through Rasmus.

He watched the three for a while, trying to get a fix on

what was up with her and her two fiends. Harsh he knew, and he didn't feel Harsh at all, and Harsh had once been his brother in slavery. The witch and the warlord were all lovey, and both of them were trying not to let the other one know they were gaga over each other.

That got him to thinking. If she made herself all soft and easy and sweet for the warlord, which she did—the way she looked at him when she thought he wasn't looking was downright sickening—then why not for him? Obviously, she liked to get done by a fiend. And he was a fiend. How perfect was that?

His cell phone rang. Rasmus. He waited until the last possible moment to press the headset button and pick up. "What the fuck do you want?"

The happy threesome headed for the shoe department. Carson hung back, and Xia's heart beat harder. But Nikodemus came back for her and even kissed her. Totally giving her tongue. Things got a little hot for a bit, but the warlord pulled away and they rejoined Harsh.

"Temper, temper," came Rasmus's voice over his Bluetooth headset.

How the hell had Harsh gotten free of Rasmus? He thought about snatching Harsh and working him over until he gave it up. But a Harsh who wasn't mageheld anymore was dangerous. He didn't know what he'd face if he got down with Harsh. "I'm busy."

"Still?"

Xia had no trouble imagining the mage's face as he spoke. And even less imagining his own fingers around Rasmus's throat. Squeezing. Tighter and tighter. He couldn't get even a flicker from Harsh. Not an atom of a flicker, and all a mage's fiends felt at least an echo of each other through the mage. With a little concentration, he could feel his fellow magehelds out in the parking lot. But not Harsh. The guy had really and truly been cut free. Xia couldn't remember the last time Rasmus had lost a fiend. Harsh's freedom wasn't going to last, though. Magellan was positioning his fiends in the parking lot, because he was hot to have the witch and the talisman back. Poor mage didn't get his way, and now he was all pissed off and taking it out on everyone else, including Rasmus.

"You want this done, or done right?" Xia said.

Harsh was making her try on a pair of shoes. The witch was pulling faces, but she was doing it. Following a fiend's instructions. Imagine that. When he got his hands on her, he'd have a few instructions for her.

"What I want," Rasmus said, "is for you to do what you have been directed to do. *Por favor.*" His imitation of Magellan was spot-on.

When the mage lapsed into sarcasm, you knew steam was coming out his ears. Xia smiled. At least something was going right today. His three little pigeons left the shoe store. "Fuck you, mage."

And then he hit the jackpot. They went to a salon, where he had to watch her get her hair cut short like she was some mageheld bitch for an asshole who liked his sex kinky. Not a buzz, but above her shoulders. After the haircut, she went into a booth with a slender human woman. He waited to see what Harsh and Nikodemus were going to do, which turned out to be nothing but sit around jawing and looking at magazines with pictures of human women with boob jobs and freaky hair. Fantastic. They weren't close enough to feel the witch.

He got control of the human in the booth with Carson and slipped inside. She was getting a Brazilian. He figured he had ten minutes max before Rasmus harassed him again, so he didn't waste time. He grabbed the human woman by the throat so she couldn't make any noise and started squeezing.

"Make a sound, witch, and she's dead. Pull any magic, and you're dead."

The witch grabbed the towel and covered her parts. Damn shame. He liked all those bare parts. Skin down there was so soft and tender when it was freshly naked. Interesting. She wasn't afraid of him. "What do you want?"

He shut down the human woman's mind and let her slide to the floor so he could draw his knife. The witch's magic heated up. Not focused, but shit, she felt deep with it and tinged with fiendish magic that made him feel emptier than ever. The wrist Magellan had cut was nearly healed. A mage who could heal a wound like that wasn't insignificant. If she was limited, he'd fucking hate to see what she was like when she wasn't. "What did you do to Harsh?"

Her eyes got big, looking at the blade. "I don't know."

"Fuck you, witch." He was thinking about how good she tasted. She had some Copa in her, he could feel that, too, but all that meant was she'd taste that much better. "Answer my question." His pulse sped up. "Harsh used to belong to Rasmus, and five minutes after he meets up with you, he's walking free. But he isn't yours, is he? He doesn't act like he's your mageheld. If he was, I'd feel him."

"He's not." She sat up, holding the towel over the lower half of her body. He didn't like that she wasn't afraid. Something was different, and he had a feeling if he didn't figure it out, it wasn't going to be Rasmus who killed him. The witch had severed Harsh, he was sure of it. He got his excitement tamped down. No sense telegraphing everything to Rasmus. If he was right, he was looking at his freedom.

He pressed his back against the wall. She was tiny compared to him, and in this room where he could press his hands to the ceiling without stretching, he must seem giant. Human women were funny that way. They didn't like to be at that kind of disadvantage with a man they didn't know. One of the fundamental weaknesses of their species. He steeled himself. It hurt, it hurt his soul to act contrary to orders. He couldn't really, but even thinking he would betray Rasmus was like sticking needles in his heart.

"Trade, all right?" he said. "You give me the answer to my question, and I'll see about giving you a way out of the trap you're walking into."

She looked at the woman lying on the floor, and he got a funny vibe from the witch. Almost like she was a fiend. But she wasn't, so that was bogus, but it still creeped him out.

"Yeah, right," he said. "She's my insurance. If you don't help me, she dies. And I promise it'll be painful for her."

"I thought you had to do whatever Rasmus told you."

He pulled some power, just a trickle, and traced a line along one of the edges of his knife. The metal gleamed dull blue in the light. He wished he was doing it along her skin. Delicate traceries all along her body, drawing a net that would make her his. "I do," he said.

"So?"

"I'm supposed to get you out in the north parking lot, where he and Magellan have their magehelds backing me up. Magellan's going to take you and the warlord while Rasmus takes back Harsh—"

Her eyes flashed. "He can't."

"They're mages. They can do anything they want." The human on the floor moaned. Xia looked over and put a foot on her chest like he was going to stomp down. He was pretty sure he wouldn't, but you never knew. He'd surprised himself before.

"No!"

Xia whipped his head around. She was flaring up again. Now, that had to stop or he'd have Nikodemus and Harsh in here trying to beat his ass. He pushed through into her head, and it was like butting his head against a stone wall. "Tell me what I want to know, and I'll make sure you don't get caught."

"But now I know he's out there." He grabbed her injured wrist, and she still damn near slipped away from him. He held on. She didn't feel the way he remembered. She felt better. Stronger. His orders from Rasmus helped him get dug in, wasn't that ironic?

He smiled at her from over the tip of his knife. "Dead witches don't remember much." Fortunately, she blanched and didn't consider, he presumed, that the mages might want her alive. If she concluded he'd been released from the prohibition against harming mages, well, gee. Too fucking bad.

"What is it you want to know?"

"I want to know what you did to Harsh." He took a step toward her, knife in his hand. She was a witch and therefore could not be trusted. She'd probably lie to him. But Harsh was free, and he wasn't, and the witch was responsible for that. He breathed in and smelled roses on her skin. Freshly shampooed hair with some flowery scent. Clean female skin. Naked down there. Maybe she was too cool right now, but he still had the advantage. "He doesn't belong to Rasmus anymore. I want to know how and why."

She threw up her hand and nearly lost control of the sheet. "I don't know what I did. Not exactly, anyway." His knife slipped and nicked her earlobe. Carson went stiff and wide-eyed, but she didn't complain. The smell of blood sparked hunger in him.

"No sudden movements, witch." Her heartbeat pulsed in his head, and the tart, sweet smell of her blood pulled at him and threatened to drown him. Her magic wasn't like anything he'd felt before. She felt like a fiend and a mage, and that was just crazy.

"I touched him," the witch said.

He leaned in, keeping his breaths shallow. "Then touch me," he said. His back crawled like Rasmus was listening in. He wasn't, but Xia was treading close to the kind of betrayal that would get him killed. "Touch me the way you did Harsh. Sever me, and I'll get you out of this. That's a promise."

She hesitated, then put her hand on his chest, palm flat. "I touched his chest. Like this."

Xia sucked in a breath, anticipation sending a rush of adrenaline through him. But nothing happened. Not a goddamned thing.

He stared her down. She didn't drop her lying, betraying witch eyes.

"I told you," she whispered. "I don't know how I did it. It just happened."

Fuck. He wanted to howl with disappointment. If Rasmus had released him, he would have killed her on the spot. He took a step closer, crowding her space. He thought about holding her down and checking out her freshly naked skin. "Tricks and more tricks, witch. I should kill you right now."

"I told you, I don't know how it happened!" She made a fist on his chest, fingers clenched. Her magic bubbled up, but inchoate, without purpose or intention. At the edges of her he felt the pull of his kind, and despair filled him because he could never connect with the kin again. He was going to belong to Rasmus until the mage decided to kill him. "There was so much going on, everything was jumbled, and I just did it. That's all I know. It just happened. I'd sever you if I could. I swear it."

His phone vibrated again. "Fuck you," he said into his headset.

"I've come in," Rasmus said.

Xia would have laughed if he hadn't known Rasmus would blame him for this failure. "Then the warlord knows you're here."

"He doesn't. He can't."

"You'll never get them now."

"That is not among my troubles, Xia."

He ground his teeth.

"The witch first," Rasmus said over the headset. "Then the warlord."

CHAPTER 23

Nikodemus dropped his magazine when the hair on the back of his neck sizzled. His spine flashed red-hot. "Mage," he said.

Harsh looked up from the paper he'd pulled from a stack, eyebrows raised. "There's nothing—I feel him now." He put away the pen he'd been using to do the *New York Times* crossword and got to his feet.

"Not some weak-assed mage, either." The air vibrated with the magic he was pulling. "Rasmus, unless I'm very much mistaken." Harsh didn't like that much. Nikodemus felt that right away.

"You're not. And if Rasmus's here, then so is Xia," Harsh said.

"We can probably count on Magellan, too, along with his buddy Kynan Aijan." He tossed his keys to Harsh. "Get the car and bring it around there." He jabbed a finger in the direction he meant. "Doors unlocked. Be ready to punch it when we're in." He grabbed the other fiend's arm. "Stay the hell away from Rasmus, you hear me?"

Harsh barely acknowledged him before he went off at a run. Nikodemus hoped he wasn't sending him to be owned by Rasmus all over again. He didn't know for sure if Harsh was protected by his link with Carson.

As for him, his body was in fight mode: primed, balls tight, senses alert. Everything felt light. He was walking an edge, all right. He headed for the back of the salon, past the women looking through lotions and oils and poofy sponges and straight for Carson's room. He had a fix on where she was the last time he felt her, but he got nothing from her now. Nothing at all. It was all he could do to keep his human form.

He pulled power before he burst into the tiny room, as much as he could safely handle and then a little more. He welcomed the edge. If he tipped over, too bad. A human woman lay insensate on the floor, mentally stripped until she'd collapsed. Nikodemus stepped over the human.

Carson sat on the table, her hand on Xia's chest like she was trying to push him away. Xia snarled at Nikodemus, teeth bared. The mageheld was as close to leaving his shape as any fiend could be and not have changed. Xia reached behind his back and brought out a blade that gleamed with the years of malignant magic poured into its making.

"We're busy, Warlord," he said, eyes on Nikodemus. "So just fuck off, all right?" He laughed. A corner of his mouth curled. "Guess your witch likes what I do for her."

Nikodemus didn't wait. He had Carson on tap, and that meant he could feel Xia. Not full-on, but enough to surprise the crap out of him. He let loose with a shot of heat focused straight at Xia's chest. The fiend hit the back wall with a crash, but he shook it off. Too late. Nikodemus saw his opening and was halfway through it. Drawing on Carson, he cut Xia off from his magic. Shit, Xia was a fucking monster. He snatched Carson's jeans and threw them at her. "We need to get out of here."

She rolled off the table, jeans clutched in one hand, but turned toward Xia. The mageheld might not be able to use his magic right now, but he was still a goddamned big and powerful freak. Nikodemus figured he had about five minutes, maybe six, before Xia broke the physical freeze he had on him.

"Get dressed, Carson. Now."

She gave Xia another look before she shoved a leg into her jeans. He had the fiend immobilized, but not much more than that. She hopped a couple of times because she was staring at Xia. At this rate, he was going to have to carry her out bare-assed. At last, she got her jeans on and shoved her feet into her shoes.

"Sweetheart! Let's go."

She swung to Xia. "But I can feel him, Nikodemus."

"Carson." He reached for her, and when his fingers closed on her he got a blast of her magic, disorganized but rapidly taking on coherence. It didn't go anywhere. Couldn't. But the fiend-magic in her was something else, and it was transforming something freaky.

She stood her ground and closed her eyes, concentrating. She leaned toward Xia. The mageheld blinked. "I can *feel* him. I couldn't before, but now I can."

"What the freaking eff are you doing?" He tightened his grip on her wrist. She reached for Xia, who was as likely to kill her before, during, or after he was done balling her brains out.

"I can do it now," she said. "You need to let him go, Nikodemus. I can't do this if he doesn't have his magic."

Xia arched back, bowing away from her as much as he could. "Fuck you, witch. I'd rather die than be your slave."

Nikodemus was just about at the end of his ability to keep Xia down. "Carson, we don't want to be anywhere near this guy when he breaks free. In his state, he could take down the building."

"Let me try!"

"Carson, now!" And he hauled her out of the room.

Xia broke free before they reached the side exit where Nikodemus hoped Harsh was waiting with the car. He wasn't. Nikodemus scanned the parking lot for his Mercedes. Lots of pedestrians. Cars, too. Too many people around. He didn't like this at all. Rasmus was here, not far, and that meant his fiends had to be close.

Carson was totally calm. Her gaze swung back to the mall. The change in her, her eagerness to go after Xia, vibrated in her. Her magic was coming up strong now, and it was hard for him to concentrate. He walked her to the west exit, hand on her back the whole way.

Twenty feet past the exit, the hair on the back of his neck stood up. "Shit," he said. "Magellan's here somewhere."

Neither mage would do anything out in the open. Not in a crowded mall. They'd have to be foolish or damned good or both to think they could pull magic out here in the open. But Magellan wasn't even trying to hide his power anymore, and that was worrisome. Nikodemus didn't like knowing there were fiends he couldn't feel. It made his skin crawl.

He drew on Carson and, through her, got that echo of what it was for a mage to feel the kin. The contact with her opened up a psychic floodgate. This was a lot like what had happened with Kynan. His connection with Carson let him access her magic, and her magic resonated around fiends. There were two on top of the wisteria-covered trellis between the mall and the main parking lot. He looked up. Their black dusters flapped in the afternoon breeze.

Fifty yards away, his Mercedes was stopped behind several cars waiting for a woman with a double stroller to cross in front of them. Crap. The two clowns on the trellis were drawing attention. Rasmus was around, too, but not showing himself.

One of the two on the trellis snarled at them. Harsh was too far away. Nikodemus put a hand on Carson's back, and at the first break in traffic he walked her onto the parking lot, away from the trellis. The three guys in leather walked along the diagonal walkway. Nikodemus tightened his grip on her elbow. These guys and more somewhere with the mages. "Carson, can you sever any of them?"

Her eyes dilated. Wide open to stimuli. She was on. Totally chilled. Totally focused. Someone had turned on the magic spigot in her. "I think so. But I need to touch them to do it." She narrowed her eyes. "I don't think it works any other way."

Three more fiends appeared at the other side of the lot. All of them wore leather pants and dusters like they were auditioning for *Highlander.* And then one of them vanished. Fuck. A human teen with baggy pants halfway down his ass froze. His eyes bulged, showing nothing but whites. He screamed without pausing for breath, arms windmilling. Spittle dripped down the side of his mouth as he bobbed and pitched, and then he dashed straight for Carson.

He absolutely could not touch a human, not in the middle of a crowd. The best he could do was put himself in front of Carson and take the brunt of the physical attack. At the periphery of his vision, he saw Harsh corner the Mercedes, keeping in the inside lane. The equivalent of a city block away. The kid shrieked like his head was on fire, and all while he battered Nikodemus to get at Carson. Two of the leather-boys stopped, but a third circled around. A fourth dropped from the roof. Did they think no one was going notice someone jumping from twelve feet in the air and just strolling off? And then Carson juked around him right when he expected the kid to blast them.

She stuck out her arms, and the human boy crashed into her palms. They went reeling, the both of them. Nikodemus caught her in time to stop her from cracking her head on a cement column. His connection with her was enough to feel what happened. Her magic separated the fiend from the kid the way a hot fire incinerated paper. The indwelling fiend burst away, damn near destroyed by the impact. The kid hit the ground hard. He lay limp, barely breathing. The fiend kept shrieking. His fellow magehelds grabbed him when they realized he was losing it. All around them, humans stared. A few pulled out cell phones and started dialing.

"Fucking awesome, Carson." Nikodemus grabbed her. "Now, run!"

When Harsh saw Nikodemus and Carson running, he gunned the engine and ran the car up the sidewalk. Behind them, the fiend who'd taken the kid collapsed. Two other fiends darted after them, realizing too late they were made and had lost any advantage they might have had. Tires squealed when Harsh hit the brakes, and Nikodemus got a nose full of burning rubber. Carson jumped for the car and yanked open the rear door. Nikodemus dove inside, and she threw herself in after. Harsh floored it.

In the back seat, Carson wriggled around until she struggled to sit up. She stared out the back window, transfixed by the chaos. "Oh, my God," she whispered.

"Seat belt, Carson!" He pulled her down and grabbed the belt. *Click.* "You can't sever even a puny-ass fiend if you get killed going through the windshield."

As they shot the red light, Nikodemus looked out the back window, too. Magellan was calling back his fiends. The goofs in the dusters were gone. Across the street from the mall, a tall fiend stood next to a man in a suit. They weren't too far away for Nikodemus to recognize Magellan and Kynan Aijan.

CHAPTER 24

Nikodemus was strung high as a kite after they got back to the farmhouse. He wasn't entirely sure of his control over anything. One thing was sure now, Carson's fealty was as solid as any normal fiend who'd pledged to him. Maybe more. She was his. And that gave him the shakes if he thought about it too hard. Magellan's witch was sworn to him. If the other warlords found out about this, they'd probably start assassination plans the minute his back was turned.

He followed Carson upstairs, leaving Harsh to unload the car of their purchases and make sheep's eyes at Fen and Iskander. In her room, Carson stood by the bed, arms wrapped around her chest, focused on the floor. He moved toward her. "Carson—"

Her head came up, and she took a step back. Her usual serious expression didn't mask her fear. "What happened to me?" She held up her hands. "I'm trembling still at the thought of what Magellan and his fiends could have done to you. If any of them had touched you, I would have killed them with my bare hands." She dropped her hands. "I'm not a killer. I'm not."

"It's your fealty to me," he said. He had to work to keep his voice even. No big deal. This was no big deal. He leaned against the door, one knee bent so the sole of his boot was on the wood. "Stronger than I expected, but that's all it is." He hooked his fingers through his two front belt loops. No big deal. Right. "I'm bound to protect you, and you're bound to protect me. That's how it works."

She opened her mouth to say something and apparently thought better of it. "I need a drink of water," she said.

He watched her march to the bathroom, listened while she got a drink. *Clunk.* That was the cup hitting the sink. When she came out, she said, "What happened to that boy?"

"You separated him from the fiend who took him."

She leaned against the wall by the bathroom door and stared at the ceiling. "Okay," she whispered in a trembling voice. She ran her hands over her head. "Okay." Then she looked at him. "But is he going to be all right?"

"Probably." He walked over to her and slipped his arms around her waist before she had a chance to take a breath. "You didn't kill that kid. Chances are you saved his life. The mageheld sure as hell didn't give a rat's ass what happened to him."

"Magellan is after us." Her eyes fixed on him, big and intensely green. "He's after you because of me. And he's not going to give up."

He dropped his head to her shoulder, getting up close and thinking about her being naked in his arms, which he really shouldn't do. "Look," he said after a bit. "You don't make my life any more dangerous than it already was. That's just a fact, so don't get all broken up about Álvaro Magellan having a hard-on for me. Mages are always looking to snag a fiend. It's been that way for longer than I can remember." He sighed, and Carson put her arms around him, holding him close. "If we don't figure out how to change that, pretty soon there'll be more of us who are mageheld than free."

"So what now?"

He shrugged. "We go on. I meet with the other warlords and do my best to convince them we need to work together." Her body felt good against his. He nuzzled the side of her neck, breathing in her scent. "You smell good, Carson." Her body softened against his, and without thinking, he opened his mouth over her. His teeth scraped her skin. Not enough to draw blood, but still, the desire was there. He bit down a little harder. Her arms tightened around him. They could do this. He could control himself enough to have plain vanilla sex with her.

When he lifted his mouth from the side of her neck, he definitely heard the moan in the back of her throat. He put a hand on her cheek. "Don't look so serious," he said. Her eyes were pools of still, green ocean. She gazed at him as if she'd fallen overboard and he was the one with a rope. "This isn't life or death, Carson. It's not what was going down with Harsh the other day, the three of us. That was serious. Out of hand. What happened at the mall today was serious. You and me like this isn't. The two of us are just good together."

Right. Him feeling like she was the only thing that mattered was no big deal. She studied him with that serious look of hers that made him so hot for her. She was back to low tide, so he couldn't be sure where she was emotionally. Not without going where he shouldn't. A tiny white scar ran into the lower edge of her bottom lip, a diamond of pale white in the red. She licked her lips, and he stared at her mouth, thinking things he shouldn't. He leaned closer and invaded her space on purpose. His skin prickled: the hair up and down his arms came to attention, almost like he was going to change form. "For a human woman, Carson," he said in a voice thick with reaction, "you manage to rev me up on more than the physical level."

"Is that bad?"

"I like it." More than liked it. And he liked the way she thought so hard about everything. For her, every decision was a momentous one. She was getting to him. He was thinking more about her than he was about himself. "So," he said. "Are we going to?"

Very serious again, she said, "Do you have condoms?"

"The kin don't get STDs."

Her cheeks pinked up. "What about pregnancy? Do we need to worry about that?"

"I'm not fertile in this form. If we ever make it when I'm shifted, then you can worry about me getting you knocked up."

She licked her lips again and blinked several times. Her skin went two shades whiter. Nikodemus put his hand on the nape of her neck. *Zing.* The contact went straight to his gonads. Her lower lip rolled underneath her upper one and came out glistening. "Well," she said. She put her arms around him. "Then I guess we are."

"How do you like it, Carson? Slow and sweet, or sweaty and rough?"

"That depends on the moment, doesn't it?"

He pressed his thumb to her damp lip. "We'll try it both ways, then. I just want it to be good for you." He dropped his hand to her shoulder and made a circle with the pad of his finger. And while he did, his imagination drifted. He saw himself shifted to his other form, his finger trailing down her body. His back itched with the idea of being in his most elemental form. With more effort than he liked, he brought his thoughts back to right now.

She watched him with familiar caution. What calculus was behind those eyes now? She grimaced, and her gaze locked with his. Yeah. He could definitely see himself shifted, touching her naked human skin with his fingers so as not to accidentally draw blood, gliding along her body, lungs pulling in air, his cock hard and sliding in while he delved deep into her head, soaking up all her emotion. His spine tingled all the way down his back. She had some control, too, so she wasn't going to just let him roll her like a drunk in a doorway. Not that he would.

He leaned back long enough to jerk his T-shirt over his head and drop it to the floor. This close to shifting, he didn't like clothes against his skin, and he was close. Convenient, since he needed to be out of his clothes to have sex with her anyway. He stroked her forehead with the pad of his index finger. "You know, Carson, you could come into my head if you wanted."

"I could?"

"Yeah. Wanna try?" She nodded. His magic wanted to taste the well of blackness churning in her almost as much as he wanted her physical body. His fingertip pressed gently, about an inch above the bridge of her nose, and like that, their link came alive, easier now because the fiend-magic in her was sworn to him. As a warlord, he almost never let someone in like this. "Just think about being in me."

To his surprise, she came on, soft but sure, no barging in, no breaking down of barriers. Just—insertion. And Carson was there. With him. His blood sizzled with the effect of her being in his head. She was one hell of a rush. Sweet and lush, a siren's call to the ever-ravenous side of his nature.

She pressed her palms to his torso and spread her fingers, driving him right to the edge of his control. "Is this all right?"

"Hell, yes," Nikodemus said. Her hands were cool on his skin. Human skin. His skin was still human. "I like that you're not tall," he said, because he needed something to keep him from changing. He turned toward the wall, crowding her, pressing her against the cool surface, his palms braced above her shoulders. Much as he liked her hands sliding down his torso—God, did he like it— he was shaking with the desire to change and that would scare her right out of the mood. "Perfect."

He lowered his head and kissed her. In the back of his head, the alien, human presence of her stirred, shimmering beneath everything else, pulsing through his body. Something in him answered until he felt the burning sensation that meant he was about to lose control. He broke contact and threw back his head, his pelvis pressed against her until the energy that presaged his physical change drained away.

When he was reasonably sure he had himself under control, he went back to kissing her. Hard this time. None of that sweet and tender crap. His tongue swept into her mouth, answering her heat. He got a hand between them and worked at pushing up her T-shirt. This had been coming on for so long it was a relief to know they were finally going to get it done. They separated enough for him to get the shirt off her.

"Oh, hell, yes," he said when he saw the flash of her skin. Her bra was industrial-strength cotton and hideous. No lace anywhere. But there was no disguising she was stacked. Not obscenely or anything, but nice, really nice. Really, really nice. She was too slender for bombshell status, but he felt like someone had gone and made him a human woman who pushed every sexual button he possessed. Real hips, real breasts, a flat stomach, and skin that had never baked in the sun.

He got a hand behind her, palm to her back. A quick pull forward and she was pressed against him, her soft, bare skin against his chest. Her presence in his head electrified him. He tingled beneath his skin, his back rippled, and again he had to pull away just to keep from going berserk with her.

Her lips parted, and he cradled her face with one hand and with the other worked at the back fastening of her bra. *Pop.* Yeah. Body armor about to fail. "I love your mouth," he growled. Her pupils were big and black as midnight, pools of black surrounded by green. "I love it so much I'm hoping you like to give head." He worked at her bra. Three damn rows of hooks, and the last one just wasn't going to unhook. "Do you, Carson?" His voice went low and soft. She was there in his head, so she knew exactly what he was thinking and feeling. "Tell me you're a cocksucker."

But then her bra came loose and he lost track of his bad language and a few other things, too. "God, you're perfect. Round and pale and all tight." He put a hand over her naked breast, and she made a sound in the back of her throat that dove him right off the high board. He was taking them along. Too fast. He knew that, but that's how things were between them. He couldn't not go there. Then his mouth was on her, licking her, sucking, hot and damp, and her reaction sent him out of his mind. Her nipple came erect in his mouth and under his tongue and, just, Christ, he was in heaven.

He ran his finger along the waistband of her jeans. He hardly knew where to touch her. He kissed his way up her throat, letting his hand take over where his mouth had been, and when he got to her mouth, he slid his lips over hers and kissed her, and her mouth opened under his like a dream. She kissed him back and at the same time pushed his hand away from her pants. With a wiggle, she came in closer and ran a finger up his fly. And then she popped the buttons of his jeans.

He pulled away and turned them so his spine was pressed against the wall, and, *thunk,* his head hit the edge of the door. He toe-heeled his boots off, and she got her hand around him, fingers warm and then tightening around him just so.

"Holy fuck, Carson." His hesitation about this encounter was living in some other time zone now. She did it. She went down on him, and she knew exactly how he liked it, too. He adjusted his position so it was easier for her. "I'll return the favor, I promise. Oh, Jesus, that feels good."

Her tongue went the length of him, magic. He grabbed her hand and extended her arm out. He got a picture in his head that didn't do much for his good-boy hopes. A picture that, when he peeked at her, was more or less what was in his head except he still looked human. She ended up propping her hand against his abdomen, and he kept himself from exploding in her by drawing another line from her shoulder to the tip of her index finger. He managed it twice more, got all the way to her ring finger before she blew the top off his head.

He lost it. His control dissolved and his body started to change, and he was so close to his natural form that he nearly slid all the way there. Only he didn't. He caught himself in time. Well, not quite, because when she stood up, he saw a thin line of blood on her shoulder. He kissed the scratch. Her blood tasted of salt. He bit her. Just a little. Just enough to remind him that what he wanted to do was taboo. A fiend wasn't supposed to take a human who knew he was shifted or who was going to remember afterward.

"My turn," he said. He walked forward, forcing her to walk backward. All the way to the bed. He grabbed her upper arm when the backs of her knees hit the mattress. His hand slid toward her fingers, letting her lie back. He knelt on the mattress with his knees on either side of her hips. Her body was luscious. He curled his fingers around her wrist and drew another line. He put his mouth by her ear. "I started out thinking this would just be fucking, but it's gotten a little out of hand. You know, do it and get you out of my system. So, yeah. Maybe it's be a little more than that. Okay? Just so you know. You okay with that? Because I am."

"Yeah," she said, tugging him toward her. "I'm okay with that."

He let go of her wrist and applied himself to getting her naked. She was already barefoot. Pants, gone. Ugly cotton undies, gone. "You," he said, breathless with the sight of her, Brazilian and all, "are amazing." And that was the last thing he said for a long time. She tasted good, and when she got close to orgasm, the link between them vibrated. He let her relax between peaks, took her almost to the edge and backed down until she was writhing. "What happens if I leave you like this?" he said when she was damn near there. He used his knee to nudge her legs apart.

"Don't you dare," she said, all wild-eyed and panting.

"You sure?" he asked. "'Cause I think you're going to come apart. Are you? Wouldn't that be bad, coming apart in my arms?" He shifted his body down and blew on her heated skin, right there on the very spot. He had a hand cupped over her bare ass, soft, so incredibly soft. "I think maybe one little—"

She tasted good. And oh, yeah. She shattered, and she was still so deep in his head, he shattered, too.

Her heartbeat slowed and throbbed in time with his. Two beats. One heart. He pulled himself over her, wanting this never to end. He hadn't been this intimate with a human in longer than he could recall. One hand skimmed the outside of her arm, and his fingertips sizzled with the heat of the magic flowing out. He'd forgotten just how exhilarating it was to be possessed like this.

Carson opened her eyes, and he found himself looking into them, still resonating with magic, still connected, the two of them. She whispered, "That was incredible."

"No shit."

Her eyes were dark green, with thick ebony lashes, and Nikodemus could see all the way inside. She groaned, a soft sound, breathy and redolent with desire. One of her hands touched his chest. His magic flowed into her, twined inside her, and he pulled more until his body was taut with it and their skin crackled with energy. He slid inside her, into heat and wetness. Her eyes opened wider, head thrown back. She clutched his arms and pushed herself toward him.

"More," she said.

He had to concentrate to maintain his form. He filled her with his body and slid further into pleasure. "You're not ready for what I am," he said. A reminder to himself, more than something she needed to know. She fit him tightly. With one hand on the bed beside her shoulder he moved. The pleasure belonged to them both. Carson arched her back. His free hand slid around her waist to the place where her spine curved, underneath so that his fingers slid over her skin, skimming the layer of warmth. He fell a little deeper into her head, took on a little more magic. He could feel the magic in her, but it was the human part of her that pulled him in.

His fingertips danced along her spine, along skin warm and pliant and smooth, and he could feel passion rising in her, another trait of humans that called to his kind. The scent of her arousal, the sheer physicality of her rising desire, curled around him. He was at flash point, the edge of his ability to maintain the corporeal form that allowed her to see him as human.

He went deep in Carson's head, past the barriers, inside, touching her, surrounding himself with the pulse of her life force. He dipped his head, and his mouth found the hollow at the base of her throat, the place where he could feel her pulse, hear it, pulse with it, taste it. Her body radiated heat. He opened his mouth and tasted her skin, touching the tip of his tongue to her. He came out of her because he wanted to last longer. He kissed her shoulder, turning her onto her stomach. He found the scratch on her shoulder, and he sent a pulse into it so that the blood welled up.

Only a little. Such a sweet, bitter tang against his tongue. The skin across his back rippled. He was so deep in Carson's head he never wanted to come out. She was dark and sweet, and her magic tainted everything. He flexed his hips, and the slide into her racheted his pleasure again. She made a little sound in the back of her throat. "Carson," he whispered.

He could drink her forever, stay in her forever. She moved her hips again.

"Carson, I need you not to move."

She groaned. She was as gone as he was, and that just—you know, what male didn't get extra turned on when a women lost it with him? He wasn't going to, but he got her turned around and he went into her from behind. For quite a while he thought he was safe, that her backside against his belly was enough, that sliding into her again and again like this was enough. But it wasn't. It just wasn't. He slid backward off the bed, shaking. He was so close. So close to changing because his body and soul wanted her. If he did, it would feel good. Beyond good. She turned over, eyes questioning.

Mine. Mine. Mine. Mine. Mine. The words became a roar in his head.

She held out her arms.

"I'm not supposed to do this with a human. We want it," he said. "We all do, but—"

"What?"

"Something wicked," he said. His cock ached to be inside her. But if this was going to end here, he needed to be in control. "Something bad. Something very bad. Something you might not like." *She's human,* he thought. And the wickedness of his urges cranked him even higher. "Otherwise, we have to stop. I'm sorry."

She tipped her head and considered him, and their connection attenuated.

He swallowed hard. "I am not walking away from you. And I'm not lying." She misunderstood what was happening to him. She thought he was abandoning her, cutting her off again. "I'm trying to keep you safe."

She sat up, and he waited. He wasn't any better off. His fucked-up and depraved desire was still there, and he was working hard to keep her safe. "Safe," she said. "From what? I know what you are, Nikodemus."

"You don't know what you're doing to me." Idiot that he was, he walked back to the bed.

"I know you make me feel good. I know you're different. Not human. Not like me." Her hair fell over her ears, and she was drop-dead sexy, the way she looked at him all shy and with her mouth so thoroughly kissed. He started to lose it. His body came to flash point. "Don't let it end like this. Not when I know there's more."

"Carson—I can't promise you won't get pregnant. Not like this."

"I could be dead by tomorrow. And we don't even know what I am now."

She ran a hand along his flank to his hip, and in his head he was seeing the two of them again, her all small and pale and him not human anymore, and she was working him. "Please, Nikodemus. I need you." He lost his sense of human shape when she looked at him from under her lashes and he got a full dose of her green eyes. "Don't say no," she said. "Please?"

"I don't want to frighten you," he said, thinking maybe there was still some way to avoid this fiasco. Although, actually, maybe he wouldn't mind it if she was afraid, just a little. "But I can't maintain. This form. I'm sorry, I just can't. If you don't want that, we have to stop—" His words stopped on a gasp because she'd just touched his thigh high up enough that maybe the location qualified as his groin. "—now."

"I'm not afraid of you, Nikodemus." She touched his hip again. "I'm not afraid of you at all."

Okay.

Well.

Just fuck it, then.

"I'm going to take away the light." He said it slowly, giving her time to find a *no,* in case it was in her and she just needed time. "You won't be able to see me. Are you all right with that?"

She nodded.

The lights winked out. He took away all the light. All of it. His magic had always been dark-edged, and he embraced it because this was his source, the essence of his nature. His back rippled, and he shifted.

Yes.

Slowly, he became aware of his body and its state of arousal, and then hers. He saw perfectly in the dark. The human shape of her, her eyes staring hard, unable to penetrate the blackness. He smelled her skin and her arousal, and he caught the tangy scent of blood from the accidental cut on her shoulder. He knew she felt his shift. They were standing too close for her not to have felt the push of his magic. But she couldn't see him.

He lowered himself onto the mattress, over her. His perceptions always changed when he shifted; his experiences were rawer, harsher. A little fear wouldn't be a bad thing to feel. Just a little. Just enough to wind him up. Her palms brushed him, stilled, then moved, and she drew in a breath. A gasp. He let her feel the difference of texture and heat. And oh, there it was. Fear, dancing along her skin as her sense of touch fed her information about what he was. A growl pooled in the back of his throat, a bass vibrato.

Her palms followed the outside of his arms. Since he had his weight on his hands, his muscles were taut. She got to his elbows, and her hands drifted to his back. There was no way she didn't feel the difference in size. "I'm not afraid of you," she whispered.

That was one big fat lie. She was afraid, but she was dealing with it, and if he thought he was hard before, he was wrong. His cock hurt, he was so wound up. She let her head fall back. His mouth followed, finding the cut and letting her feel teeth that were sharper than before.

And then he did it. He slid his inhuman body inside her human one and it was perfect. Raw. Primal. He thrust into her, again and again, and it was incredible, doing her like this, knowing she was feeling the difference in his body, the changed texture of his skin. Human body under him. Human skin under his fingertips, touching him, a human woman's breasts cupped in his palms. He could see the difference between them. He didn't need to imagine anymore. He wrapped his arms around her and rolled until he was on his back.

Carson arched, breathing in hard as he went deeper inside her, and the sound did it for him. A breath and a gasp at once. Her desire mingling with his magic, calling him, pulling him deep into their connection. His desire meeting hers, power and desire tangling. He touched her everywhere he could reach.

Click.

He swore even as the wave of passion came over him. His leg came up, his inner thigh pressing against her side because he was holding her down on him now, then pushing back, arching into her downthrust. Setting in deep every way he could. His fingers touched her belly, and she felt the prick of his nails, jumped at the contact. His senses spread out, interlocked with hers. His experience of the world turned sharp and visceral. He had a fiend's receptivity to emotion, and she had the thoughts and physical experiences of a human.

Her fingers trailed along his shoulders and sent a shiver of arousal through him. Right to his balls. And then she opened up to the energy that gave a fiend power over the physical realm.

He sat up, keeping her on him, and she threw her arms around him to stay balanced. Without even thinking what he was doing, he lowered his head to her shoulder and scored her cut a little deeper. She flinched. She was much, much smaller than he was now. Distracted, she couldn't feel him tracing more lines across and along her body, in this position, her spine, too, so human, lovely, soft. No point holding back. They were well past anything acceptable.

"I want to see," she said into the darkness.

"Are you sure?" He leaned her back until her shoulders were on the mattress. He angled his hips. It didn't take her long to lock her thighs behind him. More lines. More sparks of pale gold into her skin. His mark on her. He was done kidding himself about that. They were permanent.

"Oh," she said. And it was a sound of passion. He'd stroked her just right, hit just the right spot inside her.

He gripped her hips and rose up to go deep inside her, and he loosened his hold on the lights. Carson's eyes opened. Blinked. Focused. She didn't recoil, which he didn't expect, anyway, but he got the jolt of her reaction. What caught him off guard was his response to knowing she could see him, see what was inside her human body.

God help him, he kept his eyes on her and said, "Fuck me harder, Carson."

CHAPTER 25

Carson headed upstairs to the attic to look for the guns Harsh said were up there. Another attack by Rasmus and Magellan was practically assured, and Nikodemus wanted them prepared if the mages found the farmhouse. Guns weren't as good at killing fiends as, say, magic, but a good shot could kill a mage and at least slow down a fiend. So here she was, in the attic, looking to see if the guns were where Harsh said they were.

Nikodemus was on the phone again, but five minutes ago he'd nodded enthusiastically when Harsh mentioned his weapons stash. Then his cell rang. Again. He'd been returning and making calls for hours now, trying to get the other warlords to agree to a delay and a change of venue for their meeting. Warlords, she surmised, were a paranoid and stubborn lot. He certainly hadn't been having any luck until Harsh started making the calls and taking messages for some of the return calls. A warlord with an executive assistant who didn't let you get to the boss got results. Fen was sulking at the table, picking at the remains of dinner when she wasn't looking at Carson like she hoped she'd drop dead. Lovely, that. Iskander had lapsed into another of his silent periods.

The attic was cool and clean. Dim, too, since the windows were shuttered from the inside. She yanked on the dangling lightbulb chain. Ah. *Clean* was perhaps somewhat relative. Cobwebs adorned the ceiling and clouded the windows, but at least the dust wasn't too bad. A Persian rug covered most of the floor and cut the chill, too. Not that she felt the cold much lately. By now, she was starting to figure out that Harsh liked to indulge his champagne tastes. A fifty-thousand-dollar rug in an attic was just about typical. Like the thousand dollars he'd dropped on a pair of fancy oxfords.

Cardboard storage boxes were stacked to the ceiling on one side and crates over in the other corner, next to a wooden bed frame and a dresser with a broken mirror. Interesting; someone was using the place to get away from it all. A wool blanket and a pillow were laid out on the rug with a stack of paperbacks beside them. A dog-eared U.S. Army and Marine Corps *Counterinsurgency Field Manual* was on the top of the pile. A little light reading there.

She crossed the room to open the window. She ran hot ever since the talisman, a degree or two above normal. Harsh was constantly checking her temp. She was almost never cold. Moonlight poured through the window, scattering pale beams across the rug and walls. Outside, barn owls hooted.

She headed for the crates, which was where Harsh said he'd last seen the guns, and pried the top off the first. Whoa. Harsh hadn't been kidding when he said he had weapons. Heckler & Koch. Another of the crates was filled with ammo, packed in coffee grounds. Something in her head tickled, almost a vibration. She was still getting used to the ways she'd changed since the talisman, and her awareness of fiends was one of them. The sensations tended to come and go, but some of the freakier side effects seemed like they were permanent. Not needing to sleep as much. Or getting an icy sensation in her head when there was a fiend around. She turned.

Iskander stood with his hands on either side of the doorway. Right. She glanced at the blanket and pillow. Iskander wasn't sleeping with his sister anymore. He was staying here.

She was used to being outsized. Most everyone was taller than she was. Iskander, though, was a big man. Taller than Nikodemus and heavier with muscle, too. Xia's size. He kept his hands above his head, and with his short sleeves there wasn't any missing the muscles of his arms. He looked like he could throw a semi. She wasn't wild about being alone with him. Fen she could take or leave, but Iskander freaked her out sometimes. She reacted to him a lot like the way she'd reacted to Xia.

"You," she said and was relieved that she didn't get any weird vibes from him. With her luck, Fen would be up here any minute, threatening to take her head off for being in the same air space as her brother. "I'm not going to save you when Fen finds you here with the big bad dangerous witch."

The lines down his face glowed, as if they'd been tattooed with phosphorescent ink, which was almost as unsettling as her awareness of him flaring even hotter than usual. But then, he was broken, like her. "Magellan's witch," he said. His voice sounded rusty.

Her skin jumped all down her back, because usually the cobalt stripes down his cheek were more alive than his eyes, but right now, his eyes glowed, too. He left the doorway and walked inside, into one of the shafts of moonlight. Carson stood up, wiping her hands off on her thighs. "What do you want, Iskander?"

Their gazes met and *wham!* She lost her sense of perspective again. The corners of the attic blended in with the floor and the ceiling, and the colors all ran together. She shook her head. Her breath caught in her lungs. Her body felt electrified. She blinked, and her vision stopped streaking with color. Iskander's hand gripped one of the support posts. With her vision going out on her, she couldn't be sure, but she thought his fingers looked longer than they ought to be, with talons instead of nails. She tried to track his hand as it slid slowly down the post. A thick splinter sliced his index finger. He flinched, and the weird connection between them wavered and then vanished.

The room went back to normal, and so did Iskander. A normal man, if normal meant six-four and 230 pounds of muscle. But not everything was normal. The sliver had opened a bleeding cut. The scent of his blood hollowed out her stomach, and she couldn't move. That was another change to cope with, the way certain things set her off. Like Nikodemus shifted. Like the scent or sight of blood. Bright, bright red and such an intense scent.

In all her life, she'd never seen such a beautiful red, or smelled anything as rich and deep as Iskander's blood. She walked to him, a matter of three or four feet. "You need a bandage," she whispered. She held on to normal as hard as she could, but she wanted a taste of his blood, and that wasn't normal. Not at all.

"Witch," he said, and it was a sneer.

The same interior light that made his tattoos glow lit his eyes. Blue streaked across the black behind her eyes. The streaks solidified and became the pattern etched onto Iskander's face. Straight through the blue-black of his pupil. His striped eye filled her head. She was losing her sense of balance again, and she had to fight to hold on to the shape of the room and keep everything in three dimensions.

Whatever else was going on, she recognized that she'd fallen into this exact state of hyperawareness with Xia. With the mageheld fiend, she just *saw* how to sever him from Rasmus. She saw Iskander in much the same way now. All she had to do was call up his magic, bring it up from deep within those cobalt lines, and touch it. Touch his magic with hers, and he wouldn't be broken anymore. She focused on the stripes on his face and fell into the space between the stripes. The sound of barn owls hooting disappeared. The wind stopped rattling the windows. Her mental sense of Harsh and Nikodemus dampened.

Her ears felt full, and she swallowed hard to clear them. They popped, and the pressure returned to normal. But the attic remained dead still. She could almost touch the magic that had wanted to sever Xia. She was aware, then, of another magic, magic she couldn't touch. What filled her now was different, its source not mageborn but fiend, dark and deep and touchable. She reached across that wide, vast pool that had opened up for her with Xia.

Iskander's eyes flickered from dark blue to cobalt and

then back to pale blue. She smelled his body, the earthy outdoor scent of ashes and wood smoke. Hunger rose in her, a sharp and gnawing need to have Iskander belong to her. The sensation come at her hard, flowing over her, through her, a river of need. Her skin sizzled, the tips of her fingers vibrated. She reached out and pressed her palm flat against Iskander's chest.

Yes.

A current of magic, electrified and searing hot, leapt from her, and she followed it because only Iskander would satisfy the hunger. The fiend's eyes went wide. Outside herself, she heard him make a soft exclamation. The sound meant nothing to her.

His body bowed toward her, his head back, throat tense, muscle and sinew stretched taut. She moved forward, closer, opening herself to the power. An image formed in her head, of her in Iskander's arms, her drinking from him, tasting him, touching his magic. She knelt, and Iskander came with her as she followed the connection outside herself and into him. She held his head between her hands, and Iskander tipped his chin toward her, eyes open. His irises were sky-blue, the left one bisected by the first line of color down his face. With a greedy joy, she saw exactly how to make him hers.

She set the fingers of her right hand to the top of each stripe. Slowly, she drew her hand down, following the lines, modulating her magic on nothing but instinct. The stripes turned from ashy gray to faint blue, deepening to cobalt. She saw the nature of his binding, the tie to Fen and through Fen, something else. Someone? Something that didn't belong. Something that threatened his sanity. She understood now what Nikodemus had been talking about with Harsh. Iskander had been blocked from his kind for too long. Like Harsh, he'd been slowly dying from the isolation with no hope of release.

He wasn't mageheld, she knew that much now. She'd felt several mageheld fiends when Rasmus and Magellan were at the mall, and Kynan and Xia had given her an up-close and too-personal shot of what a mageheld fiend felt like. Iskander didn't feel like that. She went deeper. His body, still taut, had relaxed enough that she didn't feel like she was touching a statue. His skin was warm, and now he was leaning into her, staring at her, past the lines and into her eyes. A live connection to him sizzled through her. The room whirled, dizzied her, and then Iskander was there. Fully present in her head and so real she could barely hold on.

She reached into him, quivering with power and the need to make him hers. His bond with Fen pulsed, edged with something bleak and poisonous: the source of whatever was wrong with him. When she breathed in, the air smelled bitter. A metallic taste coated her tongue. Iskander was cut off from everything but this one remnant of his sister. And even there, he'd built a wall between him and his twin, between him and the poison that leaked back. Carson caught flashes of what he'd been like before his bond with Fen had changed. Making love with her, touching her fiery red hair, his twin's sleek body arching under him, the perfect melding of their minds and their power. Harsh was in his memories, too, touching him, caressing, kissing, three minds and bodies intertwined. When they had been whole.

Carson sent her magic into him, and like some idiot savant who didn't understand yet possessed the knowledge, she saw what she needed to do and how to do it. She severed his link with Fen. Mercilessly. Without remorse or hesitation. He was free of the poison and all that remained was for her to bind him to her. If she didn't stop, Iskander would be hers the way Kynan belonged to Magellan.

How wonderful to have all that power at her command.

Could she really do something that ugly to another living being?

Her ears rang, a painful, shattering howl, caroming around the inside of her head. When it stopped, Iskander's hands were pressed to her temples, covering her ears, and she was shaking. Normal now. The war in her was over, and she had managed not to destroy herself or Iskander.

She touched the stripes on his face, traced them one at a time. His mouth parted, and Carson touched his lips with the side of her finger, top then bottom. She didn't feel his magic at all, yet his cobalt blue irises sparked with life, fully aware for the first time since she'd come here. The lines down his cheek sizzled with the same unearthly blue.

He raised his gaze to hers, and she got a jolt when she tried to disengage and couldn't. Iskander touched his neck, drawing a finger along the pulse of his vein. Blood gathered on his fingertip. A ripple of cold air slid past her, lifting the hair on her arms. She leaned away, but he held her in an iron grip.

The blood-twin's magic was coming back, and she was caught in some kind of psychic knot with him. No matter what she tried, she couldn't break the connection. Her bones went cold as his magic folded around them both, full and dark and overpowering.

Carson was dreadfully, horribly aware of Iskander in

her head, every minute growing darker and more resonant. He was coming to grips with his altered physical and mental state. No longer a blood-twin, but no longer broken, either. What was it Nikodemus had called them? Psychotic. Unstable.

And she'd just unleashed him without anybody to back her up.

CHAPTER 26

Carson's mental link with Nikodemus flared up. Hot and disturbing, a distracting falling-off-the-edge thrill. She couldn't move. Not even a twitch of a muscle, even though the muscles along her spine screamed from the effort of holding her upright and away from Iskander.

"You aren't going to break into her head, Iskander."

That was Nikodemus's voice. Low and even. Completely and utterly calm, as opposed to the panic that held Carson immobile. Iskander rose. He was tall, tall, tall. His presence shivered through the room. She couldn't disengage from his eyes. Her head tipped back. There had to be a way out. But he was still looking for a way in, and she was afraid if she tried anything, he'd find it.

"She is a witch," Iskander said. His voice was hoarse. His magic washed over her and raised goose pimples on her skin. "An enemy."

"And kin." A floorboard creaked, and movement darkened the moonlight that flooded the room from the open window. "You trying to tell me she doesn't feel like kin to you, too? Let her go, Iskander."

"You've bound the witch to you," he said.

Nikodemus walked into Carson's line of sight. Iskander topped him by a couple of inches, but Nikodemus came to a stop, arms crossed over his chest, unconcerned by Iskander's physical size. "I said let her go." His hand whipped out and caught the side of Iskander's head. "You must have a death wish pulling this shit." He brought his head toward Iskander. "She's mine, fiend." Iskander's eyes flashed again. He took a step back, but Nikodemus didn't let go of him. His voice dropped to a whisper. "I'm not even going to count to three."

"Warlord." The locks around Carson's head loosened. Nikodemus opened his hand, and Iskander's hair fell away from his grip. Iskander touched his first three fingers to his forehead and bowed. She still sensed them both, but Iskander was no longer trying to break her down.

"Whatever was wrong with you, you psychotic freak," Nikodemus said, "Carson fixed it. You think we can't use that on our side? You think that's not a power that can save us?"

Iskander knelt at Nikodemus's feet, head bowed. "Warlord."

He was big. Bigger than Nikodemus was, and if she didn't know Nikodemus's power, if it weren't flowing through her right now, she wouldn't have been sure which one of them would win a fair fight. Nikodemus cocked his head at the kneeling Iskander. "You wanna tell me what you mean by that?" he asked. "Be real clear, because there's no going back."

Iskander touched his first three fingers to his forehead before he turned his head to one side, stretching his neck taut. "There will be a battle between fiends and the mages," he said. "And I choose the warlord whose witch freed me."

"What about your sister?" Nikodemus softly asked.

The stripes down his face glowed intense blue. "I am free to choose, Warlord," he replied.

"Just what I've always wanted," Nikodemus said. "The psychotic half of a pair of blood-twins. Last chance. You sure?"

Iskander began to speak in a soft voice that sounded like silk in a dark room. Magic coated the words, colored the intent, and worked into the very air they breathed. Carson didn't dare move. Iskander might have stopped trying to break down her mind, but he hadn't disengaged from her, and she found herself a spectator to the ritual that forged a connection between a fiend and a warlord.

When Iskander finished the words, Nikodemus scored the fiend's neck with a now-sharp nail. Blood flowed with crimson heat and a copper scent, rich and pristine. A longing to taste it wracked Carson. She was already on edge with Nikodemus's magic flooding through her, and this about sent her off a cliff. He pulled Iskander to his feet. With his fingers tangled in the hair at the back of Iskander's head, Nikodemus drew the fiend toward him. Off balance, Iskander's arm snaked around Nikodemus's hip, stabilizing them. Carson was there, too, experiencing with him the taste of Iskander's blood and the thrill as the fiend's bond of fealty was forged. She felt as well Iskander's reaction as the bond eased the desolation that had eaten away at his soul while he'd been cut off from his twin.

Nikodemus drew back to score the inside of his wrist and offer his blood to Iskander. The fiend's eyes flashed a dozen shades of blue, and Carson felt Iskander's magic filling her as he bent to Nikodemus's wrist. The taste and smell echoed in her. Her heart thudded slowly as the bond solidified. This, she realized, was what Nikodemus needed. Kin loyal to him, who could be trusted.

When Iskander lifted his head from Nikodemus's wrist, he bowed, again pressing three fingers to his forehead. "Warlord," he said.

Nikodemus put a hand down and pulled Carson to her feet. He rested a hand on the back of her neck. "She's mine, Iskander. And I am hers. You understand me?"

"I feel her as kin," Iskander said, and it was both an admission and an expression of relief. His eyes met Carson's, and he was a flicker in her head, and then more. Iskander's magic was definitely off, like his mind, too long twisted to be anything but permanently bent, but there was no denying he was a powerful fiend. He'd been isolated for so long, cut off and unable to interact with his power, that he greedily reached for Nikodemus now. His need to connect with the kin became a river. His mind touched Carson's, too, jittering like Fen's eyes. Unstable.

Nikodemus brushed a finger along the line of the blood-twin's jaw. The air around them rippled with their magic, sweeping Carson along in the connection. She lost sight of Iskander, but his presence in her head burned with sensual heat. She lost Nikodemus, too. He was still in her head—none of that had changed. Both were in her head, or maybe she was in both their minds. She tried to find Nikodemus's face in the shadows, but every time she thought she saw one or both of them, she lost them.

"Nikodemus?"

The light rippled again, or maybe it was that her vision returned to normal, because she could see them both as clearly as if the sun were pouring in the windows. Iskander slid his arm off Nikodemus's shoulders. Nikodemus captured her in his arms, caressing her throat with the tips of his fingers.

She felt at home, and though Iskander was there, the deeper connection for her was with Nikodemus. The two of them, Nikodemus and her, shared their stronger link with Iskander. Together, they brought Iskander along. He'd been so very isolated all these years. Even now Iskander missed his sister, the years-long coexistence with a being that was an extension of him. Without that, he'd been slowly losing himself. And this, Carson realized, this link between the three of them was a step toward healing him. He needed touch, physical and mental, with creatures of his own kind. He needed to learn how to interact with fiends other than his sister.

Iskander removed his shirt with fluid grace. Moonlight shadowed the muscles of his torso and then his thighs as he shucked his briefs. Naked, he touched his finger to his heart, then drew a line along the midline of his chest from throat to navel. A dark blue line rippled in its wake. In the dim light, his eyes glowed cobalt blue, and the base of Carson's spine liquified as she watched.

The blue line down Iskander's midsection wasn't going away, and she watched it, fascinated and horrified both. Iskander crouched. The energy gathering in him pressed the air from Carson's lungs. He stretched his arms over his head, palms reaching for the ceiling, and stood to his full height. She had to move to see him and tip her chin upward. Power resonated in him, along the connection between the three of them.

And then Iskander changed. His body rippled. For a moment, she thought he'd disappeared. She blinked and then blinked again. He absorbed darkness so absolutely, the contours of his body were lost unless she turned her head and looked at him from the side. His eyes glowed hot blue, the only color left to him aside from the unrelenting shifting blue-black of a body that gleamed cobalt where the moonlight slid over him. Even his hair was blue-black, shoulder-length curls of inky blue darkness. Iskander remained in his balanced pose. He was made to fight, formed to be lethal. He was bigger now, his body physically larger. Menacing. And she couldn't dismiss her suspicion that he intended the menace.

The thing was, she liked it. She liked the menace. Was this what Nikodemus meant about her responding to fiends? Looking at Iskander made her hungry. The fiend's mouth curved into something that might be a smile.

"Yes, Carson." Nikodemus braceleted her wrists and, too quick for her to track, brought her arms up and back so that she ended up with her hands clasped behind his neck. Because of his height, she was stretched up. He pressed a hand into the small of her back, and when she arched in response to that pressure, he reached around her and slid both hands under her shirt again, slipping up her stomach to cover her breasts with his hands. In her ear, with Iskander present with them, he said, "You have on too many clothes."

And he proceeded to undress her. Her shirt and bra, gone. Then he cupped her breasts and dropped his head to her shoulder, his teeth scraping along her skin, not drawing blood, but close. He could so easily hurt her. One hand returned to the small of her back, pressing until she had to let go of him. He caught her around the waist in time to stop her fall to the floor, but not gently.

His hands on her telegraphed his strength. He could have been much rougher. Her breath caught.

In her peripheral vision, she caught a glimpse of Iskander moving toward them. Nikodemus hooked his fingers in her flannel pants and jerked down hard, taking her underwear with them. His mouth on her breast was firm, just on the edge of too rough, his tongue over and around her nipple wickedly agile. She felt the pull all the way to her core; she felt Nikodemus and Iskander and herself all in the same mental space.

"This won't be sweet or tender," he said.

"I don't want sweet or tender." She brought his head to hers, and when their mouths met, her stomach soared. She felt his teeth against her lips, and when he opened his mouth over hers, she swept her tongue inside. Her body ached for him. He reared back. His eyes glowed black, backlit with silver. The wetness started a quiver in her belly and an ache in her breasts. Her heart pounded too quickly. "Nikodemus." She felt Iskander echo her. Her hands lifted, caught in Nikodemus's hair, and tangled there in curls like silk across the backs of her hands. "Nikodemus, please."

"This isn't safe," he said. His voice came from deeper in his chest, lower down, harsher. "We are not safe like this."

"I don't care." Carson pressed her palm to his chest.

Inches from brushing his mouth with hers, he pulled back.

"Nikodemus." She moaned his name. Her hands lifted, caught in his hair, and tangled there in curls like silk across the backs of her hands again.

"Iskander," Nikodemus said. "You need to shift back. Now."

"Warlord." Her sense of Iskander receded. He was back in full view, as the man she knew, blue stripes on his face, but with eyes that were alive.

Nikodemus touched her forehead with an index finger and he was there in her head, taking over. The sensation of his connection with her flared, and then the silver-to-black of his eyes disappeared, too. Even the shadows around him vanished. Nikodemus was inside her. Really inside. All the black shadow of him was inside her, taking her feelings and racheting them up unbearably. He used her body from inside. Iskander knelt and touched her, his hands sliding the length of her body, alive in her head. Nikodemus took all her sensations and fed them back to her with his.

She gasped when she felt Iskander touch the magic from the talisman. The very action made her aware of the magic she couldn't touch, of the poison that had gathered there year after year until there was no hope for the magic she'd been born to. Her body reacted differently, and her vision was different, too. She felt Iskander's teeth against her lips, and with her reaction came Nikodemus's. When he opened his mouth over hers she swept her tongue inside. Iskander needed the augmented psychic link that came with physical touching.

With a slow movement, Iskander covered her body with his. The heat of his body startled her, then the pressure of his chest against her torso jarred her. He kissed her, one finger of a hand around her nape finding the physical remnant of the talisman's entry into her and stroking over it. Carson brought him into her embrace, touching him, letting him kiss her harder and then kissing him harder yet.

She could feel Nikodemus in her head, taking her

to the edge of sensual collapse. Iskander fit his body to hers, and though he was brutally big, she was ready. His forward press into her came in a relentless pressure of her body accepting his. She lifted a knee and he surged forward. When he was in, all the way in, a cry gathered in her throat. He felt right, exactly what they needed. And then the slide, the withdrawal and surge inward. She felt him in her body and Nikodemus in her head, ramping them higher and tighter. He grabbed her hands and pressed forward, getting deeper inside her, and while he did, she matched him.

"Nikodemus. Warlord." The words came from deep in Iskander's chest. Heat built in her all over again, a wave of climax rushing at her. Nikodemus controlled the wave, plunged them both into it, built it up. Iskander's eyelids lowered, hiding the burning blue pupils. The stripes down his cheek glowed softly. She held him as tight as she could, following the muscles down his back, feeling them flex and extend and release. He had her pinned, thrusting hard and harder. His forward flex into her brought a scream rushing up and, in time, in response, a growl rumbled through the air, thrummed through every inch of her body. He wasn't close enough, not deep enough.

His burning hands slid under her shoulders. He rolled onto his back and she went with him, still with him inside her. The pressure was almost more than she could stand. She was beyond the point where she should have come. Her inner muscles clenched around him. Iskander grabbed her head and tangled his fingers in her hair to pull her to him. His mouth covered hers, tongue thrusting. Inside his mouth, the wet was hotter than she expected. The shiver of orgasm built in her. Her hands slid around his back, down the curve of his spine, to his hip. He came first, with a keening groan that emptied into her body and swept her along with him.

She felt Nikodemus disengage from her body, and when she could see him again, he knelt in front of her, back straight, hands resting on his thighs. She blinked, and when she opened her eyes again, he shifted the way Iskander had. Solidly there, yet elusive in the shadows so that she had to pay attention physically and mentally in order to see him.

His fingers, resting on his thighs, ended in gleaming ebony talons, and his face was all severe lines and austere planes and hollows. Unyielding and possessed of none of the delicacy of his human shape. His nose slanted down to his cheeks with a wild and aggressive plunge. Teeth gleamed like ivory between lips that took a harsh turn at the edges, despite the lush and sensitive lower lip. His body was male, hard-muscled and broad, yet he retained at least a suggestion of the elegant proportions she knew from his human form.

Iskander stood, and she caught a ripple in the moonlight as he shifted and then vanished, only to reappear as a part of her connection with Nikodemus. Nikodemus's eyes turned more blue than gray, and on his cheeks faint blue stripes glowed. She reached out a hand until her fingers touched him. The pads of her fingers brushed over exquisite softness, supple skin that warmed her own. More than once when Nikodemus blinked, she lost sight of him altogether. If she weren't touching him, she might have believed she was alone. His heart beat strong under that impossibly soft hide. When she moved her hand, her ring finger slid over his nipple.

His head dropped back, and he arched his torso toward

her. She obliged the silent request by bringing his nipple to a peak. His breath hitched in the back of his throat, and he growled. In her head, she felt Iskander, twinned with Nikodemus. Her answer was to lean forward and touch her tongue to Nikodemus's nipple. His hand left his thigh to hold the back of her head. She moved forward, between his spread thighs, resting her hands on his shoulders. His nipple peaked again under her tongue. The shape of his hand on the back of her head felt wrong. Head-rush wrong.

He put a palm on the back of her head, but the other hand molded the curve of her lower spine. Not fingertips, but talons rested on her back. Talons. She shivered, and between her legs the heat grew unbearable. He had a way of arching his fingertips so that just the pads caressed her. The slightest adjustment set the curved talons against her skin. She looked down and saw his ink-black arm around her waist, not touching now except for one talon making another circle in her navel. Nikodemus was foremost in her head, but Iskander was there, too. His other hand pushed into the small of her back, moving toward her shoulder blades until she arched again. Both hands now, traveling the line of her shoulders, along her arms to her hands. The entire time, he and Iskander were in her head, taking up her emotions and sharing theirs.

One of his thighs slid between hers, moving outward and separating her legs, and he was pushing to get inside her. Her pulse hammered, and her sex quivered with anticipation of his body. She cried out because he wasn't getting inside. He grabbed her by the hips, got himself placed at her entrance, and pushed hard. Harder. The head of his cock slid in. He didn't wait for her to relax, he just drove in hard. Harder. She was wet for him, ready for his power. Her entire being ached for him, and her belly raced with him and his drive into her.

Above her, his chest heaved, the burst of air from his lungs sounded in her ears, and then, when his head dipped, his breath flashed hot against her shoulder. Her skin slid against his hot and leathery hide. He shifted his weight to one arm and leaned away to cover her bare breast with his palm, tightening his fingers on her until she felt the prick of his talons.

Dangerous he might be, but she trusted him. She just did. He thrust hard, wonderfully deep. In her head he brought her along with him. Desire rose in her, as hot as his skin, as hot as fire. He pulled out of her and, on his knees brought her up to him, his erect cock between them. With a snarl from deep in his chest, he lowered his head. His hair brushed her shoulder before whispering along her side. She looked up and met the silver-blue rounds of his irises. His emotions flowed through her. Her breath hitched from the impact. He felt in flashes of red-orange heat.

She slithered free of his grasp, and before he could touch her again, she sat up and put her hands on his chest. For a moment, Iskander's eyes looked back at her, but then his eyes flashed back to familiar gray. Black eyelids closed over his eyes when she pushed him until he lay on his back. He bent one knee and slid his calf around the inside of her thigh. She wanted to explore him until he was as aroused and desperate as she was. She wanted him to feel pleasure.

Everywhere she touched him, muscle was close beneath his skin, and she was wet, so wet and aching for him. She kissed his neck and worked her way down to tongue his nipples. His body bowed against hers, and he, with a hand cupped to her backside to steady her, slid a finger between her legs, into the dampness of her. She cried out.

Silence filled the attic. He let go of her and pushed up enough to raise his torso and look at her. His legs remained twined with hers. Black-to-silver-to-blue eyes held hers, wary. He settled his weight on just one arm to grab her chin with the other. Nikodemus sat up all the way, and she slid down to his lap. He spread his thighs and opened her over him, but far from his cock. He slipped his hands between them. She thought at first he meant to lift her over him, but he didn't. Both his index fingers dipped into her, sliding in wetness. Her breath hitched. He worked her inside with his fingers and outside with his thumbs until she was teetering at another release. Each rise to that peak came faster and harder and less controlled. Hot breath puffed against her cheek when he leaned forward and whispered, "Tell me you want this, Carson."

She looked up and willed her focus to remain on his face, but it wasn't easy, because of the way he kept disappearing into shadows. "I do."

"Warlord," he whispered. "Say that."

"Touch me, Warlord," she said. She watched his hand, long-tapered fingers ending in talons, settle around her breast. "Please, I want you to touch me." He did. "More," she said.

He put his other hand to the side of her head and pressed until her throat stretched taut to one side. With a talon, he scored her skin and fit his mouth over the breach. His arms wrapped around her, folding her against him as he turned her onto her belly and caressed the nape of her neck. Like Iskander had, he stroked the spot at the top of her spine, and she nearly came apart. He curled a hand around her waist, holding her. And then he was inside her head with Iskander. Desire ripped through her like fire, scorching her, taking everything there was of her and burning it away in the heat. She howled as he pulled his body over hers. One arm snaked around her waist, pulling her upward, against his belly.

"You can take this," he said. All her sensations, physical and emotional, redoubled.

His cock was enormous and hot, but she was wet for him, and when he put himself to her, he slid in smoother than she expected. And harder. And slower. And better. Along her back, the heat from his body kept a layer of sweat between them. His hair fell over her head like a black veil. Other than the sounds of their bodies sliding and meeting, they were silent. No words at all. He used her mind the way he used her body, taking, absorbing, wringing her out. Orgasm welled up in her, threatening to break until she screamed and begged him to finish it before she simply shattered. She begged him to make her come, and God, his cock pounded her, hard and hot, but she did not break.

When she came back to herself, Nikodemus was there, a comforting, familiar presence in her head. Iskander had separated from them. She still sensed him, but not as fully as before. She pressed a kiss to Nikodemus's collarbone, and he slid an arm around her and held her tight.

Iskander said, "Fen's gone."

CHAPTER 27

Downstairs, Harsh looked at the three of them and said, "I don't know where the hell Fen went. She's just gone."

"Yeah," Nikodemus said. "We know." He wanted to pull Carson into his arms and break a few more taboos with her. But he didn't. Instead, he walked into the kitchen and waited, his body quivering with longing to return to his true form. He waited for Harsh to come into view.

"Is she gone because she's in a snit over Iskander being mine now, or for some other reason?" They sat at the table and, after hashing it out a bit, they figured out that Fen had disappeared at roughly the same time Carson had brought Iskander back.

Magellan's witch, for fuck's sake, a woman he'd once wanted to kill on sight, had brought back two fiends who'd been cut off from the kin. Once was maybe some kind of freak accident. But twice? A mageheld and a fucked-up blood-twin. Beside him, Carson slipped her hand into his.

"Think about it," Carson said. "If a fiend is mageheld, he can no longer connect with fiends who aren't, isn't that right?"

"Yeah," Nikodemus said slowly.

"And you can't feel him anymore, right? When we came here, you could feel them. Iskander and Fen, right? They seemed fine because you could feel them?"

"Sure," Nikodemus said.

"Of course," Harsh said at the same time. Iskander leaned against his chair, arms crossed over his chest.

Carson looked at Iskander. "But you and Fen, Iskander. Didn't you guys make a package deal? Not separate, but one?" she said, cheeks coloring, She glanced at Nikodemus but quickly looked away. He wished he could be impolite and just go looking for what was in her head right now. He did the next-best thing and pulled her closer. Her fingers curled around his, and she gave him a tiny smile that about slayed him. "So, maybe I'm wrong, but don't you feel blood-twins as if they're one entity instead of two?"

"Where are you going with this, Carson?" Nikodemus asked. He was getting a bad feeling about this. Really bad.

"Two of them, sensed as one." She frowned, staring hard at Iskander. "But what if one of them is mageheld? What happens then? Do you feel nothing from them, or do you only feel the one that isn't?"

"Shit," Nikodemus said, because he totally saw what Carson meant. "She means we mistook Iskander for Iskander and Fen. We assumed what we felt when we got there was a pair of blood-twins. She's saying, what if Fen was mageheld all the time?" He looked to Harsh. "You knew them before—did they feel different to you?"

"Yes, but you could see something had happened to Iskander. I thought whatever was wrong with him was the reason they felt different, and besides—"

Nikodemus cut him off with a wave and brought his thoughts back. "Our first order of business is to find out where the hell Fen went and why."

"We don't know if Fen ran," Harsh said. *Poor sap,* Nikodemus thought. He just didn't want to accept that his former lover was probably mageheld. "Or, if she did run, why she did so. Her location and current state of mind are unknown." He tapped his fingers on the table. "It's possible severing Iskander from Fen has harmed her. She may be outside somewhere. Hurt. Or too confused to get back."

"Iskander," Nikodemus said. "What happened to send you off the deep end like that?"

Iskander bowed his head, eyes shut tight. He took a breath, and when he straightened, his eyes were pure blue flame where his pupils ought to have been. "I don't know. Not with certainty. It was sudden."

"Were you and Fen together at the time?"

He shook his head. "For months, I could do nothing, say nothing. Feel nothing. What is the human word for this?" He frowned. "Catatonic." He looked around the table. "Fen kept me from dying." He pressed his palms on the table, fingers spread, and watched Nikodemus from lowered eyes. Cobalt fire burned in his pupils. "Do you really understand about blood-twins, Warlord?"

His voice carried a hint of growl. Iskander with his magic restored was a formidable creature. The stuff of nightmares. As part of a whole blood-twin, he and Fen must have been righteously scary. Iskander sat straight, leaving his hands on the table. The muscles of his upper arms tensed. "My sister was trying hard to bring us back. More than once she nearly succeeded. I was lost. Alone, and I have never been alone." He took a breath. "And then you came. I felt you, Warlord. I felt Harsh and even Carson."

"We have to consider the worst case," Carson said.

"Yeah," Nikodemus said slowly. He didn't like where this was heading.

She looked at him. "She knows you're meeting with the warlords, Nikodemus. If she's mageheld, then whoever it was, he probably knows, too."

"We have to call off the meeting," Nikodemus whispered.

Harsh shot from his chair. "It's too late." He looked at the three of them. "They're already here. They called about five minutes before you came downstairs."

"How much did Fen overhear?" Nikodemus asked.

Harsh sighed and started pacing. "I'm not entirely sure."

"We know Rasmus and Magellan are here. We should assume one of them has control of Fen." She leaned toward Nikodemus, earnest concern on her face. He liked when she got all intense like this. "What if they have the warlords already?"

"Then we're fucked."

"Unlikely," Harsh said. "They'd rather take us all at once. Me. Carson. Nikodemus."

"Plan A," Nikodemus said. "Harsh, you contact one of the warlords while we're driving into town. If we're lucky, you'll get a hold of someone who'll relay a warning." His mind raced with scenarios.

"No guarantees of that," Harsh said.

"Plan B is we show up and do the meet-and-warn in private." Plan A was best-case scenario. Unlikely as hell, but you never knew. "Harsh, you're with Iskander on the meet-and-warn. Carson and I will set up the mages to think the meeting's someplace else at some other time. If it works, keep the warlords occupied long enough for me to deal with Magellan and Rasmus."

"Is there a plan C?" Carson asked.

"Yeah." He grinned. "We improvise."

How Fen disappeared was explained when they opened the garage. Nikodemus slammed a fist against the garage wall. "She fucking stole my car!"

Their only choice was the rusty pickup parked behind the barn. The keys were gone, but Iskander hot-wired it, and in eight and a half minutes, they were on the way into town.

Carson rode in front with him, and Iskander and Harsh got comfy in the bed. He was going to rip Fen a new one if there was so much as a scratch on his Mercedes. There was a reason Nikodemus favored expensive new cars. The Chevy was a heap, and some of the coils in the seat poked through the material. A bungee cord held the radio in, and another kept the glove box shut. When Carson fastened her lap belt—the pickup was too old to have shoulder belts—he gave the Chevy some gas and they bounded down the driveway. Without, it felt to him, the benefit of the modern invention of shock absorbers. Through the rearview mirror, he saw Harsh on the phone.

In town, Nikodemus pulled the pickup into a parking lot behind a bar called Kodiak Jack's. Perfect. While Carson wrestled the passenger door, Nikodemus disconnected the wires. When he got out and closed the door, the driver's-side window plunged down. He used his palms to bring it back up. "A bar's as good a place as any to fake a meeting," he said. "Too many humans for anyone to pull serious magic. Safer for everyone. Any luck, Harsh?"

"No." He handed back Nikodemus's phone.

"Plan B it is." The wind off the Olompali River lowered the nighttime temperature several degrees. He was glad for the coolness. The truck's window slid down again, but this time when Nikodemus brought it back up, it wouldn't stay. He shrugged and left the truck with the window open. "You'd have to be fucking desperate to want this piece of junk, anyway." Nobody smiled. Harsh dusted off his trousers.

"Harsh," Nikodemus said. "You're the point man on the warlords. Make it look good. Iskander, you're his backup. We'll meet you there if we can. Everybody got it?"

Harsh and Iskander nodded. Three fiends and a witch, and nobody was worried she'd betray them. They all knew she was rock solid.

Nikodemus grabbed her head between his hands. "If there's trouble, you improvise, okay? If we get separated, don't forget you're a witch. You come across any magehelds, they can't touch you. Sever them if you can. If there's trouble and you can't pull, get the hell out."

Who was he kidding about this? She was totally under his skin. Like it or not, he was emotionally, physically, and psychically committed to her. He pulled her up onto her toes and kissed her long enough and hard enough that he almost forgot they had an audience. When he stopped, his hands tightened on her. Her eyes went big and wide. He waited, but all she said was, "I'll be careful, Nikodemus."

It was kind of stupid for him to be standing here afraid to say what he really meant. "You get yourself hurt, and I'm coming after you to knock some sense into you, you hear?"

He wondered if she knew that meant, *You're the only one for me, Carson. The only one.*

They watched Iskander and Harsh walk away.

CHAPTER 28

Carson and Nikodemus walked toward the concrete ramp up to the street-level entrance. She tried to set aside her feelings, but she couldn't dismiss her nerves. The whole idea of going any place where Magellan could get at them was, in her opinion, terrifying. Wind sliced through her, raising goose bumps on her skin even though she hardly felt the chill. On the sidewalk around the front of the building, a neon sign blinked red. *Kodiak Jack's*. *Kodiak Jack's*. *Kodiak Jack's*.

Nikodemus opened the door and let Carson inside. A woman who had to move away from the door gave herself whiplash looking at Nikodemus. He did look good in his usual faded jeans and a tight black T-shirt that emphasized the power of the body in it. Warm air hit her from inside, ripe with the scent of bodies and spilled beer. Music and the sound of conversation rose up, loud enough to hurt her hears. Six other people waited to show IDs to the bouncer.

Two women ahead of them in line got an eyeful of Nikodemus and kept turning back to look at him. Long, lingering looks. One of them broke off from her friends to shove a card into his hands. "Just in case," the woman said with a look at Carson. "You might get bored."

Nikodemus didn't return her smile. "I don't think so," he said.

The others got their IDs inspected and walked into the bar. Nikodemus handed the bouncer his license. He was already nodding to the music. Carson's mouth went dry. She grabbed Nikodemus's wrist to stop him and went up on tip-toe to whisper, "I don't have any ID."

"No problem," Nikodemus said in a low voice. He turned and came in close to her until they were chest to chest, with his emotions hammering at her. He put his palm on her back, on the bare skin between the top of her jeans and the bottom of her shirt. When he got his ID back, he handed it to her and put a hand on the wall, leaning over the bouncer. Cold air rippled down Carson's arms as if the door was open, even though it wasn't. Hand shaking, Carson handed over Nikodemus's ID.

The bouncer compared the picture on the ID to her. Carson smiled at him. "Enjoy," he said as he gave it back.

Nikodemus took his ID and they walked inside. Carson's pulse bumped another ten beats per minute. Kodiak Jack's was wall-to-wall people. She had trouble distinguishing one person from another. Colors were too bright for the level of darkness, and much of what she saw refused to form anything but incoherent blobs of color. She blinked hard, but the only result was that she was dizzy when she opened her eyes again.

Nikodemus took her hand, and slowly, her vision

cleared and the blobs of color formed tables and chairs and people. The floor was dark planking and messy with bits of paper, napkins, and just plain dirt. The live music was excellent. *Ryan Huston,* said the posters tacked up on the walls. Huston was singing something slow and a little sultry. Swaying couples jammed the dance floor.

There wasn't any open space. And people were staring at them. Women drooled at Nikodemus. Understandable. His hair was loose, long enough to reach well past his shoulders. He looked more than a little dangerous, actually. A chill rolled across her shoulders, and when she turned to Nikodemus, he had a look of concentration. He was pulling magic, proofing the place, as he called it, so he'd feel the disturbance if any of the magekind came in.

At the bar, he ordered something that sounded to Carson like *la frog.* His twenty-dollar bill vanished into the bartender's hand. "You, Carson?"

She shook her head. Men were checking her out, and that kept her from concentrating the way she should have been. She wished she were wearing anything but her new clothes. Her pink and green polka-dotted shirt didn't reach the top of her low-rider jeans, and she didn't like the exposed feeling. She tugged on her shirt, but there was no hope of covering her navel.

The bartender gave Nikodemus a glass of something, and he drank it down in one swallow. Nikodemus eyed her. "You look fine," he said. He hooked a finger in the waist of her jeans and pulled her toward him. With the way her vision had been acting up lately, Nikodemus's eyes looked backlit with silver light. "Wanna dance?"

"I thought we were supposed to be doing recon."

He looked around, then looked her up and down. "There are no free fiends in here besides you and me."

"I'm not a fiend."

Nikodemus smiled. He still had his finger hooked in her jeans. "Yes, you are." He shook his hair back behind his shoulders. "There are also no mages here besides you." His smile disappeared, and he tugged her closer. "So, mage, do you want to dance with the big bad fiend?"

"I don't know how."

"It's a cinch, Carson. And I'd love to dance with you."

Nerves made her misinterpret the first tingle down her spine. All these people unsettled her. The second time, she recognized the sensation for what it was. Carson's heart felt like someone was squeezing it. Nikodemus stiffened at the same time. "There's a mageheld here somewhere," she said. She faced the crowded interior, scanning the people for the source of her uneasiness. "Not far."

Nikodemus leaned a forearm on the bar and tapped his fingers on the surface with a speculative expression. The bartender came back. "Bottle of Laphroaig," Nikodemus said. He threw down a hundred dollars. "Wait," he murmured. "Whoever it is will feel your magic pretty soon. Let him find us."

Carson turned around and there was Fen, fifty feet from them, her red hair pulled back into a long ponytail rather then her usual braid. She hadn't yet seen them. She couldn't tell if Fen was mageheld. If she was, why the still-long hair? She didn't like the anomaly. Too much was at stake. Carson tapped Nikodemus's hand and inclined her head.

"Guess it's our lucky night," he said when he saw her. "You get a chance, you sever her, okay?"

"Okay."

Fen noticed them, Carson first. The color drained from her cheeks when she saw Nikodemus. She walked toward them, eyes jittering. Nikodemus moved too fast for Carson to see. By the time Carson realized he'd moved, he had Fen's arm in a firm grip. The air chilled another two degrees.

Carson grabbed the bottle and Nikodemus's glass, and the three of them walked from the bar to a table that was, what a coincidence, emptied of patrons as they approached. He brought Fen along—she was holding a beer in one hand—while moving in close to her and keeping a tight grip on her.

Carson put down the bottle and glass and extended her hand to Fen, palm up. "You stole the warlord's car," she said. "If you're smart, you'll give up the keys so he doesn't decide he needs to take care of you himself."

"Drop dead, witch."

"Give it up," Nikodemus said. "Or I'll take them from you. And you won't like how that happens, I promise you."

Fen glared but dug in her pocket for the keys, which she dropped onto Nikodemus's outstretched palm. He put them in his pocket. "Thank you."

They sat. Fen next to Nikodemus, Carson across from them, but he pulled Carson's chair close to his. His magic was crazy hot, seething with his reaction to Fen. He broke the seal on the Laphroaig and poured himself half a glass. "When is Rasmus coming, Fen?"

"Who?" She crossed her slender legs. "Never heard of him."

"Liar." He took a drink. The back of Carson's throat burned like she'd swallowed the stuff herself. "When are you meeting him?"

"What are you talking about? I'm not meeting anyone."

"You aren't very convincing." Carson leaned across the table and grabbed Fen's arm. She'd been hoping to sense what she had to do to sever Fen, but she got nothing. "What mage has you, Fen? Rasmus or Magellan?"

"You're crazy," Fen said. "I came here to get away from her." She jerked free of Carson. "Thought I'd find a human to spend a few hours with."

Nikodemus leaned over Carson, his front overlapping her back, and placed his finger across Fen's mouth, caressing, a man admiring his lover's lips. He draped his other arm around Carson's shoulder. "That is a lie."

Fen glared at Nikodemus's arm. "Why are you touching the witch like that, Warlord? Maybe you're the one who's mageheld."

Nikodemus's head shot up. "There is a mage here."

CHAPTER 29

Sure there's a mage here, Warlord." Fen looked longingly at her empty beer bottle. "Her."

"Fiends, too," Carson said.

"Yeah. The warlord and me."

"Not just you two. Magehelds." The skin along Carson's arms and over the back of her neck prickled unmistakably. "At least six more." Did that mean this was working? Did Rasmus and Magellan think the meeting was going to be here? What were Iskander and Harsh doing now? Had the warlords been warned, or were they too late?

"Magehelds?" Fen made a show of looking around. "I see humans." She leaned in and addressed Carson, her eyes jittering. She was just as psycho as her brother. "Prey. For kin. But no fiends. You don't know what you're feeling, witch."

On the stage, Huston finished his song. When the applause and wooting finally died down, he set aside his guitar and left the stage for a break. There was a moment of excruciating silence during which nobody spoke. Carson didn't get anything from Fen other than her sense of what Fen was: a fiend who was not free.

Nikodemus found the darkened spot at the very top of Carson's nape where the talisman had condensed, and brushed a fingertip over the sensitive skin there. He leaned in. "Can you sever her?" he whispered.

She reached for her magic, but without even an atom of longing to take Fen, nothing happened. She was, in a curious way, as cut off from Fen as the mageheld were cut off from the kin. She wanted to jump up and do something, anything but sit here feeling like a failure.

Fen jumped as if she'd been goosed. "Leave me alone, witch."

"There's nothing," she said. "Just . . . nothing." The fiend still had long hair. That had to mean Fen wasn't mageheld, didn't it? And yet, like her brother had been, she wasn't free. Not mageheld, but all the same Carson knew Fen had ties to a mage. She just didn't understand yet what those ties were.

Music came over the bar's sound system: Keith Urban singing about a woman taking back her cat. Nikodemus kept one hand wrapped around his glass and the other on the back of Carson's neck while Fen put out a hand and reached for him. The tats on her arms put off a faint glow. Nikodemus leaned his chair back, glass in hand, just out of her range. A furrow appeared between Fen's eyebrows. Her crystalline blue eyes just couldn't stay still.

"What's the matter?" she said. "You afraid to let a fiend touch you?"

"You're a psycho," Nikodemus replied evenly. "You think I'm going to let some mageheld psycho used-to-be-a-blood-twin touch me without permission? If you do, you're fucking deluded."

Fen touched her hair, smoothing down the already smooth sweep of red over her head. "Is Iskander still alive, or did your witch kill him?"

"He's back among the kin," Nikodemus said.

"How?"

"Carson." His expression didn't change, but his fingers tightened on his glass. Fen raised a trembling hand to Nikodemus's cheek, but just when she would have touched him, he averted his face. Her hand remained suspended for a heartbeat, then dropped. "You can touch me like that after you're sworn to me, Fen." He shook his head. "Not before."

"What has the witch done to Iskander, Warlord? I can't feel him. Not even a little."

He lifted his Laphroaig to his lips and emptied his glass. "I told you. He's free now. And sworn to me. You want him back, you know what to do."

Fen's mouth twisted, and she turned her attention to Carson. Her gaze skittered across Carson's face. No love there. None at all. "As free as your mage allows him to be, you mean?"

"He's free. Like Harsh is free now." He dropped his arm to Carson's shoulder, and Carson settled against his side. "Of you." He scanned Fen, and Carson felt him push magic at her. Nothing happened.

"Right." Fen held her empty beer bottle by the neck and suspended it over the table. "It starts out that way." *Clunk.* The bottle hit the table. She picked it back up. "You think you're free, that the mage would never do anything to restrict or control you." *Clunk.* She shook her head, eyes jittering madly. "But it's never that way." She reached for Nikodemus again and, again, he moved just out of her reach.

"I said no touching," he said in a low voice. "You want contact, you have to swear fealty to me."

"You're a fool if you think your witch is going to let you stay free. Sooner or later, she'll betray you."

Nikodemus set his empty glass on the table. With lightning speed, he leaned forward and wrapped his fingers around Fen's wrist, not a caress, but an iron grip that trapped the fiend's arm in the air between them. "The way you betrayed your brother tonight?"

The air around them turned hot. Carson squeezed Nikodemus's thigh. "She's pulling magic."

"Shut up, witch." Light flashed on Fen's silver bracelets. "This has nothing to do with you."

Nikodemus shook off Fen's attack. "You ought to know better than to pull in a room full of humans. But why would I expect better from the fiend who betrayed all of us." Fen tried to free her arm, but his fingers tightened. Her tats glowed copper-red wherever his hand didn't cover the bands. "You betrayed Iskander, Fen. Your blood-twin. You left him high and dry." Nikodemus took a deep breath. "To be a mage's servant?"

"I'm no one's servant."

He let go of Fen's arm like it made him sick to touch her. "What have you told your mage about us?"

"I didn't have to tell him anything." Carson saw the emotion in Fen's eyes, and she understood at last why she didn't resonate like other magehelds. Fen had willingly gone to the mage. "He already knew."

Carson's nerves came shuddering to attention again. Even the backs of her knees tingled. Fen tensed, and Carson felt her pull again. Her magic jittered, unstable, like her eyes. Nikodemus registered it through Carson, and that's why he was prepared when Fen let loose at him. His head snapped back. The humans behind him shouted, and one of them fell off his chair.

A pulse of recognition had Carson looking at the entrance, where six men had just come in and were making their way through to the interior of the bar. Fen looked, too. Mageheld fiends, every one of them. Nikodemus couldn't feel them except through Carson, but Fen did all on her own, or she would never have looked. And that meant she must have some connection to the mage who held them.

Four of the fiends wore Desert Storm camo. They looked like army grunts, with black boots and bloused pant legs, short hair half an inch shy of a buzz. What they looked like was muscle. Xia walked at the front, with a sixth keeping to shadows so dark not even Carson's improved vision could make out his features. He was tall, though. And he had the kind of power that gave her gooseflesh. Question answered. Fen's bond was with the Danish mage Rasmus.

She tried not to stare at Xia with his please-come-close-so-I-can-kill-you smile. His leather pants fit smooth over legs that did total justice to the material. His boots were scuffed, well worn, and metal-toed. His long-sleeved shirt fit snug to his torso and belly. He looked mean. He looked like he could eat nails for breakfast, lunch, and dinner. And enjoy it. A gorgeous man if you didn't mind the attitude. He scanned the room, and Carson got a wide-open dose of what he was. Her entire body quivered as her power came to life.

The sixth fiend came out of the shadows. Like Xia, he wore leather. His face was turned from her, but as he scanned the bar, eventually, inevitably, she saw him. Her heart thumped hard against her ribs, because the sixth mageheld was Durian. Nikodemus heard her intake of breath and touched her arm, calming her. Fen's bracelets jingled, and Carson looked at her in time to see her copper tats glowing again.

The six got within ten feet of her, and the feeling she'd had at the mall hit full blast. Xia and Durian set off her reaction the way Fen hadn't. Because, she thought, Fen was not held against her will. Carson didn't take her eyes off Xia. A lot of heads turned to watch their progress. Despite Durian, Xia was primary in the group, that was obvious. He was the fiend the others deferred to, even Durian. Xia was the one she ached to sever.

They were the primary attack force, sent to blend in among the humans because they would be invisible to the warlords and any fiends the warlords brought with them. Xia and Durian made a formidable pair, between them capable of holding a warlord long enough for Rasmus to act. And if you added Kynan into the mix? Why bother with any other backup?

She watched Xia scan the crowd, eyes moving, pausing, assessing, moving on. Carson tried to center herself, find her magic, and have it ready. She knew she was trying too hard but didn't know how to make herself relax under pressure. She couldn't fail. Her oath to Nikodemus wouldn't tolerate failure. Taking Xia away from Rasmus would cripple the mage. She had to find a way.

And then, Xia saw her. Or came close enough to feel her magic. Whichever it was, his eyes found her and locked with hers. Everything else faded into the background. Xia kept his electric blue eyes on her as he approached with Durian and the lesser fiends. The last time she'd seen him, she was certain there was no way he could come back from the horrific injury Magellan had done him. The last time she'd seen him, she hadn't been able to feel his magic. Now she could, and it frightened her almost as much as Xia's. How was she going to deal with two fiends like that?

The fiends stopped, Xia in front, Durian just behind, the other four at the rear. Xia's mouth twitched. He looked Fen up and down. "Rasmus said we would find you here." A Bluetooth headset curled around his ear. "I have her," he said. His eyes unfocused a bit, and he nodded at whatever was being said to him. "As you said. The warlord, too." When his eyes focused again, a spark of energy jumped from him to Carson, but it didn't offer her a way in yet.

"Glad to see you survived, Durian," Nikodemus said. Durian didn't reply.

"He wants you." Xia used his chin to indicate Fen. "Outside." He listened to something again. He blinked, and his eyes went from electric blue to black and then returned to blue. Too blue. A painful blue. Carson shuddered. "On her way."

Fen nodded and, with a lingering look at Nikodemus that the other fiend ignored, left. When she was gone, Xia smiled at Nikodemus. "Warlord." He kept his arms crossed over his formidable chest. Nikodemus got up. He wasn't as big as Xia, but somehow he radiated power that Xia couldn't hope to match. "I bring you in, Warlord," Xia said to Nikodemus, "and Rasmus might decide it's time to reward me." He laughed. "Maybe with the witch."

One of the camo-clad fiends moved forward, but Durian lifted a hand and the fiend stopped. Like Xia, Durian topped the other fiends by an inch or more. "Not here," Durian said. He grabbed the other fiend by the shirt and pushed him back. "You know this can't happen here. Among humans."

Carson's magic flared again, and she reached for it before she lost it. She could see the shape of his magic. The way in which Xia was bound to Rasmus was there for her to see. Just when she thought she had it controlled, her magic cut off so hard and fast it hurt.

Another slow smile appeared on Xia's mouth. All the fiends felt her magic. They knew when she was building up. She just hoped only Nikodemus knew she was spiraling out of control. "Fucking witch," Xia said.

Carson left the table and took the three steps needed to stand in front of him. Adrenaline shot through her. Oh, yes. His magic called to her. In her chest a familiar burning sensation started a streak of pain through her head. She crossed her arms, too. "Witch?" she said. "As in rhymes with?"

"Carson," Nikodemus said. "Not here. We're drawing attention."

She ignored the curious looks from the people in the bar. She could do anything she wanted. As long as Xia and the other magehelds were dealing with her, they weren't after the other warlords, and that was the entire goal of this encounter.

Xia mouthed another word at her. His eyes were pools of black. Not blue. Black. Big dilated pupils surrounding black irises. She wanted to dive into them and go swimming in all that magic until she found the part Rasmus had put there. And then she'd destroy it.

"If I were," she said, "what does that make you?" She

opened up to instinct the way she had with Iskander. "A thieving mageheld bastard?"

Xia tracked her from her chin down, lingering on her hips. "You're too little to be pissing me off like this," he said. "I could break you with one hand."

Carson was so focused on Xia she hardly had space in her head to think about the fact that she and Nikodemus were outnumbered. For her, right now, with Xia keeping just out of her reach, with her magic surging and waning, that didn't matter to her. "You're not released." She leaned in, reveling in the buzz of his magic and waiting for the next wave to catch her so she could touch him and sever him. "You can't touch me."

Xia stepped forward until his chest was inches from her. "Fuck off."

Her head swam, so hot with magic she could barely stand. She had the wave and rode it hard. Nikodemus grabbed her arm and her concentration shattered. "Not here." Nikodemus said. "We can't. Not around humans."

"Time to go," Durian said. The mageheld fiends formed a box around her and Nikodemus, and in a clump, they headed for the back of the crowded bar.

Xia leaned toward Carson on their way out. He whispered, "If I were free, witch, you'd be dead."

CHAPTER 30

Xia lead the group down the hallway toward the back exit. The witch settled down, and he was immediately distrustful. He didn't like the way she felt like mage and kin both. That ought to be impossible. His life was fucked. Feeling the kin was impossible.

The witch glanced at Nikodemus, and Xia wished he could tell whether they were communicating. Was the warlord her mageheld? If he was, they were probably planning something right now. Except Nikodemus's hair was still long, and he didn't know of any mage who took a fiend and left his hair long. He concentrated on the sensation of heat in his chest—that was coming from the witch—and on the fiends around him. He got nothing from Durian. The big fiend of Magellan's was a cool son-of-a-bitch, but his four couldn't stop fretful glances at the witch. Any fiend was uneasy around a mage. You never knew when one was going to fuck you over. Made sense they'd be uneasy around her. They all knew who Nikodemus was, too, and his gofers were legitimately frightened of the warlord. He hoped they didn't freak out of control. He needed the muscle.

The cycles of the witch's magic were more severe than ever, set off, he guessed, by the number of fiends around her. He didn't like it much, either, though for different reasons. They were heading someplace dark and lonely, and he was worried about what she might do. Durian was newly held, still adjusting to being fucked for the rest of his life, and though he had no choice but to follow whatever orders Rasmus gave him, the fact was, Durian belonged to Magellan. If Durian broke with Rasmus, no great tragedy, and that meant Xia would be an idiot to rely on Durian. He didn't like this at all.

In the narrow corridor, Xia turned around and brought the entire group to a halt. He slammed Nikodemus against the wall and grabbed a handful of his hair. The warlord's eyes glowed, and if Xia weren't mageheld, he had the feeling he'd be frying. The only thing saving him now was the fact that they were still in the bar, surrounded by humans. Otherwise, he had no doubt the warlord would kill him.

Xia pulled out his knife and held it to the handful of his hair. "I don't know why she's letting you keep this. Maybe I should shave you for her. What do you think, fiend?" Nikodemus's eyes burned silver-black. Xia leaned closer. "You think I don't know you're up to something?" He shot a glance at Carson. "Try anything, witch, and he's dead. Durian!" Durian stepped up. "Hold him. If the witch does anything, break his neck."

Durian pulled. Xia felt the echo across his skin. That should keep the witch from trying anything. Durian put Nikodemus in a headlock, but that lasted all of ten seconds. The warlord broke free. Fuck. Xia started walking again. Faster now. Durian had the sense to keep close to the warlord while they continued. After a detour through a storage room filled with mostly unopened cases of liquor, they reached a narrow door, bolted shut. Xia raised a leg and kicked the door hard. It popped open onto a short path, past the employee smoking area to a set of wooden stairs leading to the darkened parking lot below. With Durian, Nikodemus, and two of the lesser fiends in front, down they went. A few humans in the parking lot looked up and then away. Fucking losers.

They headed for a chain-link fence enclosing a storage facility. Xia pulled out his knife and sliced through the metal like it was warm butter. No one would see them take down Nikodemus here. No way. But it was going to take four plus Durian to manage it, and even then, unless Rasmus got his ass here fast, the warlord might just fry them all. The poor fucks. Looked like the new mageheld's slavery was going to be short-lived. Some guys had all the luck.

Willow trees overhung three sides of the enclosure, and the side Xia had cut through was blocked by a construction Dumpster. Behind them, cold air blew off the river. His skin crawled as every mageheld fiend present pulled magic. In his chest, Xia felt the witch's magic burn out of control. His magehelds maintained their box, though, and headed across the compound to the river, where a rotting footbridge spanned this narrower section of the waterway.

He tapped his headset. "Ready," Xia said when the connection came on. "Durian will take care of him until you get here." He listened to Rasmus's instructions. He could hear Fen in the background, saying something about killing the witch. As if Rasmus would kill a mage. The mage sure as hell wasn't going to kill Magellan's witch. Not when Magellan wanted to do it himself. He grabbed Carson by the upper arm and jerked her so hard her feet left the ground. His arm went tight around her neck as he gave Durian his final instructions. "Take care of the warlord." He hesitated while the mage yapped in his head. The warlord's eyes glowed an unearthly silver. Time to stop listening to stupid instructions. "He gets out of hand, Durian, you kill him, got that? Rasmus will just have to deal."

"Of course," Durian said.

Carson flailed her legs, but it didn't do her any good. In the dark, the warlord's eyes flashed to black. "You know what to do, Carson," he said. "So find a way."

"Which is nothing," Xia said. He slid his arm tight around Carson's waist, wrist cocked so the tip of his knife touched her side, holding her so the warlord could see how easily his little witch could be dead. Xia headed for the footbridge. Carson twisted in his grip.

"Nikodemus!"

"Shut the fuck up!" He turned and saw one of the weaker fiends go flying and hit the ground with a thump. Bunch of fucking loser fiends. Durian wasn't completely healed, and Xia thought it likely Nikodemus would decimate the losers before Durian was forced to give up and kill him. Xia hauled Carson around. Time to distract the witch. "Rasmus and Magellan know where the warlords are meeting." He laughed. "He's probably shaving them right now." He brought his head closer to hers. "Let's go watch."

That got to her, all right. Her magic hit the sky, a total turn-on to him in any state. Their hips touched, and all the while they walked, darts of her magic raised goose bumps on his skin. He smelled her body, warm and dark and soft. He copped a feel, and she elbowed him hard in the kidney. He kept walking, sure-footed despite the rotting wood. They made it across and, once up the stairs on the bank, took a sharp left to a one-way street with a warehouse on one side and a garish yellow gingerbread Victorian next door. The warlord's Mercedes was parked in front, where Fen had left it when she first drove in to Olompali with the news that the witch had taken her brother.

A side entrance got them into the Victorian. The stairwell was narrow, with one landing and a turn, so he couldn't see straight to the top. Xia put a hand in the middle of her back and pushed. "Up," he said.

Her foot hit the middle of a step.

"I said, up." He wanted this over, he wanted his part in the treachery of his kin to be done. The warlords upstairs wouldn't feel him, but they were going to feel the witch pretty soon. Start a little panic there before he arrived to serve the evening's capper. They'd all be too distracted to do anything when Rasmus and Magellan attacked.

"I can't see."

Oh, boo-hoo. If she could use her magic like every other mage, she would have been able to see, and he wouldn't be here with her, all alone in the dark. Xia slipped an arm around her throat and tucked her hard against his pelvis and torso. "Up," he growled. She grabbed his arm with both hands and tugged down to get a breath. Magic seeped under his skin, dark and wild and barely under control. That got him going. Her magic was fucking amazing. His dick got hard fast. He pressed himself against her so she couldn't miss his condition. Maybe she'd want him to do her. His grip against her throat relaxed just the tiniest bit. His other arm stayed around her waist as he walked her upward into the darkness.

"Let go," she said.

"I belong to the mage Rasmus," Xia told her. "Not the mage Carson. I don't have to do what you say. So shut the fuck up." The point of his knife sliced through her sleeve and nicked her skin. He smelled blood, and damned if he didn't get a sense of excitement from her, too. The part of her that felt like kin surged through him. "Back it down."

"I can't. I don't know how."

"Bullshit," he said. His arms tightened around her.

"Let go of me, you freak." She bucked hard and managed to unbalance him enough that he stumbled back. But he didn't let go of her.

"I could do you right here," he said, his mouth up close and tight against her ear. One of his hands slipped under her shirt. She was soft. Rasmus almost never let him have sex. How long had it been? Years and years. But the witch was different. He needed the witch worked up for maximum effect when they got within range of the warlords, and if that meant letting a fiend have at her, Rasmus was willing.

He touched her bare skin, palm flat, hips rolling against her. He slid his other hand up and down her side, from her thigh to her belly. "He's letting me do this. He likes it when they're afraid of me." His breath hit warm against her throat, cold on the inhale, like he was breathing in her power. "Are you afraid of me, witch?"

"Yes." Her voice was too matter-of-fact for him to believe her. "But if you want to be free of Rasmus, Xia, stop trying to scare the pants off me."

"Like this?" He thumbed the top fastening of her jeans. He felt the button pop open, and his dick got harder. The more he touched her, the more Carson felt like kin. She opened herself to him, no walls or barriers, and it was, for a moment, as if he'd never been taken.

"Let it happen, Xia," she whispered. And it was freaky the way she felt like kin. "I freed Iskander. That's two. You need to be three."

"How about I do you right here? With Rasmus taking it all in. Because he's here. Close enough to be in my goddamned head. He wants to know everything that happens between us." His hand moved again, lower, over her belly. He bumped her hips to give him access. "I promise you, witch, he won't let me feel a thing."

"What do you want, fiend?" she asked. She faced him down like she was twice his size. He got a blast of her mage-magic, enough to roil his stomach. "Sex or freedom? You decide. 'Cause I'm telling you right now, you can't have both."

"You already failed with me." He fisted the knife against her shoulder, and she flinched. There was no flat side to his blade. Edges bit into her skin, tearing her shirt, abrading her skin until the scent of her blood rose up. He let go of her and she turned, keeping her back against the wall.

"Let me try."

The stairwell was dark, but he saw just fine. Her eyes were big and wide open. While he watched, she touched her abraded shoulder. Her fingers came away with blood clinging to her skin. She didn't wipe her hand off on her pants or anything human like that. No, she licked off the blood, and her eyes closed like she was savoring the taste.

"Is this what you want?" he asked. He touched his blade to the inside of his elbow. A light touch, feather light, but his blood welled up.

The witch breathed in, and at that moment, he would have sworn she was kin. He extended his arm to her. And she took a step toward him. Her mouth settled on his skin, hot and damp, tongue sliding along the cut he'd made. She groaned, and a taste of copper danced in his mouth, echoing her reaction. He arched against her, frantic to touch her, frantic to touch her magic. But she pushed him away, and he took a step back, hands up. She shuddered, and her magic flared up. He hissed and jerked like he'd been bitten. Her eyes were wide and killingly green.

"Don't move," she said. "Don't." She put out a hand and spread her fingers over his chest, and it was like someone touched two electrified wires. A circuit closed. Pain roared through him. He couldn't get enough breath. No air. He didn't have air to breathe. Rasmus was there, in his head, shrieking, so that it felt like his eardrums were bleeding. Xia clapped his hands over his ears. His knees buckled.

The witch sucked in a breath, and he could breathe again. His lungs emptied on her exhale. She came to life in his head, fully alive because her magic was there. His heart beat erratically, in time with hers, then off, then back to him. Shit. What the fuck was that?

"You moved," she said. She was plenty pissed off, and wasn't that just like a mage, to get pissed off like that. "You ruined everything."

The only mage in his head now was Rasmus, and he wanted the witch in range of the warlords five minutes ago. The compulsion to obey jacked him up. He turned her around and pushed her up the stairs again. "Shut up. Just shut the fuck up."

At the top of the stairs, the back of his neck flashed cold as ice, as if he were connecting with the kin again. He wasn't. He couldn't be. The witch's feet stopped moving. Xia pushed her toward the door. She put a hand on the wall to balance herself. He didn't feel anybody in the room, even though he knew there were four warlords. Four more to betray.

CHAPTER 31

Carson's chest burned hot. She couldn't see, and she didn't know anymore which way she was facing. Her stomach felt like a rock, and inside she raged with the need to touch Xia, to sever him from Rasmus. Her palm hit something. The wall. Had to be the wall.

At last the sensations cleared enough that she could see again. She was on the landing right before the door, still on her feet. Her hand pressed so hard against the wall her wrist hurt. The cut on her shoulder oozed blood, a thin trickle that excited her and therefore, she knew, excited Xia. She watched the doorknob turn. A slice of light widened until it crossed her face. She blinked and moved her head out of the direct light.

"Carson?" Iskander stood in the opening, hands on his hips, one foot keeping the door open.

"It's a trap," she said.

Xia grabbed her hair and pulled back, the blade of his

knife across her throat. "Shut up, witch. Let us in, fiend, or she dies here. Right now."

Iskander stood aside, and Xia stepped out of the stairwell and into the room. The stairs opened into an apartment that, if she had to guess, she'd say took up the entire floor. From behind her, Xia shot home the deadbolt on the door. He looked around the room. "Take my advice, why don't you, and get the hell out of here while you can." He tapped his headset. "In," he said.

The other warlords, two men and a woman, jumped up from their chairs. Harsh was here, too, on his feet like the others. The level of magic in the room shot sky-high, and Carson was the only one able to feel all of it.

"You all right, Carson?" Harsh leaned in to grab her arm, pulling her against his side.

"You shouldn't have let us in. Rasmus's after Nikodemus. Iskander, you have to go after him. Go!" The words tumbled out of her throat, tripping and wrapped in cotton. Her chest burned hotter. Breath caught in her lungs because she was still timed to Xia's respirations. She struggled to get enough air. God, her head felt like it was going to explode. To the upper right of her field of vision, the air streaked deep purple. Her eyes recovered from the light enough that she could make out Harsh's expression even with the streaking colors across her eyes.

Outside the house, a mage moved in, near enough that Carson felt his magic. Dark and foul, the sensation set her teeth on edge. Magellan or Rasmus? She didn't know which. If she didn't sever Xia soon, she might never, and Rasmus would have Nikodemus. She faced Xia and centered herself despite her whirling emotions. Her body didn't move, but the sensation of forward motion made her knees wobbly and her head spin. She couldn't let

Nikodemus down. She wouldn't. This time the magic coursing through her wasn't alien and out of control. Not entirely, anyway. Heat boiled in her chest and flashed along her arms and into her palms. A roar of inchoate rage from Xia deafened her.

The backwash caromed off the walls like a crazed bird in a cage. Xia lunged for her, knife hand outstretched. Time slowed. His knife scraped along her skin, raising a thin red welt that supernovaed in her body. Through the pain, her focus remained on Xia. She flexed her wrist, and the knife turned aside. Xia's shock was etched into his face, and when she shifted her weight, her palms landed on his chest and his expression froze.

Yes.

Xia blossomed inside her. She fell into a labyrinth of hatred and power. Her magic bloomed, too, taking control, directing her, showing her how to take Xia away from Rasmus. She forgot who and what she was. Her magic rushed out, white-hot. She tried to rein back and couldn't. The inside of her head reverberated. Colors bounced off her closed eyes. Her palms burned.

Flick.

The world blinked, and in the crazy upside-down moment, Xia burned through her. The magic that bound Xia to the mage Rasmus pulsed angry orange, bitter to scent, acrid to taste, a chancre in his body that seared inside him and formed the seat of his overweening hatred.

Xia stared at her with wild eyes. His irises and pupils were the same inky black, two deep, open, infinite wells of hatred. His strength was exactly what Nikodemus needed. She pushed inside, back toward Rasmus's hook into him, the magic that held Xia bound to Rasmus. She touched the mass, and it was a foul and rancid thing to know. The part of her that was inside Xia surrounded the acid stain Rasmus had used to bind Xia to his will and separate him from the kin.

"What the fuck do you think you're doing?" Xia grabbed her wrist and squeezed. But he didn't push her away.

She surrounded the sickness that robbed Xia of his freedom. The fiend yelped and thrust his hands into the space between her arms. With an upward and outward motion, he broke their physical contact. The world ripped apart, and she went tripping head over heels. She blinked and looked down at a woman with pale skin and dark hair. Her eyes shimmered in the light.

"Fuck you, witch," Xia whispered. But he was speaking inside himself. Not to the woman in front of him.

She fell out of Xia's eyes, momentarily blind. She howled in rage because she hadn't done what she was supposed to. Her body quivered. Heat bubbled up again, burning white-hot in her belly and chest. She stared fiercely at his eyes, but try as she might, she couldn't fall inside them again. She bared her teeth at him. He backed into the room, a wide, open living room, and kept going until he hit a wall, just missing a gilt-framed photograph.

"Do it," he said. He brought up his knife, red with her blood. He sounded fierce, but he was shaken. She felt it in her bones, the quaver in his voice broke over her. "Do it this time."

On nothing but raw emotion, Carson reached inside Xia for the knotted magic that tied him to the mage Rasmus. Fast. No wasting time. Xia was too big and too strong for her to have even a moment's hesitation. She knew where to strike now. Heat burned in her hot as fire, scouring her, but she grabbed hold and let the flames take her. She sent all that heat out of her body and into the knot of magic inside Xia.

Xia threw his hands up in the air. His arms slapped against the wall. A framed picture crashed to the floor. Glass shattered. His eyes opened wide, staring at her through a grimace of pain.

The knot resisted, pushed back at her, but she refused, refused to let go. She wanted Xia free of Rasmus. He must be free. What Rasmus had done to him was anathema, and it had to be ended. Sound rang in her ears, vibrating until she couldn't hear anything else. She examined what was happening to her and discovered she could focus the heat if she thought about it. So she focused it on that ashen, vibrating morass. She severed him.

When it was over, Xia's back was to the wall and his eyes were on her, big and round and black as pitch. Sweat dripped down his face. His clothes were untouched, but his chest heaved, ribs bellowing, mouth open. His eyes glowed. Carson's stomach heaved, but there was nothing to come up. Time came back to normal, and she realized only a few seconds had passed. Enough time for the warlords to pull enough magic to fry her into ashes. The only thing stopping them was Iskander, standing near her, crackling with power.

Xia's knife fell, spinning away in a blur of blue-gray. The fiend touched his chest. His legs trembled, and she could see him pressing hard against the wall to remain upright. One foot slipped from under him, slid in the glass on the floor, but he caught his balance again. "What did you do?" His voice came out in a croak. His legs splayed. "What have you done to me?"

His eyes rolled up in his head, and then he hit the floor with a thud.

The kitchen window screeched open, and everyone in the room turned to see Nikodemus drop lightly onto the floor. "Good evening, warlords," he said. He brushed some dust off his chest. "Sorry I'm late."

Nikodemus walked over to Xia's knife, and then back to the unmoving fiend. He shoved the knife into the sheath at Xia's waist. "Goddamn, Carson," he said. "I had no fucking idea you could do something like that. I felt that all the way on the other side of the river."

One of the warlords crouched, hand extended. Nikodemus rolled his eyes. "Cut the drama, Mir. You aren't pulling rank here, and you know it. Iskander," he said. "I need you to do a little cleanup for me. Across the river, back behind the Dumpster. You can't miss it. Better take the window, though. There's mages out front."

"Warlord." Iskander bowed.

Carson's head was clearer now. The burning in her chest was subsiding. She stepped toward Xia. He looked dead. But inside, she still resonated with his magic, and she felt him. The way she did Harsh and Iskander. From where she was, he didn't look like he was breathing. Like one of those cases of excited delirium, when a perp dies while the cops are trying to restrain him. Her heart pounded hard against her ribs. He lay so still she was afraid he was dead despite her connection to him.

"You all right?" Nikodemus asked. He slid a hand under her forearm, steadying her. His ruby earring glittered as he turned his head to address one the warlords.

"Sure," she said. She wasn't, but she didn't think it was a good idea to let the warlords think anything different.

Another of the warlords stood in the middle of the

room, arms crossed over his chest. Both the males were typical fiends. Athletic bodies, muscled, with hair past their shoulders. One of them wore his hair in dreadlocks, the other had his straight hair tied back. The female warlord, tall and long-legged with a dagger at her hip, stood apart from the males, her long hair corkscrew curly. She slid her dagger free and crossed to a black leather sofa, where she sat, legs tucked underneath her.

Harsh picked Xia up out of the glass as if the fiend weighed nothing at all. His head hung over Harsh's shoulder, his body limp as Harsh carried him to a smaller sofa, away from the warlords. His headset fell off his ear and dropped to the floor. Nikodemus walked over and crushed it until it was nothing but bits of plastic and broken electronics underfoot.

The dreadlocked warlord looked Carson up and down and said, "Well, Carson Philips, that was an impressive trick."

Carson didn't like the way everyone seemed so jumpy and on edge. Even Nikodemus felt tense to her. He hadn't let go of any of his magic.

"Nikodemus," said the woman. She drew her dagger. "It is one thing to have your mage outside. Dangerous play, but if she's only your plaything—" She shrugged. "I commend you for gaining control of her. A lesson for us all, to be sure. But Nikodemus, it is quite another for you to let a mage into this room. On this night." She ran a finger along the flat of her knife. "Betrayal will get you and your plaything killed."

CHAPTER 32

Carson was telegraphing so fiercely Nikodemus knew exactly what she was thinking. Which was that they were in deep shit. He didn't disagree with the sentiment. But none of the warlords did anything, despite Siddique and her dagger. No flash of light, no deadly punch to the heart. No total oblivion, which he was only mostly sure he could avoid. He stayed in the middle of the room, about five feet from where Xia was now sitting with his head in his hands.

The air shimmered around Siddique, the female warlord, and Nikodemus gathered his magic, ready to blast her from here to Napa County and back if he had to. Xia felt the push, too, and his head whipped up.

Siddique pointed at Xia with her knife. The air around him flickered. Goose bumps rolled down the backs of Nikodemus's arms. Everybody was jacked up now. Xia leaned forward, middle finger raised to Siddique. Couldn't fault the fiend for his nerve. There weren't many of the kin who'd chance making an enemy of a warlord.

"Fuck off," Xia said to Siddique. "I'm not your creature."

"I would be nice to you if you were," Siddique said. "Very kind." She pulled her legs up and underneath her, holding her knife sideways with both hands, tip between two fingers, hilt between thumb and forefinger of her other hand. She looked at Xia from over the blade. "Just whose creature are you, I wonder?"

"I can feel you. You can feel me." Xia looked at Carson, and Nikodemus didn't think he imagined that Xia paled. "I guess that makes me freelance." He glared at Siddique. "I'm not looking to join up anywhere."

Siddique lowered her hand. Behind him, Nikodemus felt Harsh, pulling magic just enough to make sure the warlords understood Nikodemus had support. "How . . . disappointing."

Nikodemus smiled and draped an arm around Carson, bringing her in close. "Maybe you should go home, Siddique. I'll deal with the others."

Siddique turned her attention to Nikodemus. Her lovely, pointed-chinned face was curious but edged with the malice so typical of her. "Is the mage under your control, Warlord?"

Mir, the warlord with dreadlocks, sat next to Siddique and took her hand in his, raising it to his lips for a kiss. "There is a great deal for us to learn from one another. For this reason, I'm glad for the opportunity for us to speak to Nikodemus."

Nikodemus rolled his eyes. He would say that. Mir wasn't as mean as Siddique, and the fiends sworn to him were half the number Siddique had. Nevertheless, Mir had a habit of prevailing against poor odds. He looked around, settled his attention on Carson, and smiled.

"If only we were in private, I'm sure we would hear a most fascinating story." Mir's gaze shifted off Carson to Nikodemus. He let Mir probe. The inquiry was delicate, razor sharp, without more energy than was necessary. "Your newest companion, if I'm not mistaken," he said, "is Magellan's witch."

"If I was her mageheld, you wouldn't feel me as kin," Nikodemus said.

"She's still a witch," the third warlord, Huijan, said. Always the quiet one. He had a reputation for striking first. Wherever he thought he'd do the most damage.

"You sure about that?" Nikodemus said. He looked around the room. "You don't feel her as kin at all?"

"She should be killed," Huijan said. "You should have killed her."

Nikodemus leaned against Carson. "I won't say I didn't have the same thought when we met. But did any of you feel Xia when she was on her way here?" He looked around the room and saw varying expressions of distrust. "I'd say the answer is no. You felt her. But not Xia. And now, Xia is kin. You saw her sever him. She did the same for Harsh here. I don't know of many mages who go around releasing the kin from their slavery. Do you?"

Siddique spread her arm across the black leather sofa. "Why don't you prove you're free of her influence, Nikodemus, and kill her?"

Mir and Huijan exchanged a look, but they didn't demur. Their silence was assent to Siddique's suggestion. Warlords could be a bloodthirsty lot. Which was part of the problem.

"I can't." Nikodemus kept his arm around Carson. Siddique hissed, and out came her dagger again. He raised his other hand in an apologetic gesture. "She swore fealty to me."

"Fealty?" said Mir. His eyebrows drew together.

Nikodemus returned Siddique's poisonous glare. Warlords understood power first, battle second, and politics last. "She's under my protection, warlords. Harm her, and I will crush you and everyone you love into the ground. Harm me, and she'll protect me with her life. You might be proof against most fiends, but are you proof against a mage?"

That last was a calculated risk, since he figured the warlords didn't know about Carson's limitations as a mage. One of Huijan's black-as-night eyebrows lifted. "How did this happen?"

"I found her, and we worked things out from there."

Xia left the sofa and walked the perimeter of the apartment. He had his knife out, and he was flipping the weapon end over end, first catching it by the handle, then by the tip of the blade. Over and over. Unerringly. And quite the unusual weapon it was. Nikodemus hadn't seen anything like it in years. Not one blade but dozens, winding over each other in a mind-bending pattern of mercilessly sharp edges. It took years of magic to make a blade like that.

Siddique watched Xia prowl and, after a bit, lifted her dagger and balanced the length of the blade on her index finger. "I can do tricks with knives, too, fiend."

Still flipping the knife, Xia ignored Siddique and continued his walk of the room. He spent a lot of time looking at the framed photographs on the wall on either side of the windows. Scenes of the town from a hundred and fifty years ago, mostly. A few country panoramas, the occasional shot of livestock.

Mir's gaze held Nikodemus's. Of the three warlords, he had the least strength, but his subtlety of understanding made up for the lack. He rarely misstepped. "I feel it now. She is, indeed, your creature."

"Like I said."

Siddique stopped playing with her dagger to take Mir's hand. He brought her fingers to his mouth for a brief kiss. "There is something different about the mage's magic." Nikodemus felt the warlord probing at Carson. Gently, but an inquiry nonetheless. He didn't get far. Nobody did with Carson. "I have heard of this happening. Only once, but I am certain there have been other cases in which a fiend has transferred permanently into a human. In that case, however, the fiend was in possession and stayed so until his unwilling host perished."

Carson kept her cool.

"In your case," Mir said to Carson, "the fiend does not control you. You have assimilated, fiend and mage." He frowned. "I wonder if it is accurate to say you are still human?" His mouth curved, but somehow it wasn't a smile. "I'm curious, Nikodemus. When you are in possession of her, how does her magic affect you?"

Nikodemus smiled back, and his wasn't a smile, either. "She's a fucking head rush, Mir. Like you wouldn't believe."

Mir started to pull his magic again, and Nikodemus didn't like it one bit. Siddique was back to playing with her dagger, partially unsheathing it and drawing a finger along the edge. She put her bloodied finger in her mouth. Nikodemus tucked Carson closer to his side. "She's had a long day, and I'm worried she's going to get cranky if we don't wrap this up soon. Is there a deal or not? Or are you going to stick to your old ways and watch as more and more of our kin fall to the mages until there are none of us left?"

He was offering them what fiends lived for—battle against an enemy. For centuries the magekind had been the greater threat to fiends than their infighting. They clung to the old ways, staying separate, fighting between themselves, and dividing and fatally weakening the strength of all fiends.

"This requires thought," Huijan said. "Discussion."

"A waste of time," Nikodemus said. "You're in or you're not, and if you're not, you might as well march out there and give yourselves up to the nearest available mage."

Xia faced the window and parted the blinds with the tip of his knife, peering into the darkness. He flipped his knife into the air and caught it by the tip. "There's a limo outside." He looked at Nikodemus. "A nice shiny stretch limo." He cocked his head. "If you ask me," he said, "it looks like it came here all the way from Tiburon."

Beside him, Carson stiffened. "Magellan," she whispered.

The flicker of magic around Siddique flashed into white heat and condensed to nothing. Nikodemus felt it heading for Carson, malignant and gathering force. Xia had his knife extended and he was laughing, but the sound was bereft of mirth. Nikodemus pulled his own magic, and Carson opened herself to him so he could pull even more. She didn't know shit about fiends, but there was nothing wrong with her instincts. Sometimes a good improviser beat a great tactician. Nikodemus struck, and

Siddique's magic crashed into a wall of granite. Even Xia reeled under the impact.

Carson shot to her feet and shouted, "Windows!"

Magic came through the glass, ugly and perverted, and if Nikodemus hadn't been warned by Carson's shout he'd have been too late to do anything at all. Magellan's attack was silent and deadly. All three of the warlords jumped to their feet as their connection to their sworn fiends vanished. Magellan's attack was a cover while the other mages took the warlords' fiends. Nikodemus still had Harsh, though, and suddenly his odds against the warlords didn't look bad at all.

The *shingg o*f Siddique's dagger being freed to the air was nearly lost in the sound of her rolling off the sofa. Blade in her hand, she headed straight for Carson. Mir and Huijan pulled, too. The room threatened to combust as Siddique attacked.

Nikodemus flexed his body and sent heat into the dagger as the backwash hit hard. All the air went out of his lungs in one tremendous whoosh. As he fell, he didn't know if he'd managed to change the warlord's trajectory at all. Magellan's strike clouded everything. He saw stars, and while his eyes refused to cooperate, he heard Xia's knife cut through the air. A body fell boneless to the ground. Nikodemus smelled blood. Mir and Huijan pulled at the same time, raising a counter to Magellan's attack. Harsh added his power to the effort.

Magellan's power slowly dissipated. For the moment, thanks to Carson's warning, the combined magic of the warlords had repelled Magellan's sortie. But it was only a sortie. Things were bound to get much, much worse.

The blood belonged to Siddique. She lay on the floor, the hilt of Xia's knife protruding from her throat. Already her eyes were glazed over. Nasty little fucker, that blade. Xia said something, and the knife was back in his hand.

Mir had his hands pressed to Siddique's throat, but blood was done spilling and there was no point. Nothing was left of Siddique's dagger but the handle, still gripped in the warlord's hand. "You're dead, fiend," Mir said. He pointed at Xia. "Dead."

Xia's eyes went from black to blue. "Go ahead," he said in a voice that shook with rage. "Give it your best shot." His eyes glittered. "We'll see which one of us is dead after you try."

"If you want an alliance between us, Nikodemus," Mir said, "then give me the fiend."

Jesus H. Christ! Didn't they ever learn? Nikodemus said, "He's not mine to give. But even if he were, I'd have to decline. Siddique attacked us." Anger welled up. Fury. "I warned her, and still she attacked. When she went after Carson, she went after me. I would have killed her myself for her attack on any kin who have sworn fealty to me. Xia saved me the trouble of killing her myself."

"Believe it or not," Harsh said. He was at the window, looking out from the side in order to keep himself a smaller target. "We have bigger problems right now."

Nikodemus went to the window, watching the street below, where a gray-haired man stood by a limo. He focused himself and made goddamned sure of his facts. The anticipation of battle rose in him. "Looks like Magellan brought a few of his friends to play."

Carson came alive in his head. Her exhilaration was back, thrumming through them both. A hunter, that's what she was. His pulse sped up as he realized what that meant. Get Carson within ten feet of a powerful fiend, and she went feral. And, of course, recent events had her in full bodyguard mode, too.

"Who is it?" Nikodemus asked her.

She sat up straight, pale, but eyes green as anything. "Kynan."

The windows flexed.

"And Rasmus," Xia said.

Nikodemus risked a longer glance out the window. "How many fiends did Rasmus bring with him tonight?"

Xia sheathed his knife. "Including Durian and me, twelve."

Nikodemus didn't have time to think about that. Until Carson got her hands on him, Durian was one of the enemy. "Any apprentices?"

"One of them's talented."

"Three mages, then." Xia nodded agreement. "Carson, how many fiends do you feel?"

"How can she tell if they are mageheld fiends?" Huijan asked.

Nikodemus put his back flat to the wall. This was the future. Fiends working together against the mages. Let it be so. "She's a mage, Warlord. She feels us whether we are kin or mageheld. How many, Carson?"

"I need to be closer to be sure." She closed her eyes. "Fifteen? Maybe."

"Fifteen, then," said Nikodemus. "Durian and Kynan are the only two we need to worry about." He met Carson's gaze. "Any chance one of them is Iskander?"

"I don't think so." She touched her chest. "I still feel him." She gave a tight shake of her head. "But there's no way to be sure."

Mir and Huijan stayed at attention. He hoped they saw

what Carson brought to them. "Any others that get you going besides Durian and Kynan?"

Carson shook her head. She paced a tight circle, hands on her hips. "Get me out, and I'll take care of them."

"How?" Nikodemus said. He'd been in tighter spots than this, but not by much. The windows flexed again. Magellan had taken care of the warlords' fiends and now he was after them. A jagged crack shot across the middle window.

Her expression was calm, but he knew inside she seethed. "I'll sever them. Every fiend I can get my hands on. That leaves you to deal with Magellan and the other mages."

"Two coming up the back stairs, four from the font," Xia said. He cut off Mir's objection. "I can hear them, Warlord. They're not even trying to sneak up on us."

"Good soldier, Xia," said Nikodemus. He couldn't help noticing the way Xia stayed near Carson. Since he came to, he'd never once let anyone get between him and Carson. He doubted Xia was aware of what he was doing.

Xia nodded at him. "Somebody had to pay attention, Warlord."

"If you decide not to freelance, you let me know. Recommendations for getting Carson on the street?"

Xia responded exactly as if he were one of Nikodemus's sworn fiends. He tipped his head. "Out the window."

"We're on the second floor, Xia, and she's not a fiend. She can't drop that far without getting hurt."

Xia rolled his eyes. "Lower her out the window, don't drop her. Form a chain. You hold her ankles, I'll hold yours. But you and I stay here." He looked at Siddique's inert form. He motioned to Harsh. "Throw her body down the stairwell. That should startle them. Give us a few minutes extra to get her out."

Nikodemus laughed. "I like the way you think."

Xia looked at Carson. "Well, human?"

She was totally up to the challenge. "Which window?"

"Kitchen. Here." Xia unfastened his knife and clipped it to Carson's belt. "Take this."

"What do I do with it?"

Xia patted the hilt of his blade. "If you see Rasmus, stab him with it."

CHAPTER 33

Carson's heart banged against her ribs when she landed feetfirst in the alley. Definitely a breathe-through-your-mouth situation here. She picked her way past upended trash cans and broken bottles and made it to the street.

There were two bars on the street, and at both places people gathered, trying to get in, she supposed. Parking was at a premium around here, and cars trolled the streets for a space. A squad car rolled by. Considering it was well after midnight, there were a lot of people on the streets. They walked in mixed-gender groups, holding hands, laughing, and flirting. They were her age, mostly, thought some barely looked legal. Until tonight, she'd never been in a bar. She didn't know what it was like to have friends or to go out for an evening just to have a good time.

On the sidewalk, she tried Nikodemus's trick for deflecting notice from herself. She leaned against the wall, gathering herself, waiting for the shiver of fear to leave her. The air was crisp and wet with mist off the river, and she breathed deeper until the stench of garbage was gone. The fear didn't go. Several people, humans all of them—how did she know that? *Well,* Carson thought. She just did. They were human, and the men and women in the group walked past her, talking among themselves.

No one paid her any attention.

She pushed off the wall and headed past the iron-fronted buildings that gave the town its late nineteenth-century charm. What would it be like to be one of those laughing women, holding hands with a handsome young man, or flirting with someone she thought she might like? Xia's knife was clipped to the front of her jeans, and every so often the handle touched her bare skin and sent a shock of dark magic through her. At the corner where she needed to turn to get onto the street where Magellan stood guard, her skin prickled.

Mageheld.

As if someone had flipped a switch, her senses sharpened. She saw better, farther, and in such fine detail she had a disorienting moment in which her brain couldn't accept the stimuli coming at her. *Breathe deep. Relax. Let it come.* The world settled and came into new focus. How sad, she thought, that she had so little in common with her own species. No matter how much she wanted to be normal, she never would be. None of the humans noticed the fiend standing there, and yet for Carson, the fiend set off a vibration in her chest.

A woman this time, which was unusual for Magellan. She wore a light wool pants suit, with a white shirt and a green scarf instead of a tie. Now, that was like Magellan, to dress his fiends so distinctively. The fiend was leaning against the sidewalk side of a blue Ford Ranger with a gun rack mounted in the back window. She had her arms crossed over her chest. This time when the hilt of Xia's knife touched Carson's skin, the tingle amped her up even more.

Carson continued toward the fiend. She had to get close enough to touch her. She listened hard, expanded her senses, and overshot her target. She reined back the instinct to look too far. All she needed to know right now was how many fiends were in the immediate vicinity, whether her current target had backup, and how close it was.

Three. She felt three pinpoint areas of awareness: the woman by the Ranger, and two males. One was in a crowd of people spilling from the bar down the block, and another sat in a black Mercedes SUV. Not close enough to help their comrade. Carson narrowed her focus to the woman and moved down the street like a shadow. When she was nearly to the pickup's front bumper, she let up on the stealth. The woman's nature sang in Carson's ears, and before she was an arm's length away, Carson knew how to sever her. She had Xia's knife in one hand, and she was appalled to find herself prepared to use it, to take a life should something go wrong. But if she couldn't follow through, Nikodemus and the others would be taken.

The woman's eyes widened when she saw Carson. She pushed off the pickup. "Carson Philips?"

"Yes," she said. The woman was young. A very young fiend. What if she resisted? What if her tie to Magellan was stronger than the lure of freedom? Carson walked right up to her, got inside her natural defense zone, and pressed the palm of her hand to the fiend's sternum. Power flowed out and Carson followed it, pushed herself inside and destroyed Magellan's magic. It wasn't hard, because she'd only recently been taken. She wasn't very powerful, and Magellan hadn't needed to use much magic to secure her. The woman staggered. Her back hit the door of the pickup. To anyone watching, they looked like one woman helping another who'd had too much to drink. Carson liked the magic roaring through her. She liked the power. Better than liked it. She was drunk on it.

She ramped down her excitement. The woman was severed from Magellan, but if Carson wanted to, she could do deliberately what she'd nearly done with Xia. She could take just a little more—just the merest nudge, and the fiend would belong to Carson. Her creature to enjoin instead of Magellan's. Whichever fiends she took, she could send them after Magellan and Rasmus and they'd have to do it. They'd be mageheld, true, but working for Nikodemus instead of Magellan.

Their eyes locked, hers and the fiend's, and the knowledge of what this moment held for them both blossomed between them. Freedom, or one servitude for another? How sweet it would be to own a fiend, to have a ready source of magic to draw from and a servant who would always do exactly what she wanted. How sweet to take Xia's knife and slide it oh so gently along the fiend's skin to free a well of blood, to taste copper warmth in her mouth and down her throat. The dark longing filled Carson until she shook with it. Stepping in close and still gripping the woman's arm, Carson released her magic into the fiend.

The darkness in Carson whispered that she could finish by taking the fiend as hers. For Nikodemus. On his behalf and for a good cause. She shuddered and fought her impulse to continue. She stumbled back, gasping as the magic receded. She squared her shoulders and recited

Nikodemus's cell number, sending it into the fiend's head with enough emphasis that the string of digits would stay in her memory. "Leave a callback number if you want to join us."

The woman sagged against the truck, hands pressed hard against her chest and gasping for breath. Her eyes were wide open and dilated. *Not too late.* "I'm cut."

She backed up again and let the fiend's vulnerability close up. Opportunity faded, and she thought that, still, it was not too late to take what she wanted. The fiend nodded once, and that was that. "Go," Carson whispered.

She stood near the Ranger, a bone-deep chill shivering through her. Only when the fiend had vanished did Carson realize she was gripping Xia's knife. She stared at the twisting metal curves of the blade. The thing was thirsty. It ached for the taste of blood. *My God,* she'd been so close to taking the fiend. The knife's longing remained, tight in her chest, a voice whispering that she could take the next one, taste the next one. *Nikodemus,* she whispered, *I need you.* The abyss was no farther away than Xia's knife, a chasm between her and what this night required of her.

Carson slid the knife into its sheath and opened herself again. The second fiend was easy to locate in the crowd outside the bar. He was closest and most likely to have a view of the woman who was no longer at her post. She overplayed him and nearly lost him when he jerked away from their initial contact. She juked with him, and in the crowd no one thought anything of a couple up against a wall, touching. She severed him. Easy. The one in the car was simple, too. She let him see her, and he got out and chased her. Oh, he was easy. Easy to free. Easy to make hers. But she didn't. She resisted the pull, but it was a little bit harder than before.

The fiend in the SUV had figured out something was wrong and was crossing the street toward the bar, scanning the humans for one that didn't seem to belong. Carson waited. Before long, the street was clear. She proceeded clearing the other streets. Eleven fiends in all. Some of them she knew from the Tiburon house. Some were new.

As she worked her way toward Magellan, she felt Kynan, a distant point of darkness. By the seventh, she'd learned it was safest for her to take her time assessing the fiend, but once she knew what to do, she needed to work quickly. By the seventh, she was quicker at all of it, better, smoother. The abyss threatened every time; each time took more strength to resist.

She came around the corner, the rush of her last taking still heating her veins. Her sense of Nikodemus turned hot. He wasn't far away, and he was pulling magic. And it made her careless. Worry kept her from opening to her surroundings the way she should have.

"Carson," someone said.

The world stopped dead, and when it restarted, nothing felt the way it ought to. Álvaro Magellan, the man who'd had her stolen from her family, stood about five feet from her, Kynan just behind him. She shut down her power. She needed to surprise him, take him off guard, and she really, really needed not to let her hatred of the man take over.

Magellan's expression was pleasant. Bland, even. Kynan frowned and looked at her through narrowed eyes. That was perhaps Magellan's greatest skill as a mage, she realized, to look so pleasant and harmless even when he was destroying lives. He had Kynan, after all, to terrorize or murder for him. She had no difficulty separating Kynan's power from Magellan's. The magic surrounding Magellan felt different.

"Well, well, Carson," Magellan said. "You seem to have recovered since last we saw each other."

She looked around, frantic, because she knew in her bones something was wrong, and she didn't know what it was. "I haven't got the talisman with me," she said.

"A great pity, Carson. But you will tell me where it is presently. Oh, and by the way, your companions won't be able to see us," Magellan said mildly. A different kind of magic than she was used to slid around them. Her head started to hurt, a familiar, debilitating pain. "Nor will they hear you."

He gestured to Kynan, and the fiend came forward to clamp a hand on Carson's upper arm, shifting her so her arm was tucked up behind her, painfully tight in her shoulder. Kynan goose-stepped her to Magellan's limo. He kept her arm twisted behind her back and used his palm on her head to get her in the back. A police car went past them, and she tried to whip her head toward the cruiser.

Carson tasted iron in her mouth, dry and heavy and bitterly metallic, when Kynan got into the back seat of the limo with her. He kept her prone and her arm twisted back. Xia's knife pressed into her belly. She couldn't see, because her head faced the back of the seat and Kynan's body kept her from moving. Carson tried to block out everything except what she needed to know about the fiend. She needed to know how to sever him. Her fear of Kynan went deep, and nothing was as easy as it had been with the other fiends.

The back door opened again, and someone else got in with them. He spoke from the seat opposite. "A warlord, Carson," Magellan said softly. "Nikodemus himself, no less." His familiar voice flowed like iced velvet. "An impressive acquisition for a witch with no ability."

She managed to lift her chin. "Go to hell."

"Kynan?"

The fiend eased up on her and turned her head toward the rear-facing seat, where Magellan sat with one leg crossed over the other. "One wonders, Carson, which way your relationship with the fiend goes." His steel-gray eyebrows rose. "You don't have the magic to control a fiend of his ability. No, we think, Kynan and I, that it must be Nikodemus who controls you. Until he becomes bored. At which time, I assure you, he will kill you. Such is the manner of fiends." His attention shifted above her, to Kynan, whom she could not see. "How long do you suppose, Kynan, before Nikodemus realizes we have her?"

"Not long," the fiend said. He kept one hand on her head and the other on the middle of her back, pinning her to the seat. "Half an hour at most, I think. The others will not defeat him."

Magellan's magic settled down, and Carson's concentration improved. She blocked out Magellan as best she could to concentrate on Kynan. "I suggest you use the time wisely, Kynan. The sooner Nikodemus is induced to come to her, the better."

Above her, Carson felt Kynan's body still.

"I shall wait outside," Magellan said. She heard Magellan kiss Kynan. The fiend's body tensed even as he leaned toward the mage. They separated. "Do with her what you will."

"Mage," Kynan said.

"Take your time, of course. But do not terminate her until Nikodemus is mine."

"Yes, Mage."

The locks disengaged. Cold air filled the car, and then the door closed with the heavy thunk of metal against metal. No one would see what was going on. The windows were black. Carson shut down her panic. She had to concentrate on Kynan and parsing out the steps for freeing him from Magellan.

He flipped her onto her back, and she'd been so focused on his magic and finding the way in and warning off Nikodemus that she didn't realize until then that he'd taken Xia's knife from her. The blade hissed as he pulled it from the sheath and held it, glittering edges between them.

Kynan laughed. He grabbed her wrist and squeezed until her eyes watered. Her fingers went numb. The fiend released her, and when Carson sat up, he moved to the seat across from her. She focused on Kynan, who was just now examining Xia's knife. He sat like Magellan did. One leg crossed over the other, crossed wrists on his knee. "You can't get out, Carson. He's sealed the doors." His gaze dropped below her chin. "No one will hear you scream."

Kynan's magic frightened her. He felt like Nikodemus, dimensioned so she could barely follow the ways in which his magic occupied space. The knots woven into him by Magellan's bond were far more complicated than anything she'd encountered tonight. She couldn't visualize the knots well enough to think she had any hope of severing him. Not quickly enough to matter. And now the hot sensation of Nikodemus flared up in her head. He was pulling power again, and she weakened her guard against Kynan in order to give Nikodemus access.

Kynan uncrossed his legs and jammed his feet on the seat on either side of her. His gorgeous eyes flickered with orange fire. His suit was Luigi Borelli, a charcoal wool with a stark white shirt and golden-brown sevenfold tie. Everything came handmade and made-to-order from Naples. Kynan's measurements never changed, of course. Nothing but the best for Magellan's fiends. "You feel different. What did Nikodemus do to you?"

She resisted the impulse to cross her arms over herself. Let him stare all he wanted. "I don't know if I can explain it."

He unfastened his tie and dropped it on the seat. "I've heard you severed another fiend from Rasmus." He unbuttoned his suit jacket. "First Harsh, then Xia. Is that true?"

"Yes."

"When you touched Xia before, he told me nothing happened." He unfastened the top buttons of his shirt, exposing golden skin above a white undershirt. Carson pressed her spine against the seat. He continued unfastening his shirt. When he finished, he untied his shoes and slipped them off. He raised his head, mouth turned down at one corner. Carson sought his eyes, needing to lock gazes with him to find her way in. His gaze was cold. Dispassionate. What Kynan wanted didn't matter. He was bound by Magellan's command. Carson sat up. Her hand shook, a well of old pain renewed. Bright droplets of blood ran down her arm from the abrasions left by Xia's knife. His eyes flickered. She knew what blood did to a fiend, and that flicker in Kynan's eyes was the first true thing she'd seen from him.

"And me?" He removed his jacket and unfastened his belt. With catlike grace, he slipped out of his trousers. He wore boxers, and those were soon gone. Carson's heart pounded in her ears. She knew now that fiends preferred to be naked when they changed form. They didn't have to be, but they preferred it. She wasn't sure she could handle Kynan in shifted form. His shirt and undershirt were next. His eyes stayed on hers, and she gazed into them. "What would happen if you touched me?" he asked.

"It depends," she said, "on whether you're helping me or fighting me." Carson took a breath and, with fear hammering at her, offered him her wrist.

He hesitated, and Carson waited. At last, he wrapped long fingers around her elbow and tugged. His mental energy focused on her wrist, on the color and scent of her blood. She moved to his seat, looking for a way in. Kynan slid his hand along her forearm until he cupped the back of her hand and raised her wrist to his mouth, touching her skin, but not her blood. Not yet. "What else did Nikodemus teach you?" he said in a low voice.

"More than you know."

With a smile curving his mouth, his tongue flicked out, and she raised up when he closed his lips—almost a kiss—and tasted. They shared his body's reaction, his heightened arousal pulling them both along. He reached for her with his other hand, pressing her shoulder against the chill of the window glass.

"What about you?" she whispered. "Don't you want your freedom?"

When he lifted his head from the freshly bleeding cut on her arm, Kynan bent his head to one side, exposing his throat. He ran the blade across his skin. Just the slightest touch, and blood welled up. He waited, beautiful eyes fixed on her. Carson leaned forward in the unbearable closeness of the limousine, Kynan's scent in her nose, and pressed her mouth to the cut on his throat. Tangy and sweet. Her body sizzled with the taste. His fingers fumbled at the fastening of her jeans, sliding the zipper down.

Carson managed to wriggle out of his grasp. "No."

"Why not?" He slid a finger along her lower lip and came away with a drop of bright blood. Carson's mind reeled with the intensity of his magic and the echo of Magellan. She could follow that link, she thought, and end up back at Magellan. Losing Kynan would damage the mage, and she needed to do as much damage to the mage as possible. She closed her eyes and concentrated on that. And then she was in his head. Not much, but enough. And then more. His hatred of Álvaro Magellan would burn the world if ever he was free.

"I can sever you," she said.

"How are you doing that?" His hand, the one still clutching Xia's knife, pressed against her head. Three fingers loosened to thread through her hair. Carson was in his mind, and he knew it and allowed her to stay. "You're not of the kin. And I am not free."

"Yes," she said. "I am kin. And mage." She slid further into Kynan's mind. Her new magic, centuries old but new and untested for her, reacted to Kynan with a power that brought a cry flowing up from her throat. She fell hard inside, and then she didn't see Kynan anymore. She sped through the thoughts in his head, separating the magic that was his from the magic that came from Magellan, and then she smiled.

"Impossible," he whispered. "It's not possible."

She leaned forward and touched a hand to his cheek.

"I know how he did this to you. And I'm going to put a stop to it right now."

She severed Kynan in a single, brutal slash and kept going, coming perilously close to making him hers completely. Kynan's magic caromed toward her, blowing over her like a hurricane. The part of her magic that wasn't fiend billowed out, interfering with her vision. Kynan came in, landing her back in her body, gasping for air. He kept pushing magic at her.

"Stop," she said. His body flexed over hers. His rib cage heaved as he fought for breath. "Kynan," she said, desperate not to be pulled along into something that could come only at the cost of her relationship with Nikodemus. Her desire to take him burned hot, so hot she didn't know how to stop. He would be hers, a weapon she could direct against Magellan and Rasmus both. She could help them all if she made Kynan hers.

Kynan lifted his head, staring into her eyes as he continued to feed into her head. His mouth twisted. "Better your creature than Magellan's."

"No." Nikodemus needed her to sever Kynan, but she needed never, ever to cross that line and make a fiend her mageheld. The heat of the connection between her and Kynan blasted her, but she shut it down because that way led to an evil that would never leave her.

If she did this, she'd lose Nikodemus.

Kynan's body arched, and he let out a whoosh of air. She stared at his hand around her arm. "Let go of me, Kynan. Please."

He sagged against the seat, hands pressed to his chest. "He's gone." His eyes opened wide, but Carson stayed disengaged from him, and when he tried to slip into her head, she walled him off.

"It's over, Kynan."

He looked at her sideways. "You didn't take me. Why?"

She shrugged. "Because it's ugly and wrong, that's why."

"But I have a connection with you, I feel that."

"You're not mageheld."

"Impossible," he said softly, touching his chest.

The limousine rocked, and she went cold because Nikodemus was pulling hard from her. He was out there facing Magellan, and he needed her. Her heart clenched like a fist around rock. With a cry, Carson pushed at the door, fumbling at the lock mechanism because her head was bursting with the pain of Magellan's magic exploding around her. Kynan grabbed her arm from behind. She turned back and snarled at him. "If you want to pay me back for setting you free, Kynan, then you make sure nothing happens to Nikodemus."

"Mage," he said. "Or are you fiend?"

"Both," she snapped.

Kynan reached around and released the door lock. She kicked the door open. He was here, Nikodemus was here and Magellan was lying in wait, quite possibly with Rasmus, too. Maybe he didn't have Kynan anymore, but he was still formidable all on his own. Overhead, the sky boiled black, starless, fathomless. She half fell, half scrambled onto the street. Kynan hit the pavement beside her. He was still naked, and she knew he was close to changing.

Nikodemus crouched on the hood of the limo while Magellan stood with a hand raised toward him. Carson's throat closed off because she could feel Nikodemus slipping away from her. Sheer panic propelled her forward.

Without Kynan, not even Magellan had the power to bind Nikodemus—she knew it, and by now so did Magellan. He wasn't trying to take Nikodemus anymore. He was trying to kill him.

She dove for Magellan, her vision streaking in brilliant orange and purples. Her breath caught in her lungs; she couldn't feel her skin. Panic brought her up short, froze her with the terror of having made an error at the cost of Nikodemus's life. Her magic couldn't touch Magellan. All she found when she tried to enter his mind was blackness. An impenetrable veil.

She could not do to a mage what she was able to do with a fiend.

She pushed her mind, all of her self into Nikodemus and found him, joined him completely and without reservation. She didn't care if she died keeping him from Magellan. She didn't care what happened to her. Nikodemus left his crouch, his body flexed for a leap, but Kynan reached Magellan first, a blur of motion that wasn't human anymore. Xia's knife flashed once in his hand, then clattered to the pavement as Kynan went tumbling backward.

Magellan reeled as he straightened, blood pouring from a wound in his chest. His gaze found Carson, and heat seared the inside of her head. She knew Magellan. She knew his magic and that he was after her now. And she was vulnerable to him because of the fiend in her. The first of his bindings wrapped around her, slowed her mind and her will. She watched his smile spread and heard Nikodemus shout as she went under. Such despair, she thought. His love for her pierced her heart.

She was trapped in a sickly sweet coating of magic that tied her to the mage. Every particle of her being protested at the loss of her freedom. A howl scoured her throat as she realized that Magellan was binding her to him, taking her. She was going to end up mageheld because she couldn't see how to sever herself from Magellan. Her heart froze with a brand-new fear: that, through her, Magellan would find a way to take Nikodemus.

Magellan's mind wrapped itself around hers, bidding her to take Xia's knife. The pain of resistance shook her body. Magellan wanted her to kill Nikodemus, and a part of her quivered with the desire to do so. She clamped down on that part of her mind, trying to wall off the compulsion the same way she walled off her mind when she wanted to keep someone out. The effort ripped at her soul. But she'd rather die than harm Nikodemus. And that, she thought, was exactly what was happening.

The blade glinted in the streetlight, a peculiar, glowing blue-gray. From the corner of her eye, she saw Kynan transform from his human body and leap at a second form. Not Magellan. Her will broke. She darted toward the knife, and immediately the pain released her. With the knife in her hand, Carson faced Nikodemus. She roared and pried her fingers open. And then she collapsed as her disobedience to Magellan began to dissolve her.

She lay on the pavement, quivering, fighting off the wave of agony working its way through her. Her lungs refused to work; drawing breath was like trying to breathe in a vacuum. Her last sight was of Nikodemus standing over Magellan. His arm held back, frozen for an exquisitely clear instant. Then he finished the arc through the chill night sky and came up for another, blood glistening on the blade. The sky turned white. No sound. No scent of blood. No color but blinding white at the very moment that she felt her life and Magellan's end.

CHAPTER 34

$\mathcal{N}$ikodemus pulled Carson into his arms, cradling her to his chest. "Don't let me be too late," he said. His voice broke along with his heart. In the distance, a siren wailed.

"Warlord?" That was Kynan Aijan. Nikodemus ignored him.

He didn't feel anything from Carson, but after a moment of sheer panic he realized she was still breathing. She was the color of chalk, though. He stood up with her in his arms.

"Warlord," Kynan said. "Get her out of here." He glanced behind him at Magellan's body. "I'll clean up."

"See you back at the ranch?" he said, sending the other fiend a mental image of how to get there. Kynan nodded, and with that, Nikodemus left.

The sun was coming up when he pulled the Mercedes behind the farmhouse. By then, Carson had recovered enough to sit up on her own, but she hadn't said anything yet. For now, he was okay with the silence. But inside he was cold with the possibility of the damage Magellan might have done to her. He held back his connection with her because he wasn't sure where she was, after everything that had happened, and he didn't want to intrude or make things worse.

"How bad is it?" he asked.

"I'm okay," she said in a croak.

He bent his head to the steering wheel. She wasn't damaged the way Iskander had been—her mind was intact. But she wasn't reaching out to him, and he didn't dare check for himself. God knows humans could be even funnier about their mental privacy than their physical privacy. He took his time locking the car. If she wanted, she could go into the house by herself. He didn't want her to, something he didn't understand until he felt the twist of a knife in his heart when she walked away.

"Hey, sweetheart," he said. "Wait up."

She turned, and he knew right then, without anything more than looking at her face, that something was wrong. Seriously wrong. He caught up to her and put an arm around her shoulder. "Hey, Carson. What's the matter?"

She shook her head. "Not now, okay? I just want to get inside."

"Sure." When they got to the kitchen, Harsh was grinding coffee beans and pulling ingredients out of the fridge. Xia had the small of his back against the kitchen counter and was staring at the table. Glaring, actually, at Kynan in his sissy Italian custom-made suit. Iskander was next to Kynan, but with eyes that were alive behind the cobalt stripes. It hit him then that every fiend in the room was bound to Carson in one way or another. Harsh. Xia. Iskander and Kynan. And him. Him, too. Maybe he didn't need the other warlords at all. Maybe he could start his fight against the mages right here. Right now.

He threw his keys into the bowl by the door, and they all jumped like he'd set off a bomb.

"How the hell did you get all these freaks back in one piece, Harsh?" Nikodemus said. Nobody looked happy right now.

"There's a lot of room in the back of a pickup," Harsh said. The espresso machine whooshed, and he didn't say anything more, or if he did, Nikodemus didn't hear it.

"That explains the hay." Carson picked a strand from Kynan's hair. Nikodemus tried to catch her eye, but she avoided him. Kynan stared at Carson like she was ice cream and he was chocolate syrup.

Harsh pulled an espresso and drank the stuff straight from the little silver cups, one shot after the other. In the silence that followed while Harsh was reloading the espresso machine, Xia said, "Give me back my knife."

Kynan turned his attention from Carson to Xia. He reached down, below the table, and came up with the knife. The blade caught the morning light and threw rainbows across Carson's face. She blanched. If she was chalky before, now she didn't have any color at all. Kynan balanced the point of the knife on his fingertip and smiled. "This is one hell of a blade, fiend."

"Give it back to him, Kynan," Nikodemus said. And Kynan, even though he was a warlord himself, did as he was told.

"It's a good knife," Kynan said. "It likes blood." He flipped the knife, caught it between his thumb and forefinger, and flicked it at Xia.

Xia caught the knife without even blinking. Nobody, not even Kynan Aijan, out badassed Xia.

Carson dropped her head and held it between her hands. Nikodemus thought about a gentle mental nudge to find out if she was okay but decided he'd better not. This wasn't like the other times he thought he'd been in love. He wouldn't have laid down his soul for any of them. Carson was his soul, and he was intensely aware that he had the power to hurt her. And he couldn't do that to her. "I hate that thing," she said. "I hope I never see it again."

In the kitchen, Harsh lined up coffee cups and scooped foamed milk into the line of cups on the counter. He had the griddle on, too. Something smelled good. Harsh brought out the first cap and gave it to Carson along with the sugar and a look at Nikodemus. "Does anybody know for sure what happened to Magellan?"

"The warlord killed him," Kynan said with a nod at Nikodemus. He jerked his head in Xia's direction. "With that one's very fine blade."

Carson's head came up fast. Like she felt guilty about something. But what the hell did she have to feel guilty about? Hell, she'd practically saved the day all by herself.

Kynan leaned against the back of the chair, arms over his chest. His tie was hanging out of the pocket of his suit coat, but he still looked damn good. His hair was buzzed, but what he had looked to be medium brown.

"You're sure he went down?" Iskander asked.

Harsh gave Nikodemus a perfect cap, he knew from the smell and the weight. He put another in front of Iskander and went back to the kitchen to flip pancakes. "Yes," Kynan said. He smiled. "I burned his body to ash, so yes, I am sure Álvaro Magellan is dead."

"How about Rasmus?" Nikodemus asked.

Iskander lifted his coffee and breathed in. "He escaped, Warlord."

"What are we going to do about that?" Carson asked.

Xia swiveled his head to get a good look at Carson. "We?" he said. "What do *we* have to do with anything? I will find Rasmus and kill him."

Kynan put down his cappuccino. "Who freed you, Xia?" He gave the fiend an evil-eye glare. "It wasn't any fiend in this room. Why are you talking to her like that?"

"She's human. She has magic." Xia lifted his hands, fingers spread. "Therefore, she's a witch. I don't like humans, and I hate witches." His lip curled. "As far as I'm concerned, we should cut her loose. One of us should have killed her when we had the chance."

Harsh slammed down a plate of pancakes. "Funny, I don't notice Carson forcing us to do anything, Xia. I can sure as hell remember Rasmus doing that."

"Fuck off and die."

Harsh shoved Xia's chair with his foot. "No one's keeping you here, fiend."

"It's a matter of time before she gives in to her natural impulse to control us." Xia pointed at Carson. "She's a mage. She can't help herself."

Interesting, Nikodemus thought. If anything, Carson looked even more miserable now. What the hell was up with her? "Jesus, Xia," Nikodemus said. "Doesn't anything improve your mood? You're fucking free. Take a minute to smell the roses, you freak."

Harsh handed out plates. "Why? He'd only stomp on them. Carson freed him. If he still hates her, then he can go to hell. He doesn't belong here." Harsh sat down and stabbed his fork into the stack of pancakes and dropped them onto his plate. "Not with us."

Carson licked her lips. "Xia is right." Everyone looked at her. "It makes me sick," she said. "Sick to my stomach to think about what mages do. But you know what?"

They all looked at her, spellbound even though she wasn't doing anything but staring them down.

"Xia, you can hate whoever you like, but do it on your own time. Not ours. The same goes for you, Kynan." Her stare pinned each of them in turn. "The only question is how many of you are loyal to Nikodemus? Because if you want even a chance at defeating the mages and getting back a few more of your own kind, then your people need him."

He always had liked a woman who could take charge. His woman. Nikodemus leaned back and let her wail on them.

She pointed at Xia, then Kynan. "The rest of us have sworn fealty to Nikodemus. Yes, including me. If you two are going to stay, you need to do the same." She gave Kynan and Xia a withering glare. "Your choice, but if it's not, you need to go now. Right now."

They were all getting juiced up, and there was something to be said for the condition. Xia cocked his head and stared hard at Carson. Carson elected to sit down and butter her pancake. Nobody said anything, and she looked at them like she didn't get what was up. "That's it. I'm done talking. Harsh, please pass the syrup." Harsh passed the syrup. "Now, can we just eat like normal people, please? After that we'll say good-bye to whoever's going."

For a while that's what they did. Mostly civilized. And

then the food disappeared, and the coffee was gone, and Kynan went down on a knee to Nikodemus.

"You're a warlord, Kynan," Nikodemus said. He was thinking maybe he'd be happier if Kynan decided to walk with Xia. "You could go out on your own if you wanted. You sure you want this?"

Kynan touched the tips of three fingers to his forehead. "I fight with you and Carson."

He swore fealty, and then the blood exchange was done. When Kynan was back on his seat, Nikodemus stuck out his hand to Xia. "No need for you to hang around any longer. No one's going to make you do the dishes before you go. Thanks for your help last night, and take care."

Xia glared at him. And then he astonished everyone by going down on one knee. He swore fealty in a clear, unemotional voice. When it was done and sealed, Nikodemus said, "I'm glad to have you on our side, Xia. But if you ever touch Carson again, I'll rip off your head. Clear?"

"Fuck you."

"Probably never." He looked at Kynan, too. "Same goes for you. Understand?"

"Of course." And then, Kynan got up to help Harsh clean up in the kitchen, Iskander went upstairs, and Xia went outside to sit on the back porch, and just like magic, Carson and Nikodemus were alone.

"Carson?" he said. "Don't you think it's time we talked?" His chest tightened a little. " 'Cause it's driving me crazy wondering the hell is wrong."

She came around to his chair and took his hand. She started to say something but didn't manage to get it out. He waited. "About Magellan," she said.

"He's dead, Carson." He might never forget the vicious

joy he took in taking down the mage. He'd do it all over again if he could. "He's never going to hurt you again."

Her fingers were warm in his palm. "He had me mage-held," she said.

"Yeah, I know." He pulled her closer. "That's not a feeling I ever want to have." He reached up and thrust his fingers through her hair. "I felt it happen," he whispered. "You were gone, and my whole life ended right there."

"He wanted me to kill you."

"Makes sense." He brought her hand to his mouth and kissed her fingertips. "But you didn't." He was starting to see the problem, and he was afraid of saying the wrong thing. He pulled her closer, but she resisted.

"Part of me wanted to."

Nikodemus licked his lips. "That's the way being mageheld works, Carson. The fuckers make us do things we'd never do otherwise." He frowned and then brought her in close, whether she wanted him to or not. "There's no way I'd blame you for anything you thought or felt while Magellan had you locked down, so if you're worrying about that, you can stop right now." He held her, watching her eyes. "Besides, you didn't kill me. I saw you going for the knife, and you didn't use it on me."

"But I wanted to." Tears filled her eyes.

"So fucking what? You didn't." He brushed away the tears. "Look, I'm no good at this emotional shit, so I'll probably fuck this up. You're not Magellan's mageheld. You're safe now, I'm safe, and that's all that matters. That, and that I love you."

She wasn't calming down. "What if it happens again? What if some other mage ends up getting to you through me?"

Nikodemus pulled Carson onto his lap. "I could get

run over by a Mack truck tomorrow. Or you could. Or we both could. Maybe that's not the most romantic way to put it, but it doesn't make sense for us to give up being happy now because something bad might happen later." He held her so she pretty much had to look at him. "Don't do this to us, Carson. We belong together. I belong with you."

"Nikodemus—" She relaxed a little, and he put an arm around her and brought her into his embrace.

"I need you," he said. "So far you haven't given me anyone low-level. At the rate you're going, I'm going to have a clan of nothing but warlords and psychos like Xia and Iskander. Not that I'm ungrateful, but it's a lot of work keeping them in line."

"You need me to run your day care, is that what you're saying?"

"Maybe I need to clear something up," he said.

"What?"

"For the record, Carson, in case you didn't know, when a fiend says I love you, it means you're the only one. It means I hope like hell you're not going to break my heart and commit to someone else." He brushed her hair behind her ear. "I do love you. If you leave me, I'll never be the same."

"No," she said. "No. I thought maybe I was too messed up to love anybody, but Nikodemus, I don't know. Maybe I am too messed up. I'm not normal. I never have been."

"Like I'm Mr. Normal myself." He laughed and kissed her shoulder. "I saw what you did tonight—last night—whenever the hell it was, and I'm alive because of it. You were his mageheld, Carson. If you'd been a normal fiend, you would have killed me. But you're not. He couldn't force you because he didn't own all of you. And the part of you that was still free, which, by the way, was the mage part, kept you from offing me." He kissed her forehead. "I love you, Carson. I love you because you're fucked up and brave and you turn me on. Now, do I have to say it for you?"

"No." She took a deep breath. "You're the only one. Whatever happens, you're the only one for me, too."

"Yeah?" He frowned. "Gee. That's actually kind of disappointing."

She rolled her eyes. "All right, then." She put her arms around him, and his heart got bigger than his chest. "I love you, too, Nikodemus.

Nikodemus curled his fingers around her waist and drew her toward him. He opened his mind and his heart to her. "That's a goddamned fucking relief to hear. Because you're not Magellan's witch anymore, sweetheart. You're mine."

THE DISH

Where authors give you the inside scoop!

From the desk of Carolyn Jewel

Dear Reader,

What was that line Shakespeare stuck in one of his plays? Oh, yeah. *Hamlet,* act 1, scene 2. "There are more things in heaven and earth, Horatio, than are dreamt of in your philosophy." Even if you're not Horatio, and chances are you're not, that's a true statement. When things go bump in the night, maybe it's not the cat knocking stuff over.

Maybe there really is a monster drooling under your bed.

Right. There are things out there maybe you don't know about. Say, for example, the mages in MY WICKED ENEMY (on sale now). A mage is a person who can do magic. Real magic. The kind that can get you killed. Or save your life. Depends on your point of view, I guess. Then there are demons and, more specifically, fiends. They're not people, but they can do magic, too. My advice is watch out for both. Here's the thing you need to know about fiends, though: most of the time they look like normal people. You could walk down the street and never realize that wicked-hot cutie sitting by the coffee shop window isn't human and that if he wanted to, he could destroy your life. Could be your boss isn't human (I've had one or two bosses I'm convinced didn't have a check mark in the human category). For a fiend, learning how to pass for normal is a survival skill. Didn't used to be that way, but it is now. That's just a heads-up for you. Here's another one: they're good at it because they have to be. They end up enslaved to some effing mage if they're not careful. And sometimes even if they are.

With the magekind, it's hard to tell where you stand, mostly because they started out human. They don't have as much trouble pretending to assimilate. Human but not very, if you see what I'm getting at. It's enough to make you wonder, isn't it? I mean, do you even know who you are? Really and truly? Be honest. Maybe you just wake up one day and realize your entire life has been a lie. The man who raised you is a mage who crossed over to evil centuries ago, and now everybody and their brother wants you dead.

Maybe you get headaches. Bad ones. You know, a flash of pain from the supraorbital process down to your maxilla. Hurts like heck. And they're getting worse. And worse. Then you see stuff that turns your stomach. So you run.

Right into the monster's arms.

It could happen. It happened to Carson Philips in MY WICKED ENEMY.

Watch yourself out there. That's all I'm saying.

carolyn jewel

www.carolynjewel.com

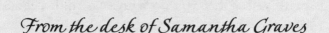

From the desk of Samantha Graves

Dear Reader,

When I wrote my first romantic suspense, SIGHT UNSEEN, I discovered that I loved exotic locales. The research was intense, but that only made these amazing places more amazing.

In my latest book, OUT OF TIME (on sale now), I got to visit Mexico with all of you. I have never been there, but someday I'd love to see it for myself. In lieu of that day, I did the best I could with guidebooks, videos, travelogues, maps, photos, and even an online Speed Spanish class. What did we do before the Internet?

My fascination for Mexico turned into Jillian's passion, as well. She embraced this culture and its people with an open heart. Her wide-eyed appreciation became a symbol for how she viewed life and people—seeing the beauty in everything.

Simon's dislike for Mexico has nothing to do with the country itself, but with the betrayal he experienced there—a betrayal that marred him with a cynicism that shaped the rest of his life.

During the story, both characters must face the truth as Jillian begins to see the ugliness and Simon begins to see the beauty. It could have been Mexico or Guatemala or Santa Barbara—all places contain both ugliness and beauty. What you choose as truth is up to you. What you do with that truth defines you.

In the end, Jillian didn't let the ugliness change the fact that there is beauty, and Simon didn't let the beauty change the fact that there is ugliness. They simply found their common ground, accepting both as part of life and choosing to see the truth in their love for each other.

I hope you enjoyed both.

All the best,

Samantha Graves

www.samanthagraves.com

P.S. In case you were wondering, *"Quite mis ropas"* means "Take my clothes off." Happy reading!

♥ ♥ ♥ ♥ ♥ ♥ ♥ ♥ ♥ ♥ ♥ ♥ ♥ ♥

From the desk of Paula Quinn

Dear Reader,

Few authors get to see their characters come to life before their eyes, but I did. You met Graham Grant, the hero in A HIGHLANDER NEVER SURRENDERS (on sale now), in my previous release, LAIRD OF THE MIST. I met him in Grand Central Terminal. The Scottish Village there hosts a fashion show that was about to begin. I like kilts. I'll watch.

Donning a kilt of black leather and matching jacket that he held closed at his chest, model and former rugby star Chris Capaldi stepped onto the stage like he owned it. His tousled mop of deep amber hair eclipsed killer green eyes that sparkled with confidence and a hint of wickedness. All he did was smile and a horde of women behind me started whooping and cheering in a dozen different languages. Oh, yeah, he knew the ladies were digging him, and he fed the frenzy by sliding the jacket off his bare bronze shoulders and curling his sulky mouth into a grin so salacious I swear every woman in attendance sighed at the same time. Grand Central was never so hot.

There was my Graham Grant. Six feet three inches of pure rogue.

Chris has graciously agreed to star in my next Grand Central Publishing release about a notorious rogue and a beautiful rebel he can never have. From the moment Graham meets the bold and passionate Claire Stuart, he wants to take her, claim her. But Claire has far more dangerous undertakings ahead than surrendering to a wickedly alluring Highlander. Amid betrayal, honor, duty, and ultimately love, she must put this vision in his place in order to save her sister's life, and her own. Pick up a copy of A HIGHLANDER NEVER SURRENDERS and journey with Graham to a place that has remained untouched until now—his heart.

Enjoy!

All the best,

Paula Quinn

www.paulaquinn.com

Dear Reader,

Poor Xia. He hasn't had an easy life. You may have noticed he has kind of a bad attitude. I don't blame him, though. People get on his case all the time because he's not so easy to be around. Put yourself in his shoes. (Which I've had to do, in case you were wondering.) He was betrayed by a witch and ended up mageheld for more years than he wants to count. As it turns out, having his freedom doesn't mean his life magically goes back the way it was. His old life is gone, you know? A tough situation for anybody. Not so fun. Plus (and he doesn't know this yet) he's about to meet the love of his life. She's a witch. Like the woman who betrayed him. Rats.

For more information about Nikodemus, Xia and the others, check out my website at www.carolynjewel.com. You'll find character backgrounds, scenes that didn't make it into the final version and other cool stuff I happen to think of or that people suggest. (Hint! Hint!) If you have questions or comments, e-mail me (please!) at carolyn@carolynjewel.com. And thanks.

Want to know more about romances at Grand Central Publishing and Forever? Get the scoop online!

GRAND CENTRAL PUBLISHING'S ROMANCE HOMEPAGE

Visit us at www.hachettebookgroupusa.com/romance for all the latest news, reviews, and chapter excerpts!

NEW AND UPCOMING TITLES

Each month we feature our new titles and reader favorites.

CONTESTS AND GIVEAWAYS

We give away galleys, autographed copies, and all kinds of fun stuff.

AUTHOR INFO

You'll find bios, articles, and links to personal websites for all your favorite authors—and so much more!

THE BUZZ

Sign up for our monthly romance newsletter, and be the first to read all about it!